THE YEAR MRS. COOPER GOT OUT MORE

A Great Wharf Novel

Meredith Marple

CINDER PATH PRESS

First Cinder Path Press paperback edition, October 2015
ISBN: 0996732411
ISBN: 9780996732413
Library of Congress Control Number: 2015953183
Cinder Path Press, Sarasota, FL

To my husband, Gary

ACKNOWLEDGMENTS

It took many kind, generous, and experienced people to guide me through the writing of this, my first novel. If I've neglected to thank anyone in particular with my remembrances below, I can only beg you to forgive me.

Thank you to my magnificent editors—to Pat Carda for critiquing my first draft and setting me on the right path to flesh out the whole story; to Caitlin Alexander for critiquing my ninth and tenth drafts, being gently stern and not letting me off the hook, ever; and to Krista Smith for pouncing on the mechanics and not hesitating to alert me to some oversimplifications I'd hoped to get away with (if some of those are still left, it's entirely my fault); to Carl Lennertz for suggesting the perfect place to end chapter one, and for being a cheering section when I desperately needed one.

Thank you to my Maine writing buddy, Sandy Neily, for hours upon hours of close attention and patient counseling to free me from my pedantic inner editor, and to my Florida writing buddy, Rickie Gordon, for reminding me to look for the excitement.

Thank you, Eric Bell, for reviewing my sections on the Great Wharf Police Department and preventing me from misrepresenting how Maine law enforcement (its procedures and its people) might work in the situations I imagined. Any errors in the end result are mine.

Thank you, John Middleton, for explaining how the *real* Seashore Trolley Museum operates, and for forgiving my allowing Richie to behave badly. (Just for the record, I understand that Richie would be subject to a fine; the museum curators would demand it. He may be allowed to mount a free-standing plaque adjacent to the car, but the curators or Board of Trustees would need to approve the text of the plaque.)

Thank you to published authors who lit the way—to Lily King, for the week-long workshop that showed me both how near and how far I was, that summer in 2011; to Johanna Moran, for untold commiseration plus convincing me I still didn't have the right title, until I did; to Susan Streeter Carpenter, for marking lots and lots of places where a scene (show) could replace the tell.

Thank you to all my caring readers across different drafts (I tried not to foist more than one version on any one of you): Anne J., Curt S., Dottie B., Ellen M., Gary M., Jon R., Judi H., Lydia R., Marlene B., Mary M.B., Nancy R., Nancy S., Pat M., Pat W., Sandy K., Susan L., Susanne C., Tina M. And a special thank you, Karen G., for listening to me read aloud three drafts … unbelievable.

Lastly, thank you to my husband for usually obeying the sign on the door to my writing (slash laundry, slash guest) room—"Do Not Disturb: Future Bestselling Author At Work." It's up to me to deliver on that last part.

Credit: Map of Great Wharf drawn by Daniel Reeve

Route 1

toward Biddeford

Newman Lane

Wyeth Road

KENNEBUNKPORT

Seashore
Trolley
Museum

Log Cabin Road

Hips Way

Rose

Burnham Bog
(Great Wharf Land Trust)

Pleasant Street

Temperance Way

harbor

A T L A N T I C

O C E A N

Garden Path Lane

proposed
cinder path

Olympia Snowe Blvd

GREAT WHARF

rd Ogunquit

C A N A D A

U S A

MAINE

N E W

Y O R K

VERMONT

N E W

N

HAMPSHIRE

Portland
Biddeford
Kennebunkport
Ogunquit

et not to scale]

MASSACHUSETTS

Key: // break in road map
— · — town line
⠒ traffic lights

My dear, have some lavender,
or you'd best have a thimble full of wine—
your spirits are quite down, my sweeting.
John O'Keeffe, 1798

Everything will change when your desire to move on
exceeds your desire to hold on.
Alan H. Cohen, 21st century

EPISTOLARY EXCERPT FROM
UNPUBLISHED MANUSCRIPT:
RUNAWAY LEGACY

By certified mail postmarked May 26, 1999

Dear Mr. Gallant MacPherson,

Please excuse this unusual means of contact from two people who probably mean nothing to you. We're not asking for money!

We had a daughter who disappeared the day after her eighteenth birthday. She wasn't kidnapped or anything; she left a note saying good-bye. We'd like to say she "ran away from home," but that would imply she was still a child. Friends and neighbors, so careful not to hurt our feelings for years beforehand, have since enlightened us. Mary was no child.

We'll spare you the details of the suffering we went through after her departure. Suffice to say, the little girl we had nourished and watched over and encouraged in all she did didn't return the favor. We searched for years, hoping to reconnect, and we paid a great deal of money to more than one private investigator to dig up and follow clues.

Last week, our most recent PI told us she had located a man (you) who had been married to our Mary for eight years and with whom she had a child. That would be your daughter Caitlin, one year old now. We despair of ever seeing Mary again. In fact, we'd just as soon not—she never once contacted us after leaving home. But we wonder if you might be willing to include Caitlin's natural maternal grandparents in her life.

You may wonder why you should ever bring us into your daughter's life. After all, you may think, Mary must have hated us to leave us behind forever and without another word. Perhaps you were married long enough to Mary, and hurt enough by her eventual rejection, to understand that it was nothing we did, just as we bet it was nothing you did either.

Might we meet? We live less than an hour away. All our contact information is on the enclosed card.

Sincerely, and with high hopes,
Vera and Sergeo DiMatteo

1

July 2014

*In which Mallory Cooper skirts an issue but makes
good on two promises, even meeting Angie Weller.*

SHOULDERS BRUSHING, MALLORY and Dwight Cooper
focused on the swivel television between the dining and kitchen areas. It was their habit during dinner to watch the local Maine news out of Portland.
Their town of Great Wharf, like a playful kitten's paw,
reached out to claim a tiny portion of coastline south
of Kennebunkport.

Five minutes into the broadcast, Mallory said,
"Dare we hope? It looks like no new bad news tonight.
I mean, just updates on old bad news. How refreshing!"

Dwight murmured his agreement, but Mallory knew he was just biding his time until he finished eating. He'd been wanting to say something ever since he got home. But she had hurried him into washing his hands and sitting down to catch the start of the news. She had, as usual, looked forward all day to seeing him. He was her anchor, always had been.

At the first commercial, Mallory picked up her plate and flatware, swung her legs over the bench, and walked to the counter. She laid her things by the dishwasher, then turned and asked, "Ready for more wine?"

"Not yet. Still nursing this one. Why'd you jump from the table so fast?"

"I didn't jump, just got out normally."

"Yeah, normal like a scared jackrabbit."

"What would I have to be afraid of?"

"Mal, you telegraph your emotions in all sorts of ways. Thirty-six years and three grown kids later, I've learned how to read you."

Mallory harrumphed and refilled her wine glass. Turning to face Dwight again, she waved it slowly in an arc from left to right in front of her. "Did you notice the amazing cleaning job I did on this room today?"

"It always looks clean in here. Sorry. Tell me what you did."

"I washed under the counter edges, and I dusted everything, including the leaves on the fern. I even risked life and limb on the stepladder to dust the overhead light. Little did you know while you were chatting with tourists at the trolley museum that your wife was *this* close to a fatal fall." She held her arms out from her sides and made a show of swaying, careful not to spill the wine.

Dwight shook his head. "You really need to get out more, Mal. I'm starting to think you're hiding out in here, like someone in the witness protection program. Or an actual hermit." He chanced a grin over his nearly empty plate, but a question hung in the air. Mallory gave him a lopsided smile. She didn't want this conversation. She grabbed the sponge and swiped it across the sparkling counter.

"Sorry, babe. I'm just concerned."

"Tell you what—I promise to do something out of the ordinary tomorrow."

"Outside the house and away from the yard?"

"I promise."

* * *

The next day Mallory put on her most comfortable walking shoes and left the house twenty minutes early for a doctor's appointment that Dwight knew nothing about. In the spirit of her promise, though, she planned to tack on a detour to Byways Gift Shop. That would add ten minutes to the walking time. Another ten minutes in the store should be enough to form an impression of the proprietor, a woman named Angie Weller.

Mallory's neighbor had been after her to do this. This neighbor watched the townspeople of Great Wharf the way some people watched soap operas—with a vengeance, Mallory thought. She hated the gossip mill that Doris Hillobenz ran. But she'd hate it more if Doris were to decide her immediate neighbors needed extra scrutiny. So Mallory had promised Doris she'd meet Ms. Weller and report back.

"Please do, Mallory," Doris implored, having cornered her at the mailbox to make her request. "I know you don't like making unnecessary trips. You've always been careful where you put your time. But this Angie Weller is quite the mystery woman. I can't find a single person who's ever seen her outside her shop. I've heard she goes to Rotary sometimes, but I'm not in that crowd, being retired and all."

"Why do you care, Doris?" Mallory knew it must be driving Doris crazy that she hadn't dug up any dirt yet. Not that Doris would admit that.

Doris stopped a glossy magazine from slipping out of the pile in Mallory's hands. "I've been in her shop, of course. I think things are overpriced, but I guess no more than anywhere else these days. But she watches every move I make, as though I'm going to steal something. Just see what you make of her. Humor me?"

"Okay, I'll humor you. I won't be running right over there, but I'll let you know."

That was two weeks ago.

Leaving the house now, Mallory checked for the small folded knife at the bottom of her oversized purse. She felt silly about this, but local news stories recently attributed more violence to increasing desperation in a down economy. Sure, these stories centered in Portland, with a higher than usual jobless rate. But a few burglaries had occurred this summer closer to Great Wharf, and, well, better safe than sorry.

Even so, she fretted about the sharp object. What if it sprang open while she was rummaging for her cell phone? The thought of bright red blood dripping into her purse, let alone coming from her own finger, gave her a shiver.

Blood was on a lengthening list of things that made Mallory queasy, including elevators and crowds and, most recently, driving her car. But blood headed the list because the sight of it had actually made her faint once. Usually it just disabled her, like when Dwight cut himself last week and asked her to get a Band-Aid. Her gaze fixated, instead, on the crimson bubble and she couldn't move from her chair.

Dwight got his own Band-Aid. Later he said, "You didn't used to freak at the sight of blood, Mal. You used to handle the kids' accidents just fine. What happened?"

"I don't have a clue." She avoided his gaze, but in fact she really didn't have a clue.

Dwight, sweet man, had dropped the subject. Last night's conversation, however, was a sign that he wasn't going to keep dropping subjects. She needed to get back in control of herself, if she only knew how.

* * *

Three blocks out, with four blocks still to go, Mallory's progress slowed. Having walked fast at first, she took delight in midsummer Maine's best day so far. Breezy and warm, the air carried the invigorating sweetness of newly cut grass and the oddly pleasing sound of power mowers getting it done. But as she neared the tourist-dependent downtown, the crush of people threatened to ruin her plans. A wave of dizziness made her steps unsteady. She stared at her feet in a head-down position that made her look despondent, she knew, but it helped steady her. Now if she could just get her ears to ignore the ludicrously carefree chatter and laughter of a vacationing horde.

She called on a reliable escape mechanism, which was to replay the joy of being hired for an art museum job four years ago. She had latched onto it like a student sculptor handed a free hunk of marble. Assisting the events manager helped her get beyond the deathly quiet at home after all the kids had moved out. She created checklists and email templates that could be replicated with minor tweaks. She gloried in bringing such efficiencies to the job. Her good work, however, created a built-in obsolescence.

Two years in, her paid position was eliminated. Now volunteers used her checklists and tweaked her templates. She considered switching to volunteer status herself, but paying off the second mortgage for the kids' college tuition remained a priority. Unfortunately, few places were hiring, and her age didn't help. Despite glowing reviews from her former boss and many of the artists, she had been turned down for one position after another.

"You're excused." An annoyed voice penetrated Mallory's musings as her shoulder hit someone else's in an oncoming wave of people. Embarrassed, she didn't stop to apologize. The person had to be two or three people behind her by now. She kept her head up as she crossed Wyeth Street—the busy main drag—and made her way one more street over to Newman Lane. Just turning the corner onto Newman relieved the worst of her tension. Shade trees predominated, and homes mingled with businesses. The noise dropped almost in half.

Mallory thought about kissing the ground but refrained and kept walking. Newman Lane would eventually take her to her true goal for the day, her doctor's office. It was located on the other end of the block, at the corner of Newman and Olympia Snowe Boulevard. Halfway there Mallory spotted the sign for Byways Gift Shop. Her breath caught and she considered walking right past. But then she felt resistance from her more steely self. (Where have you been? she wondered.) Today she would make good on her promises to Dwight and Doris.

The contents of the display window screamed New Age. Crystals, angels, and tarot cards dotted the surfaces among garden statues and multicolored T-shirt piles. Front and center, on a small ledge attached to a poster of *The Wizard of Oz*'s homesick Dorothy, rested an elixir called Spirits-Up.

"Sweet Dorothy," she whispered. "Don't worry; everything will be okay. Just hang in there." She remembered saying exactly that to each of her three children as they struggled through teen angst so many years before. Only this time the reassurance was for herself.

Upon opening the door to the shop, Mallory first noticed the tinkling bell that announced her arrival.

Next she breathed in the uplifting scent of citrus plus lavender, which reminded her of her backyard garden. She looked around for the proprietor and thought that might be the woman behind the cash register. Just two other people browsed the aisles. She took a few uneasy minutes to do the same, feeling like a spy. Finally, she grabbed an "Over the Rainbow" music box—a packaged one beneath the display—and headed to the register.

The woman's badge identified her as Angie Weller, Store Proprietor. Mallory's eyes widened at how easy it had been, after all, to honor Doris's request. The woman said, "You look surprised. Do we know each other?"

Mallory had to find a pretense. The truth was a combination of things. She had not expected to meet the proprietor—her quarry—so fast, and she had not expected to find such an attractive woman. Doris hadn't said a thing about her looks. Angie Weller was petite and buxom with deep red pixie-styled hair, a creamy complexion, and penetrating black eyes.

Mallory recovered quickly. "No, we don't know each other. I'm just pleasantly surprised to find no line. I haven't been in here before, and I found what I needed right away."

"I bet you'd find many more fun items if you browsed a bit longer."

Angie's bright voice made it sound like an invitation, but Mallory didn't like feeling put on the spot. The instant she felt her dislike start to form, she lectured herself that the woman was just trying to make a living.

"I'll have to take a rain check on that, since I'm due for a doctor's appointment up the street." She nudged the music box toward the cash register and put her credit card on the counter.

Angie placed the card on top of the register for safekeeping. "Which doctor?"

Again Mallory felt jarred, now because of the personal question. "Jim Beall. Do you know him?"

"Can't say I do." Angie finally took hold of the box. "I've been so busy getting this store up and running the last two years that I've been bad about getting to know people. If someone doesn't shop here or work on behalf of town businesses, then it's a good bet I haven't met them yet."

She waved the scanner over the bar code until the beep sounded. Then she put the scanner down but kept her hand on the box. Mallory caught a whiff of musk and watched a nostalgic smile play across Angie's lips.

"It's funny—I once knew a James Beall. Different time and place. Very different. Maybe I'll make an appointment with your Dr. Beall anyway." She looked away for a moment. Then recomposing herself, she glanced beyond Mallory to make sure no one was nearby and whispered, "After the shoplifting incident last week, I'm probably due for a stress check." Her black eyes softened in what Mallory read as a plea for sympathy.

"Shoplifting? Here? In Great Wharf?" Mallory said too loudly.

Angie jerked back and gave her a warning stare. But then she seemed to forgive and said, still sotto voce but no longer a whisper, "The worse the economy gets, the more shoplifting goes on." Angie slid the purchase into a plastic store bag. "It's not nearly as bad in my store as at the grocery and clothing stores, but I get my share. In between my last two inventories, I lost three T-shirts, two decks of tarot cards, and a crystal geode. I think it's only one or two people. I have a few I'm keeping my eye on."

Mallory's insides wrenched. "That's horrible. What's our corner of the world coming to?"

Angie's flawless face turned into a scowl. She leaned close to Mallory and spat out, "I have a few I'm keeping my eye on. I'll get them before they take advantage of me again."

Mallory was taken aback by the abrupt shift in Angie's demeanor, which changed yet again. Angie straightened her back and added without emotion,

"With tax, your total comes to six sixty-two. Credit or debit?"

"Credit." Mallory couldn't wait to leave.

Angie swiped the card fast, punched a few keys, tore off the receipt, slapped it on the counter, and tossed down a pen.

Mallory signed quickly, put her copy of the receipt in the bag and the bag in her purse, and left without another word. She could feel Angie's eyes following her.

2

JULY

In which Mallory lies to her doctor; Doris Hillobenz
is a bother; and being online has pluses and minuses.

As Mallory walked up the block, she wiggled her fingers past the Byways bag in her purse to check the location of the knife. The interaction with Angie Weller had left her unnerved. It wasn't just the shoplifting. Maybe she was feeling jealousy. The woman ran what appeared to be a healthy business and she was breathtakingly beautiful. Two things Mallory wished she could say about herself.

More detailed comparisons emerged. Angie's deep red pixie had great style compared to Mallory's shoulder-length dull brown and graying straight cut. Angie's perfectly adorable body came from a different planet than Mallory's slightly drooped carriage. Angie's black eyes grabbed the world directly while Mallory's blue eyes hid behind a pair of outdated bifocal specs.

Exactly what would she report to Doris Hillobenz?

Her reverie was broken by the door to the doctor's office suite. In the waiting room, Mallory's thoughts turned to how she would lead into the consultation. And would Jim tell her to give up her wine? She suspected the wine had been saving her life in this unsteady world. Even familiar noises—the ice machine in the refrigerator, a car door slamming across the street—made Mallory jump or squirm. In a way, her hometown of Great Wharf felt under siege.

Great Wharf. The name made Mallory shake her head. You couldn't even see the water from downtown, unlike in other tourist towns along the coastline. You had to walk or drive a half mile from Wyeth and then another half mile down Rose Hips Way. The pier, once you got there, seemed longer than the harbor was wide. No, the true draws for Great Wharf were its proximity to other towns on the water and the lower cost of its inns.

Still, Mallory loved her town, as much for its relative invisibility as for its ordinariness. She realized now that being ordinary these days might include being less safe than before. She wished Dwight spent more time at home. Besides his full-time work in building management, he was a devoted volunteer at Seashore Trolley Museum in Kennebunkport. She didn't begrudge him his passions, but her own—the children and her last job—didn't need her anymore. What was left to protect? Or to protect her?

Sleeping in a bit later and sipping a bit earlier, Mallory knew she needed help. She had made the appointment weeks earlier. Jim Beall had been the Coopers' general practitioner for twenty years. They shifted to first names after the Coopers' children were grown. Even though Jim and the Coopers didn't socialize outside office visits, Mallory considered him a friend.

In the exam room, Jim sat next to a clean counter with a new computer on it, holding an old clipboard on his lap. Mallory, fully clothed for the consultation, launched into her topic. "I don't recognize myself, Jim. I'm spooked by normal noises. I'm starting to rely on Dwight to feel safe. When he's not home, my heart beats faster, and I get dizzy sometimes, lightheaded. I probably just need to get out more and get some exercise."

Jim gave her a kind smile. "It sounds like you're hyperventilating. Don't worry; whatever's going on, we'll get to the bottom of it. You've had a lot of changes in the last few years, with all the kids leaving and your job going the way of the economy. Your symptoms may be nothing more than your spirit heaving a sigh of relief. It can finally wreak a little havoc of its own."

Mallory loved the idea that her inner self was making itself known. She sensed it had a lot to say. This was Jim at his reassuring best. His rumbling baritone voice made him sound especially wise, and his silver hair belied his age; he was still some ten years away from retirement.

Jim riffled the pages on the clipboard and then scrolled at the computer. "Everything checked out fine when you had your physical seven months ago. You're in excellent health. You turned fifty-five this year, right?"

Sigh. "Yes."

"Well, maybe you're just feeling blindsided by the years sneaking up on you. Until you find another job you like, it's perfectly normal to be wondering what's next."

He looked again at the clipboard and computer. "I do see you've put on a few pounds. You're right to consider getting more exercise."

"What about alcohol, Jim? Am I drinking too much?"

"How much *are* you drinking?"

Mallory scrunched her face and pretended to consider the question. With no work or children to focus on, she often managed five glasses of red wine—up to a bottle a day. Since Dwight shared her appreciation for wine and since she did the shopping—not to mention that Dwight didn't usually get home until seven or eight at night—he hadn't noticed the change in her habits. Mallory was suddenly embarrassed to give Jim the real number.

"Two or three glasses a day. Red wine."

She noticed him jot a note on the clipboard paper even as he kept looking at her. "I wouldn't worry too much," he said, "but it wouldn't hurt to cut it down to one or two glasses. That would get rid of some extra pounds. But just as important, get out of the house and do some walking. Tire yourself out a little. Try that for a few weeks; then give me a call and let me know how it's working for you. Okay?"

"Okay!" Mallory was thrilled Jim hadn't told her to stop drinking altogether.

Jim got up and put his free hand on her shoulder. "You're physically healthy, Mallory. I think you've entered a new phase in life that may take some adjusting to. Be kind to yourself."

"Thanks, Jim. I'll try."

"Say hello to Dwight for me."

Mallory's head drooped as soon as she merged with the crowd. Her straight hair became protective blinders.

She hadn't told Jim she was fearful of driving or even leaving the house. She hadn't told him—couldn't tell anyone—about her worry that Dwight might be losing interest in her. And who could blame him either? But he was usually only home for a late dinner and sleep. Was he avoiding her? Or worse, having an affair? Although both were possible scenarios, neither one made sense to her. Their history of talking things out with each other argued otherwise. And they still enjoyed making love, just less often.

She didn't raise her gaze again—except for quick glances to sidestep trouble—until she heard the jarring notes of Dwight's alarm clock. The neighborhood mockingbird had started imitating the sound in May, two months ago. The bird's presence meant Mallory had left the crowd behind. She looked to the sky. A lone cumulus cloud made her think of a ewe separated from her flock. Then she looked straight ahead and was buoyed by Temperance Way's familiar sights. Approaching number 18, home, she felt the magnetism of her walkway gardens.

A nice young man named Richie Trent had been helping this spring and summer. Dwight wanted Richie to feel useful during a stretch of unemployment he was in. Mallory understood that by taking Richie under his wing, Dwight had eased the sting of Jess not being around. She felt the same way. She had tried to get Richie talking on several occasions, but he was reluctant to say much about his home life. Mallory guessed he was embarrassed, at age twenty-one, to be still living with his mother. So she didn't push him. He was a hard worker, strong and polite.

Stepping onto the first slate flagstone, Mallory announced, "There, good doctor, I've had some exercise."

From the other side of the driveway hedge came Doris Hillobenz's high-pitched voice. "Were you talking to me?"

Mallory's jaw tightened. "Oh, hi, Doris. No, just talking to myself."

Doris leaned heavily on her cane as she rounded the front of the hedgerow. She limped across the driveway to plant herself across from Mallory, who had stopped midway up the garden walk. "Why talk to yourself when you have a perfectly good neighbor to talk with?"

Mallory put on her best welcoming smile. "You're looking well, Doris. How's your knee?"

"It's getting there. Heather, my physical therapist, says the surgeon did a good job, but she keeps reminding me that I need to lose more weight if I don't want the same thing to happen to my other knee. And I keep telling her that my weight has nothing to do with it. Both my parents were hefty people and they never had any problems with their knees."

While shaking her head, Doris raised and lowered her cane, forcefully striking the asphalt twice. Thud. Thud. "It really bothers me when a twenty-five-year-old thinks she knows more than I do about my own body, even if she did get a degree in it. I hope my Cassidy never feels free to talk to me that way."

"I'm sure she won't. Cassidy is a very sweet girl. Now, if you'll excuse me, I really need to see to something inside." Turning, Mallory felt her spirits rise again as she approached her safety net.

"By the way, I've grown kind of fond of this Wedgwood color you used on your house. Will you be keeping it when you repaint?"

Mallory pivoted to face Doris again. She forced herself to keep smiling and put a lilt in her voice as she reported, "We haven't decided yet."

"I remember your husband saying he would always associate the new color with the day Carol left for Canada. The house had just been painted the week before."

The cordial quality the Coopers maintained with their neighbor had been carefully cultivated. No one wanted to get on Doris's bad side, lest the whole town hear unflattering details for months to come. But now Doris was coming dangerously close to pushing Mallory's annoyance button. First of all, Dwight should never have voiced in front of Doris how he associated the house color with Carol's departure. Mallory hated for Doris, of all people, to have that sort of knowledge about a very personal emotion. Also, they wouldn't be able to pay for a new paint job for at least another two years. Still, that would be only one year beyond the recommended five-year schedule. If Doris Hillobenz had a complaint to make, she should just come out with it instead of hinting, hinting, hinting.

Mallory swallowed and took a moment to center herself. She swung her head as though to look at the paint on the house, but she looked at the yard. The results of the intense work blossomed on all sides. This version of Maine in July carried the comfort of a mother's lap—not Mallory's mother but the mother she wished for, and the mother she hoped she was to her own kids. Carpeting of sweet snow alyssum (dream mother) provided a heavenly aroma and a textured canvas for orange begonias (eldest child), yellow butterfly daisies (middle child), and purple hurricane daylilies (youngest child). By the house—so near now!—a hummingbird flitted in and out of the majestic Black and Blue salvia (Dwight).

Fortified, Mallory replied, "Yes, the house changed to blue only four years ago. It's holding up pretty well, don't you think? I really have to run, Doris. Give Cassidy a hug for me. Take care of that knee!"

She threw the last comments over her shoulder as she leaped up the three brick steps to the front door of the old colonial, swiftly unlocked it, and entered the dark-wood womb of the vestibule. Shutting and locking the door after the word *knee*, she turned and leaned back with her eyes shut. The old walnut wood smell was pure welcome.

* * *

Mallory entered the front hall and dropped her keys into the pewter dish by the stairs. The familiar clinking, like the mixed wood and clothing smell of the vestibule, epitomized home. Opposite the stairs, her grandparents' old settle, with its high back and well-worn maple wood, beckoned her to take a sit.

And so she did, placing her purse beside her. The Byways bag peeked out, reminding her she hadn't told Doris about meeting Angie Weller. She shook her head and muttered, "What am I going to tell her anyway? That all Angie did was make me feel worse about myself? Or unnerve me half to death?"

Mallory removed and opened the bag. To get to the music box, she had to reach past a flyer Angie had thrown in with the receipt. Crapola, she thought. She opened and wound the music box. The tinny rendition of "Over the Rainbow" added more endorphins to the ones released by the vestibule, keys, and settle. She rested her head on the settle's high back, closed her eyes, and hummed along.

When the music slowed and stopped, she rewound the handle and retrieved the flyer. Mostly it listed items being discounted during July and August, none of which interested Mallory. A text box at the top advised customers to be sure to read Angie's call-to-action letter to the editor in the next *Great Wharf Gazette*.

Mallory taunted out loud, "Maybe I will," tilting her head to the left, "and maybe I won't," tilting her head to the right.

A text box at the bottom gave information about "Free Revolving-Door Art Classes." Oh! Now this was interesting. Monday evenings from seven to eight. Come when you can, don't when you can't. Informal instruction by Angie Weller in all manner of media, from charcoal to acrylics and more. Free except for materials, which can be purchased at a discount at Byways.

Mallory felt a push-pull. She had some talent for drawing and had always wanted to learn to paint. Maybe in a small group like this she could focus on the piece in front of her and ease back into the world again. Going to and fro would be in daylight during the summer months. Still, when she really thought about doing it, fear quickened her breath. She folded the flyer and put it with the music box next to the pewter dish. She'd think about it later.

She headed toward the kitchen. Her pace quickened as she neared the only modernized room in the house. The lemon-yellow walls and shiny white trim always brightened her mood. The open floor plan included a fireplace with an expansive hearth; an eat-in area with a picnic-style table; and a wide, horseshoe-shaped cooking area. The laundry room was down a short hall to the right. At the start of the hallway and opposite the cooking area was the home-office alcove housing Mallory's computer.

More than once, Dwight had told her she should take Jess's or Carol's room for office space, as he had taken the room vacated by Panda, their eldest, when she left. But Mallory wasn't ready to do that. Her excuse was that the limited space in the alcove ensured she wouldn't end up buried in paper like Dwight was. But really, Mallory didn't want to feel shut away. She liked being in her favorite room in the house. Memories cradled her—the screen door banging as the kids asked when dinner would be ready, and the million and one meals they had shared around that table.

She looked at the decorator clock over the fireplace, last year's anniversary gift from Dwight. Only 4:08—too early for wine? She usually had a glass with lunch but had forgone that today, knowing she'd see

Jim. Maybe she could wait until six. She decided to throw in a load of laundry and check her Facebook news feed first.

The familiar smell of the spring-sweet detergent tickled her nose and her mood. There had been a lot more laundry when the kids were around. The speed of her task made her realize that as laundry decreased, time on Facebook increased. "Someone should do a study of that," she said aloud as she sat down at her computer. She didn't used to talk out loud so much. "I think Harvard should do a study of that." Now at least the comment held more weight.

The newest Facebook postings were by two museum friends, each posting about the thwarting of a robbery there. Mallory commented, "How scary!" and "Glad you're okay!" She missed being in a work environment, sharing the excitement when something unusual happened. At the same time, reading about the robbery made her stomach churn. She left the computer to check that the front and back doors really were locked.

When she returned, she saw that Carol had just posted a picture of her freshly painted kitchen, a spirited green. Mallory commented, "I'll try to find a matching potholder!" Imagining the smell of another kitchen's fresh paint gave her a lift. She looked forward to the time her middle child might meet the right guy, but she didn't worry about Carol's ability to enjoy life.

Mallory typed her own Facebook update. "Just back from doctor, who says I'm in excellent health for someone my age. Is that a compliment?" She paused. Did it sound like bragging? Would people think she was fishing for compliments? Oh, who cares, she thought.

But she did care. She deleted it. In its place she posted, "Shoplifting's on the increase, I hear, but I still pay the asking price. Does anyone ever admit to shoplifting? (No, I'm not implying anything.)"

She liked that one.

Moving on to her emails, Mallory scanned the senders and saw that one was from her uncle. Her chest tightened, and little explosions of static electricity erupted in her head. She shut her eyes and took some deep breaths. Uncle Bill was seventy years old now and emailing with greater frequency. Without opening his email, Mallory closed the browser and poured herself a glass of red wine.

3

JULY

*In which Jim Beall's friends Richie Trent and
Sheila Nies bring balance to his life.*

Dr. Jim Beall assumed, as he always did, that his
office manager, Cora, had locked the front door
on her way out. The back door was in his office and
gave him direct access to the parking lot and his reliable old Camry. As Jim got into the car now, he tried to
remember the last time he felt this drained after work.
Oh yes, it was last night, Thursday. And Wednesday,
the night before. And Tuesday ...

Having his own practice, he had hoped, would
mean having control over his work hours. When he
first opened his office in Great Wharf, twenty years

before, he planned not to take on too many patients. Over the years, though, one thing led to another—one patient begged him to add her whole family, another pleaded for his brother, and so on. Jim acknowledged that he was a softie; he couldn't say no when people needed help. Nowadays he doctored from seven in the morning to eight at night, six days a week, and sometimes more. He had almost laughed out loud when, earlier in the week, he heard himself advising Mallory Cooper to de-stress. He knew he didn't follow his own advice.

Waiting at the traffic light to turn onto Wyeth, Jim checked the dashboard clock and decided he had time for both a shower and a quick bite. He lowered the windows to enjoy the evening's breeze. The satisfied murmuring of vacationers as they sauntered to and from their dinners further relaxed him.

Jim was grateful to be in good health. He prescribed exercise for himself as well as his patients. He went to the YMCA every Sunday afternoon and also during the week whenever a patient cancelled near lunchtime or end of day and no paperwork pressed on him.

Last Sunday, five days ago, Jim was halfway through his routine, counting to himself in a second set of bicep curls, when he spotted Richie Trent in the doorway. Jim had first gotten to know Richie through the Great Wharf Community Players, in which Jim was once active. They discovered they both enjoyed weightlifting, and Jim recommended the local Y. Until last month he had worried that the lack of a full-time job was wearing Richie down. But then Richie, who had been with the Players for about two years, finally landed a role. Since starting to rehearse the part, Richie had become more talkative during their YMCA meet-ups. Jim hoped the morose Richie was gone for good.

"Hey, Richie, over here," Jim called with a wave.

Richie waved back. "I'm surprised to see you here, Jim. I thought the Y had banned old people."

"No, they're waiting till next year when you get your first gray hair."

"Ha! You'll never see it. I'll snatch it out first. Or your cataracts will blind you to it."

The two bantered until Richie started his own lift routine; then silence was the unspoken rule. They'd each be counting their reps or thinking about something else or nothing else. It was a free space they respected.

When Jim finished his workout, he used the alcohol-soaked antibacterial wipes provided by the Y to swab where his hands had been. On his way to the shower room, he passed by Richie and said, "You're starting to stink, man, so I'm heading out."

Richie laughed and then asked, "Will you be coming to the premiere of *Rumors* Friday night?"

"Wouldn't miss it. How did the dress rehearsal go?"

"Really great." Richie kept doing leg lifts while he talked. "This play's a winner. Come backstage and say hi before it starts, if you get there in time. I'd like to introduce you to Zoey, the woman who got me into theater to begin with. Also, Ma will be there, and Amanda, who works with Ma and Zoey."

"Will do, Richie. See you then."

This memory of Sunday's conversation spurred a thought process that now accompanied Jim through his brisk after-work shower and an oregano-infused microwaved meal of frozen lasagna. Jim wondered if, at tonight's premiere, Richie planned to fix him up with one of those women. Experience had taught him this might well be the case. And he wasn't necessarily against the idea, either, as long as the word *commitment* didn't enter into it.

Jim's parents had both been doctors, so he knew how easily the profession could consume a person. He adored his parents, and they loved him. But usually a housekeeper fed him dinner. He was familiar with loneliness.

There had been only one romantic interest in his life, during college. Her name was Beverly. Jim always felt a twinge of nostalgia when he remembered how they met. He savored this memory while he rapidly sudsed an orange-scented soap up and down his arms. A tall, lissome blond had sidled up next to him in the cafeteria line, tapped his shoulder, and said, "You're colorblind, aren't you?"

"Uh-oh. Is it that obvious?"

"Both my brothers are colorblind. They're always putting bad shades together. Just like that shirt and sweater thing you have going there."

Thanks to a few shopping trips with Beverly, Jim's college wardrobe improved. And thanks to Beverly, Jim got a taste of the deep trust and grounding that can come with the right relationship. And now he regretted not having more time to keep sudsing with the revived memory of their love in his head.

Between her junior and senior years Beverly transferred out to nurse a sick sister a thousand miles away. The sister died several years later, but Jim and Beverly never did see each other again. By then, she had met someone else and was heading into married life and motherhood. Part of Jim mourned. A larger part celebrated. This early in his medical career, he would have found it nearly impossible to be the active, involved parent he would want to be.

Convenient friendships and more than a few torrid one-night stands satisfied Jim's healthy animal side through medical school and his residency. After seven years of residency in Cleveland, Ohio, Jim moved to Great Wharf. He had dated often enough by then to know his reputation: extremely attractive but impossible to pin down. Even the most determined females concluded there was something in Jim Beall's character that fought true intimacy. He started informing women about this on first dates. For some it was a turn-on. For others it caused an argument. For all, he just meant it as a truth that needed to be gotten out of the way. He enjoyed being with people, and he loved sex. But he wouldn't get involved beyond a superficial level.

Toweled off, Jim put the frozen lasagna in the microwave to cook its five minutes while he dressed. Matching numbers sewn into different items told him the pieces that went well together. His friend Sheila Nies had helped him with that soon after they met, two years ago. In Sheila he found a kindred spirit who, likewise, wanted to keep relationships undemanding. She wasn't a classic beauty in any sense of the word. But she was a good psychologist, devoted to her work. And like Jim, Sheila enjoyed people.

She complained to him, "The hardest part of my job is keeping likable clients at arm's length. You have it easier. You can focus on a physical ailment and pretend to have another patient waiting in the next room.

But I have no assistant and only one room, and I'm probing deeply into the person's psyche to boot!"

Sheila and Jim became friends with benefits. They enjoyed each other's company intellectually, and they both had robust sexual desires. They figured they were a perfect match for the time being. There would be no commitment beyond showing up when a date was made, or calling if something interfered.

* * *

Insistent beeps from the microwave alerted Jim that his dinner was ready. He finished buttoning his favorite shirt, a black Tommy Bahama with a silver sailfish design, bought on a winter trip to Florida years ago. He slid his feet into Birkenstock sandals. He wore closed shoes at work, but he wore the open Birkenstocks almost everywhere else—especially in Maine's soul-nurturing summer months. If he could have gotten away with walking naked in them, he would have.

The heavenly smell of steamy, bubbling lasagna greeted him in the kitchen. While he ate standing up, he replayed the keystone conversation he and Sheila had that still gave them the giggles.

"We'll have to be careful," he had pointed out, "not to let people see us together. It's too small a town to invite gossip about our relationship. If our clients think of us as a couple, they'll be asking about it constantly. Asking us to their homes and all, you know."

"You're so right!" Sheila agreed. "I'm willing to let you be my doctor if you're willing to let me be your psychologist. At least then we can get some regular privacy. Don't you feel the need for monthly sessions with your shrink?"

"Yes! And I think you'll have a condition of some kind that requires regular checkups. Nothing contagious or weird. I'll come up with something."

And that's why Jim Beall was whispered to have had a childhood trauma he wouldn't talk about, and Sheila Nies was whispered to have back pain from a childhood battle with scoliosis improperly treated at the time. Jim knew their ploys had worked when one of his patients, infamous town gossip Doris Hillobenz, ran the information by his office manager for confirmation. Good, reliable Cora let Jim know the rumors about Sheila's physical health and Jim's mental health. She quickly added, "I told Mrs. Hillobenz it was none of my own business and shouldn't be hers either."

Jim swallowed the last bite and put the dirty plate and fork in the dishwasher. He looked forward to de-stressing with his friend Sheila again soon. Two years of friendly hookups with no other expectations had forged a strong bond of friendship between them. He had a small gift for her, a bookmark from Byways

Gift Shop. Sheila had raved about Byways as the place where she bought greeting cards.

"It's an inviting little shop," she told him during yesterday's afterglow conversation. "As you know from the cards I pick for you, it has a quirky selection for friends and lovers."

Sheila drew an imaginary figure eight with her index finger on Jim's bare thigh. "I've decided to go to Byways Monday evenings to perfect my charcoal drawing techniques. Angie, the owner, offers free come-at-will classes in July and August. I didn't run into any of my clients, at least during the first session, so it should be a good way to relax with my sketch pad."

"Free classes? What does this Angie get out of that?" Jim trusted Sheila to have picked up on any ulterior motive.

"She asks that participants buy art materials from her shop when they need them. She has a whole section of chalks, watercolor paints, acrylics, and so on, and how-to books. I'm sure she's hoping to create word of mouth and to sell other items at the same time."

Jim said, "Promise to be a model and I'll show up myself sometime."

"Promise me you won't!" Sheila gave him a slap on his thigh just as her cell alarm went off, signaling it was time to get back to work. Before she left, she said, "Don't you dare show up. But the next time I need to increase my client base, I'll remember what you said and offer Angie my live-modeling services." She walked out the door with an exaggerated booty swing.

Jim had used lunchtime that day to walk down the block for a look at Byways. The bookmark he bought read, "Lying is the strongest acknowledgment of the force of truth." He wondered how Sheila would apply the quotation to their secret relationship.

The cashier wore a name tag identifying herself as Angie Weller, Store Proprietor. She was a petite spitfire whose age he was hard-pressed to guess. She asked him, "Are you buying that for yourself or as a gift?" He avoided a direct answer by saying, "I just like that quotation, and it didn't seem right to browse so long and leave empty handed."

She gave him his change with a meaningful look, her fingers sliding along his open palm. "There. Your hand's not empty anymore." Jim enjoyed Angie coming on to him, but he simply nodded and left anyway. On his walk back to the office, he chuckled at the thought of letting Sheila know she might have some competition.

4

JULY

*In which Jim meets three new women who may
or may not have designs on him.*

ONIGHT, TIRED BUT refreshed, Jim had the premiere of the play to attend. He arrived in time
to head backstage and say hello. The Great Wharf
Community Players had been in operation for six
years now. Ten years ago, a wealthy patron had committed to matching all donations the group could raise
over a two-year period to purchase and renovate an
old stable, changing it into a playhouse. It took two
more years to get the building smelling more like saw-
dust than manure. Captioned photographs lined the

sparsely furnished lobby, displaying the histories of both the stable and the playhouse.

Jim had been in a couple of productions himself. His silver hair, six-foot-one-inch height, and deep voice made him a natural for authority roles. He had never tried out for a lead role because he knew his schedule would get in the way. The troupe needed to know they could count on him when he did get involved. Even for the small parts, an understudy was always ready.

Opening tonight was the Players' rendition of the Neil Simon play *Rumors*. Jim howled when Richie told him Doris Hillobenz had a role. Much of the script involved people making up stories, specifically to explain what had happened to the host of a party. Before the opening scene, the party's host—a deputy mayor of New York—shot his earlobe off, possibly in a suicide attempt gone awry. To protect their host's reputation, the guests make up stories to keep the police and media off track. Mrs. Hillobenz would be a good fit in a role that required telling tales.

Richie was cast as the deputy mayor's accountant, Lenny. He'd be wearing a baldness wig and glasses to look older than his twenty-one years. Jim couldn't wait to razz him about playing an older person. He peeked behind the red velvet curtain. The frenetic activity backstage reignited in him the warm feeling of camaraderie he loved about amateur theater.

"Hey, Jim!" Richie spotted him and gestured for a high five. "Glad you could make it!"

"Hi, Richie." Jim delivered an extra-strong high five. "What happened to your hair?"

"I thought it would help our friendship if I learned how it felt to be as old as you."

Richie's attention shifted to a short woman with wild brown hair walking by. Grabbing at her sleeve he said, "Zoey, this is my friend Jim Beall." To Jim he said, "Zoey's the one who got me interested in the Players to begin with, even though she wasn't involved herself. She let me be the guinea pig, and then she signed on for this season."

Jim judged Zoey to be forty years old and carrying fifteen extra pounds. He watched her expression change—from minor annoyance at being diverted from her goal to a warm smile (for a friend of Richie's? for Jim himself?). She held out her hand. "I work with Richie's mother doing medical and legal transcription work."

"You do?" Jim's bushy eyebrows flew up a good half inch.

"Yes. Why is that surprising?"

"Because of my medical practice. I'll bet my office manager has used your services. What's the name of the company?"

"Best Transcriptions—it's located in Biddeford."

"I'll ask Cora. From the work I've seen, Best Transcriptions would be an accurate name."

"Well, thanks! Listen—it's great to meet you, but I have to go help with the scenery." Zoey shrugged her shoulders to indicate helplessness and then tapped Richie's arm.

"Yeah, I need to go too. Thanks for coming, Jim. Hope you enjoy it!"

"Break a leg, but not really. I have enough to do."

Jim made his way to a row of folding chairs with an empty seat. After sidling by the people closer to the aisle and before sitting down, he looked around the rest of the audience to see if there was anyone he should wave at. Sure enough, he exchanged waves with several of his patients, including Mallory and Dwight Cooper. They were seated in the very last row near the door.

Jim settled in for the play. Zoey wasn't his type, which would be taller and thinner or at least athletic. Not that he was looking anyway. He didn't think Zoey found him especially interesting either, or else she would have given him a clue with a certain look or touch—instead of a quick howdy-do-and-back-to-the-races, an expression his mother used to use. Maybe Richie really hadn't had an ulterior motive when he invited Jim to visit backstage.

Jim didn't know any of the people seated near him in the audience, but they all enjoyed small talk until the lights dimmed. He was asleep by the second scene.

At intermission, he asked a neighbor to fill him in. He didn't want Richie to know he'd failed him. The neighbor said the actor playing Lenny had been very funny and his timing was perfect. These were the words, then, that Jim drew on when he went back-stage to congratulate Richie afterward.

"You did a great job, Richie, and your comic tim-ing was perfect." Jim had to shout to be heard over the postperformance din.

"Thanks! Everyone was so on tonight!" Richie waved his arms wide. "Listen—I have to take care of a couple things before leaving, and Ma's waiting to drive me. Would you mind introducing yourself to her and Amanda, and sort of keep them entertained until I'm ready to go? It shouldn't take more than fifteen minutes."

Jim heaved an internal sigh. "Sure. Where are they?"

"They're waiting in the front row. The blond is Amanda, and the brunette is my mother, Jean. Ma's been hoping to meet you. She's always complaining that I don't have enough friends, so be ready for her scrutiny."

"And who's Amanda again?"

"She works with Ma, like Zoey does. Ma calls Amanda and Zoey her A-to-Z friends."

"That's another clue, besides her being a transcriptionist, that your mother likes words. I'll bet she does crossword puzzles too."

"Yeah, she does! Your ancient wisdom continues to amaze."

"If you live long enough, you'll come across smarter than you are too. See you in fifteen."

Jim maneuvered back through the throng, slid by the heavy closed curtain, and started his descent to the audience floor. On his way down he spotted Amanda and Jean standing in conversation with each other. This gave him a moment to form his own impressions.

Amanda was the modern-day personification of a 1960s Miss America. In fact, her wavy blond hair and willowy height reminded him of his college love. She seemed much younger than Beverly, though. That's when Jim realized he was now thirty-five years older than when he'd been with Beverly. When he looked again, he saw that Amanda wasn't much older than Beverly had been when they'd been together. He smiled ruefully at the trick time had just played on him.

Looking next at Jean Trent, Jim felt a lightning-fast hitch in his forward motion, as though his feet had—suddenly and for only a split second—landed on a moving walkway headed in the other direction. It happened so quickly he hardly even noticed it. Just enough to feel puzzled for a fraction of a second. Richie's mother was slim and nicely proportioned, with light brown hair and freckles. What Jim noticed most as he neared the women were Jean's large smoky-green eyes. Hypnotic. Almost frightening in how deep they might probe.

"You must be Jean and Amanda."

His deep voice startled them. He quickly shook hands. "I'm Richie's friend Jim Beall."

"Oh!" both women exclaimed at the same time. Jean said, "It's such a pleasure to finally meet you. You've been a bright spot for Richie during this uncertain time. There must be some karmic connection. Do you feel it?"

Jim felt his usual cringe when someone assumed he leaned toward Buddhism—or any organized religion. "I don't know about karma, but I think very highly of your son. He's a great kid."

Amanda added, "I've only met Richie twice now, but the first time was just after one of his workouts at the Y, and he mentioned you then. It's great to meet you."

Jim again took in Amanda's beauty as he nodded at what she said, but his eyes went back to Jean's eyes. He had to make a concerted effort to turn his head toward each of the two women in turn. Paying careful attention to individuals was a skill he had developed as a good doctor known for his bedside manner.

"Well, it's great to meet you both. I met Zoey backstage before the play, and I know you three work for Best Transcriptions. I'm pretty sure that's the company my office manager uses for our work. She's very happy with the results."

Jean and Amanda beamed at each other. "That's good to hear," Jean said. "We never get a chance to talk with customers directly. Of course, that's fine with us when the customer has a complaint."

Jim chuckled at the conspiratorial look Jean gave him. "Sounds like the relief I feel when Cora is the one to handle billing complaints."

During this exchange Jim had noticed out of the corner of his eye the progress of Doris Hillobenz toward their group. She had descended the steps from the stage—mincing, careful not to twist her healing knee. Her adopted granddaughter, Cassidy, helped her. They'd been standing there now for less than a minute.

Doris leaned into the group. "You know, I used to work as a transcriptionist myself. I was very good at it. And even if I felt sick I still kept to the schedule. Why, when Cassidy here was two years old, she ran a fever and started throwing up, but I finished the job in front of me before taking her to the emergency room. Kids are resilient, but if you have a tyrant for a boss, your job can disappear just like that."

"Hello, Mrs. Hillobenz, Cassidy," Jim said. "Have all of you met before?" He ignored the story of bad parenting since Cassidy had somehow made it to high-school age and Doris had no other little ones to bring up. She had lost her only child, Cassidy's mother, to a car accident that killed both parents when Cassidy was only one year old. Doris and her husband at the time had adopted Cassidy immediately.

"No, we haven't," Doris said, "and I thought I knew everyone in town."

Cassidy's face was flushed, but whether from embarrassment or excitement Jim couldn't tell. She was a little overweight, and having to cope with a grandmother like hers might even have led to high blood pressure. He would double-check that at her next physical.

Jean said, "You may know everyone in town, but we're from Biddeford. My son Richie is Lenny in the play."

Jim let his eyes stay on Jean while she introduced herself and Amanda. There was something profoundly touching about Jean. He tried to memorize her face and mannerisms, planning to analyze the effect later. At the moment, a rationale for staring wasn't needed.

Amanda said, "Doris, you were hysterical in your role tonight. Good show!"

"Thank you, Amanda. Cassidy here thought I played my part as well as that Oscar winner Kathy Bates would have. Jean, did you know that my Cassidy and your Richie know each other from the trolley museum?"

"No, I didn't. How do you like it, Cassidy? Richie loves it."

"It's great, Mrs. Trent." Cassidy nodded vigorously. "Everyone's so nice there? I'm learning a lot about streetcars, and people too?"

"Like what?"

"Well, for instance? My volunteer friends and I all thought Richie was really stuck up, because he never said hi for so long? But he isn't stuck up at all." Cassidy made this pronouncement while she waved to one of her girlfriends at the back of the room. "That's the girl I was telling you about, Gram. She's the one with a crush on Richie, not me." Cassidy glanced at Jean and added, "I mean, I think he's great? But I'm not stupid about it. I know he's too old for me. I'm only sixteen and he's …"

Returning his attention to the conversation, and knowing Richie's age, Jim almost couldn't resist answering the dangling question on Jean's behalf. He had been Cassidy's doctor for fifteen years. It was fun seeing her in this informal setting.

Jean said, "Twenty-one. And it's true that Richie doesn't have a stuck-up bone in his body. He's just a bit shy at first. I'm glad you and your friends are getting to know the real Richie. And you're right; five years is way older when you're in high school."

Doris said, "Well, I'm glad to meet Richie's mother. I know Richie as an actor, but I've also seen him helping with the yard work at the Coopers' place, next to mine." She placed her hand gently on Jean's and said, "Maybe you could give him some motherly advice about not taking his shirt off when he's working there. I caught Cassidy staring out the window at him the other day."

"Oh, Gram," Cassidy moaned. She put her head down and brought a hand up to hide her eyes. Jim wondered if the others noticed the Hello Kitty faces on Cassidy's fingernails. She had always wanted a cat.

"Anyway," Doris continued when Jean didn't promise to have a talk with Richie, "I saw the Coopers in the audience, but they skedaddled out of here while we were taking our bows. Don't you think that was rude, being my neighbors and all?"

She looked around for agreement. No one responded, but Jean said, "I wish I'd known they were here. Richie speaks so fondly of them both."

"Well, Mallory's become quite the hermit since the last of their kids left home. I do what I can to encourage her to get out more, but she doesn't listen to me. I asked her to check out that new Byways gift shop—to let me know her opinion of the owner, Angie Weller. Near three weeks ago and still not a word from her. I might as well be talking to the walls."

Again, no comment. Doris took Cassidy by the hand. "Well, we have to get going. My knee's bothering me, and I need to be strong for tomorrow night's performance."

Jim said, "Take care of that knee, Doris. By the way, how do you like your orthopedist?"

"She's a Miss Know-It-All, but I guess she's as good as the next one. I wish you had specialized in knee surgery, though."

Jim thanked an invisible god of choices for that one.

5

JULY

In which Jean Trent makes Richie talk; Richie hatches a secret plan; and Jean's A-to-Z friends help her wake from a long sleep.

MORNINGS BEAT EVENINGS for Jean Trent. She liked to get up before the sun, brush her teeth, shower, and greet the day fully dressed. This pattern held true whether she was in an upward or a downward mood swing. Jean had a youthful appearance at age forty-eight. She had the slim body type often associated with swimming, her own choice of exercise when she made time for it.

From her seat at the kitchen table this Monday morning, Jean heard Richie shuffle into the bathroom.

She felt a swell of pride at how well he was handling the tedium of job hunting without letting all the rejections get to him. She took a sip of green tea and wished for the trillionth time that Edward, Richie's father, could see what a fine man Richie had turned into.

Richie's handling of his current situation led her to wonder about the ups and downs she experienced in her own moods. Were they chemical or situational? She didn't used to have these strong swings. They had started about a year after Edward's death. He had died when he grabbed a live wire hidden by litter. The fatal shock to his system sent a debilitating shockwave through the whole family system, though Richie had been affected more than the other children. Richie was so sensitive that he even found a way to blame himself for what had happened. A school counselor eventually opened Jean's eyes to that, but Richie refused to talk about it.

Jean's first priority after Edward's death was to keep the family on solid footing. They lived in Massachusetts at the time, and fortunately most of the kids had finished high school or college. Mainly Jean worried about Richie, the youngest and then in tenth grade. She would never forget the late-morning call from a school administrator telling her that Richie had started a fistfight. He had never gotten into any physical trouble before. It was the latest, though, in a series of problems. He had been swearing in class, drinking and smoking marijuana with undesirable companions, and generally being at odds with himself and others.

Jean finally gave him an ultimatum: Turn yourself around or I'll make sure a judge turns you around. She didn't just threaten; she gave him an opportunity. She told him about a school in the next town over that had a career and technical program she thought he'd enjoy, if he wanted to make the switch. Her boss had mentioned the school to her in another context, but she thought it might be a sign from the universe. At least it made sense to her.

To her surprise, Richie jumped at the chance. He went online and checked out the school. The options excited him. He even talked with students and teachers there. Finally, he spoke with someone in the placement office and decided to become an electrician.

At last, a year after Edward's death, Jean could attend to her own grief. After holding it all together during work hours, she collapsed every evening on the living room sofa. She knew Richie and his sisters and brother could manage the rest. After half a year of that, her kids banded together and convinced her to see her doctor. Finding nothing wrong physically, the doctor recommended a psychiatrist who might prescribe medication to help Jean fight the crippling malaise.

The psychiatrist told her there was no "magic bullet," but with his help Jean regained a sense of purpose. She took up swimming for exercise. She scheduled get-togethers with friends after work to keep herself more outwardly oriented. She became used to ups and downs as part of her reaction to the different meds and to life since Edward's death.

After Richie got his electrician certificate, and three years after Edward's death, Jean decided to kick-start a new life for herself. She would move to Maine, where she'd still be within driving distance of her children but far enough away to experience something different, whatever that might be. Her psychiatrist encouraged the change and referred her to a colleague in Portland, Dr. Eli Sterns. Jean found an affordable apartment in Biddeford, just north of Kennebunkport and only a twenty-minute drive from Portland.

Richie moved with her to help with the transition and to expand his own horizons as well. Before the move Jean lined up a job with Best Transcriptions. Richie applied for certification to practice as an electrician in Maine. He landed a full-time position with a start-up company, Hank Sanborn Electric. He enjoyed the work, but the company went out of business at the end of the year. Now Richie's unemployment benefits were still helping, but nothing like a regular job.

Jean did her best to think positively, to see the current situation as just part of a cycle that would turn upward again. But she could feel the melancholy looming.

***

Richie finished his shave and stepped back from the mirror to analyze a quick flexing of his tanned abs. Then he leaned in close to the mirror again. A blackhead? No, just a tiny piece of lint from the black face towel he had just used. Whew! He hated to think he'd been sporting a huge blackhead when he saw Amanda Friday night, before he and Ma left after the play.

He turned on the shower. Waiting for the water to heat up, he turned back to the mirror, yawned, and flexed his abs some more. Not for the first time he wondered if Amanda could possibly think of him as a boyfriend.

Along with his mother's freckles, Richie had the pocked complexion left by virulent acne in his teenage years. The cratered skin struck people as rugged, not unattractive. He chalked their conclusion up to his barely controlled shock of light brown hair and a slim but strong body. He realized people were also responding to his quiet demeanor. The bantering with Jim Beall was exceptionally outgoing for him. Normally, barring a pressing need, he responded more than initiated. The combination of looks, freckles, scars, and reticence made him appealing to men and women alike. His ma told him he came across as trustworthy. Could all this be enough to reassure and attract Amanda?

The golden tan from outdoor work at the Coopers' place was an added plus. Richie was grateful to Dwight for both the tan and a number of freelance job referrals. They had first met in January, thanks to an emergency at one of the buildings Dwight managed in Portland. The electrical repair company Dwight usually relied on was backed up, but he had made note of Richie's flyer at the Great Wharf Coffeehouse. With a shared background in building maintenance, Richie and Dwight hit it off right away. When Richie told him he lived in Biddeford, Dwight commented that the trolley museum in neighboring Kennebunkport might like to know about him.

"I've been volunteering there for years," Dwight said. "They're always looking for donations of time, not just money. As long as you're not working full-time, you should offer yourself up to help with their restoration or guide needs—as time permits, of course."

"Yeah, as time permits. I've got plenty of time these days." Richie tried not to feel sorry for himself, but the lack of regular work and any kind of love life was eating at him.

"What I'm thinking," Dwight added, "is you'll meet some guys involved in the building trades and make other connections that could mean paying jobs later."

Richie decided to try it. And on top of his getting the role with the Players, Seashore added more purpose to his days. So far, so good. As soon as he got a real job, though, the first thing he planned to do was ask Amanda out. If he could wait that long.

He wiped the steam from the mirror, turned on the whiny exhaust fan, lowered the water temperature, and stepped into the shower. The clanging of the old pipes reminded him of his current project. He was helping to restore museum car 48, an old cable car from San Francisco built after the 1906 earthquake.

Seashore Trolley Museum was largely outdoors, with open car barns for the main displays. The museum had horsecars, cable cars, fancy parlor cars, double-deck cars, and much more. It also offered air-horn-blasting open-sided trolley rides around the property. While Richie lathered up, he pictured the rusting old streetcars that weren't housed in the car barns. Bright yellow, dark green, and dusty red trolleys nestled higgledy-piggledy among a mix of deciduous and fir trees. There the cars waited to reach the top of the repair list or to sacrifice parts to others. Richie liked those cars the best.

* * *

Yawning even after his shower, Richie dragged himself into the kitchen and found his ma doing her crossword puzzle while eating a bowl of granola. Being a vegan, she ate it with rice milk instead of cow's milk. The refrigerator included both kinds, though, because Richie had not made the switch when his mother did a few years back. He did like the granola, but not before his coffee. If he could just get that coffee poured, he'd have the strength to move on.

"Now, Richie, don't lie to me, but what's a three-letter word for falsehood?"

"Funny, Ma." He had to smile.

"Before starting my puzzle today, I read some of the *Great Wharf Gazette* you left on the table. There's a letter to the editor from someone named Angie Weller. Do you know her?"

"No. Why? What'd she write?" Richie turned the Clean sign over to Dirty and opened the dishwasher, knowing this meant he would have to unload the dishes now. When it was run at night, his ma usually unloaded it the next morning before he got up. He made an "ugh" sound.

Ignoring his grunt, Jean said, "I gather this Angie person runs a gift shop there in Great Wharf. She's proposing that the town put in a cinder path to encourage visitors to enjoy more of the less frenetic parts of town. Have the Coopers said anything about it?"

"Nope."

Jean rattled the paper. "Dear Editor," she read. "As the owner of one of Great Wharf's more successful shops, I'd like to propose a way to bring even more visitors to our wonderful town. My idea would translate over time to more visitors during the whole of non-snow season, not just the high summer months. Let's build a cinder path that people can walk along as an optional route paralleling Olympia Snowe Blvd. The path could run through the neighborhoods from oceanside's Garden Path Lane all the way to Newman Lane, on the far side of Wyeth."

Jean looked over the paper at Richie as he finished emptying the dishwasher. "I'm surprised the Coopers weren't talking about this when you worked on their yard yesterday, since their neighborhood might be affected."

"Nope. Maybe they hadn't read it yet."

"It sounds like a great idea to me, but I'll bet a lot of people will be opposed for any number of reasons. Let me know if you hear anything. I, for one, would love a path like that to walk on."

"Sure, Ma." Finally Richie was done with the unloading. Time for coffee.

"On to my next topic then." Jean removed her reading glasses. "The theme of this week's crossword puzzle is different kinds of people movers. Do they have any cable cars at the trolley museum?"

"Yeah, they do." His fingers took hold of his Hank Sanborn Electric coffee mug, the last item in the dryer rack. The cold enamel brought a shiver.

"Do they know where they came from?"

"Yeah, they do." He placed the mug on the one-cup coffee maker, inserted the French roast flavor packet, and hit the brew button. "This gift from big bro has made me his slave for life."

"See if you can find out—do they have a cable car from the old days in San Francisco?"

"Weird. I'm working on one right now."

"That is not weird; that is fate. There are no such things as coincidences. The universe brings us clues about how to connect the dots. If that museum has a streetcar from that period, it could be the very car that killed your gramps G-squared. Maybe it wasn't enough just to name you after him. Maybe something else needs to happen."

This thought hit Richie with the power of a spike being driven into a railway tie. His great-great-grandfather had died after being hit by a runaway San Francisco cable car sometime around 1910. His mother's mother's father's father, Richard C. Laskey, was the man for whom Richie—full name Richard Laskey Trent—was named. His mother liked to do what she could to bring things full circle, to give things closure.

"The circle of life," she liked to say, "is what it's all about. To everything there is a season. Sometimes it just takes a little bit of creativity to figure out what season it is and whether the next one has begun."

Had his hands been inside the instrument of death? Wasn't unemployment hard enough without having the power of your very name questioned?

Richie knew his mother had planned to bring closure to her ancestor's early demise by naming a son after him. As it worked out, the honor had to wait until her fourth child. Child one was a son who would carry his own father's name, and then two daughters. By the time Richie was born, she had just about given up hope. But now, all twenty-one years of Richie's life had been lived with the comforting assumption that Gramps G-squared rested in peace.

"I'll check into it, Ma."

Maybe she was right. Maybe nothing was ever really over and done but always part of a pathway in some realm. The concept of closure was a comforting one, but it turned out that being closed in one category didn't mean being closed in another. To bring closure on behalf of Gramps G-squared, he might need to do something more than carry the name forward. An idea germinated.

With Richie's reassurance that he would check on any streetcars from San Francisco, Jean left for work feeling a little more lighthearted. She noticed the upbeat feeling and wasn't sure whether to ascribe it to having a new question to be answered or to the new medication Dr. Sterns had prescribed. She almost exchanged her gray blouse for a purple one, but she was late so she stayed with the gray.

As she steered her old green Cavalier into the Best Transcriptions parking lot, she spotted Amanda and Zoey chatting near Zoey's car. Amanda rented a room in Zoey's house, and they usually drove in together in Zoey's car. Jean called out the window, "Wait for me!" The fourteen-inch height difference between her A-to-Z friends no longer caught her attention.

"Thanks for waiting." Zoey and Amanda were spray-cleaning the car windows when Jean arrived. She marveled at their energy. "So, Zoey, the play was spectacular. Did you think Saturday's performance went as well?"

"A smash hit all around." Zoey moved to the back window. "What did you think of your son's acting job?"

"Now what do you think I thought? He was great, of course."

Zoey reached toward Amanda at the side window to give her a teasing nudge. Then she looked at

Jean and said, "I heard you two met Jim Beall. So did I, backstage. What did you think of that blue-eyed doctor?"

"Such a handsome man! Didn't you think so, Amanda?" Jean shifted her look upward from Zoey to Amanda.

"A real looker. Almost as handsome as Richie. In a different way, of course."

Jean's short bob of hair bounced as she angled her head with the question, "Do you think Richie's handsome, Amanda?"

"Yes, I do." Amanda put her hand to her forehead, as though deep in thought. "At least I think I do. It's hard to remember what he looks like without the baldness wig. Let me see that picture you carry of him again."

While Zoey and Amanda put the cleaning materials back in the car, Jean pulled a packet of family photos out of her purse and flipped to Richie's graduation picture. They all huddled over the picture as though they had never seen it before.

Amanda said, "I know he's tall, but how tall?"

"Six feet three inches—two inches taller than you."

Amanda said, "Uh-huh," but stepped back from the huddle. Jean worried she might have gone too far with her last comment.

As the women started walking across the parking lot, Amanda said, "Now, Jean, I know you'd like me and Richie to get together, but you know I'm just out of a bad relationship. I'm still nursing the wounds. And, well, Richie should be focusing on getting a job, right?" Amanda gave Jean a reassuring hug and then finished, "So yes, he's gorgeous. But let's leave it there for now, okay?"

Jean agreed. "You're right. Forgive an anxious mother?"

"Of course. Now, back to Jim. Do we know if he's married?"

No one knew for certain.

Jean said, "Remember that Hillobenz woman's comment about the sexy gift shop owner?" Amanda nodded. "Well, maybe Jim will be running right over to check her out now."

Zoey said, "How can we keep tabs on this potential intrigue? Jean, you're closest in age to Jim, and Jim's a friend of Richie's. I think you should make it your assignment to find out if Jim's married—and if not, whether he'd prefer you or the gift shop owner."

"Whoa, Zoey!" Jean stopped short of the door to the building. "You sly creature, you! And here I was thinking Jim might want to get to know Amanda. I mean, what man in his right mind wouldn't?"

Amanda said, "Yuck! He's way too old for me."

And Zoey said, "Jean, it's time to take off your blinders. Take a look at what's out there, and while you're at it, take a look at your gorgeous self."

Jean opened the door for the other two. "I must admit, Zoey, you have got me thinking. See you guys at lunch." The women headed to their cubicles.

Lately, Jean had found herself thinking more about death. She was doing it again now, on her way to her cubicle. Her thoughts on the subject were more philosophical than morbid. Her mind skipped to it now because she felt totally alive and grateful to be so.

She remembered when, last year, she went with Richie to a funeral back in Massachusetts, the second funeral of his life. A good friend of his from high school, a friend with an even greater aptitude for troublemaking than Richie had shown, died while participating in a life's dream—running with the bulls in Pamplona, Spain. The odd nature of the fatality was the only thing that helped Richie accept this first death of a peer, a peer who had romanticized "death by goring" as a cool way to go.

Cool way to go? Jean shook her head as she remembered the first time Richie voiced that opinion. It's true that some deaths take a long time. And some are way more painful than others. But she'd never been able to wrap her mind around a concept that basically made light of death. She made sure to say as much to her son. Death wasn't something to romanticize. It was something to stave off, to avoid, to fight as long as possible. Even though she had her battles with melancholy, she never seriously considered suicide. Something in her trusted that there would be an upswing and it would be worth waiting for.

She hadn't dated anyone after Edward's death, with the exception of a few disastrous fix-ups. Maybe it was time she thought seriously about falling in love again. Edward had been gone five years, but she still felt a twinge of guilt at the thought of dating someone. She had not, however, been able to get Jim Beall's handsome face out of her thoughts this past weekend. Was he available? Would he look twice at her? And would this new thought process turn into an upper or a downer?

6

JULY

In which Mallory spills her coffee, voices a minority opinion in class, and welcomes a gentle giant to the neighborhood.

THIS MONDAY MORNING, per usual, Mallory Cooper hardly glanced at the front page of the latest *Great Wharf Gazette*. She counted on Dwight and Doris to alert her to local news in near real time. Dwight commented on what the news meant for or about the economy. Doris suggested the light it might shed on townspeople's "business" in all other regards.

Mallory got her own rush each week from the op-ed pages, where letters to the editor shed light on what was truly pleasing or bothering people in town. Today she spotted Angie Weller's name among the writers. She started reading that letter first, her coffee mug halfway to her lips.

After what seemed like just the blink of an eye, the mug lay on its side, empty. Coffee that hadn't seeped between the table slats coated the surface like pond scum. Her bathrobe was soaked. She looked at the clock over the fireplace. Five minutes had passed.

Mallory stretched one arm to the napkin holder and took out several napkins. She sopped up the film of coffee and then left the table to put her bathrobe in the washing machine. She cleaned up the rest of the mess, put the mug in the sink, and started toward the stairs to shower and dress. Even if she didn't go out that day, she'd at least get dressed.

Passing by the little table in the hallway, Mallory stopped to wind the music box. She retrieved the Byways art-class flyer from under the box and carried it upstairs with her. Humming to the sound of "why then, oh why can't I," she thought maybe she could learn acrylics while painting a cinder path. The challenge would be to get some color other than gray into the piece. Even fifty shades of gray wouldn't lift the memory into a happier place.

* * *

At 6:40 that evening, Mallory paced the front hallway. All day it had been in her mind to go to Angie's seven o'clock class. But two minutes ago, as soon as she had raised her hand to the front door, she had stopped and backed out of the vestibule. She wound the music box and started humming. She paced into and out of the living room, down the hall, into and around the kitchen, and then back into the hallway. She decided that as soon as the tune started to wind down, she'd leave the house before it stopped altogether. She could do this.

On the third winding of the music box, Mallory held her breath and left the house just before the tune ended. Shutting the door behind her, she swallowed hard and stood on the stoop a moment. A rustle in the flower bed signaled a rabbit's alarm at her arrival. She wished she could put its fears to rest, and yet the animal was just operating on a healthy instinct. Ignoring her own instinct to go back into the house, she took the steps down and kept walking. It got easier with the physical activity. It would be daylight for another couple of hours. She could do this.

As the sidewalks became more crowded, she squeezed into herself and tried not to bump into anyone. She forced herself to look up more than usual. She hummed her new mantra ("why then, oh why can't I") aloud, not caring if anyone heard her. It helped more than she ever imagined it could.

Outside Byways stood a sign promoting the free Monday-night classes. When Mallory walked in, the tinkling bell caused the people already gathered there to turn and look at her. She counted six women and two men. She didn't know them. A relief—no need to chat.

Just as she took a seat—the only one left and smack in the middle of everyone—Angie appeared at the front of the room. She wore a colorful, low-cut painter's smock that didn't need to be high cut because there was no blouse to cover. Mallory wondered if that was true, or if the blouse was low cut too. How, she asked herself, can someone look sexy in a smock? Ah, she answered herself, awesome cleavage might be a factor.

"Welcome, everyone! I recognize some of you, but I see some new faces too. Do you all have the materials you need?"

Mallory raised her hand but, in a rush of nerves, didn't wait to be acknowledged. "I want to learn acrylics. I know I'll need gray. Or black and white—however that works. And canvas or whatever to paint on. And a palette maybe? I don't know. Help?"

Mallory despised sounding ignorant and helpless. Why had she talked herself into doing this? Oh yes.

Dwight wouldn't be home until eight thirty. And she did want to learn acrylics. And she especially wanted to release some energy around the idea of a Great Wharf cinder path. To what end wasn't really clear. In any case, she would sit in this shop from seven to eight and see what happened. Dwight would be proud of her, getting out again, and so early in the week.

Angie said, "Sit right there, and I'll bring over what you need to get started. Everything's 10 percent off during class time. Everyone else okay for materials?" Murmurs of assent. "Tonight we'll be creating images of the Maine coastline, so start imagining yours while I get this budding artist her materials. Don't put anything on your paper or canvas yet."

Mallory blurted, "I didn't realize we'd be told what to paint, but I guess gray will still figure in. I'll probably need some blue too."

"Don't worry. Be right back." Angie swirled away— a bit too dramatically, Mallory thought.

Angie quickly reappeared with the materials in hand, including small tubes of black, white, blue, green, yellow, and a vibrant pink. "I predict you'll want a splash of color for beach roses. May I take your card and ring this up while you get set up?"

Mallory reached into her purse, carefully, and handed over her credit card. "Will you be providing some instruction?"

"Oh yes, just as soon as we finish this little task. In the meantime, please write your first name on this name tag. I'm sorry I've forgotten it. I remember you bought the music box last week."

"Yes. I can't tell you how many times I've played it." Then Mallory added, "Such a sweet tune," but Angie had already turned toward the checkout area, though she did call back, "I agree, a lovely tune."

Under her breath, Mallory spoke toward the retreating figure, "Mallory, by the way. My name's Mallory."

She caught a giggle to her right. A plain, middle-aged woman sat there already at work with a charcoal sketchpad. The woman had begun despite Angie's admonition not to start yet. This bit of rebellion impressed Mallory.

The woman pointed to her own name tag. "My name's Sheila. Angie's kind of brusque, but we can't really complain about that when she's giving us free lessons."

"Oh, believe me, I can still complain. I've become quite an expert at it." Mallory hadn't come here to meet others, but she was glad to focus on a single person amid the array of strangers. This Sheila was her opportunity to start fomenting dissension.

"Sheila," she said, leaning toward her, "did you read Angie's letter in last week's *Gazette*, about building a cinder path here?"

"Yes, I did. I think it's a great idea. Anything that encourages people to get out and walk in their neighborhood can only have positive outcomes. Don't you agree?"

"No, I don't!" Everyone swiveled toward Mallory's outrage.

"Sorry. I just think a cinder path will cost too much money and invite trouble on top of that."

"What kind of trouble?" a woman asked from behind Mallory.

Mallory turned to face her. "What kind? You name it! Who will police the path, make sure no drug sales are taking place, no pedophilia, no—I don't know—whatever! Doesn't this scare anyone else?"

Sheila said, "I think you might be watching too much news. The path would be well lit, and well traveled by well-meaning neighbors. Why would it be any different in that sense than taking a walk down your normal side street?"

Mallory changed tactics. "Well … who's going to pay for the construction and maintenance?"

Returning with Mallory's receipt and card, Angie joined the discussion. "I'm so glad you raise that question, Mallory. And I'm happy to learn people did read my letter and are discussing it. My thought is that somehow we in Great Wharf could start a nonprofit group called Friends of the Cinder Path or something and do fundraising. Membership dues could pay for the maintenance."

"What would members get in return, assuming perfect strangers can walk the path anytime?" another classmate asked.

"Well, that's something people need to think about, I guess." Angie walked to the easel at the front of the class area and held a black marker to the blank sheet. "For now, let's get to work with tonight's theme, creating a coastline image in your particular medium."

Mallory leaned over toward Sheila and whispered, "Brusque."

Sheila nodded but kept her face turned toward Angie. Mallory's heart was racing. She'd been itching for a fight, and now she needed to calm down. She was glad to have other colors than gray to work with. Glad to draw anything but a cinder path.

Angie wrote "Objects" at the top of the easel pad and "Emotions" halfway down. "Let's brainstorm a little before I set you free to create. Call out some coastline words for me to write in either of these categories."

The class exploded with suggestions. Mallory struggled to refocus. Painting was the fun reason for being here. And she did want to justify the $47.28 on the receipt Angie had given her. At least she could tell Dwight that the price included a pretax savings of almost five dollars.

* * *

Walking home down Olympia Snowe Boulevard, between Pleasant Street and Temperance Way, Mallory heard a moose. She recognized the sound from childhood vacations in the Moosehead Lake region of central Maine. Never had she heard one around Great Wharf. She likened the sound to the love child of a power lawn mower and a nose blower with a deviated septum.

If you were going to hear a moose, then dusk in July was a good time to listen for it. But here in Great Wharf? Humorist Tim Sample, she recalled, said tourists to Maine have three plans for their visits. They want to see a lighthouse, eat a lobster, and see a moose. Mallory knew that to see a moose, they'd generally have to travel farther inland and northward than Great Wharf. But she also knew that along the southern coastline there were more moose-vehicle accidents per square mile than anywhere else in Maine.

She decided the sound she'd heard must have come from Burnham Bog, ten acres of conservation land paralleling the boulevard on the other end of Temperance Way. It was full of greens a moose could thrive on.

Mallory's list of fears did not include a contented moose. In fact, she found the sound soothing—a reassurance that the natural world might persist despite human intervention. She worried, however, about a gentle giant unfortunate enough to haunt the sometimes mean streets of southern coastal Maine.

7

JULY

*In which preoccupation makes Dwight Cooper a
walking target for Elizabeth Easley.*

DWIGHT COOPER EASILY dodged Great Wharf's foot
traffic, which hardly compared to that near his
company's location in Portland. Still, Great Wharf was
noticeably more crowded today, a Friday, than earlier in
the week. People flocked northward from the Boston
area on summer weekends.

Moving now toward the hardware store, Dwight
had family on his mind, a family besides his own.
Yesterday he had found a newborn cat family in one of
Seashore Trolley Museum's streetcars. The squealing
kittens couldn't have been even a day old. He alerted

the groundskeeper, who promised to rope off that aisle and keep visitors at a distance. The mother cat, a calico, had become a museum mascot of sorts since she had first shown up a couple of weeks ago.

The groundskeeper would run the idea by management, but he and Dwight predicted that the calico would raise a litter of mouse catchers. Being surrounded by woods, there would be more than enough food once they were weaned. In the meantime, nature could take its course. If the kittens survived, more power to them. The episode might even translate into a feel-good story for *Down East* magazine. Free publicity for Seashore Trolley Museum!

Dwight imagined the world from a newborn kitten's point of view—all sounds and smells and jostling. No sense of danger. Not yet anyway. This thought brought Mallory to mind, and her increasing sense of danger outside the home. He worried that it was only a matter of time before she'd feel unsafe inside the home as well. Her promise to get out more gave him hope. She had told him about going to the art class this past Monday, but since then, as far as he could tell, she had remained home and garden bound.

Dwight's preoccupation came to an abrupt end when a kid's errant Frisbee sailed over the street crowd and hit his head. He reached down to grab the bright orange disk. A woman behind ran into him and almost brought both of them down. But she was young and athletic, and she recovered quickly. Dwight, in the meantime, slapped the ground like a befuddled flying fish.

"What the …?" Then he noticed the strikingly beautiful, mocha-licious woman who had caused his fall. Embarrassed, he said, "I stopped too fast, didn't I? What an idiot."

Dwight didn't even notice the kid retrieving the Frisbee with a "Sorry!" and racing off again.

"Oh dear." The vision put her youthful, light brown hand out to help him up, and he took it, knowing he wouldn't put any weight on it but wanting to touch it.

As he pushed himself up, he couldn't take his eyes off her. Her thick, curly auburn hair gleamed in the late afternoon sun. She had hazel brown eyes that promised humor on top of kindness. Dwight was reminded of Mallory when he had first met her, even though Mal's hair was darker and her eyes were blue and her white skin rivaled bathroom porcelain. The resemblance lay in the way this young woman tilted her head but still looked right at him. She really seemed to care.

Dwight suddenly realized how much he missed his wife, who had turned into a stranger over the last few years. He wanted to recapture her in this woman. He had never been unfaithful to Mallory, but he craved this person beyond reason.

"Listen," he spoke after the smallest of hesitations. "Don't take this the wrong way, but can I buy you a latte?"

The vision finished adjusting the angle of her shoulder bag. He couldn't tell if she was annoyed or interested or indifferent to his invitation. She gave him a sidelong glance and asked, "What's your name?"

"Dwight Cooper."

"Are you a Great Wharfian, Dwight Cooper?" Now she was looking right at him.

"Do you want me to be?" He laughed so she wouldn't think he was just being flip. Flirting yes, flip no.

"Yes." Her self-assurance in voice and posture made Dwight question his own capabilities.

"Does *ever since second grade* count?"

"Good enough. I'm Elizabeth Easley and, yes, you can buy me a latte."

"Outa sight," he practically whispered. Then louder he said, "Allow me to escort you to the Great Wharf Coffeehouse, Ms. Easley." He crooked his arm for her to put her hand through.

She shook her head the way an amused mother does when her child resurrects an outgrown behavior. "That's okay. Which direction? And, please, call me Elizabeth."

Dwight's heart raced as they walked two shops up, where he held the door open for Elizabeth. He asked her to land a couple of seats while he ordered the lattes. Watching her from the line, he was relieved when she sat at a table two seats away from the window.

"Here you go. One luscious latte for one very forgiving woman."

"I think you're the one who needs to forgive me. I was looking up the street and trying to imprint a picture of the town's quaint shopping district on my brain. I was totally unconscious of the crowd in front of me."

Elizabeth stirred the foamed milk into the rest of the glass as she talked. She blew on the drink before tasting it. Dwight stared at her glossed lips.

"So, Dwight, what's your role in this sweet town?"

He blinked away from her lips and said, "Well, I don't really have a role in town, unless you count our home on Temperance Way."

"Our?"

"My wife and I are empty nesters now, but we raised three great kids there."

"What do other people do in Great Wharf besides gawk at your famous neighbors in Kennebunkport now and then?"

"We leave the gawking for the tourists. The former president's family isn't there most of the time, of course, but that doesn't stop every visitor from taking the slow drive by the turnoff to their house, trying to get a glimpse. Have you taken that drive yet?"

"No, I haven't. But I admit planning to after I leave town today."

"When are you leaving—and why?"

Elizabeth's smile acknowledged his implied invitation. "I'm a freelance journalist. I'm just in town to interview some local retailers and service companies about what it's like to pin your livelihood on a seasonal tourist town. Then I go back to my loft in SoHo … I'm just kidding about that part. I live in a studio in an unglamorous part of Portland. How I wish it were New York City."

"Funny, New York's the last place I want to live."

Dwight had been talking from the left side of his brain while the right side enjoyed the sight, sound, and scent of this beautiful woman. Could he add touch and taste to capture all five senses? In this semi-trance state, he reached over to Elizabeth's wrist and tapped it lightly with a forefinger. "How did you get such beautiful skin? The color is an exact match with these lattes."

With neither a flinch nor a smile, Elizabeth explained, "My maternal grandfather came from Jamaica. His family moved to the U.S. when he was ten years old, and he became a citizen at eighteen. He met my grandmother in college. When they married in the early 1960s, it was like front-page news back then—or would have been if the papers had even had the nerve to print it. Interracial couples were shunned, so they had a tough time of it. Then he was drafted and got killed in Vietnam. I wish I could have known him."

"Is your grandmother still alive?"

"She died last month." Elizabeth's eyes moistened. "She was a wonderful person."

"I didn't mean to upset you. This all started because I had to comment on what lovely skin you have." He tapped her wrist again, but this time he watched in some horror as his finger caressed it a bit before he yanked his hand back.

"I'm sorry. I shouldn't have done that."

"Apology accepted." Elizabeth reached around to retrieve her shoulder bag from the back of the chair. Dwight steeled himself for the good-bye. She reached into the bag and said, "Dwight, do you mind if I take a few notes while we talk?"

"Oh! Not at all. As long as the notes aren't about my pitiful attempt to flirt with you."

"Don't be offended, but it's not breaking news that you find me attractive. If I thought it was, my editor would suggest I write for a gossip tabloid and let the *Herald* know when I wanted to report real news again. No, what I'd like is your impression, as someone who's lived here a long time, of the tourist trade in town. Do you feel positive or negative about it?"

Dwight admired Elizabeth's self-assurance and nonchalance in a situation that would make most of the women he knew blush. Damn but she was attractive. He almost missed her question.

"Positive," he blurted. "This town needs tourists like a calendar needs July and August. The drop-off in their number the last few years has been steep, and we've lost a few retailers. This year's been a little better, but the improvement didn't come soon enough for some."

"And what business are you in?"

"My own business isn't tied to tourism. I own and run a building management firm in Portland."

"Named?"

"PCJ, for my kids' names—Panda, Carol, and Jess. Right now, the company is six employees strong, including the live-in superintendents in two of the five buildings we're managing." Dwight hoped the numbers were big enough to impress.

"You mentioned being an empty nester now. What are your kids up to?"

Dwight's heart and face lit up. "Our oldest, Panda—a childhood nickname that stuck," he explained with a grin, "got married a couple years ago and is living with her husband in Vermont. She eloped, so that was a tough time for all of us, but we like him fine now that the dust has settled. Our youngest is Jess. He's a Marine in the Middle East, so worrying about him is part of how we move through each day. We never worry about our middle child, Carol, but we sure miss her. She moved to Montreal and took Canadian citizenship. She just couldn't stand it when George W. won a second term. She had the impatience of the young."

"How old was she when she moved?"

"It took her a long time to put everything in place. She was twenty-five when she finally landed a job there and moved."

"And how old is she now?"

"Twenty-nine."

"Two years younger than me."

Dwight cleared his throat, knowing the conversation would continue without the effervescence he'd felt at the start. He changed the subject. "Well, back to your interviews. Be sure to include Byways Gift Shop over on Newman Lane. My wife has mixed feelings about it. About its owner, really. The owner is running a free art class every Monday night during high season. Mallory tried it out this past Monday and started learning acrylics. At the same time, she's pissed off—forgive my French—because the owner wrote an op-ed piece suggesting that Great Wharf build itself a cinder path. That might add another dimension to your article."

Elizabeth made a note and then said, "In fact, I have already arranged for an interview with that owner. Her name's Angie Weller, and I'm headed there after this latte. I didn't know about her cinder path idea. Thanks."

When they drained the glasses, Elizabeth gave him a friendly yet pointed look and said, "This has been delightful, Dwight. I wish I could get to know you and your family better. Maybe we'll get that opportunity if I can make building management a thread in the article I'm writing. Or I may interview you and Mallory together sometime about making ends meet in a down economy. Would she participate, do you think?"

Dwight did his best to hide his disappointment. "She might. Here's my cell number." He wrote it on the coffeehouse napkin. "Call anytime."

Dwight waited for Elizabeth to put her pen and notebook back in her bag. Then he stood up and, with his usual gallantry, motioned for her to precede him out of the restaurant. He never noticed Doris Hillobenz waiting in line, where she was dying to know what the Portland reporter—that her physical therapist, Heather, said was in town—might want from Dwight Cooper.

8

JULY

In which an interview progresses in the aisles of Byways; and Mallory is interrupted while composing an email.

AFTER LEAVING THE coffeehouse, Elizabeth walked toward Newman Lane. Before switching her thoughts to the upcoming interview, she replayed the one she'd just had.

She estimated Dwight Cooper's age as mid to late fifties even though he still had a full head of hair and the physique of an athletic forty-year-old. She had thought he was forty until she studied his face. His deep brown eyes added both confidence and compassion to his looks. He had creases—around his eyelids, his nose, his mouth—that may have originated in sunlight and outdoor work but seemed graven in a love of humanity.

The creases were his statement to the world: This man loved life and just as deeply feared losing it or anyone he loved in it. He carried on his shoulders the uneasy fraternal twins of love and responsibility. And then, when he talked about his children, Elizabeth's suspicions were confirmed: a family man, through and through.

She wasn't sure whether her interview with Dwight would become part of her article. She might need to contact him and set up an interview with Mallory to round out the coverage from a family's point of view. On the other hand, given Dwight's attraction to Elizabeth, she should probably stay clear of the Coopers altogether. She didn't want to stir what might be a troubled pot. She'd have to wait and see where the article took her.

Now she stood in front of Byways Gift Shop. She took a couple of pictures of the window display and made a few notes before entering the shop. Seeing no one else who looked like they worked there, she assumed it was the proprietor, Angie Weller, finishing up a sale at the cash register. Elizabeth jotted while waiting: "deep red pixie, heavy eye makeup, maybe 5'7" (any heels?), C cup, bright pink top." These notes might not make it into her article, but they'd help her remember her first impression—among other things, not shy.

A loud clatter made her look again toward the register. The customer, a tall young man, maybe in his early twenties, had knocked over a display of some sort. Apologetic, he left quickly, locking eyes briefly with Elizabeth on his way out. Elizabeth went over and introduced herself to Angie Weller.

"I hope that young man didn't cause any breakage."

"No, everything's fine."

Angie came out from behind the counter, and Elizabeth noticed she wore three-inch spike heels. So, five foot four.

"Let's wander the store while we talk, Ms. Easley. I hate to say it, but I've had to be on the lookout this summer for shoplifters. I find there's less trouble if I'm walking the floor when I'm not busy with a customer."

"That's a shame. I was going to ask you how difficult it is to operate a retail store in a tourist-dependent town in a down economy."

Angie nodded. "These first two years of operation certainly haven't been easy. My prior experience was all in a different state. I was in retailing but not in a tourist-dependent situation. My first year here in Great Wharf, I experimented with print and radio advertising. This year I'm trying out different window displays and aisle layouts. I'm getting very good at learning what works. Oh—and social media! Be sure to visit the Byways Facebook page and click on the 'Like' button there. I hope you'll tell your readers to do the same."

Elizabeth made a note to visit the page herself but said, "I wish I could, Ms. Weller, but the newspaper editor would delete the request immediately. We're not allowed to write anything that might be construed as advertising instead of news."

"Call me Angie. May I call you Elizabeth?"

"Please do, Angie."

"Will your editor allow you to refer to me as Angie instead of Weller?"

Elizabeth cringed inside. She didn't need to aggravate her interviewee. "I'm pretty sure that will fly. I'll write it in a way that indicates you'd prefer to be called Angie."

Angie's piercing black eyes softened a little.

"You know," Angie said, "the locals have only moderate interest in what I sell here. They come in mostly for the greeting cards and herbal essences. I do count on the locals to buy the more expensive gifts now and then. Tourists don't like to trust or pay for shipping the heavier items. But I count on the tourists for most everything else. It's thanks to them that I plan to see profitability each August. I start sleeping a lot better than earlier in the summer."

"Tell me—why would tourists gravitate to this store on Newman Lane instead of spending their money on Wyeth Street?"

Angie looked right and left before answering. Elizabeth wasn't sure whether that was to make sure no one heard her or to check that no one was shoplifting. Since Angie's eyes had been shifting a lot during this interview, there was no way to tell. Elizabeth found herself disconcerted by the constant watchfulness.

"I offer an excellent range in prices, from tchotchkes starting at twenty-five cents to large garden sculptures topping out at two hundred dollars. And to boost the mood of each person entering the store, a diffusion of citrus and lavender essence wafts down from just inside the entrance whenever the door opens. I'm sure you noticed that yourself."

"I did. Loved it! So, the pricing and aroma help explain why customers spend money once in the store, but why do they come in to begin with?"

"A lot of people dislike the crowd scenes on Wyeth. That reduces the competition right there. Also, it's the only New Age shop in town, and so New Age buyers seek it out."

"I did notice that the easiest display to spot in the store window is the red and gold banner promoting an elixir called 'Spirits-Up.' It's hard to miss the bright orange bottle, especially when it's set next to a huge black-and-white photo of a dejected Dorothy in *The Wizard of Oz*."

As she put this long sentence together, Elizabeth was looking at her notes and then added the word *Strategy* and underlined it. She took a quick breath and concluded: "So I imagine anyone who is at all homesick or unhappy while traveling will want to come in and check out this Spirits-Up concoction. And while they are in the shop, they'll pick up some gift items too. True?"

"You're so right," Angie agreed but placed her small, multi-ringed hand on Elizabeth's note-jotting hand. "But I hope you won't reveal my strategy with Spirits-Up, please! It's hard enough finding ways to outdo the competition."

"Don't worry," Elizabeth reassured her. "I don't need to name the actual product or describe the nature of the display to get the point across that you're a savvy marketer."

"I'll count on that, then. I hope the point of the article will be what a terrific store this is. One of a kind, you know."

Elizabeth had no idea yet what the point of her article would be, but it never hurt to let an interviewee predict a glorious outcome.

"About the store being one of a kind," Elizabeth said as a segue, "I haven't interviewed her, but I do know there's another alternative offering in town. A palm reader named Madame Selene."

Angie frowned. "She's not competition, though. She doesn't sell products. Besides, her place is two more streets into the less affluent part of town—farther from the ocean and not a place you might just happen upon. No, her clientele is mostly locals. I do refer people to her now and then, if they ask me about that sort of offering."

"Do you get a commission of some sort?"

"Not at all. I do it as a favor to a fellow businesswoman."

Elizabeth didn't know if she'd be interviewing this Madame Selene, but she welcomed Angie's viewpoint. "You do recommend her, then."

Angie stopped their slow walk-around with a jolt. "Did I say that? No, I did not say that. Be careful what you put in quotation marks, Elizabeth."

"You don't recommend her, then?"

"Not saying either way. All I wanted to point out is that she's not a competitor. Byways Gift Shop is one of a kind."

"Got it. I'd like to ask you about the op-ed piece you wrote, proposing the town build a cinder path. Have you had any reaction to it?"

Angie started walking and looking around again. "Oh my, yes, have I! I'm quite excited about it because I think it could be a real draw for tourists and neighboring townspeople alike."

"Any negative reactions?"

"Not a single one I've heard. People love the idea."

"Good for you. If you're right and the path becomes a draw, that could help your business, too, by getting more people into the area. Another tally for your marketing savvy."

Angie made the self-congratulating motion of blowing on her fingernails and rubbing them on her blouse. "You said it; I didn't." She grinned. "I've already started planning a new window display for the day the path is christened."

"What will it be?"

As my dearly departed mother would say, "That's for me to know and you to find out."

* * *

Dwight completed his errand to buy duct tape at the hardware store. Purchase made, he slipped behind the wheel of his pickup, a 1998 black Ford Ranger that had never given him a moment's worry. He was, however, worried. Who the hell was that guy he played earlier, sitting with Elizabeth Easley in the coffeehouse? He glanced at himself in the rearview mirror to imagine what that beautiful thirty-one-year-old might have thought. Maybe he should ask Richie about his chances with the Community Players, if they were going to put on a play about a midlife crisis. What if someone had seen him with Elizabeth? What would he say to explain?

Was he really having a midlife crisis? Wasn't he too old for that? He turned the key in the ignition, and the familiar sound of the robust, reliable engine calmed him. He had always associated his own abilities with those of his machines. We're on the same wavelength, he thought. Simpatico.

He merged cautiously into the slow line of traffic and headed toward home. He didn't want to admit it, but he knew that Elizabeth and he would never match the level of connection that had always existed between Mallory and him. He thought about how taken he had been by Mallory when he first saw her, thirty-eight years ago, on a playground swing. She was watching over a little boy, who was, at that moment, fascinated by the goings-on around a large anthill ten feet away.

With the boy momentarily stilled, seventeen-year-old Mallory swung herself high. Her long, dark hair swung with her, revealing her face and then covering her face, revealing and covering, revealing and covering. She wore a broad smile and looked up at the sky, down at the ground, over and over. Dwight watched happiness in motion. He was as attracted to

the happiness as to the pretty package. What was revealed was heavenly. He doubted that what was covered could be anything else.

Dwight was at the playground because he was part
of a summer-job work crew. He made his way over to
the swings and pretended to be checking the stabil-
ity of one of the legs, which he told her looked a little
loose to him.

"Should I stop swinging?" she asked him.

"No, I'm sure it's safe enough for now. Keep going.
You look like you're having fun."

"I am. I always have fun when I'm watching over
Charley there."

"Are you two related?" Dwight asked. He held his
breath, hoping she wouldn't say he was her son.

"Uh-huh. He's my nephew. I take care of him on
weekdays after school lets out, until my brother or his
wife gets home from work. This is Charley's and my
favorite place when the weather's nice."

She stopped swinging and looked directly at
Dwight for the first time. "I haven't seen you here
before."

"No, I'm new on the crew—home for the summer
from college. I just finished my sophomore year. You
are so beautiful."

"Wow. Thanks. You're very handsome."

Now, as he steered the truck into their driveway, Dwight smiled over the first time he had shown this house to Mallory. He had graduated that year. They had been married six months and were living with his parents. The newlyweds were getting anxious to move into their own place because Mallory was now three months pregnant. When the time came, they wanted to bring the baby home to a place of their own. It was the dead of winter, ice everywhere. Dwight had spotted the house a few days earlier while driving to one of the snowbird properties he managed for the winter.

The real estate agent, a woman in her sixties, told him the house was too big for them and in need of too much repair. She acknowledged their plan to raise three children, but right now they were a struggling young couple with a baby on the way. As the Coopers saw it, however, this house had the perfect four bedrooms. Granted, those bedrooms—and the kitchen, bathrooms, hallways, floors, and ceilings—did need a lot of work. The front steps were missing entirely, having been removed by the owners, who didn't have the money to repair them. When Dwight and Mallory entered the back, the storm door fell atilt off the top hinge with a monstrous creaking sound. The agent cringed, but they just laughed. They got the house for their price.

The work, done over the decades as finances and muscle power allowed, was all worth it. Dwight winced as he remembered some of the meltdowns over failed contractors and disagreements over style or cost. But Dwight and Mallory loved their home, which operated nicely these days under normal maintenance attention. They had endured. They would always worry about money, but they managed it carefully. They had never lived hand to mouth.

Dwight's back straightened as a thought grew into determination. Before getting out of the truck, he made a dinner reservation for two at Spears, a swanky restaurant on Mallory's bucket list. She had added it to the list when she lost her job. He made the reservation for Valentine's Day, seven months away. They had only two tables still open when he called. He told them he wanted the reservation as a surprise for his wife. They promised him his secret would be safe with them.

Dwight brought up the calendar on his smartphone and entered the information. Scrolling back and forth, he saw that the only other nonwork entry before that distant one was the *Rumors* play they had gone to a week ago. When he saw that lonely entry, he had two thoughts. First, both he and Mallory needed to get out more—she for any reason at all, and he for anything other than volunteer or paying work. His second thought was how agitated Mallory had become after the play ended. She had practically run to the car. But then the trip home went fine as they revisited the scenes that had made them laugh the hardest.

Dwight got out of the truck, grabbed the hose he'd brought home to repair, and lugged it to the back of the house. As he rounded the corner to the backyard, the peeling paint reminded him where some of their savings would be going in a couple of years. But the front and back yards looked great this year, thanks to the time they had put in with Richie Trent. Dwight laid the hose by the side of the garage and looked through the screen door to the kitchen. There she was, hunched over, typing at the computer. He walked in with a smile and a "Hi, beautiful!"

Mallory screamed and flew back from the keyboard. "Damn but you scared me!" Then she quickly regained control of the keyboard and exited the email she'd been creating. "Damn."

"Sorry, honey," Dwight said. "You must have been somewhere far away. Anyone I know?"

"No, no. It's nothing." She put the computer in sleep mode. "You're home early. Is everything okay?"

"Yup, but I have some equipment repairs to work on in the garage. I stopped in town on the way home and picked up more duct tape." Dwight took a glass out of the cupboard and started filling it with water to take with him. "Did you know two more places are closing on Wyeth Street?"

"No! Which ones?"

"The dry cleaner is gone, and Ralph's Optometry has a 'Going Out of Business Sale' banner in the window. Now may be a good time to get those new frames you've been wanting."

"It's scary to learn that two more shops are going down." Mallory shook her head. "Thank God your work is thriving. People will always need good building managers, and PCJ has a wonderful reputation. I check the online comments every now and then just to make sure no one's said anything mean. All I see is praise."

"Thanks for keeping an eye on that, Mal. Well, I'm going to change into my grubbies and set to work in the garage."

"When would you like me to put dinner on?"

"How's two hours from now?"

"Perfect."

Dwight was relieved that, so far, no one seemed to have called his wife because they had spotted him with Elizabeth. Otherwise, he knew Mallory would have said something immediately. One thing about Mal: she didn't let things stew inside. At least not between them. She did let things stew from her childhood, and he didn't know how to help her with that. He just tried to be there for her when she was ready to peel another layer. She and her mother shared all the warmth of a judge and jury. And something festered between her and her uncle that she had never shared, except to say Bill was an a-hole.

EPISTOLARY EXCERPT FROM UNPUBLISHED MANUSCRIPT:
RUNAWAY LEGACY

January 1, 2000

Dear Gallant,

We want to take a moment to send you this special note of thanks for including us in little Caitlin's life the way you have done. We are breathing easier than we have since Mary's disappearance nearly fourteen years ago. To know that we have a grandchild, and to know that she has such a loving father looking after her, is more comforting than words can say.

You live up to your name.

Gratefully,
Vera and Sergeo

9

JULY

In which Richie brings Cassidy Hillobenz into his confidence, discovers Byways, and makes his mother a special tea.

MEWING SOUNDS? RICHIE extricated his long body from under the San Francisco cable car, Seashore's number 48, to figure out where the mews were coming from. Listening as he turned full circle, he zeroed in on the Glasgow double-deck trolley, number 1274. Tourists were allowed to walk up the winding steps to the upper deck, but a rope now kept them out of the lower deck. Richie stooped under the rope and started walking down the aisle. The mews were louder now.

Under the third seat back on the right side, he found seven still nearly hairless, still blind little kittens. They were working away at the swollen nipples of mama cat, the well-fed calico he had first seen the week before, a cat others told him had become a much-appreciated mouser. Now Richie realized she hadn't been well fed at all, just very pregnant. She looked thin and done in now. Most litters—he knew from watching Animal Planet—top off at five kittens.

Richie quietly removed himself from the nursery and went looking for some milk, or at least some water. The high schoolers working at Seashore always brought their lunch. He found Cassidy Hillobenz, who volunteered after the short school day every Friday.

"Hey, Cassidy, how're things?"

"Great, Richie! How about you?" Cassidy blushed.

Richie would have flirted over her blush, but Cassidy wasn't his type. She was too young, to begin with, and he suspected she weighed more than he did. Mainly, she talked too much about movie and reality stars, as though they were more important than the local or national news of the week. But what Richie did like about Cassidy was her kindness. She loved people, and he figured she probably loved animals too.

"I'm good. Listen—I need to let you in on a secret. First, do you have a shallow bowl or dish or know where I can get one?"

"A secret?"

"Yeah. But do you have some container?"

"Oh, yeah. If it doesn't need to be pretty or used in a microwave, I could clean out a tuna-fish can or something. How big does it need to be?"

"I don't think it matters."

Richie told her what he had found, and they started walking back toward the double-deck trolley.

"I've never been allowed to have a pet," Cassidy confided. "Gram is allergic to cats and says dogs are too much work. We did have a goldfish once? I love it when the front covers of magazines at the supermarket show actors with their pets. Gram says that Mr. Amaldi, next door, once gave a guinea pig to a woman he had a crush on? But Mrs. Amaldi found out about it and threatened to kill him. I don't know if Gram meant kill the guinea pig or Mr. Amaldi."

Richie would have bet on Mr. Amaldi but kept quiet and just nodded. When they reached the double-deck trolley, Richie said, "Remember this is a secret, so keep your voice down when you see them." After a group of visitors walked on to the next trolley, Richie slipped under the rope. Cassidy followed. He led the way down the aisle and then pointed under the third seat.

As soon as Cassidy crouched down, both her hands flew to her mouth. She squealed as quietly as she could.

"Oh, they're such babies, Richie! Look—their eyes aren't even open yet."

"That's why I don't want anyone interfering with them. I guess we should tell the grounds manager, but if he's not an animal lover I don't know what we'll do."

"We could picket."

Richie stifled the laugh he knew would only confuse Cassidy. "The main thing for now is not to tell anyone. And sorry, but especially don't tell your grandmother, okay? She's kind of a talker."

"Don't worry. I've lived with Gram long enough to know when to hide things from her."

The cat family had thrown a monkey wrench (or 126 kitten claws) into Richie's plans. When he'd heard the mewing, he had been looking under the neighboring cable car to find the right place to attach a metallic plaque he had on order at a shop in Portland. Nobody else knew about the plaque or what he had planned for it. He hoped things would stay that way. He still hadn't decided on just the right spot for it, but he'd seen enough to know he'd be able to do what he wanted.

His mood was brightening, and kittens upped the wattage.

* * *

The only time Richie had made downtown Great Wharf a destination was the long-ago day when he posted flyers for freelance work. Normally when he aimed for Great Wharf, it was to the Y or Community Players, both on the outskirts of town, or via back roads to the Coopers' place. He never had to go near the main drag of Wyeth Street. Besides, when he left the Coopers', he was sweaty from weeding and mowing. He didn't feel comfortable checking out the town when he stank.

But Richie yearned to break out of his rut, and today the kittens had put him in a great mood. He didn't want to go straight home to Biddeford and—what?— watch daytime television again? So this day, instead of heading directly home from the trolley museum, and since he still smelled nice, he detoured over to Wyeth Street.

At first glance the place looked pretty much like any other small tourist town along the coast of Maine at the height of summer. The buildings were mostly two-story. A few were red brick, but more were clapboard or had weathered gray shingles. When the clapboards weren't painted a stately color, they went in a wholly commercial direction to attract attention, like the Great Wharf Coffeehouse with its peach siding and turquoise trim. People swarmed all along the commercial district sidewalks. They clumped at the ends of crosswalks and outside the doors of the popular shops. Having lowered his windows, Richie felt the buoyancy of energized voices flowing through the car.

He laughed at himself for thinking he'd be able to drive as fast as the posted speed limit of twenty miles per hour. The traffic and pedestrians made that impossible. He wanted to gawk at both the people and the storefronts, but that too was impossible. He became unnerved when he imagined a kid playfully pushing a friend into the street. Kids think that's funny until they become drivers themselves. He didn't need another accidental death weighing on his psyche.

He stopped for the stream of walkers at a crosswalk and decided to take the next right turn he could. Scanning the scene while waiting, he spotted Dwight Cooper holding the door of the peach and turquoise coffeehouse for a fine-looking woman in a shimmery blouse. Richie thought, I'd hold the door for that one too. He couldn't wait to tease Dwight about it. He realized he probably shouldn't bring it up in front of Mallory. He'd keep it for a time when he and Dwight were handling a repair or something. He was pretty sure Dwight was straight-arrow in his marriage, but just in case, he'd be careful. *Circumspect*, he thought, that's the word. Ma would be proud of me—for the thought and for the word too.

Traffic moved again, and Richie took the next turn. The voices receded. Smatterings of tourists were checking out the side streets but nothing like he'd seen on Wyeth. Three blocks away he saw a parking space open up on a quiet street and he grabbed it. After locking up, Richie gave the car a love tap on the hood, knowing that if he didn't get a full-time job soon he would probably have to sell it—his first car. Over the four years he'd owned it, he had done a lot of work on it, including painting a purple and green stripe front to back. He caressed the stripe every time he left the car.

Walking back toward town, his long legs automatically made fast progress. Still, Richie took time to notice the neighborhood. The streets, like where the Coopers lived only two more blocks away, were lined with maples and oaks. Many of the houses were small, mostly two- and three-bedroom homes. Then, closer to downtown, Richie saw more four- and five-bedroom homes. Small or large, homes or B&Bs, the structures were in good repair. The gardens begged to be noticed and praised.

This town put its best foot forward, careful not to discourage visitors when the seasons permitted. He wondered if the same would be true on the other side of Wyeth Street, and how many streets away from Wyeth it would be before he'd find the first hint of neglect. Maine was not a wealthy state, despite its spruced-up appearance around areas near the ocean views. The other side of town would be farther from the Atlantic.

Three blocks from Wyeth, other walkers started appearing, and most nodded or said hi to Richie in passing. This added to his good feeling. When he hit Wyeth, he walked toward the very center of downtown and immediately needed to slow his pace. That was okay; it gave him time to look in the store windows. The first window belonged to a shop specializing in purses and shawls. In an elegant display, colors and textures vied for attention. The next window was black, blank, empty. Richie peered in and saw the unswept floor of a denuded space. He wondered what used to be there.

Next came an art gallery featuring seascapes, and then another blank window, except this one had a letter taped on the door to the shop: *Thank you to all our faithful customers for your support. With heavy hearts, we have had to admit defeat this year, unable to keep our beloved business going. We'll miss you and wish you all the best. Gayle and Bruce Perry, Elemental Goods*

Wow! Bummer, Richie thought. Next came the Great Wharf Coffeehouse, and Richie looked in but kept walking. The shimmery blouse was easy to find, but the woman's back was to the window so he couldn't get a good look at her. Dwight had his hand on the woman's wrist. Richie didn't worry that Dwight might see him, since he could obviously only see the woman.

Richie now felt hemmed in by the crowd, his good mood gone. It was bad enough to see two shops emptied out. It was worse to read that sad letter on the shop door. And now to think that maybe Dwight Cooper wasn't the great family man he'd thought—well, Richie's spirits drooped and pulled down on his shoulders.

He finished walking the length of Wyeth Street's commercial section and saw three more defunct businesses. In an ever-worsening mood, he decided to check out the parallel street one block beyond Wyeth before heading back to his car. He found that this street, Newman Lane, had a number of residences mixed in with the shops. On Wyeth, when there were shops on the first floors, the second floors were either extensions of those shops or occupied by professionals such as attorneys and accountants. But on Newman Lane the second floors were mostly residential units. This gave the street a special feel to a potential customer, like the stores on it would be more personally relevant than the mass-appeal places on the main drag.

Richie was drawn to one store window in particular, a shop called Byways. It sported a red and gold sign promising "fast relief for *malaise*." He recognized the word that defined his mother's mood when she entered a downward slope—as she had the last couple of days. The sign also used the words *gloom* and *unease*, thus covering his own turn of mood. The sign promoted a product called Spirits-Up.

Even though Richie wasn't a big believer in signs from the universe, his mother was. And even though Richie had never used an elixir, he was curious. He got the message and acted on the impulse. He went in and plunked down ten dollars—which he might have used on a couple of imported beers—to buy one fluid ounce of Spirits-Up, the only size on the shelf.

The short woman at the cash register was possibly twice his age, but he felt an animal magnetism coming from her like an ambush of tigers. Her deep red pixie-styled hair sent a mixed signal of no-nonsense and you-name-it. She wore a low-cut scoop-neck sequined jersey. Her black eyes locked on him. She winked and said in a throaty voice, "Hi there, handsome. I'm Angie, and I own this little shop. Did you find everything you need, everything you want?"

Not normally one to stutter, Richie answered, "Um, yes, yes, thanks … Angie. Yuh." He noticed a hint of musk in the air. Angie told him the total with sales tax. She was too old for him. Cassidy was too young for him. Amanda was just right. He handed over the money and mumbled something about coming back again if the potion worked. Then, turning too quickly, he knocked a point-of-sale jewelry display facedown onto the counter.

The clatter of the necklaces was only a little more jarring than the quickly disguised look of disgust that flashed across owner Angie's face before she smiled and said, "Don't worry, sweetie. This happens all the time. Come back soon." But Richie could see that the earlier prowling tigers had settled down for a nap.

On his way to the door, Richie noticed a woman watching him from a few aisles over. She must have heard the racket he'd just made, and now he felt even more idiotic. Then he recognized her as the woman he'd seen twenty minutes ago in the coffee shop with Dwight. He unlocked his gaze from hers and sprinted to the door.

Richie came home to a dark apartment. It would have been full of light if the shades weren't drawn. He knew the dark meant his ma had surrendered to the down that had been exerting itself for several days now. The different medication regimens from Dr. Sterns weren't doing anything noticeable to lighten her mood. More than once the doctor had suggested that she might simply have a tendency toward melancholy that pills weren't the answer to. He had started encouraging her to get more exercise and do more socializing outside of work.

Friday night a week ago had been a nice high point, when Ma and Amanda went to the *Rumors* premiere in support of Richie and Zoey. In fact, Ma had seemed to be on an upswing until Richie told her a few days later what people said about Jim Beall. Word one: Mallory Cooper said Jim never dated, as far as she knew. Word two: Cassidy Hillobenz said her mother knew Jim was seeing a psychologist because of some childhood trauma. When Richie told his ma what he'd heard, he saw her face fall. That's when he realized she had asked about Jim because she wanted to date him. Richie quickly countered that Jim was a great guy and never seemed anything but upbeat and happy. But he could see his mother's mood had shifted, and now he was living with that.

Her routine now, when she got home from work, entailed lying down on the couch and zoning out in front of the TV, or going to bed and listening to the radio. Sometimes Richie could get her to eat dinner, but more often all she wanted was some chamomile or green tea. This behavior had been the norm before the move to Maine. If something didn't change soon, he'd call his siblings and get their advice. He hoped to avoid that, since he knew his lack of full-time work would be an unspoken factor in how his brother and sisters would comment on the situation.

It was true that the downs had gotten worse the longer his unemployment stretched. Not that Ma would agree. If anything, his mother placed much more blame on herself than she ever tried to stick to others. Funny, she said the same thing about him.

He whispered into her room, "Ma, you awake?"

"Hi, honey. Yes, I'm awake. Come on in."

Richie found her lying still fully clothed on top of her bed. She swung her feet over the edge and sat up.

"How was work today?" he asked. "Did you have to transcribe any obscene data?"

She smiled at his effort. "No, just the usual jargon."

"I did some more volunteer work at the trolley museum."

"That's good, hon." She took a sip from the water glass on her bedside table.

"Can I get you something to eat, Ma?"

"No food for me, just some tea."

Back in the kitchen, Richie refreshed the water in the kettle and set it on high. He pulled a boxed pizza from the freezer and poured himself a bottle of Shipyard IPA while the microwave did its magic. The first sip of ale reassured him that all was right in the world. His taste buds revved up for dinner. Hot pizza went with ale like ... like what? Ah, like leather on a Harley owner. He decided to ask Ma if it wasn't time for them to splurge on a motorcycle. Would that make her smile or just tick her off? That's when he remembered the Spirits-Up elixir from Byways.

He checked the label. There was no warning about any danger in taking it with alcohol. He squeezed the dropper bulb and watched the liquid plop into the beer bottle. No added fizz. He swirled the liquid and took a taste. Still his favorite beer. He would risk it in his mother's tea.

He caught the kettle before it screeched, and poured water over the tea bag. After making sure the tea was strong enough for his mother's taste, he removed the bag, slipped a dropperful of Spirits-Up into the liquid, stirred, and delivered.

Conversations with Jim, Dwight, Cassidy, Zoey, and others were keeping Richie socially sane. Yard work at the Coopers' and workouts at the YMCA kept him physically sane; Seashore Trolley Museum and freelancing, professionally sane; and amateur theater, creatively sane. Still, he found it hard not to focus on how bad his life (read: living with Ma instead of a girlfriend) was turning out. For the zillionth time he imagined what it might feel like to kiss Amanda. He slipped another drop of Spirits-Up into his beer and then hid the bottle behind his personal stack of sardine cans.

10

AUGUST

In which Dwight and Jim offer Mallory very different lifelines.

LATE AFTERNOON, THE first Sunday in August, Dwight came in all sweaty from mowing the lawn. "It's a scorcher out there. I'm taking a shower. I'll take a cold beer up with me."

Mallory rubbed a beefsteak tomato under the running water at the sink. "Okay, honey. It's a cold dinner tonight—tomatoes stuffed with tuna salad—so it'll keep in the fridge till we're ready."

When she finished preparing the dinner, Mallory set the table, poured herself another glass of red wine, and turned on the evening news. Big mistake, she thought, but she succumbed to her news-junkie habit anyway. A few minutes later, when she heard Dwight's footsteps on the stairs, she realized her hands were clenched around the stem of the glass. The news tonight had already included a house fire in Saco and an apparent murder-suicide in Arundel.

She jumped up from the table and turned off the TV. As Dwight took his seat across from hers, she brought the plates out of the fridge and then shook a mass of potato chips into the basket. Her hand shook a little as she poured some wine into Dwight's glass.

"You seem a little edgy, Mal. What's wrong?"

"Oh, you know, the news. When will I learn?"

"Anything here in Great Wharf?"

"No. Saco and Arundel." Mallory flapped her napkin open and placed it on her lap. "Sometimes I think I'm going crazy."

Dwight cut a wedge of the tuna-filled tomato and chewed it slowly. Then he reached for a chip and chewed it slowly too. He took a sip of wine. Then he gave a small laugh and said, "Want to elaborate on that?"

"Not really."

"Okay. Well, I've got something I want to talk about. Maybe it's connected to your insanity."

Mallory didn't know if he was joking with her or not. She just nodded to let him know she was listening.

"I've been thinking about us. Here's the thing. I've been working and growing the company, and I added on volunteering at the trolley museum. But you've lost the two jobs you enjoyed—childrearing and art events managing. And you've started disappearing."

Mallory frowned but kept her face down, looking at the plate while she chewed.

"I don't mean it's your fault. I'm as much to blame as anyone, leaving you to fend for yourself while I've just gone ahead with what I already enjoy. We don't have anything we still do together except at mealtimes, if then. And when we are together, we don't talk about anything new. What do you do at home all day? What keeps you occupied?"

The whole time Dwight was talking, Mallory's mind roiled, knowing where he was headed and not wanting to deal with it. But now here was the question she had hoped to keep ducking.

She looked up, briefly, into Dwight's eyes. But she broke the gaze to detail the truth. Her eyes darted from his face to the fireplace, the clock, the back door, the counter, and back to her plate as she talked.

"Honestly, here's what I do. I do the boring stuff I've always done. Laundry and meals, cleaning and grocery shopping. Instead of writing letters I'm do-ing emails. Instead of watching a soap opera, I go on Facebook. Instead of getting the cards out, I play computer solitaire. I play FarmVille. I even created a dog in Pet Society, for heaven's sake. I'm going stark raving mad."

"That's what I was afraid of. I didn't know any details, of course. What's your dog's name?" Dwight tilted his head, and Mallory knew he was trying to lighten the mood.

"Casper, to reflect my out-of-body feelings. Dwight," she said, shifting gears, "I saw Jim Beall for a consultation a few weeks ago."

"Why? What's wrong, Mal?" Dwight put his hand on her forearm.

"I've been getting dizzy spells and feelings of anxiety. I didn't even tell Jim everything. I've become more fearful about driving, and I drink more than I told him."

"Well, what did he say about what you did tell him?"

"He said to get more exercise."

"Are you?"

"No."

"Okay." Dwight put his fork down with a clatter and turned to face his wife. He used his authoritative voice. "Here's what we'll do. Instead of heading over to the trolley museum each day I finish work early, I'm going to head home, and you and I are going for a walk. Every day I can, without fail."

Mallory's spirits soared. Frequent walks with Dwight! She hadn't dared ask for such attention—hadn't even considered it. "I hate to take you away from your streetcars. You love that place so."

"I love you a hell of a lot more, and that's what this conversation is about. We have a lot of years left together, I hope. We need to figure out how to make them as fun for each other as we can. If we can do that, the time we spend alone doing our own thing will be more fun too."

Mallory looked down as she laid her fork by the plate. She ran an index finger along the grain of the tabletop, as familiar as the lines on Dwight's beautiful face. "That would be really nice. I'd love it, Dwight."

* * *

Jim's tickler file reminded him to give Mallory a follow-up call. It was now over a month since her visit. Before he had a chance to make the call, he and Sheila enjoyed one of their regular meet-ups. After their session—during which they hadn't said a word about either a childhood trauma or mistreated scoliosis—Jim asked Sheila, "Do you have room in your schedule for another client?"

"What kind of client do you mean?"

"The real kind."

"Oh good. For a moment there I didn't know if you were planning to spice things up or what. Who do you have in mind?"

Jim stopped putting on his socks to turn toward Sheila, still lying happily limp on the crumpled sheets in her guest bedroom. "Aren't I spicy enough for you?"

"You know you are, macho man." Sheila rolled toward him and kissed his rippled abs. Jim loved that she appreciated his time in the gym.

"Okay then!" He grinned and went back to getting dressed. "No, I'm thinking of a patient of mine, Mallory Cooper, whom I'm making a follow-up call to this week. If the conversation goes like I think it will, I'd like to recommend that she make an appointment with you. She's been a patient since I started my practice here. Her whole family has. She's an empty nester and she's been out of work for a couple of years. I think—unless our call surprises me—that she's not handling the extra time very well."

"Why do you say that?" Sheila left the bed and started getting dressed too. Jim watched her from behind and wished they had another hour. Strategically placed at the level of her T3 vertebra, just below the deepest back on any of her blouses, was a tattoo of the human brain. He had to look away or else he'd jump her bones all over again. The brain got him every time.

"Jim? I asked you why you think she's not handling the extra time very well."

"Right. I think she's drinking more than she admits, for one thing. And she's looking tired, sort of haunted. She admitted she's not getting out of the house much. I've always liked Mallory, and her husband, Dwight, too. I'd hate to see them come apart, especially if I could have done something to help."

Sheila gave her hair a quick brush with her fingers before responding. Then she said, "If I had to jump to a conclusion, I'd suspect she might have a touch of agoraphobia, which can have any number of causes. It's not impossible to turn the tendency around if it's caught soon enough. I can't diagnose yet, of course, but go ahead and send her my way. I think I'll be able to help."

Sheila opened the door to the upstairs hallway and stood on the threshold, waiting for Jim. She added, "Come to think of it, I met someone named Mallory in one of Angie Weller's art classes last month. I'll bet it's the same person. In her fifties, pepper-gray hair?"

"That would be her, yes. Come back and help me put this bed together. I don't want you getting ticked because I left it for you to do … again."

Sheila went to the other side of the bed and threw the bedding back together in a flash. While Jim caught up on his side, she commented, "The Mallory I met was quite agitated about Angie's op-ed letter proposing the town put in a cinder path. But she settled down once the class started. She was taking up acrylics. I haven't seen her in a class since, though. That would tie in if she's suffering from agoraphobia. She could find many reasons not to leave the house unless something was really eating at her."

That conversation with Sheila had taken place a couple of days ago. Now Jim had Mallory on the phone. "So, Mallory, this is your friendly follow-up call. Why are you answering your landline? Does this mean you're not following your favorite doctor's orders to get more exercise, to get out more?" While he talked, Jim corralled and rearranged loose paperclips on his desk blotter.

"I'm doing better on that score, Jim. I admit it took a while, but I've started walking about three times a week. Dwight is making sure of it. We're getting to know the darkest secrets of every sidewalk in town."

Jim hinged one paperclip into another. "Sometime you'll have to let me in on some of those secrets. Maybe there's a sidewalk or two I should get to know myself."

"Why don't you join Dwight and me sometime for our walk? We'd love the company."

Jim sidestepped the question, not wanting to mix business with pleasure. Besides, he had unwillingly heard a rumor, via his patient Doris Hillobenz, about

Dwight being seen with a young woman at the local coffeehouse. He didn't want to step into something messy that might be brewing.

"That's nice of you, Mallory, but I really called to make sure you're doing okay." Jim scrolled through the notes about her visit on his computer screen. "Seriously, are you still getting dizzy spells? Are you feeling as anxious as you were, or is it better or worse?"

"I'm still pretty anxious, Jim. Walking with Dwight helps a lot while we're walking and then together in the evening. But during the daytime I'm still not up to par. I didn't tell you before, but it's gotten so that I don't want to drive the car. I walk when I need to get something. And that's good in itself, I know, but I find excuses not to drive anywhere, anytime."

"And how's the drinking? Still two to three glasses a day?"

"I haven't been able to cut down."

"How would you describe your mood, Mallory?"

"Not as unhappy as before, but not happy either."

"How much sleep are you getting?"

"No problem there: eight hours easy."

Jim decided to act on his instinct. "Well, it doesn't sound like I can do anything more for you from a medical perspective. Tell me, Mallory—have you considered seeing someone, a psychologist?"

"No-o."

"You may want to think about it. You have everything going for you, and it's a shame not to find more enjoyment in your waking hours. I can recommend someone if you like."

"I'll think about it. Thanks, Jim."

He spoke quickly. "I know you want me to get off the phone now. But I have one more question for you. Do you know the term *agoraphobia*?"

"Yes. It means being afraid to leave the house."

"Well, that's the idea in a nutshell. It's a lot more complicated, of course, and I'm not in the mental-health business. But that word keeps popping into my mind, so I thought I'd put it in your mind instead. Think about it, and let me know if you'd like a name. I'll call you again, Mallory."

"I appreciate the call, Jim. Thanks."

As Mallory hung up the alcove phone, her thoughts were swimming. Wow. Agoraphobia? She hadn't thought about that. But it sure seemed like a fit. She sat down at her computer and typed the term into the search bar. She clicked on the first noncommercial link and started reading.

"Signs and symptoms similar to a panic attack … lightheadedness, rapid heart rate, and more … fear of being either alone or in crowded places … housebound … overdependent on others …" and on and on, much of it describing her to a tee, more and more so as she spent so much time alone and without purpose.

What am I, she asked herself, a woman or a mouse? She picked up the phone and called Jim back for a name. Then she called Dr. Nies immediately, before she could chicken out. She made an appointment for just over a week away.

11

August

In which a daughter checks on Dwight; Mallory gives in to an urge; and a slide show makes a call easier.

A N UNEXPECTED CALL from daughter Carol shook Dwight up.

"Hey, Dad, what's up?"

"Carol! How great to hear your voice!"

"You could have been hearing it a lot over the past few months. Not to sound like a whiner, but why haven't you called? Are you okay?"

"Wow, I didn't realize. I'm sorry, honey. I guess I just got all caught up with things here. No, there's nothing wrong."

"Well, why would things there get you caught up lately when they didn't prevent you from calling before?"

Dwight wondered how much to tell his daughter about her mother's troubles, but he quickly decided it wasn't for him to tell her. Besides, Mallory seemed a little happier lately. They had been walking, and she'd had her first appointment with Dr. Nies earlier this week. So why go there? Still, the teasing cheerfulness in Carol's voice reminded him that Mallory continued struggling. Maybe someday he'd hear that lighthearted tone return to his wife's voice.

"Dad, are you still there?"

"I'm here, just worrying that I shouldn't be using the cell while I'm driving. Hold on—I'm going to pull over." He stayed put in the driveway, having just arrived home when the call came in. "Okay, I can talk more easily now. So, Carol, what's new with you? Your mom told me about your latest beau. He sounds nice."

"Good change of topic, Dad, but I'll let you get away with it. I do like this new guy. His name's Buzz, but he's not going to be Mr. Right. You know how I know that already? I know because he's landed his dream job—get this—working with a research team in Antarctica. Much as I like this guy, I'm not going to follow him to Antarctica, and I know better than to sit and pine over whether he'll make it back. So I've taken to calling him Mr. Buzz-On-By, and we've agreed to move on when he leaves."

"You're very wise, honey. There are other fish in the sea. Oh, sorry."

"Good one, Dad!

With her prompting on each topic, Dwight updated Carol on how things were going at PCJ, the trolley museum, and the town of Great Wharf. She kept in touch with her siblings on her own and so she didn't need to ask about them.

"What about Mom? Still stuck with house and garden?"

Dwight started rubbing his knee with his free hand, unconsciously grounding himself to sound normal. "Mom does love her surroundings, but she seems to be making more of an effort to get out."

"Like how?"

"We're going out for walks together, for instance. We went to a Community Players show a while ago. Have you talked with her?"

"We're in pretty constant communication via Facebook, Dad. You're not geared to social media, so I start feeling more separated from you than from Mom."

"Well, there's nothing like hearing someone's voice. It's been great to talk with you, sweetie."

"Me too, Dad. Take care of yourself, and enjoy those walks."

Dwight was, in fact, worried on several fronts. Although happy that Mallory was seeing a psychologist, he figured their insurance wouldn't cover it. So he had started picking up extra maintenance work. This meant spending even less time on the streetcar work than he'd already been doing, now that he and Mal were walking. He knew she was hiding something from him, or from herself, and it ate at him.

He missed having more contact with the people at the museum, especially Richie. Richie seemed preoccupied lately, and Dwight hoped it wasn't a problem at home. And whenever he worried about Richie, it had the odd effect of doubling his worry about Jess. At least Panda and Carol were in safe settings.

And lastly, he kept finding himself picturing the lovely latte skin, auburn hair, and hazel eyes of Elizabeth Easley as she watched him across the tabletop. He couldn't stop conjuring her image, no matter how hard he tried. He still feared he might call her one of these days.

* * *

Mallory figured that she probably hadn't been the only victim of her uncle Bill's behavior before he quit drinking. She had decided to take the offensive in order to get free of the increasingly toxic feelings inside her. She knew it wasn't right, what she was doing, but she needed to feel proactive.

Thankfully, Dwight hadn't seen what she was up to at the computer that day when his "Hi, beautiful" made her scream. Under an email account with the user name "Whatchadid," she had been sending anonymous, accusatory emails to Bill every so often. She was sending one the day Dwight surprised her when he came home early and walked in the back door.

If Bill had continued harassing or had advanced to more serious abuse, he wouldn't know where the emails were coming from. It ate at her that she'd been silent about his behavior so long ago. Had her silence freed him to damage others? Her emails gave nothing away about who/what/when/where/why, but they alluded to possibilities.

"You must be a pretty sick man."

"How could you do what you did?"

"Why did you do it?"

"Have you told your wife, or are you nasty with her too?"

If he had any more culpability in him than Mallory already knew about, these random emails would drive him crazy. Good, she thought.

Sure, the emails he had been sending Mallory were full of regret and apology. But she wasn't there yet herself.

Mallory hadn't told Dr. Nies about either her or Bill's emails. But in their very first session, she had described Bill's behavior when she was only twelve. Mallory had asked Dr. Nies why this would be bothering her so much now, after she'd successfully avoided thinking about it for so many years. Together, they figured it out.

Two years ago, Bill Owens made regional news because he was retiring from a long-held CPA-management position with the state of Maine. One of the newscasts showed him with his hand on the arm of a coworker's middle-school-aged daughter as she presented an award to him.

Mallory had felt sick to her stomach watching the clip. Bill hadn't raped Mallory, but he would have if she hadn't reacted quickly and loudly. No rape didn't mean no damage. She had since endured Bill during extended-family gatherings such as christenings, weddings, and funerals. She wanted her kids to know they had family ties in life. But the last event like that had been nearly fifteen years ago. People moved away; people lived together without marrying; people stayed alive. It had been fifteen years since she had seen or really even thought about her uncle.

After her visceral reaction to the news of Bill's retirement two years ago, Mallory had started spending more time on Facebook and less time outside the house. It was a gradual withdrawal, but it definitely started then. With the children gone and with Dwight hardly ever around, she just found it easier to stay inside than to head out into the world. And the more she avoided going out, the stronger the pull became to stay home. Her agoraphobia was habit forming.

One of Bill's attacks on her had occurred on a cinder path. She hadn't told that to Dr. Nies. Maybe because she didn't know yet what to do about the whole idea of the path. It seemed like everyone in town loved the idea. Mallory knew she was transferring her anger at Uncle Bill to anger at Angie Weller. She didn't need Dr. Nies to tell her that.

* * *

Thinking about her uncle now, it hit Mallory that she hadn't called her parents in too long, maybe two months now. They had moved from Kennebunkport to Athens, Georgia, years ago, when they reached retirement age. Both were involved with cultural anthropology and wanted to be near the University of Georgia, which offered a strong program in it. The cost of living in the town of Athens was low compared to Kennebunkport, and the weather could rarely be called harsh.

Whenever she called her parents, Mallory stared at a screensaver slide show of her children. The photos were the best tranquilizers on earth.

"Hi, Mother. It's Mallory. Just thought I'd call and see how you and Dad are doing."

Panda, hugging a friend's dog.

"Mallory, darling, it's good to hear from you. We just got back from a research trip to the Blue Ridge Mountains. We're collecting data on the ecology there. So we're exhausted but impressed by ourselves."

"That's great, Mother. It's wonderful you two have something you're so devoted to. I'm still trying to figure out how to fill in the hours properly now that the kids are taken care of and I'm not with the museum anymore. Maybe I should get back into tennis. I haven't played for over two years."

Panda, pushing Jess on a swing.

"You do need to get involved, Mallory. Get yourself out there some way or other. You never did have a lot of get up and go, you know. Always so willing to let others do the outreach on your behalf. Your dad and I always thought it was so strange, since he and I are such a couple of doers and travelers. Maybe we were away too often while you were growing up. I don't know. Your sisters and brothers did fine."

Carol, standing arm in arm with her prom date.

"I did fine too, Mom. I just chose a different course than the rest of you. Academics and travel don't thrill me, but my family does."

"And now your family has flown the coop, hasn't it? How's Dwight these days? Still spending all his spare time at that trolley museum?"

Jess, waving out the window of his first car.

"Dwight does love the volunteer work, but believe me, these days he's working more than playing. Things have gotten a little tight here financially."

"I hope you're not asking for money, dear. We have to live off our interest income, you know."

"I know, Mother. I wasn't leading up to that at all."

All three children, much younger, eating ears of corn and grinning with yellow kernels on their chins and cheeks.

Mallory could barely hold the phone to her ear anymore. She clicked it onto speakerphone and hung up the receiver.

"Well, I just thought I'd give a call and make sure things were going well down there."

"That was very thoughtful of you. I know we don't call as much as we should, but we're just so busy, you know."

"I know. Take care, and tell Dad I said hello."

Mallory disconnected and put her head between her legs, hoping the dizziness would pass quickly. During her first session with Dr. Nies, while discussing her experience with and feelings about Uncle Bill, they also touched on her relationship with her parents. For the first time in her life, Mallory saw how distant her parents had always been from their children. They had been responsible enough, always making sure homework got done, healthy meals were eaten, and all, but there was no true warmth in the interactions. It was like the kids were just a checklist to be completed each day.

Mallory's brothers and sister were very much like their parents. Only Mallory seemed to need extra hugs and support. At the same time she knew she'd never get that from her parents or siblings. She'd have to go beyond them for that kind of attention. She wasn't needy; she was just on another end of the normal range from them. She had learned to hold back from asking for what she needed, afraid it was too much.

12

AUGUST

*In which Angie has a regular session with Madame
Selene DiPietro; and Richie hides a package.*

S ELENE DiPIETRO—"MADAME SELENE" and Great
Wharf's only spiritualist—held Tuesday evenings
from seven to eight as a reserved time slot for Angie
Weller, who had seen her weekly for two years. Selene
and Angie agreed that a lot of psychic readings were
smoke and mirrors, really there for entertainment.
But Selene had a gift for reading people and making
connections, leading to predictions that often proved
true. Of course, she never talked about the ones that
didn't pan out, just the ones that did.

Selene figured that by now Angie probably considered her a best friend. Angie told her they were kindred spirits, probably sisters or lovers in a past life.

Like Angie, Selene had grown up with a mother devoted to New Age objects and techniques. Where Angie's mother focused on herbal essences, especially lavender, Selene's mother focused on spiritual messages. Selene's long black hair and colorful, billowing clothing mimicked her mother's look. Angie said she loved Selene's flamboyant style. Angie's look was nothing like her own mother's, which Angie described as downright dowdy.

Angie hardly ever made reference to her life before Great Wharf. But when she did talk about the past, she vowed not to make the same mistakes. In that way, Selene mused, Angie was like everyone else she knew. But in other ways, Angie veered wide.

She talked to Selene about being a single woman, a multiple-divorcee who needed to watch over her primary retirement plan. "My biggest fear is helplessness," she told Selene about one year into their sessions. "Maybe more accurately, powerlessness. I've married, married, and married again, but the marriages failed because the husbands couldn't provide well enough even while they thought they could control me."

In Selene's opinion, which she kept to herself, Angie's idea of teamwork was for the other person to do what she said. Angie's ultimate retirement plan was marriage to a man of status with a reliable income who would make no demands on her whatsoever and would salivate at the sight of her.

Once a month Angie reviewed with Selene a list of eligible bachelors to learn of any news. If Selene hadn't heard anything around town, did she have any feelings or insights through spiritual messages with her crystal ball and tarot cards? So far Angie had crossed three of eight bachelors off her list. Gay, gay, and gay. The remaining five were probably heterosexual. Last month Angie had added a name to the list.

"Jim Beall, straight to the top of the list," Angie said. "A new customer recommended him to me just by chance—when I told her I might need to see a doctor. I was feeling the stress of the business and hoped it wasn't hurting me physically. She didn't know, and neither did I at the time, that I already knew Dr. Jim Beall. When he walked in one day and bought a bookmark, I never would have recognized him if that customer hadn't just put me in mind of him the week before. His hair has gone pure silver and he wore a gray T-shirt. The last time I saw him he was wearing a doctor's coat and wasn't even thirty years old. He had jet-black hair."

Work on the bachelor list would have gone faster if Angie hadn't been completely preoccupied the past two years getting Byways up and running. She told Selene she would have more time to devote to the list in the January doldrums.

Selene started this Tuesday's session with a question about Angie's business. "Think you'll end the season profitably?"

"Just barely. At least the shop has become a fixture in this town. The biggest draw, of course, is the Spirits-Up elixir. And then once people are in the shop, they almost always pick up more than just that little bottle. And I'm getting better at spotting shoplifters."

"When's that reporter's article coming out? Do you know?"

"No idea. At this point I'm hoping not until late next spring. Then it'll have the most impact for the selling season." Angie's eyes narrowed and she bit her lip. "I'm not sure I trust that reporter. She was awfully interested in the Spirits-Up concoction. What's in it? Why do I give it so much space in the display window? I don't want her bringing a lot of attention to that, and I told her so."

"Why do you care?" Selene was used to Angie's distrust of others' motivations. But this focus on Spirits-Up seemed an odd concern.

"Oh, never mind. I'm just being paranoid. It's not like I have any real competition, though one of those shops on Wyeth could decide to offer Spirits-Up themselves as a side item. I'd just rather not call too much attention to it."

"Mmm. Well, let's see what the cards say about you this week." Selene knew that eventually she'd get to the bottom of Angie's uneasiness, but not this evening. She dealt the cards, and the hour flew.

* * *

Richie and Cassidy kept their cat-family secret well. Richie was at the museum more than Cassidy was, but she made a point of leaving several unopened cans of food in the trolley whenever she could.

Richie would open a can and set it by the calico's head, knowing it would be emptied by the next day. He and Cassidy called the calico Mama, but they had agreed on more inventive names for the kittens, which were a grand variety of colors. Not knowing whether the kittens were male or female, they picked gender-neutral names. The two orange kittens were Wedge and Peel; the single gray-and-white one was Dust Bunny; the two calicos were Paint and Mural; and the two black kittens were Ebony and Crow.

Over the first three weeks after the kittens were discovered, the mewing got louder and Mama became more restless, taking longer and longer breaks from her babies. This worried Richie and Cassidy. What if one of the kittens got out of the trolley and was taken by a do-gooder before it was ready to be weaned? And wasn't it just a matter of time before someone—a visitor or a worker at the museum—heard the louder mewing now, or saw Mama and followed her?

Richie said they needed to alert the museum's management to the situation. Maybe management wouldn't automatically inform Animal Control. In a shelter, chances were pretty good that Mama wouldn't get adopted. Richie and Cassidy agreed, though, to take that risk for all the cats' safety.

Before they had a chance to follow through, the little family disappeared. The groundskeeper told them management had known about the kittens all along. It was why the lower level of the trolley had been roped off to begin with, to give them a chance to develop some strength undisturbed. Richie and Cassidy's efforts were not a secret, but were, in fact, appreciated. The groundskeeper had wanted to let the kittens live or die by nature's laws after weaning, but management decided that might be perceived as cruel. The little family was taken to the shelter.

Five weeks later, all the kittens had been placed. Richie brought Mama, the calico, home to his mother. Jean renamed the cat Celestine after a spirituality parable she had read many years before. The name Celestine would be pretty, like the cat, and also reflect the hopeful attitude her history signified. Besides, Jean wanted to be the only mother in the house.

Even before Celestine's arrival at the end of August, Jean's mood had been lifting. Richie assumed it was due to his secret ministrations of Spirits-Up. He knew his mother assumed that her psychiatrist, Dr. Sterns, finally had her on the right mix of meds. In any case, when Richie got home now from the museum or from an interview or a freelance job, he often smelled something great cooking before he opened the apartment door. He and Ma had divvied up the chores in the apartment, and she gave Richie a grocery list each week. She enjoyed cooking, and he was happy to stop eating frozen pizzas every night. Things were definitely looking up.

Celestine purred and rubbed against Richie's leg when he entered the apartment from the outer hallway, carrying the mail in his left hand while closing the door with his right. "Hey, Mama—I mean Celestine. How're you doing? Let me put this pile down. It weighs a ton!"

He didn't know why the mail felt so heavy. Then he noticed the brown padded envelope at the bottom. The return address was the engraving shop he had ordered the metal plaque from. He slid the package under the sofa cushion just before Jean came in from the kitchen.

"Hi, honey. How'd the interview go?"

"I think it was a good one, Ma. They're making a decision within the week, so I'll know pretty soon."

"Fingers crossed, dear. Want me to call them and tell them you're the best there is?"

"Oh yeah, that would go over big. Thanks anyway, Ma."

"Honey, I've run out of tea. I forgot to put it on the list for this week. Would you mind running over to the market to pick some up for me? Dinner won't be ready for another hour anyway."

Richie snuck a glance at the sofa and couldn't see the package from where he stood. His mother rarely sat in the living room when she cooked, preferring to read or do a crossword at the kitchen table.

"Sure. I'll be back in fifteen."

He gave Celestine, still rubbing against his legs, a pat on her back as he turned to leave. He guided her in the other direction to avoid tripping over her.

* * *

Headed in a new direction, Celestine picked up on a new aroma in the room. She sniffed her way over to the sofa and lifted her front paws up to the base of the cushion. Sniff, sniff, sniff.

"What are you doing there, Celestine baby?" Jean headed over and picked her up. "Is that a hint that it's time we had some company over to our humble abode? No one ever does sit on that couch, do they?" She rubbed the cat's head as she took her back into the kitchen to feed her.

After putting the food on the floor, Jean took out her address book to see which addresses she still needed to get. She had been thinking about having a cocktail party. She felt a growing assurance that this was a good idea. It explained her lightened heart more than ingesting any substance did.

Jean delighted in the lengthening list of people she'd invite. Amanda and Zoey were the first names. Jean had asked Richie if he'd like to invite anyone— say, for instance, Hank Sanborn, his former boss. Richie thought that was a great idea, and for sure, he said, Cassidy Hillobenz and Dwight and Mallory Cooper. Jean looked forward to meeting Cassidy, who had helped Richie take care of Celestine. And she especially couldn't wait to meet the Coopers, who had been so kind to Richie.

Finally he named Jim Beall, as Jean hoped he would. She'd get a chance to know that silver-haired gentleman better without tipping her hand. She wasn't ready to admit to anyone yet that she was looking. She would address both Jim's and Hank's cards to them "and a friend, if you'd like." She had never met Hank Sanborn, and she had met Jim Beall only once. She really knew nothing about either of them.

Along with her A-to-Z friends, her own list included her yoga instructor and the building superintendent and his wife. She didn't know any of them well, but this could be an opportunity to change that—or at least keep everyone feeling good about each other.

When she mentioned to Richie last week that she was going to have this party, she asked him about the shops in Great Wharf. Like Richie earlier, she had never spent any time walking downtown there. She planned to take a look next week, post–Labor Day, when it wouldn't be too crowded. She wanted to send handwritten invitations by snail mail but hadn't found any she liked in her usual Biddeford haunts. Knowing his mother's attraction to New Age goods, Richie had suggested Byways.

13

SEPTEMBER

In which Mallory has more sessions with Dr. Nies; and Jean expands her guest list.

N OT EVEN MID-SEPTEMBER, but fall defined the air. The cooler nights and mornings encouraged Mallory to stay in bed a bit longer than usual. She would have to walk briskly to her nine o'clock appointment—her third with Dr. Nies—to be on time. She noticed an unusual cloud formation this morning. Instead of one or two cirrus clouds in the deep blue sky, she counted ten. They were shaped like wedding veils and crisscrossed in all directions. She wondered if they were due in some way to the hurricane that had come ashore in North Carolina the night before.

She thought of Panda's elopement years ago and imagined these clouds as a reward for Mallory's acceptance of the marriage. She had been severely disappointed at the time not to be able to manage a long-dreamed-of wedding for her firstborn daughter. Over time she came to wonder if Panda had eloped because she knew her mother would take control over her most important day. Mallory suspected that she might need to loosen up when something wasn't really hers to control.

Her brisk walk actually got her to the appointment three minutes early. With speed still on her mind, Mallory tore up the wooden stairs at the side of the old Cape-style home. Her psychologist used both floors as her residence but devoted the second-floor room by the outer stairway to counseling sessions. As on the first two occasions, Mallory spotted and avoided the big crack in one of the steps. This time she thought, Cracked like me! as she gave an extra leap over the bad step. She felt pleased that she could still take two steps at a time when she needed to. She was only slightly out of breath when she knocked on the door. It bothered her that she was out of breath at all.

Mallory knew that Dr. Nies built in a full half hour between clients' sessions so people wouldn't be bumping into each other. She took that time to record her observations and reflections on the computer. The door to the office had a peephole so the doctor could see who was knocking before she opened the door.

Mallory couldn't help it—she would forever be tempted to place her index finger over the peephole after knocking. She decided not to berate herself too much; at least she never actually did it. Maybe, she wondered, this was another test the doctor had in place for her unsuspecting patients. Would putting one's finger over the hole suggest an unwillingness to be seen at a deeper level?

Just as Mallory was about to slap her face, Dr. Nies appeared at the bottom of the stairway with an orange traffic cone in her hands.

"Hello, Mrs. Cooper. I thought I'd get this cone placed before you got here. I've been remiss about getting my handyman to fix it, but at least I can keep people from breaking a bone in the meantime."

Dr. Nies placed the cone and then walked back down the stairs again. "Sorry. I'll need to let you in from inside."

So much for being early, Mallory thought while she waited. Less than a minute later, the door opened.

The room was familiar territory now. Its soft decor of browns and golds was further muted by shaded floor lamps instead of an overhead system of garish blue-white light. Mallory walked to the far corner of the room and sank into her favorite seat. Ahh. The overstuffed easy chair enveloped her body, making her feel welcome. She was aware that other clients might choose the straight-back chair or the sofa. Someday she'd ask Sheila—Dr. Nies—what the choice of seat meant about someone.

"I'm sorry, Dr. Nies, but would you mind if I started calling you Sheila? When we first met at that Byways art class, your name tag said 'Sheila' and that's how I keep thinking of you. Would you mind?"

"Say something about why you'd rather go with Sheila than Dr. Nies." The psychologist sat on the end of the sofa near Mallory, with a pen and pad of paper on her lap. She rarely made notes while Mallory talked.

"Oh, well, it just feels easier to talk about inner thoughts with someone I can think of as a friend instead of a doctor."

"Do you talk with your friends about the inner thoughts you're talking with me about?"

"Jeez, no!"

"I think we'll do better if you stay with using Dr. Nies for now."

"I see your point."

"So, how did this past week go for you? Did you still walk each day, more than just a little?"

Dr. Nies had started last week's session with the same two questions. Mallory was prepared.

"Yes, I did, but the thought of driving somewhere is still making me feel nauseous. I thought about driving to the trolley museum to surprise Dwight with a snack a couple days ago, but I had to go lie down until my stomach settled."

"Don't worry. Believe it or not, it's a good sign you even thought about doing that."

Mallory dug at her cuticles. "I felt so stupid."

"Maybe that can be your next step instead of getting behind the wheel. Make the next step that you won't feel stupid anymore for having the reactions you have. Instead, look at those reactions as the smart inner you sending messages."

"O-o-kay …"

Dr. Nies reached over and patted the arm of Mallory's chair. Mallory knew this was her way of making sure she had Mallory's attention. "Humor me. Part of your agoraphobic tendency is fed by negative thoughts. As we've discussed, you're really doing quite well. For now, focus on noticing the strengths inside you."

Mallory nodded and shifted her weight in the chair. "Dr. Nies, do you mind if I tell you about a dream I had this morning? Or do you think dreams don't really tell us much?"

"Oh no, I think dreams can be quite revealing, especially dreams that stay with us after we wake up and

move into the day. Tell me about it." Dr. Nies reposi-
tioned the pad of paper as though taking a note might
actually be called for. Mallory took that as a good sign.

"It's related to getting behind the wheel. I was in
my car, and not feeling at all afraid of being there.
Everything seemed normal. I was backing up along a
grassy strip next to a large parking lot. All of a sudden,
the car fell into a big hole behind me."

Mallory paused, recalling the shock of that moment in the dream.

"My first thought was, 'Damn! Now I'll need a tow to
get out of here.' I looked to the left and saw dirt building
up against the side window. Then I looked to the front
and saw dirt billowing fast toward the windshield. The
car grew warm. And silent."

Mallory's eyes widened, and her hands flew to
the sides of her head. "Oh my God, it was so real,
Doctor. I didn't even try to open the door. I knew
it was too late for that." She lowered her hands back
into her lap.

"I thought of opening the moon roof but then realized the car didn't have one. I started panicking then,
and here's the amazing thing to me. I had two realiza-
tions lightning fast, one right after the other. The first
thought was, 'So this is how I'm going to die—by suf-
focation.' And then as I experienced the air starting to
leave the car, I thought, 'They'll never find me!'"

Mallory swallowed, put her hand to her mouth, and took a moment.

"That's when I woke up."

Dr. Nies didn't say anything.

"So here's the thing that bothers me. It doesn't surprise me that I'm dreaming about imminent doom. I've always felt that doom waits around the corner. But why, in the end, in this dream, was it more important to me that my body be found than that I was dying?"

Dr. Nies got up and crossed the room to her desk. She put the pen and paper down and poured a glass of water, which she brought back to Mallory. Parched from the billowing dirt, Mallory downed the water gratefully.

"That's a stunning dream. It certainly cuts to the chase. We all know we're going to die, and some of us even suspect or have reason to believe we know how we will die. But let me rephrase your question and ask it back to you. Do you think you might be afraid, for whatever reason, that people will forget you when you're gone? And if so, why, in some deep part of you, do you fear that?"

Mallory's gaze settled on the empty glass as she asked aloud, "Am I afraid I'll be forgotten?" She answered right away, "Yes, I am afraid I'll be forgotten."

"And why do you fear that? Why do you think it, and why do you fear it? I don't necessarily want you to answer that right away. If you don't have an answer right away, make that something you think about this week, okay?"

"Well, I know why I think it. My parents always behaved as though their kids, each one of us, would do fine on our own and should let them go away and be on their own. It went beyond pushing us out of the nest to be independent. It was tied in with them getting their own freedom back, freedom to forget about us. My parents never call me, and they never call their grandchildren either. They just keep moving on."

"And what about that causes you fear? That's the part to think about during the week. Was there anything else you wanted to cover today? Because our time's pretty much up." Dr. Nies looked sorry to have to deliver that news. It's part of what Mallory liked about her.

"No, that's all right. See you next week."

✳ ✳ ✳

Jean Trent made the trip to Great Wharf on the Saturday after Labor Day. She parked on Newman Lane but walked over to Wyeth to look at those shops first. There were very few people. Good news / bad news. It was great not to have to shuffle and dodge, but it wasn't a good sign for the shop owners who had decided to stay open for the fall-foliage season. Even though the trees weren't turning yet, she thought there would be more activity. People didn't realize what a perfect time of year this was in Maine.

Jean walked up and down Wyeth and then treated herself to a seasonal tea at the coffeehouse. While she looked out at the people filing past the window, she was conscious how good it felt to be back among the living. Thanks to regular swimming again, which she had neglected during her down period, her muscles felt toned, plus she was enjoying a yoga class the Y offered. That, combined with whatever Dr. Sterns had last prescribed, made her feel better than she had in months.

When she returned to Newman Lane, Jean appreciated the oak and maple trees lining the street. Soon they'd be changing to the glorious hues of fall. Reaching Byways, she saw the Spirits-Up display and smiled with relief that she felt no need to purchase that product. She did, however, file its existence into the if-needed compartment of her memory bank.

As she entered the shop, a deliciously piquant aroma surrounded her, implying a wonderland of possibilities. If she wasn't careful she'd be spending money foolishly. She went directly to a petite, energetic woman at the cash register—who, according to the name tag, turned out to be the store proprietor—and asked if the store sold party invitations. The woman directed her to the stationery section at the back of the store. Jean took her time getting there, fascinated by the offerings.

She stopped in the book aisle and scanned the titles. One in particular intrigued her, and she reached for it. She almost dropped it when the proprietor spoke right next to her.

"I see you're interested in our book on road kill."

"Gross, don't you think?" Jean couldn't help flipping through the pages. "Recipes even?"

"Road kill is a perfectly good dietary inclusion. It has to be fresh—that's important. But other than that, there's no reason not to eat it. It's just like eating a chicken or hog killed at the hands of the farmer. It's like eating a wild rabbit or quail, say, and you save yourself a bullet!"

"Thanks, but no thanks." Jean put the book back.

The proprietor said, "Sorry to interrupt your browsing. Take all the time you like. I wander the aisles and sometimes can't help talking about the products. Please don't think I was pushing something on you."

"No, no, don't worry."

Jean walked over to a curtain display of dream catchers. While she enjoyed taking in the designs, she overheard the proprietor talking with one of the customers in the next aisle over. They were talking about Spirits-Up.

"Honestly, this is the most amazing stuff," the proprietor said. "I've had quite a few customers come back for more, telling me it worked wonders for them or someone in their family."

"What's in it?" the customer asked.

"I have no idea—let's look at the ingredients, shall we?"

Jean loved the idea of elixirs but wondered why she would want one when she was getting the real thing, FDA approved, from her psychiatrist. She walked over to the stationery shelves. After careful consideration, she picked out a set of abstract-design invitations in a pretty green and blue reminiscent of the ocean. That, she decided, would be the color scheme for the party. Matching paper plates and napkins were on sale, confirming her decision. At the cash register the proprietor greeted her with an extra-happy smile.

"So, did you find everything you came in hoping to find?"

"Yes, I did, thank you."

"Is there anything else you might need?"

"No, I'm all set." Jean was pleased with herself for just buying what she had come in for.

"All righty, then, I'll just ring these up. Planning a party, are you?"

"Yes, my first in many years. I'm quite excited about it."

"How lovely! And you've picked the colors I love best myself."

What the hell, Jean thought, and said, "Would you like to come to my party?"

"Good heavens! I hope it didn't sound like I was trying to get invited. How embarrassing!"

"Not at all. I'm just in the mood to meet new people, and to help other people meet new people. If you'd like to come, please say yes! Wouldn't it be fun to do something off the wall like that? Not that my gathering is going to be off the wall. It's going to be very pleasant and normal. It's just that a few people will be strangers to each other. It'll be in four weeks, the middle Saturday in October."

"Well, you know, I just might come. Send me one of these pretty invitations."

"Great!" Jean reached for one of the pens on the counter and got ready to write on the bag containing her purchase. "All I need is your name—or should I mail it somewhere other than to the store here?"

"My name is Angie Weller, and the store address will be fine. I live upstairs."

"Oh! And do you own this store, like your name tag says?"

"Yes, I do." As Angie's bosoms swelled with pride, Jean noticed them for the first time and wondered if she had just made a bad decision to invite her. Oh well, what's done is done, she thought, even if I've just given Hank and Jim something more interesting to look at than me.

* * *

"Mallory," called Dwight as he came in the front door. "Where are you, honey?"

"In here, in the kitchen. As usual, silly!" Mallory slugged down the rest of the wine she'd been nursing, and silently gargled with mouthwash before Dwight made it to the doorway.

"Mal, we've been invited to a party!" He waved a blue-green envelope in the air. "Richie handed it to me at the trolley museum today."

"A real live party?"

"Hors d'oeuvres and cocktails, at Richie's and his mother's place." He handed the envelope to Mallory, who stepped back in surprise while looking at the return address.

"Over in Biddeford? Who else is going? Anyone we know?"

"Not as far as I can tell. I didn't really feel like I should ask Richie. It would sound like I'd be basing my answer on his answer."

"Not at all. It would just be nice to know."

"We need to RSVP," Dwight said. "Will you call?"

"Sure. It'll give me a chance to say hello to his mother beforehand."

Mallory's heart raced. She could feel herself breaking into a sweat. She turned back to the sink and hoped Dwight wouldn't notice her shaking. She'd have to get a pep talk from Dr. Nies.

* * *

The next week, Mallory's session focused on getting her ready for the gathering. Dr. Nies asked her to talk about her feelings when she learned about the invitation. After Mallory described her racing heart and shaking self, Dr. Nies asked her to think back to the last time she had attended a get-together of this nature.

Mallory knew immediately when that had been, but she hadn't thought about it for a long time.

"I've been to a lot of parties, but mostly related to my kids or to my work in some way. This one I'm remembering, though, was about being a good wife and supporting Dwight in front of a new client for his building management firm in Portland. We were invited to this party so that the owner of the building could introduce Dwight to the tenants."

"How did you do at that party? Did you talk with people? What are your memories about it?"

"I felt overwhelmed at first, but then I got into the swing of it and kept up my part of the small talk. There was one strange thing, though. One of the tenants, an older woman, about eighty maybe, kept staring at me. She reminded me of my mother, the way she used to look at me to let me know I had overstayed my welcome."

Mallory made a stern face to imitate her mother.

"She used to let us kids come say hello to guests at their parties. We knew a lot of them as neighbors or as parents of our own friends. So sometimes—well, usually, I guess—I'd end up in a true conversation with one of them. And then Mother would glare, and I'd realize my siblings were long gone and I should be too. Then I'd have to get out of the conversation without seeming rude to the grown-up. It was always very awkward."

Mallory stopped, forgetting why she was back in that memory. A car horn blared. Dr. Nies prompted, "And so now at Dwight's work party, this eighty-year-old woman was staring at you …"

"Oh yes, and I felt like I needed to leave the room. So I did! I left and waited outside. Eventually Dwight came to find me, and we had a real row about it. He was trying to make a good impression on his new boss and I was blowing it for him. I cried, something I rarely did normally, and he saw I was really in pain. He let me wait for him in the car."

Dr. Nies patted the arm of Mallory's chair. "Think back now to that upsetting dream you told me about, the one where you were buried alive and no one would know where you were. I think these things are related. I think your fear in both situations relates to a feeling of never having existed in your parents' eyes, especially your mother's eyes."

Mallory nodded. It made sense.

"And now I'll suggest a tie-in too, with your uncle Bill and the experiences you described in our very first session. When he first tormented you with your parents so nearby, laughing and oblivious, you felt forgotten at that time. And being forgotten, you were susceptible to danger. You had no protection. You felt vulnerable."

Yes, that made sense too. Mallory waited for more.

"I think that your agoraphobic tendencies now are a displacement of anger at your mother, especially related to the events with your uncle Bill that never got resolved and that you never told your mother about. This was her baby brother, in a way an extension of her, which made it all the more debilitating at the time.

Also, being buried alive is how you've treated the experience with your uncle—you've buried it alive."

Mallory loved how Dr. Nies's mind worked.

"It's coming up to time you confronted your uncle, and time you told your mother about what happened."

"Oh God, no, I can't. I can't!" Mallory felt like she'd been thrown overboard by a conniving pirate.

"Don't worry. I'm not going to force you before you're ready. But start thinking about it, imagining it. You could practice the telling with Dwight first. We'll talk more about it at our next session."

14

SEPTEMBER

In which Mallory feels invigorated by a new idea;
Doris asks a favor; and the Coopers walk the pier.

DRINKING HER COFFEE and checking Facebook the next morning, Mallory felt a glimmer of hope. In honor of the feeling, she decided to change her profile picture. She pulled up a photo taken mid-serve in the final game of her last tennis competition. Just placing that photo fanned the spark of hope inside her. She ran an instant replay in her mind, putting herself back on the tennis court, beating the most formidable opponent. She recalled how amazing that felt, like a current of therapeutic electricity.

As Mallory carried that scene, she sat up straighter in the chair and felt the court under her feet. She got up and stood away from the computer and started swinging an imaginary racquet. A slow forehand, a slow backhand, then faster strokes and a few serves. Her motions were fluid, as though no time at all had passed. Actually being on a court and wielding a racquet would show how rusty she really was. But at this moment, she felt like Martina Navratilova in her heyday.

She walked to the storage closet under the stairs and dug toward the back. There was her racquet, much the worse for wear over the years, as all three kids had picked it up for half-hearted swings with friends and then dropped it again. Carol had been the only child to do something more with the game, but not until college, when she had bought her own racquet.

If Mallory was going to play again, she needed to buy one of those new models made of titanium or something. She also needed to get a new pair of tennis shoes. She wondered what people were wearing on the courts these days. White was no longer necessary, but could tennis clubs have sunk so low as to allow tattered cut-offs and T-shirts? She did a mental tally of how much money she'd need to budget just to start up again. And then what would the ongoing cost be—the membership in a racquet club?

She got online and checked out the fees for members and the costs for clothes. She called the tennis club she used to belong to, north of Kennebunkport. In the end, her research showed that getting geared up and participating again would run her about $1,200 the first year.

Dwight's hobby, helping out at the trolley museum, didn't cost them a thing. Her hobby would carry a pretty hefty price tag with it. What could she do to earn money to get back in the game? She hadn't finished college, dropping out her sophomore year to get married and start a family with Dwight. She had been so impatient in those days. How she regretted not finishing, getting her degree (in anything!), and having something to go back to now. Still, she knew just having a degree didn't guarantee a good job, or any job.

Then she remembered how she had earned money in college. She had babysat, typed, and waited on tables. She could certainly babysit now around town in Great Wharf. With her experience at the art museum, she knew online fact-finding expeditions could be hired out too. If she had fact-finding and babysitting jobs at the same time, she could ask the parents' permission to use their home computer after the kids were put to bed. She figured, worst case, once she got her name out there, she could have $600, half her goal, by the start of the new year.

Mallory picked up the wall phone in the alcove to tell Dr. Nies her new idea but then realized it could wait until their next session. She started to call Dwight's cell phone but hung up, knowing it wasn't a good enough reason to interrupt him at work. He'd be home midafternoon for their walk, and she could tell him then. He'd be happy to see her looking forward to something.

The doorbell rang. A delivery? Puzzled, Mallory left the kitchen, shut the closet door in the hallway on her way by, and then detoured into the living room to peek through the curtains. She saw Doris Hillobenz with her arm extended to a peeling area on one of the porch columns. "Don't you dare peel that off," Mallory whispered as she hurried back to the hall and through the vestibule to open the door.

"Hello, Doris. Is everything okay?" Mallory watched Doris throw the peeled piece away with an arm thrust behind her back.

"Yes, Mallory, fine. Sorry to bother you. I was just wondering ... well, Cassidy received an invitation to a party at Richie Trent's and his mother's place in Biddeford. I don't want her driving at night, and I don't know when that party will end, even though the time said from five-thirty to eight. I figured Richie must have invited you two, and I'm wondering if you would mind taking Cassidy with you. Would you mind?"

"We wouldn't mind at all, Doris. We'd be happy to have Cassidy join us. Tell her to come over at five-fifteen that Saturday." She stepped back into the vestibule, her hand on the door.

"Wonderful. I'm so relieved. Thank you, Mallory. As long as I've already interrupted whatever it was you were doing, would you like to come over to my kitchen for a cuppa?"

A cuppa gossip, Mallory thought. "I'm working under a deadline here, Doris. I'll have to take a rain check on that."

"How about tomorrow morning?"

"Maybe some other time—too hard to plan just now." She made an apologetic grimace.

"I see. Well, thanks again for letting Cassidy join you. I was kind of surprised not to be invited myself, seeing as how Richie and I were fellow cast members in *Rumors*. But you know kids these days. Course, he's a grown man, isn't he. So I was kind of surprised."

"Maybe you should throw a cast party. Sounds like Richie's party isn't for his theater connections."

"As long as that purpose isn't to start dating my granddaughter. I have to admit that's one of my worries."

"I don't think you need to worry about that, Doris. Richie doesn't treat her any differently than anyone else. He's very respectful and polite. Well, I do need to get back to what I was doing."

"Do say hello to that nice husband of yours. Is everything okay with him?"

"Just great." Mallory was taken aback by the question. It might be the first time Doris Hillobenz had ever inquired after the well-being of anyone unless she was probing for gossip to feed her mill.

"I'm glad to hear that. Well, I'll see that Cassidy gets over here when the day comes." She turned on the stoop to start down the steps. "Good luck with that deadline."

"Thanks. Bye." Mallory shut the door, wishing she really did have a deadline.

*　*　*

Dwight and Mallory had been true to their agreement. Since the end of July, seven weeks now, he had been coming home from work in time for them to go on a walk. He still volunteered at the trolley museum, but he went before or after the walk or waited for another day. They had developed a pattern that added up to a whole circumference around town every two weeks or so. Each day, they drove the car to the farthest point they'd walked the time before, and then they would walk to a new farthest point on the circumference. That would be the halfway distance for the day, and they'd double back to the car from there for the full distance. Anytime they felt like it, they'd walk a tangent beyond the town or back toward town.

For today's walk, Dwight drove toward the water. He found a parking spot on Rose Hips Way near the town dock and suggested they start walking northwest, back toward town. Reaching the local nursery would be about a mile.

Mallory agreed that would be a good goal. "First, though, let's take a walk on the pier and check out the harbor. We don't take in this view nearly often enough."

Mallory put her left hand in Dwight's right, as she did at the start of every walk. Starting out this way was a ritual they enjoyed, but it wasn't long before they took their hands back to themselves, preferring to swing their arms at their own rates.

"Nice to smell the ocean," Dwight commented as they stepped onto the old wood planks.

"Yes! It's lovely. I never get tired of it." Mallory breathed in. "Remember when we first started going to open houses just for entertainment? It was before we got serious about getting our own place. It was spring when we looked at the first property. There was a feeling of newness in the air. We had the car windows down, and then when we turned onto Rose Hips Way the smell of the ocean hit us. Do you remember that, Dwight?"

"I do." He breathed in too, raising his nose high in the air. "But I like it best at first smell. Once I picture the mix of seaweed and decaying fish flesh that creates the aroma, I stop breathing quite so deeply."

"Oh you," Mallory said, giving him a playful swipe with her left hand as she removed it from his right.

When they reached the dock's end, they put their arms around each other and gazed quietly at the scene. The water lapped against the moored boats, and a seagull stood sentinel on each one.

Mallory broke their silence. "Isn't it a riot how this huge town dock looks out at such a tiny harbor? There are only four buoys—two for full-time lobster boats and two for guests. Yup, a truly great wharf all right, if you're talking about the pier. The harbor is a joke!"

"Not to the lobstermen, it's not. And those guests, when they do need a spot, couldn't be more grateful. 'Any port in a storm' isn't a cliché when the weather turns without warning." Dwight had his hands in his pockets and was leaning forward slightly, as though keeping his balance on a shifting deck.

"Speaking of storms, is there anything else we should be doing to prepare for tomorrow's nor'easter?" Mallory hoped the question sounded offhand.

"We're as battened down as we can be, both us and PCJ's properties. We are now enjoying the calm before the storm."

"Yes, and the harbor looks so peaceful. Maybe our town's called Great Wharf because it's great there's a wharf here at all. I do hope all four of those buoys are well set."

"I'm sure the harbormaster has that under control. We should start walking."

They turned from the water view but walked slowly on the dock, enjoying the echoing of the wood planks. When they stepped off the planks and onto the sidewalk, their pace quickened.

"Dwight, I had an epiphany earlier," Mallory said, starting into her planned topic. "I was imagining myself as I used to be on the tennis court. I got out of my chair and pretended to swing a racquet. It felt so good. Well, long story short, I'm going to sign up for some tennis matches and get back in the game. What do you think?"

"I think that's a great idea! Go for it!" Dwight grinned in a genuinely happy way that Mallory realized she hadn't seen in a while, which made her sad.

"There's a bit of an expense involved, but I think I've figured out ways to pay for it so it won't hurt our budget."

"I can always count on you for that. How much expense, and how are you paying for it?"

"Sometimes I can go babysit where the children are, but I can probably also have kids come to our house too, if they're all of a family. I'll need to check the laws about that. I don't want to get into the childcare business, that's for sure. And I'll ask around about fact-finding needs at the art museum and among writers and publishers in the area."

"That sounds like a good plan, Mal. Hopefully you won't need to do that for long. Hey, can you get paid for playing tennis?"

"Don't I wish!"

When they reached the nursery they took an appreciative look at the seasonal plantings on sale but decided to do without this year. As they were leaving, Mallory noticed a chalkboard sign she'd missed on the way in.

Attention Nature Lovers!

Winter volunteers needed on Cinder Path Planning Committee.

Inquire within or visit our website at GreatWharf Plantings.com.

Meetings to be held at Byways Gift Shop.

"Look at that, Dwight." Mallory pointed to the sign. "This stupid idea is gaining momentum. They haven't begun to see all the problems. Where's this path going to go, anyway? Will the town be grabbing land by eminent domain?"

"That'll be sorted out by the committee, Mal. You should join up, be part of the discussion."

Mallory took a step back, surprised by a wave of dizziness. She put her hand to her forehead. Dwight wrapped an arm around her. "Take it easy, hon. You don't have to do anything till you've thought more about it. Just relax. Let's get back to the car. I have a couple more things to batten down tonight."

Mallory took Dwight's hand again and held it till they reached the car. They gave each other a kiss and separated as he got into the passenger's seat and she got into the driver's seat. Mallory driving home had become part of their walk routine.

15

September

In which a storm hits Great Wharf; and Jim
calls the police.

T HE NOR'EASTER HIT the next day, right on schedule by forecasters' predictions. Hurricane-force
winds of 98 mph struck in the early afternoon. Towns
up and down the Maine coast were hunkered down.
The stores had laid in enough food, water, candles, and
flashlights to satisfy the prestorm demand. People knew
the electricity might be affected and could be off for
some time. Dwight's company had spent days preparing
its properties. Both homes and businesses had board-
ed or taped windows. Harbormasters had secured the
lines and buoys holding boats and rafts in place. Many

boat owners had removed their crafts from the water altogether.

By the time the storm hit, there was nothing more to be done but wait it out and assess the damage afterward. Lightning lit the sky in all directions. Thunder rumbled first from several miles away, then closer and closer. At the height of the storm a huge crash of lightning and thunder made both Mallory and Dwight jump and drop the books they'd been trying to read.

Dwight said, "It sounds like Great Caesar's Ghost has hit Great Wharf tonight." When Mallory didn't respond, he said, "You know, like the newspaper chief in Clark Kent's office who was always yelling 'Great Caesar's Ghost' when something went wrong?"

Then he noticed that Mallory was shaking. He pulled her closer to him and said, "Don't worry—we're well protected here."

"I know, and I keep telling myself that a coward dies many deaths. But then I picture the house going up in flames or being torn off its foundation by a tornado, and I start shaking all over again."

Dwight rubbed her back and suggested a game of hangman to occupy their minds. "The only rule," he said, "is that each word has to relate somehow to peace, good health, or good times."

Mallory got a pencil and pad of paper, and they played for two hours, interrupting for chitchat whenever a word reminded them of a story in their past. When the electricity went out—only for a half hour, but they had to figure it could be all night—they went to bed and spooned until they fell asleep, encouraged by a lull in the storm.

The next morning they watched the news together. After a lead report on the surprisingly minimal local damage, a story banner going into the commercial announced: "Up Next: Local psychologist found dead." Both Mallory and Dwight stared in silence and thought the commercials would never end. Finally, the news anchor came back on.

"The broken and lifeless body of Dr. Sheila Nies was found at the bottom of the steps outside her residential office early this morning."

Mallory burst into tears.

"… probably caused by a misstep during the heavy gale winds and rain battering the town. In other storm news—"

"That poor woman! And poor me!" Mallory's gaze reeled from the television to Dwight to the ceiling and back to the television. She felt like a trapeze artist who had just slipped from her partner's grasp. She was going down.

Dwight folded his wife into his arms.

After a minute, Mallory said, "She never gave anything away about herself personally. I have no idea who to send a sympathy card to. Maybe there'll be an obituary with more information. Just have to wait and see." She sank deeper into Dwight's arms. "Those damn steps. I always hated walking up and down them. They never felt safe to me. And now look—someone who took those stairs all the time fell and died on them anyway."

"Sort of an analogy to life." Dwight stroked her hair and kissed her cheek.

"What do you mean?"

"Well, I mean, we go along living our everyday lives, doing so many of the same things every day, and, as often as not, with accidental deaths anyway, it's those very things that may do us in. I guess what I'm trying to point out is that I hope you're not going to add fear of stairs to your list of things to be worried about."

"Oh, Dwight, that's unfair." Mallory started to draw back, but Dwight held on. She said, "I've been doing better lately—really I have."

"I know, but I'm worried that with your Dr. Nies gone, you may start backsliding."

Mallory freed herself. "Well, I hope I don't, but I can see why you'd be worried about that. I guess I'd better get another shrink right away."

"Maybe, maybe not. Maybe now's a good time to reassess how much help Dr. Nies was to you. What was left undone? Are there actions you can take on your own, based on the things you already talked about?"

"Like what?"

"How do I know?" Dwight touched her hair lightly. "You're the one who was in the closed sessions with her. I'm just saying you should think about that before running off to another doctor. Why aren't you driving more, Mal? Why are you still hesitant to leave the house if you don't have to?"

Mallory knew Dwight was right, and she couldn't hold it against him. He had put up with so much the past year. She agreed that she should have shown more improvement since she started seeing Dr. Nies, even though they had only had four sessions so far. Why wasn't she further along? Why was she still afraid of going out by herself in the world?

Facing the truth, she knew she wasn't over her fears. Maybe she needed to get hold of her files, to re-read information from the sessions.

* * *

"Jim, it's Mallory Cooper. I know it's been a week since the nor'easter, but did you hear about Sheila Nies?"

"Yes, it's awful. I feel terrible for her clients. Were you seeing her, after all?"

"Yes, I was. I'm calling you because I'm wondering how I might get hold of her case file on me. I'd like to read through it and refresh my memory about her insights and ideas. Should I start with the police, or is it better if you, as my primary care physician, call them?"

"Why don't you let me give them a call and find out the answer to that in general. You probably won't be the only person to ask me about this. I have recommended Dr. Nies to quite a few people over the past couple of years."

"Thanks, Jim."

"How have you been, Mal, if I may ask with professional interest? Are you feeling less anxious these days?"

"A little. But that's why I want a look at my files. I have a feeling I've blocked out some key insight. And now that Dr. Nies won't be around to keep me on the right path ..."

"I understand. Well, I'll let you know what I learn."

Jim hung up and swore under his breath. This was an unwelcome secondary effect of Sheila's death that he hadn't anticipated. He could barely stay focused on his patients as it was. Every time Sheila crossed his mind, he had to fight back tears. He let them flow freely at home, but here in the office he had to maintain his composure.

Doris Hillobenz had come in the other day, ostensibly to update him on her burning mouth syndrome. He had diagnosed it the week before as possibly related to hormonal changes, but medical science didn't know for sure. He told her to try using just baking soda instead of her longtime toothpaste with all its added ingredients. Now she reported that her mouth felt a little better, and he said to add a weekly fluoride rinse to the regimen.

That discussion could have been handled in a phone call. But then Doris said, "I was so sorry to learn about Sheila Nies's death." And that's when Jim knew the real reason for her visit. He would stay civil, but his mind swirled with things he wanted to say. He fought back the sudden tears and said, "Yes, it's a true loss to our community."

"Were you and Dr. Nies friends?"

Jim wanted to tell her it was none of her business. "Of course, we were colleagues and both concerned with doing the best for our patients. But since we saw each other professionally as well, we steered away from close friendship." He would lie right into his grave rather than confide to Doris Hillobenz.

Waiting in the exam room while he talked to Doris was Lily Vandermere, a longtime patient with a history of hypochondria that would test the patience of Oliver Sacks. Sometimes, however, Ms. Vandermere really was ill. Her newest complaint was a pain in the side. Last month she had come in with a stomachache, which miraculously went away during the examination. She suggested he should add massage therapy to his credentials.

After Doris left and Lily's appointment began, Jim's first thought upon hearing about the latest pain was that she just wanted another massage. He tried to take it seriously, though, and he recommended that she drink more water and take daily walks.

Lily Vandermere died in her sleep that night. The family—in fact, her only relative was an estranged brother—decided against an autopsy. So Jim wouldn't get to learn what had caused her death. But he feared that he might have moved her out of his office too quickly, and he decided he needed to take some time off. He had to deal with Sheila's death. He had to get control of his emotions again.

Cora, his office manager, made the phone calls to reschedule his longer-range appointments and clear his calendar for a few days the third week in October. He told her he had some personal business to take care of, and she asked no questions. He wondered if she knew about him and Sheila, but she gave no sign.

Now, as his last duty for this evening, he picked the phone back up and dialed the police station. Then he called Mallory and told her the police had subpoenaed all the files. Any patient could ask for a copy of his or her own file, but the originals would be kept at the police station until after the coroner's report was completed and maybe until the case closed in their system. They couldn't estimate how long that might take—at least a month. In the meantime, Dr. Nies's estate attorney had a list of referrals should any of her patients wish to see it. Jim gave Mallory the attorney's number.

"Jim," Mallory asked, "wasn't Dr. Nies's death just an accident? Why would they subpoena her files?"

"Good question—and I asked it. Turns out she had reported a break-in attempt the night before the storm. An officer went over and investigated. A pane of glass had been broken on the ground-floor level. She heard it break and she turned on the hall light immediately, which seems to have scared the perp away. Chances are, the officer said, it was some kid hoping to grab something to sell for drug money. They still think her death was accidental, but just in case a patient was involved, they got the subpoena. The main thing for you is, you can get a copy of your records anytime you want."

When he hung up, Jim noticed the invitation to Richie and Jean Trent's party stuck into the blotter on his desk. Richie had given it to him during their workout the weekend before the nor'easter. He had forgotten all about it. At the time, he had accepted immediately, glad to have a reason to do something unrelated to his practice. He thought now of Jean Trent's happy freckles and smoky eyes and wondered if, even as he grieved for his friend Sheila, he would still find them so fascinating.

* * *

That night, as they got ready for bed, Mallory asked Dwight if it wasn't time to spring for a home security system. He actually laughed at her.

"You're kidding, right?"

He went into the bathroom to brush his teeth. While she put on her flannel nightgown, she told him about the attempted break-in at Sheila Nies's place. Then she added, "I've been reading the Police Blotter in the *Gazette* for a few months now, ever since Angie Weller told me about the increased shoplifting going on."

Dwight finished rinsing out his mouth. Dabbing with the face towel, he came to the doorway. "I know petty crime's been on the upswing, but nothing earth shattering." He turned, hung up the towel, and came back into the bedroom.

"Still," Mallory said as she headed to the bathroom to take her turn, "I'd feel safer if we had some kind of system, especially with one of those panic buttons."

Dwight waited while she washed her face and brushed her teeth. When she got into bed, he put his hand on the covers over her thigh and pressed down gently.

"It was bad enough, Mal, when we started locking all the doors and windows all the time. I think we're doing fine. I don't want to add another monthly expense. Let's talk about this again in the spring. If you still feel the same way then, I'll look into it."

She turned and kissed him. "Or maybe you could think about my Christmas present ..."

"Hmm."

16

OCTOBER

*In which people start to mix at the Trents' party;
and Celestine and Angie meet their fans.*

J EAN TRENT WAS ecstatic. Everyone invited to the
cocktail party had said yes, and the long-awaited
Saturday had finally arrived. She and Richie spent the
morning cleaning and pushing furniture around in
the living and dining rooms. Happily, the downstairs
neighbor hadn't complained about the noise.

Deciding to have this party had given Jean the motivation finally to change the main color scheme across
the two rooms—from a dreary beige/brown combo
to the pleasing ocean greens and blues of the invitations. Jean had even reupholstered the big chair in the

living room and the seats on the dining room chairs. She used sunset yellow as an accent color on the throw pillows and in candle groupings. Richie had cleaned all the windows, and the crisp fall sunlight flooded in.

To encourage their guests to mingle, Jean and Richie placed most of the furniture up against the walls in both the living and dining rooms. They put Celestine and her litter box in Richie's bedroom and hoped no one was allergic to cat dander, though they did work to clean away any visual and aromatic signs of cat. They hoped her insistent meows of complaint would stop soon.

Liquid refreshments were set up on one side of the dining room, hors d'oeuvres on the other side. The hors d'oeuvres included fresh vegetables with a dill dip, crackers and cheeses, olives, shrimp, and sandwich quarters of tofu egg salad and tofu chicken salad. Jean didn't want to call attention to the ingredients, but she didn't want to kill anyone either. She placed a bright yellow tent sign in front of the platter, warning "Allergy alert: Sandwiches contain soy product." The cheese and shrimp offerings were Jean's concession to the nonvegan world.

With ten minutes left before their five-thirty deadline, mother and son had finished showering and dressing. They sat on the couch in the living room to savor their accomplishment.

"Whew," Richie began. "Is it always this hard to throw a party?"

"I prefer to think it's always this satisfying."

"I gotta admit, everything looks great, Ma."

"Thanks, honey. And also thanks for all your help. The clean windows seem to be letting in more than just sunlight. In a way, they're letting in a beginning. Do you feel it?"

"Yeah, I do."

"It was fun writing and sending the invitations. As I wrote each one, I imagined what might go through the person's mind when they got it. I'm sure a lot of them, especially the women, are curious to see how we live, and I'm so pleased we can show them. The women are going to want a tour of the whole place, you know, and some of the men probably will too."

Jean talked fast. People would start arriving any minute, and she felt the need to give Richie a few last-minute pointers.

"Your friend Dwight will want a tour, being in building management himself. I'm glad we can introduce our own super to him. It was a last-minute thought to add Lloyd to the list. My yoga instructor, Bonnie, was another last-minute invite. She may bring someone, but if she doesn't you might enjoy meeting her."

"I'll enjoy it anyway," Richie said. "But I'm especially looking forward to seeing Amanda again. Is it really true she's not hooked up with anyone?"

"Not anymore. She finally gave the boot to the good-for-nothing guy she was living with a year ago. Zoey and I were so glad! That's when Zoey offered up a room in her house for Amanda to rent. And I have a feeling that Amanda would like to get to know you better too."

"Really? That's great!" Richie tossed one of the yellow pillows in the air and caught it before it landed on the floor.

"Now before you go gaga over the beautiful Amanda, be sure to pay equal attention to all the guests, and don't neglect Cassidy. She won't know most of the people, so she'll need you to introduce her."

"Don't worry—I'll be the perfect host." Richie made a dramatic sweep of hand across his giddy smile to change back into a serious man. He patted the pillow back into place.

The door buzzer sounded. Jean said, "Here we go," and bounded off the couch. She held the intercom button down. "Please give your name as the password." Amanda! Zoey! She buzzed them in to start walking up the two flights to the apartment.

"Seriously, Ma, do I look okay?"

"Mr. Studworthy if ever there was one."

Before Amanda and Zoey got to the apartment, the buzzer went off again, and the Coopers arrived with Cassidy Hillobenz. The long-awaited party had begun.

Jean loved finally meeting Cassidy and the Coopers. She was immediately taken with Dwight's kind and wise, creased face and knew there had to be a karmic connection of some kind, the way this man had befriended her son. Mallory seemed a little ill at ease at first but became chattier once she had a glass of the Cabernet in her hands. Jean, a teetotaler except for an occasional piña colada, noticed people's drinking habits. She didn't make judgments—she tended to avoid alcohol mainly because she hated the taste of it. She figured that was indication enough to leave it alone.

Jean pointed out the nonalcoholic beverages to Cassidy. "Richie told me you like Coca-Cola, but we have other sodas here too, if you like. There's also just plain water in this pitcher here."

Jean thought Cassidy was a sweetheart; she was a little plump thanks to her fondness for Cokes and Cheez-Its, as Richie had confided when first describing her last summer. But Jean was glad Richie wasn't interested in sixteen-year-old Cassidy except as a friend. At the same time, Jean wanted to pry him away from Amanda's side. He had already forgotten his promise to be a good host. After Cassidy had a Coke in her hands, Jean said, "Richie, why don't you take Cassidy to say hello to Celestine?"

Cassidy said, "Oh yes! I can't wait to see her again!"

Richie gave his ma a slightly accusatory look but smiled at Cassidy. "Let's go see our mama cat."

Amanda said, "Can I see her too? I love cats."

Zoey said, "I'd like to see her too. But, Amanda, why don't we let Richie and Cassidy have their time with her, and then you and I can go see her later? We'd just make it too confusing for the poor thing. She's been meowing like crazy in there."

Zoey's comments reminded Jean why she liked her so much. Zoey was several years younger and had no children, but, like Jean, she was a widow. This gave her an added layer of empathy for when a person (or a cat) might need some quiet attention. Zoey might also have seen the need to interrupt the spell Richie and Amanda had cast on each other.

As soon as Amanda headed over to the hors d'oeuvres table, Zoey said to Jean, "I think we may have a new romance to talk about soon."

Mallory, standing between Dwight and Zoey, misunderstood and asked, "Who—Richie and Cassidy?"

Zoey enlightened Mallory about the true romantic undercurrent in the room. Mallory confided that she was glad she wouldn't have to swallow the reassurances she had made to Doris Hillobenz a couple of weeks earlier. Cassidy and Richie really were just friends. Before Jean could add her own reassurances, the buzzer announced more company.

Jean asked for "the password" and heard Jim Beall's name in his deep voice. Her finger bounced in a blur from the intercom button to the buzz-in button. As she checked her hair and lipstick in the little wall mirror by the door, she heard Lloyd, the building superintendent, and his wife greet Jim on the way up. The buzzer sounded again, and she let in Hank Sanborn, Richie's former employer.

When the group entered the apartment, she announced the newcomers to the people still gathered in the dining room. She made a special point of taking Lloyd over to Dwight and informing them of their common interest in building management. When she turned back around, she saw that Lloyd's wife was pouring herself a drink, and behind her Hank and Jim were in conversation, waiting their turn.

Hank, Jean noticed with surprise, appeared less than healthy. He did look strong, like he worked out at the gym. He had a beer gut, though, made all the more evident by his short stature, and a scraggly gray beard and rheumy eyes. And unless he suffered from a cold or allergies, he also had a smoker's cough. Jean knew from Richie's year with him that he was a good person who treated his employees fairly. It saddened her to see that with the end of his company he seemed to have suffered a decline in health. She'd have to ask Richie if he always looked and sounded like that. Maybe he wasn't really that bad looking. Maybe it was the contrast as he stood next to Jim Beall.

The door opened to Richie's room down the hall, and Cassidy and Richie walked back into the party. Amanda said, "My turn!" and Zoey said, "Me too!" They followed Richie back down the hall. This left Mallory, Jean noticed, adrift like a polar bear on a melting ice floe. But Cassidy quickly filled the void near the only woman she knew in the room.

Jean glanced again as Richie led her A-to-Z friends down the hall, and she noticed that his hand was lightly touching Amanda's elbow. She could almost feel the butterflies coursing through both of them. After all, she had just felt them herself when she buzzed Jim in.

Another buzz and Jean heard the energetic voice of her yoga instructor. When she opened the door to greet Bonnie, she was surprised to find a group of three. Bonnie introduced her boyfriend, but no one introduced the woman standing behind them, who must have scurried in after the outer door had been buzzed open. After a moment's puzzlement, Jean remembered the black eyes and deep red pixie of Angie Weller. She hadn't recognized her in the cocktail dress.

Everyone else had assumed that a party at the Trents' place meant casual or informal dress. Not Angie. Her plunging neckline revealed more than Jean really wanted to see, and the way the flouncing angel on her necklace bounced around at the end of the silver chain was eerily lifelike—well, angel-like? Jean wondered if she was being a prude. Lots of young people were wearing low-cut tops these days. Still, not many middle-aged women were, especially to a casual gathering at another middle-aged woman's house.

All these thoughts raced through her mind in a split second.

"Welcome!" Jean forced out, as she waved her last visitor into the apartment. "I'm so glad you could make it, Angie! Did you have any trouble finding us?"

"Not at all. I know Biddeford quite well. I wonder if I'll know anyone else … do you think?"

"It's possible. Most of the guests are from the Great Wharf area, though two work with me in Biddeford. Come see if you recognize anyone."

They rounded the door into the dining room, now fully animated by guests getting acquainted or reacquainted. Jean asked, "See anyone you know?"

Jean watched people's faces as she stood there with Angie. Some people hid their reaction to the bosoms on high better than others. Richie's former boss, Hank, was the first to come over and introduce himself.

Jean left them and went to check on the refreshments just as Amanda, Zoey, and Richie came out of his bedroom.

"Richie, will you refill the ice bucket?"

"Sure, Ma."

Jean looked back at the doorway between the dining and living rooms and saw that a circle of men now surrounded Angie. In fact, except for Bonnie's boyfriend and Richie, all the men—Hank, Jim, Dwight, and Lloyd—had made their way across the room and were gazing enviously at the kinetic angel.

"It's a good thing I'm not the jealous type," Mallory said to Jean. They looked at each other and burst out laughing.

"Isn't that something!" said Jean. "I don't really know her. Her name is Angie Weller, and she owns a little gift shop in Great Wharf. Maybe you know it. Byways?"

"I do know it," Mallory said. "I bought a music box there last summer in order to keep my neighbor, Cassidy's mother, happy." Mallory nodded to Cassidy, still standing next to her, and continued, "Mrs. Hillobenz was dying for my opinion of the proprietor. Now that I think about it, I never did report back to Doris."

"What was your take on Angie at the time?"

"That she was beautiful and lucky to be self-sufficient." Mallory looked down at the wine glass in her hand and then back up at Jean again. "I was feeling sorry for myself and immediately assumed her life was going better than mine. Ridiculous, of course—no one can know what a stranger's life is like. Often we don't even know what a loved one's life is like. We all keep so many things to ourselves."

The honesty in Mallory's speech surprised Jean. Combined with her joke about not being the jealous type, it made her feel like an immediate friend.

"I also went to one of Angie's art classes to try my hand at acrylics."

"I didn't know she ran art classes. What's her background?"

"No idea. I never went back. She only ran them during July and August, trying to drum up business, I assume. And she has this crazy idea about getting a cinder path into Great Wharf, which aggravated me. Still does."

"I read her *Gazette* letter proposing that path. There have been a few letters since, from other citizens. Looks like the idea may take off. I'd use it myself."

Not noticing the flush her statement had brought to Mallory's face, Jean returned her attention to the circle of men.

"I had no idea Angie would dress like that when I invited her. I bought the invitations at her shop, and I guess I was just in a lighthearted mood or something. Oh well."

"Not to worry!" Mallory went along with the shift in topic. "This is providing great entertainment for all of us, I'm sure. And it won't hurt Cassidy here to see what fools men can make of themselves over a sensuous woman." Mallory gave Cassidy a quick side hug of affection.

"Cassidy," Mallory said, "let's go over and say hi to Ms. Weller. Then you can tell your mother your own reaction to the Byways owner."

"I'll go with you," Jean said, "and see if I can lure some of those men back into the larger party."

After Richie put the ice bucket back in place, he joined the admirers and said he didn't think Angie would remember him. He was wrong. Angie exclaimed, "You're one of my favorite customers! How nice to see you here."

Jim didn't give Richie a chance to respond. In a baritone come-on, he said, "I've been to your shop too. Don't you remember me?"

"Of course I do, Jim Beall, and I also know you're the most respected doctor in our little town." Angie's body came to full attention.

Mallory, having waited with Cassidy and Jean for a good time to interrupt, chimed in on Angie's last comment. She said, "I gave Angie your name, Jim, last summer. She was looking for a good general practitioner."

Jim's broad grin narrowed into a more professional smile. Giving Angie a quick wink, he said, "In that case I hope you found one of my esteemed colleagues."

Jean watched Angie closely and wasn't surprised to see her respond to Jim with extra warmth. Angie leaned forward, moistened her lips, and said, "I haven't committed to anyone yet. But I'm not sure I'd want to put a handsome single man to the wrong use."

Jean decided enough was enough. She had no intention of being outplaced by Angie before she'd even had a real conversation with Jim herself. While everyone was still chuckling uncomfortably at Angie's come-on, Jean put one arm around Jim and one arm around Hank, and said, "Can I interest either of you gentlemen in some incredible hors d'oeuvres?"

Over her shoulder, Jean called back, "Richie, would you mind introducing Angie, Lloyd, and Dwight to my A-to-Z friends?"

"Sure, Ma." He looked at the three and said, "Ma wants me to introduce you to the two women she works with. Can I take you over there?"

Mallory suggested to Cassidy that she go with Richie too. Then she whispered with a mock-stern finger wag, "Let me know if Ms. Weller comes on to my Dwight!"

17

OCTOBER

In which Mallory and Celestine meet Hank Sanborn; Jim pockets a number; and Angie sits awhile with Mallory.

MALLORY FOLLOWED JEAN, Jim, and Hank to the hors d'oeuvres table. She tapped Jim on the shoulder. "Hi there, good doctor!" Jean placed her hand on Jim's shoulder in a farewell gesture and moved back to the center of the room, leaving his side reluctantly. At least he would be talking with Mallory now instead of Angie.

Jim turned to Mallory and said, "I was pleased to see you here when I walked in." He lowered his voice and leaned in to add, "And I hope this is a good sign, seeing you at this sort of gathering outside your usual haunts."

"This is the first party I've been to since Carol's going-away party four years ago. I've been doing more walking and driving. Also, I'm doing some babysitting so I can afford to get back into tennis this winter. I'm not out of the woods yet, I know, but life is starting to look more interesting." Mallory placed her free hand on her chest, over her heart. "My sessions with Dr. Nies were very helpful, Jim. I only had four, but they were terrific. I want to keep improving, as a way of honoring her almost as much as for my own benefit. I can't thank you enough for that referral. She did her profession proud."

Jim closed his eyes and nodded. When he opened them again, he raised his voice and glanced over his shoulder. "Have you met Hank Sanborn yet?" The man was trying to spear a shrimp with a toothpick and having to reach behind Jim to do it. Jim stepped back enough to give Hank and Mallory space to talk. "Hank, this is Mallory Cooper, another Great Wharfian."

"Nice to meet you." Hank coughed, but at least he turned his head toward his upper arm and away from the food. He positioned himself closer to the shrimp now that Jim had moved back a step from the table.

Mallory asked, "How do you know the Trents, Hank?"

"Richie used to work for my electrical services company, but it went out of business. That's okay, though. I've got a job with the state now, as a correctional officer." Hank speared another shrimp.

"You gave up on being an electrician?" Jim asked.

"I never really enjoyed it, especially after starting my own company. The liability worries and customer demands got to me. In corrections, you just start out assuming everyone's a jerk. It's up to them to prove otherwise."

"Interesting philosophy," Mallory said. "That probably works well in your new job, but I'd hate to think it applies in general."

"Yeah, I just say it as a joke."

He speared another shrimp.

* * *

When Jean asked Richie to refill the ice bucket, she caught him before he had fully shut the door to his bedroom. The door didn't latch shut, and Celestine's front right paw shot out, opening it enough to scoot through. She was free to roam the rest of her domain. She pranced into the kitchen, where she saw Richie at the refrigerator. She shot under the kitchen table and sat there until he left the room. She took time to process the unusual smells and sounds.

Finally, she ventured forth. She hugged the doorjamb as she left the kitchen and entered the dining room. She walked close to the baseboard until she was under the draped table with all the food on it. The smell of shrimp penetrated her brain. Her nose told her exactly where the aroma was coming from. She walked purposefully out from under the table, took a nanosecond to judge her position, jumped, and made a perfect landing next to the shrimp—just as Hank's hand reached for another one.

Hank felt the fur, looked down, and screamed like a frightened child being given a second hypodermic needle. Celestine leaped high and landed, claws extended, onto the hand holding the toothpick. All heads turned in time to witness the rheumy-eyed, beer-bellied man desperately shaking his arm while the calico held on for its life. Hank Sanborn's lifelong fear of cats provoked a scream high enough to pierce the stratosphere.

* * *

Seconds after Hank's public anxiety attack, Jim felt a tap on his shoulder and turned to find Angie looking up at him.

"Poor Hank," she said with a tee-hee laugh. "I don't think he'll ever eat shrimp again."

Jim didn't want to laugh at Hank, but he did want to laugh with Angie. He liked her self-confidence. Yes, her attire was inappropriate, and he knew the women would talk about that. But she had dressed perfectly if her aim was to spark the men's interest. He actively grieved for Sheila, and Mallory's words had almost made him tear up in front of her. Even so, he had been feeling the pinch of celibacy. He could enjoy this flirtation with Angie as much as anyone with a strong libido.

He also had a strong competitive drive. He leaned down and whispered into Angie's ear. "Now I didn't say this if you're ever questioned on the stand, but Hank could do with less shrimp and more fresh air."

"Spoken like a true doctor, Doctor B." Angie giggled. Then she said, "You know, I think you've only been in my shop that one time. You bought one of the more highbrow bookmarks and then bolted. Before you bolt now too, I want to give you my card."

Angie's fingers slid beneath the fabric over her left breast and reappeared with a business card. "I've made a special note on the back just for you."

Jim accepted the card and immediately flipped it over. The word *home* was written there with a phone number.

She said, "Same address, private line."

"You don't waste any time, do you?" Jim felt a tingling sensation as he held the card still warm from its hiding place.

"I'm sure you know, as a doctor, that life is short. I don't believe in wasting time, no." Angie put her hand on Jim's arm. "Now I'm going to slip away and chat with one of the girls. Mustn't create any jealousies."

Jim pocketed the card and turned back around to see if he could be of any help to Hank.

* * *

Seeing the small lines of red bubbling on Hank's hand and arm, Mallory had left the room. She sat on a chair in the deserted living room, shut her eyes, and tried to think about anything but blood. She thought about her children, which led to worrying about Jess, which led to picturing blood on the ground in a foreign land. She thought about flowers, which led to memories of rose thorns pricking the skin, drawing blood. She thought about the drink still in her hand, which led to her opening her eyes and draining the glass.

Angie walked in and sat on the couch, facing her. "Are you all right, Mallory? You seem shaken. Was it the fiasco with the cat?"

Mallory was relieved to have an unbloodied person to look at. It was also good to have that person be a relative stranger, which required her to act normal fast. A concurrent rise in temper—because of Angie's promotion of the cinder path—brought Mallory back to full interactive mode.

"Yes, that did shake me up a bit. I tend to freak at the sight of blood. How did it turn out? Is Hank okay?"

"He's fine. Jean took him into the bathroom to tend to the scratches. It's a coincidence, I'm sure, but I used to have a calico that looked just like that one. She never attacked anyone, though, just mice in the cellar."

"What happened to your calico—die of old age?"

"No, she was in her prime, which was the problem. She got herself pregnant. Of course, that wouldn't do; I didn't have time to take care of a litter of kittens." Angie shrugged her shoulders. "I drove her to a nice wooded area miles away from the store, put some food and water down, and told her she was on her own now. I'm sure she found someone to take her in. People are suckers for kittens." Angie stopped and waited, perhaps for Mallory to agree with her.

Mallory realized she was sitting there with her mouth open. After a moment's hesitation, she said, "Oh my, well, you're right, of course. A lot of people are suckers for kittens." She felt her pulse start to race. "I mean, look at Abraham Lincoln and Mark Twain and Florence Nightingale and Ernest Hemingway and that tattooed cat-whisperer guy on Animal Planet and … Of course, except maybe for that guy, I'm pretty sure none of them were out walking in those woods. Hopefully some sucker was."

Angie's features hardened. "I do apologize, Mallory. I made a mistake sharing that story with you. Please forgive me. I was trying to think of something to take your mind off what just happened."

"No, I'm sorry. I don't know what came over me just now. I hardly know you and here I went all snarky like that. It's me who should apologize." Mallory really did feel bad. She loved cats—and dogs and birds and butterflies too. But she knew a lot of people who didn't have these feelings and yet were still good people. It was a little like having a different religion.

Angie's face softened a bit, and she asked, "Why does the sight of blood freak you out? Do you see anyone for that problem?"

Mallory was surprised by the directness of the questions. But it felt easier to talk to a near stranger than to a friend, like talking to one's hair stylist in a town other than one's own. "I haven't figured out why I react that way. I did start seeing someone to dig into it all, but she died in the storm last month. You may remember her from your art classes, at least one of them, which is where I first met her. Dr. Sheila Nies?"

"Oh my, yes. As well as attending the classes, she used to come into Byways and buy close-friend cards. No one would call her pretty. I always wondered who her 'friend' was. Do you know?"

"I couldn't say. I mean, she was very private about her personal life."

Angie sat taller and nodded toward the crowded dining room area. She said, "Maybe she and Jim Beall had something going."

"What? Wow. That never occurred to me." Mallory shook her head.

"I would have bet on it."

"Jim referred me to Dr. Nies. I thought you'd never heard of him. When I mentioned his name to you last summer, you said you knew someone by that name but not him."

"Yes, well, I've met him at this party now. And how many doctors are there in Great Wharf? They do each other favors, you know. So maybe Jim and Sheila ..."

"I suppose one could think that way." Mallory hated where the conversation had turned. There was a difference between benign and malignant gossip, but she tried to avoid it in either case.

Angie continued, "I saw you talking with Jim just before the incident with the cat."

"Yes?" Mallory was done sharing with Angie.

"I'm wondering who he's seeing these days." Angie leaned forward and looked intently at Mallory. "A man that delicious can't be celibate."

Mallory almost laughed but stopped herself. She would have a little fun. Forgetting her resolve for a moment, she said, "I think he and Jean are an item. Or maybe he and Hank. I haven't decided yet."

Angie's body sank back into the cushions, her lips pressed together. "I'm quite sure he isn't gay."

"Jean then?"

"Maybe so."

Mallory got up and said, "Hey, thanks for coming to see me, Angie. I'm feeling much better. Time to check in with the others."

Without another look back, Mallory went to find Dwight first, in case Angie watched her. Then she would find Jean. Not to tell her about the conversation—she already felt guilty about suggesting Jean and Jim might be an item—but to see how the cat had fared.

* * *

During his drive home, Jim replayed the highlights of the past two hours. The only reason he had looked forward to the party at all was to support Richie and to see Richie's mother, Jean, again. He wanted to see whether the attraction he had felt to Jean before

Sheila's death was real or not. Even if he felt drawn to her, he wouldn't act on it right away. He generally avoided that kind of attraction, knowing it could get too serious too fast. A lifetime of keeping emotionally distant had created a strong habit. Despite Sheila's status as a friend with benefits, he had found it necessary now and then to do a fast soldering job on holes she pierced in his armor. Her death had shaken him far more than he would have predicted.

When he saw Jean at the door, looking so open and happy to see him, he had almost turned and run back down the stairs. But, of course, he was more mature than that. He acted naturally, not giving a clue to his reaction. Then, when Angie Weller arrived, he had someone else to think about.

Jim shifted his weight behind the wheel to reach into his pocket and retrieve the card Angie had slipped into his hand. She didn't beat around the bush, that one. Jim put the card back in his pocket, not certain he'd follow through on it. There was something odd about Ms. Weller. And titillating as hell.

Then a deep laugh rumbled out of Jim's throat as the image popped into his head of the cat clinging to Hank's hand. At first he had felt bad for the cat, and then he had worried that Hank might have a heart attack. He'd never seen anyone with such a strong feline phobia. For the umpteenth time since Sheila's death he wished he could share a story with her. She might have suggested he send Hank her way. His laugh changed to a heavy sigh, and a tear crept down his cheek.

* * *

Meanwhile, on their own trip home, Dwight drove as Mallory and Cassidy kept up a steady stream of chatter. The mood in the car was encouraging. It reminded Dwight of having the family together, when Mallory and the girls would get onto a topic of no interest to him or Jess except for the wonderful mood of hilarity.

"Did you tell Celestine there was shrimp on the table, Cassidy?"

"No!"

"Are you sure? Because it seemed to me that was a put-up job."

"Oh, Mrs. Cooper, you're having fun with me, aren't you?"

Mallory giggled and admitted that's what she was doing. "But I have to say that cat displayed an amazing sense of purpose and timing. Poor Hank. He may never eat shrimp again."

Dwight realized Cassidy might never have seen her older neighbor enjoying herself in this way. For a couple of years now, she'd only have seen Mrs. Cooper working in the garden or shoveling snow or heading into the house in a sour mood.

Cassidy said, "I felt so sorry for Mama—I mean Celestine? She was scared to death. Mr. Sanborn shouldn't have flung her around like that. She could have been hurt real bad when he threw her down. I went to help her but she ran and hid under the couch in the living room? And ..."

Dwight stopped listening. He had so enjoyed watching Mallory hold her own at the party, with no repeat of that scene years and years ago, when she waited for him in the car. He even saw her having a quiet conversation in the living room with Angie Weller. He dared to hope they might become friends. Her other friends had moved away over the years. She hadn't made new ones except people at work, and so she hardly ever saw them.

Lately Mallory's and his walks together were high spots for both of them. But two steps forward seemed to bring a step back. The other day he had found her folded in front of the computer crying. She wouldn't talk to him about it. He thought she must still be working through the loss of her psychologist. Tonight's chatter with Cassidy reassured him, but he wondered what harm Dr. Nies's death might have done. He had watched Mallory empty three glasses at the party, and he knew she'd have another at home tonight.

For his part, thoughts about Elizabeth Easley hardly ever struck anymore. Despite his fears, he was more confident now than he had been during the summer that he and Mallory would survive the darkness. His workload had eased up, and he was enjoying more time at the museum again. Lindsey, his super-reliable office manager, always knew how to reach him if anything urgent came up. Mallory's plan to join a tennis group and find ways to pay for it herself was a good sign. He just hoped someday soon she would share whatever it really was that had made her cry at the computer.

18

OCTOBER

In which Jim visits Byways, begins a promising dinner date, and discovers the truth behind an old lie.

JIM WALKED DOWN Newman Lane, the side street by his office, to pay a visit to Byways and Angie Weller. He was feeling pretty good, now two days into his three-day hiatus from the office that Cora had arranged for him. The party at Jean Trent's the past weekend had lifted him from some of his funk, and now, after his first true days off in years, he felt he might be ready to live again.

He awoke that morning from a dream that reminded him he was overdue for a tune-up. In the dream he got one from Angie. Once fully awake, Jim knew the woman he really wanted was Jean. But he knew that a few dates with someone of Jean's caliber would quickly get complicated, and he wasn't ready for that. Not now, maybe not ever. He had kept true intimacy at bay ever since Beverly. He and Sheila had come as close to love as he could allow himself.

Sheila's death had dragged him to a bleak ocean floor and held him there until his lungs were ready to explode. Now, easing upward toward sea level, he could feel some of the sun's warmth again. Someone like Jean might cause him to try breathing before he had fully surfaced. He could drown.

Angie, on the other hand, could keep his body actively happy while he continued his recovery. The way she had flirted with him at the party promised that a good time might be in store. He did so want a good time. He put thoughts of Jean away, and just in time. Here was Byways.

As he opened the door and smelled the citrus-lavender, he remembered the bookmark he'd bought for Sheila last summer. The unexpected memory became a hurdle to jump on his way into the shop. The only noise in the empty store at ten in the morning was the bell that tinkled with the door's opening. Jim stopped just inside the door to read a hand-printed sign on an easel.

Weekly Cinder Path Meetings!
Wednesdays 7:00–8:00 pm
Come talk with your neighbors. Drink some tea
and eat a lavender brownie.
A cinder path will entice more visitors and busi-
nesses to Great Wharf.
Goal = Submission of plan to town council by end
of February

Several of Jim's patients had sought his opinion about the path. He answered each time, "What's not to like? It will encourage exercise for some people and face-to-face conversations for others. It will enliven downtown too." It impressed him that Angie seemed to be proactive in the planning.

Before he had a chance to look around for something to buy, the dream-catcher curtain jiggled and Angie walked out. She stopped short with a fleeting stunned look. Her hands adjusted the neckline of her jersey and checked the position of today's angel necklace. Then she walked slowly toward Jim, keeping her black eyes on his blue eyes.

"Good morning, handsome. I didn't expect to see you so soon after the party. Are you here for business or pleasure?" She stopped with less than a foot of distance between them and tilted her face up.

Jim said, "I guess that depends. I could find some-thing to buy, or I could take you to dinner tonight. Do you have a preference?"

"Let's see." Angie looked toward a far corner of the store and then back up at Jim. "I can't think of a thing in the store you need except me."

* * *

Even though Great Wharf had a fine restaurant on the water, Jim took Angie to Kennebunkport's Hurricane Restaurant in Dock Square. More expensive than he wanted, it was also less likely to be frequented by his neighbors.

"My oh my!" Angie gushed after they were seat-ed. "I've certainly heard about this place but never dreamed I might enjoy a meal here. And I certainly never dreamed it would be with you. It will be quite a trick to repay you." Then Angie added, "And I don't mean the kind of trick a lady has no business knowing about." She wiggled in mock discomfort.

"Rest assured, I don't misunderstand you." Jim let his gaze meet hers and then drop to her breasts, show-cased in a simple low-cut oxblood dress. A different angel played in the cleavage than he'd seen at the party, and this necklace had another figure as well. A leering horned devil waltzed with the angel.

"Nice necklace."

"I don't put this one on display very often."

"Don't you think Great Wharfians can handle it?"

"They could handle it, but I like to pick who's handling it."

Jim reached across the table and down the small distance required to take the waltzing pair in his fingers. His hand kept brushing her skin while he rotated the pendant.

"Angie, you are one luscious piece of work."

"It's good to be appreciated." She leaned into his hand, shut her eyes, and moaned for his ears only. Then she smiled and said, "Feed me."

Dinner talk took over as they ordered and toasted each other with wine (a bottle of Napa 2006 St. Supéry Merlot) that complemented their mutual choice of beef tenderloin (bloody rare). Jim felt his body relax in a way it hadn't since Sheila's death. The evening was going per plan. He looked forward to enjoying Angie's company through dinner and just maybe into the night. With her flirty manner and her beauty, Angie couldn't be more different from Sheila on the surface. Turning the conversation to careers might help him get closer to what made Angie tick.

Jim voiced his usual warning. "I don't date much. In fact, I have a reputation for avoiding intimacy. It's true too. I don't have the time for it. My practice keeps me going twenty-four seven."

As he talked, he watched Angie for her reaction. And as she listened, she cut her next bite of steak, slipped it into her mouth, and chewed slowly. They kept their eyes on each other. He waited for her to say something. She didn't, as though she were chewing to the count of thirty.

Jim cleared his throat and then went a little further. "So, that sometimes pisses women off. But sometimes it makes a woman happier to know me. I just thought I'd get that information out of the way. I'm not a catch. I'm an overworked physician with a normal sex drive. Is that too blunt?"

Angie swallowed the meat. Jim stopped himself from commenting on how fully tenderized it must be by now. He waited for her to answer his question. First she cut another bite of steak. Before putting it in her mouth, she said, "You can't be too blunt with me." Then she started chewing again.

"Good, good. You must be very busy yourself, running Byways. Tell me—how did you get into retail to begin with?"

Angie swallowed fast this time. She lifted her chin with pride. "I had just struck out on my own after high school and didn't know what I really wanted to do. I knew I wanted to make money, but babysitting wasn't going to cut it. I wanted to make big money. Without a college degree, that was going to be a challenge. Touch typing and a few basic business courses in high school and adult ed got me an entry-level job with a widow whose husband had always managed the back-office needs. You know, filing and accounting and such. She was good on the customer-service and product-buying side. I got good basic training working with her for a couple years."

Angie pumped her index finger toward her head and said with a grin, "I found out I'm really smart!"

"Was that a surprise to you?"

"No one had ever given me credit for anything. My parents never thought I'd make it on my own. Mom told me to find a rich man with gumption, like a Rhett Butler. Well, once I learned that I was smart and could take care of myself, I figured I could have my cake and eat it too. I'd make my own way, have my own career, and on top of it find a rich man with gumption. I got married three times looking for that guy."

Jim didn't want to talk marriages, so he brought the subject back to careers. "What led you to decide on a New Age sort of shop? Is that what the widow ran?"

"She ran a Hallmark store, so not much New Age there. No, I grew up with essences and crystals. My mother was big on everything New Age. The thing I associate most with my childhood is the aroma of lavender. Mom used the plant in and on everything. Lavender sachets and potpourri, sprigs of lavender in dried flower arrangements, even lavender lemonade and lavender brownies."

"Just lavender?"

"It's the most all-purpose natural essence of them all. It tastes good, smells divine, and soothes an aching spirit. It's the only thing about my home that I remember happily. It's not that it was a bad home; it just wasn't any fun. Talk about clueless parents." Angie grimaced. "Anyway, that's all over and done. I do think it's why I kept getting married, though, sort of to put as many experiences between me and that stifling place as I could. I go by the name Angie Weller, but it's really Mary Angela DiMatteo MacPherson Petrecca Weller."

"So, Ms. Mary Angela, I take it DiMatteo was your maiden name?"

"Yes, the DiMatteos of Cleveland, Ohio."

Jim's eyebrows shot up. "No kidding? Cleveland's where I did my residency."

"I know."

"You know?" Jim pulled back slightly, touched by a stealth cold-air pocket.

"The truth is, I was a candy striper at Lake Erie Memorial Hospital when you were there."

Jim cocked his head. His eyebrows nearly touched over a deepening furrow. "You've been keeping a secret from me. What's the whole story here?"

"I'd love to tell you all about it, but why don't we go somewhere more private?"

Jim suspected his hoped-for pleasant evening was about to take a nosedive. He cued the waiter to bring the check. While they waited, Jim stayed silent. Angie excused herself and went to the women's room. She returned after the bill had been paid. Jim held her coat for her. Instead of taking her to his place, as he had planned, he decided to take her to a quiet local bar. This bar had booths with high backs, designed to give customers the privacy so many of them wanted.

After they settled in and had after-dinner drinks in front of them, Jim said, "Tell me."

"You look so upset, Jim. I hope you don't think I'm about to blackmail you or something." Angie's voice was soft and sweet, and completely unbelievable.

"Tell me, Angie."

"You don't remember me, do you?"

"No, because we never met before I came to Byways to buy that bookmark, and then the party at the Trents' place."

"We not only met before, we made love."

Jim raised his hands, palms forward. "No way."

"First of all, you can't pretend you didn't have sex while you were a resident." Angie rolled her eyes. "Nurses and doctors talk, you know, and I was very good at checking the contents of my cart just around the corner. Oh, the things I heard, and not just about you. But you were the one I admired the most, because I'd seen you stand up to authority on more than one occasion. You had the ethical backbone of a saint, and the more I saw you in action, the more I wanted to run my fingers up and down that backbone."

"Angie, get to the point." Jim sat with his back up against the booth.

"You did it with a candy striper. You thought she was over eighteen. You thought so because that's what she told you."

"Only one striper ever, and she sure as hell was over eighteen. She didn't look anything like you. She was slightly pudgy. She had long, dark brown hair. Her name was Mary."

Even as Jim said this, he remembered that his one-time-only striper had had the same flirtatious approach as Angie. He'd succumbed late one night after a harrowing day in the OR. They'd done it in a broom closet on the tenth floor. Three minutes, tops.

"Oh my God, it was you, wasn't it?" His shoulders sagged and his head shook back and forth. "Mary Angela, aka Mary, aka Angie." He leaned forward and said in a quiet voice, "I've never treated a woman like that before or since."

"It makes no difference what you've done with others."

"I had no idea you weren't eighteen. You said you were. You acted thirty."

"I was three weeks short of eighteen. At the time it seemed close enough to say I was eighteen. But now, of course, I know better." Angie smiled sweetly.

The compassion he'd been feeling disappeared.

"What do you want, Ms. Weller?"

"No need to get angry. Please don't get angry. I guess I shouldn't have teased you this way. I just want us to get to know each other again, but this time as equals. I think we could have a future together. You have to admit we enjoy each other's company."

Jim gave a sigh of relief. She wasn't going to hold that momentary past against him. She wasn't going to tell others about it. She just wanted some love and hadn't gone about it the right way. At the same time, Jim remembered his uneasiness about Angie after she had given him her phone number at the party. He should have paid attention to that. It would be smart to stop it here.

Angie was looking at him with a questioning gaze.

"Angie, I made a mistake back in Cleveland. I'm happy to hear you say it was your own lie that's to blame. I think you're sexy as hell, obviously. But I don't think we're suited to each other in the long term."

"But—"

"No, I hope you'll forgive me, but let's go back to the way things were while we still can. I promise to shop at Byways now and then, and maybe I can send another doctor your way. There are a lot of younger men who would love to get to know you."

Angie set her mouth in a submissive pout. "I've tried other men. I only want to attach one more name, and I thought Beall would be perfect. I still think so. Why don't we let this evening simmer awhile and talk again when you feel ready? You know where my shop is, and my residence is right over it."

Angie slid out of the booth and got her own coat. Jim paid the bill and held the door open for her. At one point while they were walking to the car, their elbows touched. Jim took two quick steps to the side. Neither of them spoke on the drive to her place. She got out of Jim's car and said, "I look forward to seeing you again, Jim." He shook his head as he drove away.

EPISTOLARY EXCERPT FROM
UNPUBLISHED MANUSCRIPT:
RUNAWAY LEGACY

April 6, 2007

Dear Caitlin,

It was wonderful to see you over the holidays, to see your father again, and to meet your new stepmother, Blair. Just think, now you will have three sets of grandparents! All of us love you dearly and think you are very mature for a nine-year-old. We will be sad not to see you as often as we did before. But we know your dad has to go where the jobs are, and in his new line of work that turns out to be Florida, not Ohio.

Who knows—maybe we'll look for work there too. Your grandfather Sergeo just lost his job with the car dealership. The recent merger meant that most of the sales force in his old company was let go, including him. I'm still working in telemarketing from home, which I can do anywhere. Don't hold your breath, but we'll see what we'll see. Let your dad know we'll be in touch before making any big decisions.

Love,
Nonny Vera and Nonno Sergeo

19

NOVEMBER

In which Jean trusts Dr. Eli Sterns; the police question Jim; and Jim rejects a new patient, sort of.

JEAN WENT BACK to get an extension on the prescription for her mood stabilizing medication in November. She described her successful party to Dr. Sterns and hoped her excitement didn't smack of overreactions or misinterpretations. She liked this doctor for his no-nonsense style. While in everyday life Jean appreciated humor and surprise to keep things interesting, in her psychiatric sessions she just wanted candid straight talk. Tell me what you think and help me move on.

"Jean, you sound excellent," said Dr. Sterns. "You planned and gave a solid party, plus your son was very helpful. I'm going to recommend we reduce the dosage on your medication this time and see how it goes."

"Are you sure?" Jean hadn't expected this recommendation. "I never want to go back to the despair I felt." She hugged herself.

"Well, let's try reducing it. You should call me immediately if you feel yourself slipping, of course, but give it a try."

"Okay, I guess. Do you foresee a time when I won't need any meds at all?"

"Yes, I do. I believe that your problems have stemmed from the shock of the unexpected loss of your husband and your inability to properly grieve while you still had to watch over the family. Then you moved to a different state, a different job, and added to that a lot of worry about your youngest child and whether he'd land on his feet after losing his job. You've undergone so much change, it's no surprise you've spent some extended time feeling down in the dumps."

Jean listened to this focused description of her last five years and knew Dr. Sterns was right.

"There is one major aspect of your case," he continued, "that has always been a strong influence on how I view you and your chances for recovery. And that is your own aversion to suicide as an option, no matter how down you have felt. You must tell me if that changes, Jean."

Dr. Sterns's words left her simultaneously hopeful and scared, but she trusted this psychiatrist. What both she and the doctor didn't know was whether the prescription he was writing would be a reduction in dosage of a medication or, in fact, a placebo. Jean had agreed to do a clinical trial in order to get the treatment at reduced cost, and at any time the double-blind study might have switched her to a placebo. As far as her neurological system was concerned, she could already be medication free.

Jean left the doctor's office with the prescribed pills doled out by the office nurse. She would play by the rules of the game she had agreed to. Driving home, she whistled "Who's Afraid of the Big Bad Wolf?" The tune would stay in her head for days afterward.

Richie sat with Celestine on the couch. He had long since removed the hidden package, which now resided under the shoes in his bedroom closet. Celestine had been spayed and was recuperating well. All seemed right in the world, all except the lack of a full-time job. The one he had interviewed for was a near miss, going to someone with more experience. But the company promised to keep his résumé on file in case another opening came up. He knew he shouldn't count on that, and he wouldn't, but he was pleased that he had done well in the interview.

Celestine purred and stretched her paw out for more rubbing.

Jean came in the door after her appointment with Dr. Sterns. As she hung her coat in the closet she asked, "Did Dwight Cooper say anything to you about the party, the next time you saw him at the museum?"

"Yeah, he did. They had a great time, and they both thought you were cool."

"Cool neat or cool standoffish?"

"Cool neat."

"I wonder why I never heard anything from Mallory. You know, guys aren't great about following up with thank-yous, but women usually are."

"Dunno, Ma."

"I think I'll give her a call. The little bit we did get to talk at the party, I thought she had a fun sense of humor. Do you have the Coopers' home phone number?"

"Yeah, it's in my cell, by the door. Go ahead and use that to call her."

Richie heard only his mother's end of the conversation.

"Oh no, this isn't Richie, but you're close. It's Jean, Richie's ma … Please don't apologize for not calling.

I know how things can get away from us, especially with the holidays coming up … Not a problem, really! Listen—I'm calling because I'm wondering if you can recommend a good general practitioner in the area. I never changed doctors after we moved here from Massachusetts, and I'm thinking it's time I got in with someone in Maine. Does Jim Beall have a good reputation? … Oh good … Oh no, everything's fine, really. I'm just doing what I should have done three years ago.

"So, how have you been? … Are any of your kids coming home for the holidays? … How wonderful. Richie and I will head down to Massachusetts for both Thanksgiving and Christmas to be with my daughter and her family … Well, it was great to meet you, Mallory, and thanks again for the referral. Maybe we can get together for a chat when I get my checkup with your Dr. Beall? … Sounds good. Thanks again … Bye."

Jean put Richie's cell back on the table and came to the couch to pat Celestine.

"It was fun to listen to that, Ma. When you call another woman you want to know better, it's sort of like wanting to go out with someone but not wanting to get rejected right away, isn't it?"

"Yes, it's a lot like that, now that you mention it." She rubbed Celestine twice more and then asked, "Is there anyone you want to ask out?"

"Smooth, Ma."

"Just thought I'd ask. I thought you and Amanda were heading toward a first date. I'm pretty sure she'd love to hear from you."

"She's so beautiful. She could get anyone she wanted. Why would she want to date an unemployed electrician?"

"Why, Richie Trent, did I raise an idiot? You're strong and handsome and compassionate and a catch for any woman. Paraphrasing a former presidential campaign manager, 'It's the economy, stupid!' You'll find a good job eventually, and in the meantime you're earning money freelancing. It's not like you're a lazy slob with no future." Jean paused, then added, "But I'm not pushing, hon. You know that."

"I know. And I'm sort of surprised you're thinking of Jim Beall as a doctor instead of a date—but I'm not pushing you either, Ma."

Celestine purred on.

* * *

Jim Beall called the police the second week in November for an update on Dr. Nies's files. Not really wanting to remind the police of his existence, he had waited longer than the month they'd estimated. Indeed, hearing him on the phone, they asked him to come in and talk to them in person after work. The police station was only a five-minute drive away. It was housed in a modern annex to a historic building that held the town offices, a couple of miles south on Wyeth. The well-fortified annex had been built in 2002 to allow the expansion and upgrade of the former police department. Five people became ten people with more attention to homeland security and counterterrorism concerns.

Police Chief Bren Burnham liked a neat desk. To keep his desktop spare, he tossed into the drawers several times a day anything that had landed on top of his desk in the meantime. For important items he used the top drawer; for less important, the middle drawer; for inane but potentially necessary, the bottom drawer. One Sunday a month, he spent a couple of hours in his office going through all three drawers to make sure he hadn't hidden something important from himself. In the process, he filtered what was there and placed papers on his assistant's desk or threw them out.

His assistant, Trudy, had mixed feelings coming into work that one Monday a month after her boss cleaned his desk. Partly she agonized over how to make apologies for his oversights when they affected the public. Partly she looked forward to laughing with her husband later about funny things that had been unearthed. Last month it was the notification of a surprise party for one of the patrol officers that

Chief Burnham thought he'd never received, so he had ranted later about not having been invited. It was just like him, though, to admit his error when he found the memo. He was a great boss.

His family lineage went back to the landing of the *Angel Gabriel* in 1635 on the shores of what was now Bristol, Maine. The night after the landing, a hurricane destroyed the ship. Descendants of William Furber, one of the surviving passengers, dedicated a plaque to the ship at Colonial Pemaquid State Historic Site in 2010. Chief Bren Burnham, descended from Thomas Burnham—who could well have been a friend of William Furber's on that voyage—was in the crowd at the dedication. More than one photo caught the chief with tears running down his stern, craggy face.

Bren Burnham considered his role as Great Wharf's police chief a personal responsibility to his ancestors to get it right. When a crime had a loose end or became a cold case, he added a notation about the case to a list he kept in the top drawer. He looked at his "Still to Be Solved" list first thing every morning. He was determined to keep Great Wharf in the top 10 percent of lowest-crime-rate towns in Maine. His staff honored that determination.

Deputy Chief Pete Churchill had been mentored by Burnham since his honorable discharge from active duty with the Navy fifteen years earlier. He could now read his boss's mind with great precision, and the chief often let him do his talking for him.

When Dr. Jim Beall announced himself to the desk officer, he was shown to a room that looked more like an austere office than an interrogation room, but Jim got the idea. While he waited, he noticed that all the framed documents on the wall had to do either with Police Chief Bren Burnham or the police department overall. Burnham's certificate of graduation from the FBI National Academy impressed him, as did three community-police partnership awards and two best-practice awards. Two men interrupted his viewing.

Chief Burnham introduced himself, shook Jim's hand, and then took a seat behind the desk. Deputy Chief Churchill also introduced himself, shook Jim's hand, and then took a chair in front of the desk, next to Jim's. Jim had seen the deputy's face around town and recognized the chief's face from newspaper stories over the years, but he had never met either man until now. When he had taken the coursework and earned the right to carry a concealed weapon in the state of Maine ten years ago, he had dealt with some sergeant.

Chief Burnham began. "We asked you to come in, Dr. Beall, because we think you can help us understand what happened to Dr. Sheila Nies. Your name comes up fairly often as a referring physician. Now we didn't think much about that at the start, but when you called to inquire about when the files would be released, we figured it was time to have a chat."

"Oh boy, lucky me," Jim offered.

"You seem like a fine upright citizen, Doc—don't get us wrong. It's just that this Dr. Nies has been a bit of a puzzle for us. There are some things about her death that don't quite mesh. We haven't been completely aboveboard with the press, and we don't plan to be, because it's still very much an active case. Do you mind if we ask you some questions?"

"I guess this is where I should ask whether I need a lawyer."

"Entirely up to you, of course. Just say the word if you want to go that route. But until you decide, I'll just get started. Where were you the night of September 27, when the nor'easter hit us?"

"That's easy. I was working late on my own files, and hoping the storm wouldn't bring any medical emergencies with it."

"How late?" Deputy Churchill spoke for the first time. He was taking notes.

"Ten o'clock or so. And then I got a call from the hospital asking if I could help out there, which I did."

"I guess their own records tell which doctors were on that night?" The chief continued to lead the questioning.

"Probably, but I don't really know."

"What was your relationship with Dr. Sheila Nies?"

"We were professional colleagues."

"Is that all?" Again, the note-taking deputy was the one to push for more of an answer.

Jim paused. "Well, that's personal, so if you're charging me with something, I guess I need to 'lawyer up,' as they say."

"No, no, that won't be necessary. We're not charging you with a thing. We're just trying to understand all the pieces we're looking at."

"So," Jim's thick eyebrows knitted together, "was Sheila murdered?" Like Mallory, Jim had assumed the bad stair step was the culprit. Now he wondered how he could have been so dense. The police thought he might have killed Sheila. He knew that most murders were committed by people the victims knew, and mostly in relationships with them. He had nothing to hide regarding Sheila's death, but he would hate for the community to learn about their friends-with-benefits arrangement. Rampant gossip could still harm his practice. And what if someone learned about the mistake he had made in Cleveland?

Chief Burnham said, "We haven't ruled out murder."

"My God." Jim's mind went into overdrive. There was that break-in. Did Sheila have another secret lover, or an ex-husband, or someone else he didn't know about? All he knew about Sheila Nies was that they clicked. They simply clicked. They were both devoted to their work, both in the field of medicine, both contented in Great Wharf. The more he thought about it, it had to be a client of Sheila's. It had to be! She worked with nut jobs, right? He knew, of course, that most of her clients were nowhere near what could be called nut jobs. Most were like Mallory Cooper, regular people with regular issues they just needed a little extra help figuring out how to handle.

"I won't be saying anything more." Jim nodded his good-bye to each man. "Do let me know if I'll be needing a lawyer."

As he walked out of the police station, Jim felt as though hundreds of eyes were focused on him. He looked around but saw only the deputy chief standing outside the interrogation room, watching. Jim wondered if Sheila had been shot. The police would already know he owned a gun and was licensed to carry it anytime he wanted.

As he got into his car, his eyes filled up. When he backed up to get out of the tight spot he was in between cars, the tears spilled over. He blinked hard and had to wipe away the overflow before he could see well enough to drive. He was shocked to realize how much he still missed his friend. He didn't confuse the feelings with love in a romantic sense, but Sheila had been a best friend in every other sense. If she had found a romantic love and told Jim their liaisons would have to stop but they could still be friends, he would have been happy for her. That was a scenario they had already discussed. But to lose her through an anonymous violent act—that felt like someone thrusting both hands into his heart and ripping away.

He would hire a lawyer immediately, maybe also a private eye. With them on his side he might stand a chance of being kept abreast of what the police were learning. But in any case he didn't need to be hassled by the police. Jim's comfortable world had just been turned on end. He had to keep working, but he also had to know what the police were doing to find Sheila's killer.

When he got to the medical building, he took the back entrance into his private office. He washed his hands in the corner sink and looked at himself in the mirror. His eyes were as red as he feared. He sat down at his desk, opened the center drawer, and pulled out a bottle of lubricating eye drops. While the drops worked on the red, Jim kept his eyes closed and worked on the tension by rotating his shoulders forward and backward. Then he took a deep breath, let it out slowly, and opened his eyes.

In the middle of the blotter was the schedule for tomorrow that Cora had left for him. He recognized all but one of the names as long-time patients. The new name belonged to Jean Trent. He winced to see Jean's name there. Even though he had arranged that dinner date with Angie—only to find out it would be socially suicidal to see her again—he did want to get to know Jean. What was she really like? Was he foolish to avoid her? If he took her on as a patient, he'd have to keep her in that category no matter what.

He decided a direct course of action made sense. He picked up the phone.

"Hi, Jean. This is Jim Beall. I just saw your name on the list of people I'm scheduled to see tomorrow."

"Yes—hi, Jim!" The melody in Jean's voice washed over him and brought an instant warmth. "I don't have a primary care physician, so I thought I'd interview a few before making a decision. I hope you don't mind. Since I've met you twice now, I felt there must be a reason and I shouldn't let it stop with the cocktail party."

While Jean talked, Jim ran the tip of his index finger back and forth over her name on the schedule. Then he picked up where she left off.

"I certainly don't mind that you would consider me, but I have a different feeling about our two meetings so far. You're someone I'd like to know better, and I don't mean as a patient. I have enough patients. What

I don't have are a lot of people outside of work that I enjoy just talking with or doing things with. What would you think about meeting Sunday noon at the new bookstore in town here? We could check it out and then get something to eat at their cafe."

Jim paused and hoped the silence on the other end didn't mean he was about to hear a shocked turndown.

"I love that idea, Jim. Will you give me the name of another physician?"

Hiding his boundless relief, Jim said, "I'll suggest several when I see you. And would you mind calling my office first thing tomorrow morning to cancel your appointment? Just say something's come up and you may or may not be rescheduling."

"I can do that."

He hung up and suppressed a shiver of fearful delight. He was still afraid of getting deeply involved with someone, and he knew Jean wasn't the type of person just out for a good time. When he had asked Angie out, it was just for a good time, but look where that had gotten him! If his choice now was to risk either sunshine with a chance of rain or heatstroke with a chance of tornado, he'd go with the sunshine.

He made a notation in his calendar for Sunday. The holidays were about to hit, and his practice would require more than ever from him. He didn't really have time to date. That fact would help him keep Jean at arm's length.

As a last task before heading home, Jim called his medical lawyer for a referral to a criminal lawyer. He sure hoped he'd never have to go there.

20

November–January

*In which Mallory mutes the news; the Coopers
learn more about their children; and Mallory has
everything to learn about her tennis opponent.*

THE THANKSGIVING AND Christmas holidays hit
along with unreliable temperatures and rising
mounds of snow. Mallory still sent a "whatchadid" accusatory email to Uncle Bill every week or two. But
now they felt more like scratching an itch than being
brutal.

Opting out of walks in the cold and wet, Mallory
asked Dwight to be a passenger in her car so she could
practice driving in bad weather again. They made a
date to do that every Saturday afternoon until her

tennis rounds were scheduled to begin in January. She felt more assured as the weeks went by.

Babysitting work had also been good for Mallory. When she couldn't walk to a job, she would drive herself, and she had even driven to a few homes in neighboring towns. Earning money for the tennis canister gave her something positive to focus on. She had succeeded in reducing her wine intake from five to three glasses a day—and none when she'd be babysitting.

One night, Mallory surprised Dwight at the start of the nightly news. The idea hit her earlier in the day, and she still liked it at 6:05. She raised the remote with a flourish and muted the sound. Dwight waited for her to make some kind of comment. What she said was, "What say we go have a quickie?"

His eyes widened. Without a word he set down the hors d'oeuvre cracker and pushed away his glass of wine. He put his hands together and raised his eyes heavenward in silent gratitude. Mallory kissed him on the cheek and left the kitchen. She heard him push the bench back and scurry across the floor into the hallway to catch up with her on the stairs.

Instead of giving her a hug, he nudged her from behind and said, "Giddyap." Then he ran around her up the stairs. She went to the bathroom before following him into the bedroom. When she did get there, he was buck naked and lying back on the pillow with a dreamy smile on his face.

He said with a welcoming wave, "Come to me, my little sex kitten."

She started to make a show of taking off her clothes as though there were stripper music in the background, but then she remembered the whole point was that this would be fast. She said, "Just a quickie this time," tore off her clothes, and slipped into bed next to him.

"Quickie or molassie, let's do it in Tallahassee."

"That's a new one."

Lovemaking had always been good between Mallory and Dwight, but what used to be more than weekly had become maybe monthly. Dr. Nies had asked whether Mallory was satisfied with her love life, and at first she had said yes, absolutely. But the topic replayed in her mind after Dr. Nies's death. She'd come to realize that Dwight probably wouldn't say "yes, absolutely" at all. This evening's surprise newsbreak was one way Mallory could tell Dwight he mattered.

* * *

The holidays were wonderful, especially because Panda and her husband, Zack, invited them to spend Christmas at their home in Vermont. Carol drove from Canada to be part of the celebration. Jess even got two weeks' leave for Christmas and New Year's. This meant not only quality time with his family but also time back in Great Wharf to see old high school buddies.

Before the family got together in Vermont, Mallory had been reading and rereading the notes Dr. Nies had filed about her. During both the second and third readings, she was startled by the clarity of what she had to do. The notes were a laser beam she had shied away from during the first reading—just as she had shied from all the ideas while Dr. Nies was still alive. With time and rereadings, she was coming to grips with Uncle Bill's behavior. She still had to open up to her mother about it. And she had to let go of her anger in the process. She felt like she was getting closer. Thinking about the harassment wasn't as debilitating as it had been before.

She broached sexual harassment as a topic with her daughters at Christmas. The three women were alone together in Panda's antique farmhouse sitting room. The small room had just enough space for a sofa, two easy chairs, and a couple of side tables and floor lamps—all purchased from Craigslist. Mallory sat in one of the easy chairs. Panda and Carol sat near each other on the sofa. The intimate setting was perfect for the conversation Mallory had in mind. She was glad she hadn't commented on the faint mildew odor.

"Girls, I have a question for you. Have either of you ever experienced sexual harassment or abuse by anyone—a boss, a friend, a relative?"

"Never," Panda said.

"Several times," Carol said.

The girls looked at each other in surprise. Mallory listened hard from her chair. She loved how different her two daughters were from each other. Panda, for instance, kept her hair long so she could either wear it free or wrap it in a braid around her head. She wore her clothes loose. Carol kept her hair just longer than her earlobes and with a gentle perm. Her clothes fit on the snug side, just right to show her curves. The girls' polar opposite comments just now didn't surprise Mallory as much as they did the girls.

Carol said, "I'll bet you've experienced it, Pan, but didn't realize that's what was going on. A lot of times, guys will try something, but if the girl doesn't pick up on it, they just go away. You've got to admit, you've always been kind of naive about those things."

"It's true," Panda said with a shrug of acceptance. "But what happened to you?"

"Nothing major," Carol said. Then she faced her mother as she explained, "There were a couple guys at work, different jobs over the years, who thought they could pressure me into sleeping with them. I learned to laugh it off or give reasons that wouldn't offend them. I didn't want to hurt my chances on the job."

Mallory asked, "But never anyone who was a friend or relative?"

"Not anyone close to us. There was that brother of a friend of Jess's—Alex. Remember Alex?"

Mallory shook her head no, but Panda said with an exaggerated shiver, "Yes! A really creepy guy."

"His older brother was even creepier. He cornered me once after school and tried feeling me up. I told him I'd tell my dad if he didn't back off." Carol gave a victory grin. "That did the trick."

"How old were you, honey?"

"Fourteen."

"Were you scared?"

"Yes, but I didn't let him see that. And I spoke loud enough for other kids who were walking home to hear me. He was just a big bully."

"Maybe so, but I wish you had felt free to tell your dad or me anyway." Mallory cringed at the image of her then-fourteen daughter being handled forcefully. She wished she could jump back in time and call that Alex boy's parents.

"I felt free to, but I didn't want you to feel you had to do something about it. You could be kind of over-protective at times. It was over and done."

"I wasn't overprotective; I was just being a parent."

Carol and Panda exchanged a look.

"What? What's that look?"

Panda scratched at her cheek and said in a small voice, "I always felt like I couldn't do anything or go anywhere without you being there or close-by. I could understand it when I was really young, but once I hit twelve or so, if I wanted to go to a matinee with Sally or Barb or someone, you still insisted on driving us in both directions even though we wanted to ride our bikes."

Mallory noticed Carol nodding rapidly while Panda spoke. Panda's voice had reached a normal range now. "You were always scared to death something was going to happen. I ended up being afraid to be out on my own. That's one of the things Zack has really helped me with."

Carol patted Panda on the back and added, "You tried that with me too, Mom. And I guess we may as well own up to this now, but it's part of why Panda eloped and I decided to move to Canada."

It took Mallory a moment to adjust. She objected, "No, you moved to Canada because of political beliefs. And Panda, you eloped because you didn't want your father and me to have to pay for a wedding. Why are you looking at each other that way?"

"Aw, Mom," Carol said, "We love you so much. And to avoid hurting your feelings we told you and

Dad those were our reasons. But it's also true that we each needed to escape your sphere of influence in a big way. From our distances now, we both feel in control of our own lives in a way we never could have if we'd stayed nearby."

Mallory looked at the beloved faces of her two favorite women. They were fully grown and beautiful. And now they sat there, each with an arm around the other—friends—waiting for her to absorb and accept their truth.

"Wow. I had no idea. It's fascinating how you experienced me. It's the polar opposite of how I experienced my own mother. I always felt she couldn't care less where I was or what was happening to me as long as I ate my meals and did my homework on time."

"So," said Panda, "I guess you overcompensated with me. With us."

"And I drove you away in the process." Mallory grabbed a tissue from the side table and dabbed at the tears pooling in her eyes. "Come back to Great Wharf. I promise to leave you alone."

Panda and Carol actually guffawed. "Ha! In your dreams, Mom," said Carol. "Seriously, we have great lives where we are. And we love seeing you as often as possible. We're just really grown up now. You don't need to worry like you used to."

"You have no idea how much I miss you. And I only mention that because it's my way of saying how much I love you." Mallory blew her nose. "So, back to the earlier conversation. I guess the answer to my original question, about whether you two have been harassed in some way, is 'not to any great extent.' I think I can be happy with that answer."

"Good," Panda said, "but why do you ask us that now, after all these years?"

"I read so much about it these days, so I thought I should find out if my daughters are carrying any such scars. I'm glad to rest easy on this one. I'm not sure I can rest easy on the new information you've given me, but I'll get to work on it. At least I'll add it to all the other work I'm doing."

"What other work, Mom?" Carol asked.

"Oh, you know, the usual. Just life. Now let's go get lunch ready." Mallory gave each daughter a hug and kiss and left the room before they could take another stab at the question.

She was impressed by her daughters' willingness to reveal their true reasons for moving away. Although it made her sad to learn she was the cause, it made her glad to see what strong and happy women her daughters were. They had the courage to tell her where she had gone wrong while she had yet to stand up to her own mother. She realized, too, that every kid responds differently to every parent. She did the best she could, and all her children knew how beloved they were by both parents. What more could anyone ask for?

By prior agreement, while Mallory was talking with their daughters, Dwight had a similar conversation with Jess, to learn whether sexual harassment or abuse was in his background or current situation. When Dwight and Mallory checked with each other in bed that night, they were reassured about all three kids.

"I'm so relieved, Dwight. And I guess I'm really ready to let go and focus on you and me now. Especially me."

"Sounds good, hon. Except for the moment—how about us?"

She snuggled closer, and the satisfied parents quietly reminded each other of another of their strengths.

* * *

January arrived with its plunging temperatures and hardened snowdrifts. Mallory prepared to make the drive to her first tennis match, at a racquet club just south of Portland. She had been practicing her game at the YMCA in Great Wharf, but the Y didn't have enough people to organize formal rounds. So she'd have to drive north each time she was scheduled into actual competition.

Dwight asked her if she wanted him to go with her for the first match. She said no but gave him a grateful kiss for asking. He was both relieved (his business needed him) and reassured (Mal was ready for the longer drive).

When Mallory arrived at the tennis center, she went to the front desk and picked up the final schedule of play. The competition was organized as a round-robin. Four women were in Mallory's division. By the end of January they would all have played against each other, and their individual scores would be tallied for sets and games won across all the matches. This head-to-head matchup of results would determine which player would move into the next round of play. Across all the divisions, four players would survive to play in the second round, which would take them into early March. At the end of those matches, two players would survive to participate in the finals, scheduled for March 11.

Mallory looked at the list of participants, which totaled sixteen women. She didn't recognize any of the names, but that didn't surprise her. She had been out of the game for so long that most of the people she used to play with had moved or retired from the game.

Or died.

She remembered Heddy, her favorite tennis competitor at the time. Heddy was lean but not mean, experienced but not hardened. Where most players walk onto the court, Heddy ran on, and while she was running she'd yell out something like "It's great to be alive!" or "How nice to play you again!" As her opponent, you'd feel like you had to rev yourself up a notch right from the start or you'd be left in her rambunctious wake.

Heddy died of pneumonia after pushing herself too hard during what turned out to be her last season of play. But Heddy was eighty-five and had done it her way. Mallory envied Heddy for her focus, her determination, her delight. She decided to imagine Martina on one shoulder and Heddy on the other. Between them she couldn't fail.

The woman opposite her on the court today was at least twenty years her junior and clearly competitive. She had her hair scrunched under a kerchief and she wore no jewelry at all. She leaned forward into each ball and had the follow-through strokes of a trained player. While she was pleasant enough before the game began, some switch flicked on as she took her position on the court. She was all about winning. And that's why Mallory had been surprised to win the first point.

"Fifteen–love," Mallory called as she kept bouncing the brand-new, bright yellow tennis ball, readying for her second competitive serve in almost three years.

After meeting the woman she'd play against today, and after a ten-minute warm-up between them, she had aced her first serve. Woo-hoo! She knew a single point was a short-lived victory, but her Martina-guardian-angel cheered from this side of the court.

Mallory tossed the ball up for perfect positioning and slammed through it with all her might. The moment she made contact with the ball, she could tell it would head directly into the net. Instead of letting that bother her, she was pleased that her inner self knew it was a bad serve right away. Her body had the memory to keep guiding her game.

Overall, Mallory held her serve and won that first game. Her opponent was basically equal to her, just slower to warm up. By the end of the first set (which Mallory took at 6–4), they were both warmed up and ready for set two. After a sweaty three sets of intense play, Mallory lost the match but felt justifiably proud of herself. With the play over, the opponents chatted a bit before going to the locker room. They discovered some common points of interest, such as suspense novels and a love for anything Maine. They felt a kindred thread and made a tentative date for coffee the next time they'd be at the tennis center about the same time.

Mallory drove home on a high. She knew that the good workout she'd just had was a powerful relaxant, to the point that she had enjoyed the conversation with an otherwise stranger. She looked forward to getting to know her new friend, Elizabeth, better.

* * *

Elizabeth Easley drove home with the same anticipation about her new friend, Mallory. She had been so focused on her career for so long that she missed having a close friend nearby. After Elizabeth had finished the feature article on retail in Great Wharf, which probably would not run until the beginning of the next tourist season, she had slipped into a slight funk. She worked on a variety of jobs every day and kept up the work because she was self-supporting just like everyone else she knew. But then she came home, took a bath, got into her bathrobe, and read over dinner, followed by more reading or a favorite television show.

Men did ask her out, but she'd had it with married men, and with single men at work, and with guys she met in coffee lines, and with blind dates. The few men she had thought were friends ended up in relationships, and their new loves were insecure with Elizabeth's beauty or independence. Her longtime female friends were busy in their own relationships.

When Elizabeth watched the US Open last summer, alone in her apartment, she thought about her lack of people to do things with. She picked up the phone that very day and got into a round-robin for the fall. Though she considered herself to be an intermediate player, the round-robin approach was new to her. She enjoyed it more than she would have predicted.

With the fall round, last season, she had found herself totally in the game to win, and she got into the semifinal before she lost on her points. When sign-ups began for the winter round-robin, she was among the first to commit. This time, however, she reminded herself that she also wanted to play to meet potential friends. So she made a point of speaking with the competing player after each game. Mallory was the second player she had met in the winter period, and the first one in all her round-robin play who had demonstrated an interest in her as a person, not just "a worthy opponent."

She couldn't remember where she had heard the name Mallory before. It bugged her that the tennis center used only first names on its assignment sheets. She had neglected to ask Mallory for her full name or to get her phone number. Sometimes, especially since 9/11, people went overboard trying to protect other people's privacy. She would ask the tennis center to make contact for her and give Mallory her last name, phone number, and email address.

21

NOVEMBER–JANUARY

*In which winter dates warm two hearts; and
Jean explains why she pays attention to karma.*

As she headed toward her third date with Jim,
Jean's heart raced like she was Cassidy Hillobenz
about to meet a movie star. She replayed highlights
from their first two dates.

She remembered how her whoop after that call
from Jim had made Celestine raise her head from a
deep sleep and look around for an answer. Jean had
stroked her fur and said softly, "It's okay, Cel-baby.
That was just your ma being really happy. I think
you'll be hearing more and more of that. The tide has
turned."

The first date had been at Book It, the Sunday before Thanksgiving. They had started by looking in the New Releases section and sharing their impressions of the books coming out just before the holidays. Finding the selection a little disappointing, they agreed that nothing matched an earlier year's November release of Stephen King's time-travel book, *11/22/63*.

"I don't usually read novels," Jim said, "but I make an exception for science fiction. I thought King's book was well researched."

Jean said, "And I don't usually read science fiction, but I made an exception for King's book when Zoey told me I just had to read it. The 1960s came alive the way he wrote it. So did the brutality in Lee Harvey Oswald, the depth of which I hadn't really grokked before."

"Grokked! I love that word." Jim beamed at Jean, and then he said with a grin, "For someone who doesn't read sci-fi, you'll be interested to learn that the sci-fi writer Robert Heinlein coined that word in one of his books. I forget which one."

They took a tour around the rest of the store and each bought a book. Jim bought a newly released hardcover about possible evolutionary benefits in seemingly innocuous genetic conditions such as color blindness. Jean bought a paperback on the remainders table, a memoir by the son of a spirituality guru.

Over lunch at the bookstore café, their conversation ranged as widely as their browsing. They had enjoyed the Drama shelf, so they discussed Jim's and Richie's separate histories with the Great Wharf Community Players. They had browsed the Cookbooks section, so Jean talked about how she and Richie were maintaining a kitchen that served them both, a vegan and an omnivore. Jim admitted that he helped keep the town's restaurants in business when he wasn't microwaving something from the supermarket's frozen foods aisle.

They had both worn jeans to keep the mood natural and unassuming. After all, Jim had set the tone in his phone call—he was looking for a friend, not a romantic liaison. As they chatted over the light lunch, however, both of them knew something besides coffee and tea was brewing and steeping.

When they parted, Jim said, "I know the holidays are going to be busy for you, so I guess we shouldn't plan to see each other again until January."

"It's true that we're leaving for Massachusetts on Tuesday, coming back early Sunday morning. We think we'll beat the worst traffic that way. Then for Christmas we'll head back there again for a week. We'll probably be back in Biddeford for New Year's." Jean was sure she had placed enough clues in her answer to encourage rather than discourage.

But Jim said, "So I can count on January?"

"Sure—or before, if it works out."

Jim gave her a brief hug and said, "Great. Call me if you find you have more time than I think you will. This was fun."

"Yes, it was. I hope you enjoy the book you bought. It would put me to sleep."

"Maybe we should see a movie next time. Maybe we have similar taste in the cinema if not in books."

"Let's try it. Well, good-bye. Happy Thanksgiving, Jim."

"Happy Thanksgiving, Jean."

Even though no next date had been pinned down, Jean knew Jim liked her. She recognized a shy man when she spent time with one. But who would have thought this big-time doctor would turn out to have a shy gene in his body? Her husband, Edward, had had one, and so did their son, Richie. Jean, therefore, knew what to do next.

She called Jim the Monday after Thanksgiving and asked him if he would like to do a movie and dinner some Friday or Saturday night before Christmas. They quickly agreed on a new Leonardo DiCaprio movie (she would pay) and dinner at a vegan-friendly Japanese restaurant she knew in Portland (he would pay). Jim would drive, picking Jean up in Biddeford, which was on the way to Portland.

That date went as well as the first, plus they both wore clothes that signaled the evening was being kicked up a notch. She wore her basic black slacks and an aqua blouse under a black jacket. He wore black wool pants and a designer sweater that, like most of his clothes, complemented his blue eyes and silver hair. He did all his clothes shopping at a store on Wyeth Street, where the shop assistants helped him pick the right look.

Conversation that night included Jim telling Jean about his youthful love for Beverly, and about his doctor-parents leaving him alone a lot with the house-keeper. He wasn't seeking sympathy, just giving her a peek into his persona. He left out his relationship with Sheila and the interest the police might be taking in him. He left out Angie and Cleveland without even thinking about it.

Likewise, Jean told more but not all. She told Jim a little about each of her children and about Edward's death five years before, and admitted that Jim was the first man she'd really wanted to get to know since then. She omitted the mood swings, which seemed to be leveling out.

At the end of that second date, when Jim dropped Jean off at her apartment, they friend-hugged in the car and then Jim said, "Let me walk you to the door. No street's completely safe after dark, and I have to say that when I picked you up six hours ago this didn't seem like the safest street in daylight either."

"Biddeford does have one of the higher crime rates in the state," Jean agreed. "In general, though, I feel safe, and especially around our apartment building ... not that you shouldn't walk me to the door."

They left the car parked in the space by a fire hydrant in front of the building. It was a moderately warm evening for December, in the high forties, with a light rain misting the air. They both had their jacket hoods up.

Under the front door overhang, Jean tossed her hood back and said, "I'd ask you up, Jim, but your car would get towed. And to be honest, if Richie's up, I don't really want to end this wonderful evening with a banter-fest between you two—much as I enjoy them. I want to keep our own night fully ours when my head hits the pillow."

That was the clue Jim needed. He put his own hood back, put his hands on Jean's shoulders, and leaned down to kiss her. He didn't fold his arms around her, and he didn't hold her close. Instead, he gave her a kiss that suggested a future.

"Good night, Jean. See you after the holidays."

"Happy New Year, Jim."

* * *

And now, January 4, whistling "You Are My Sunshine," Jean followed a circuitous route to Jim's townhouse condominium. She had given her name to the gate attendant, who checked his list of expected visitors and then told her how to find Dr. Beall's place.

As Jim had told her he would, he'd left the light on and the front door open behind the storm door so she could walk on in. No fears about safety in this neighborhood. He said he'd be busy cooking the first complete dinner he ever attempted.

"Hello! I'm here!"

"Back here in the kitchen. Hurry!"

Jean ran toward the voice and found Jim bent over the oven. He had one mitt on the right edge of the roasting pan, which was teetering on the oven rack, and the other mitt just out of his frantic reach on the counter. She grabbed the other mitt, put it on, bent down, held her mitted hand around the left side of the pan, and said, "Now, push your side back on the rack."

Jim laughed. "I guess I could have done that to begin with. What an idiot. I just panicked!"

"Don't worry; you'll get the hang of it."

"I'm not sure I'm cut out for this."

"Don't worry; you'll get the hang of it."

"You just said that."

"I thought it bore repeating."

Jim finally took a deep breath and focused on her jumping-bean freckles and the laughter in her gray-green eyes. He put both arms around her and sank into the deep kiss he had been building up to for weeks. Jean's heart still raced, but evenly; it had found its groove. She knew she was now officially in love. Not only was the kiss perfection, she and Jim were each wearing an oven mitt.

The kiss ended with Jim extending his mitt-free hand to the other counter and handing Jean a glass of chilled chardonnay. On date two, only semi-kidding, he had told her she'd have to develop her wine palate if they were going to keep dating. He picked up his own glass, clinked it against hers, and said, "Here's to a new year."

She added, "And here's to the karma that brought us together."

Jim tilted his head to the side but left his thought unspoken for now. "Let's get this meal on the table so I can quit fretting about what I might do wrong next."

Over dinner, the conversation never flagged. They covered the holidays. Jim had gone to Ohio for two weeks and spent time with several friends from his days working at Lake Erie Memorial Hospital. He told Jean about each of the friends. Jean updated Jim on each friend she, too, had seen back home, and told more about her children.

"The only downer part of the trip," Jean said, "was on the drive home, when Richie told me he's decided to sell his souped-up old car. I've sort of been after him to do that ever since he lost his job, but I felt terrible for him. He's finally agreed it's silly to keep putting money into it when we can manage with one car. He'll chauffeur me to and from work and keep my Cavalier during the days when he does have someplace to go. We'll just need to coordinate our nighttime calendars not to conflict."

Jim said, "Well, anytime I'm involved in that conflict, I'm happy to be a driver for you and me. I'm sorry for Richie, though. I know he loves that old car."

Suddenly Jim lurched forward. "Oh, Jean!" His voice pitched higher than usual and his hand reached over to her plate. "Look at that untouched slab of roast beef. I completely forgot you're a vegan." He grabbed the plate, took it into the kitchen, and brought back a clean one with more broccoli and carrots on it.

"Don't worry, Jim. I'm used to being in the minority on this. Everyone tends to forget at first. I don't take it personally."

"I'm embarrassed anyway. But now that we're on the topic, why are you a vegan?"

"It's the most personally effective way I could think of to declare war on factory farming. I don't have money to donate to the cause, or the personality to get in people's faces about it. But I can at least not support the evil process with my own eating habits." Jean stuck her fork into a spear of broccoli and held it up like a banner before putting it in her mouth.

"Evil?"

"Yes, evil." She put her hand up for time to finish chewing. Then she went on: "You don't really want to get me started on this. But the industry is hurting our earth, increasing the chances of a worldwide pandemic, and abusing many millions of helpless animals every year."

"You're right about all of that. I promise if I serve you meat again, it will be Certified Humane, not from a factory farm. Would you eat that?"

"Yes, in fact, I would. But it's almost impossible to find."

"I'll find it or buy long-distance if I have to."

"Do you have a cause of your own, Jim? You seem so easygoing and accepting of people, of everyone's eccentricities. There must be something that riles you."

Jim's posture changed from sitting well back in his chair to leaning forward with his hands on the edge of the table. "Any talk of repealing any of the Amendments to our Constitution that make up the Bill of Rights. It's not the talk that riles me, but the ignorance that characterizes so much of it. It's one thing to hold an opinion but another thing to get worked up on the basis of inaccuracies and false logic. I should let you know, though you may be of the opposing mind-set, that I'm licensed to carry concealed in Maine, Ohio, and all the states in between, plus the rest of New England. I've trained for this and I'm a safe citizen. Weapon ownership is a right granted by our Second Amendment. So, there's one area we may have spirited discussions about."

Jean said, "I look forward to discussing all ten of those Amendments with you. For now, I'll just keep my mouth shut. But thank you for showing me your own activist side. I liked seeing your face get just this side of purple."

Jim knew it was time for another topic. He extended his long legs to touch hers and said, "Tell me about you and karma. You mention it fairly often, but I'm not sure what it really means to you."

Jean started to give him her standard comments about it and then stopped herself. "I just remembered something from when I was six years old that I think explains my preoccupation with the whole thing. Can I tell you about it?"

"Of course." Jim sat back in his chair. He had been leaning forward through the whole discussion of causes, and for most of the dinner before that, enticed by Jean's openness. He loved that she wore no makeup, that she let her freckles show as clearly as she seemed to let her thoughts show. Now he made the conscious effort to relax and sit back. He kept his legs where they were, touching the side of hers.

"Like I said," Jean started, "I was six years old. My baby brother, Jimmy, had been fussing and crying for hours. I was trying to make him feel better. I gave him the antique toy car from the knick-knack shelf in the living room. He went silent while he studied it. Then I started singing 'The Itsy Bitsy Spider.'" Jean made the hand motions that go along with the tune. "But he started crying again, louder than ever.

"I thought, Mom's going to think I hit him again. I watched my hands take hold of his arms and give him a quick shake, then a big, long shake." She demonstrated with outstretched arms. "Mom walked in and yelled at me, 'Jean, put him down, right now. You're going to scramble his brains!'

"Mom held him with such tenderness, like she hadn't held me in a long time." Jean gave Jim a crooked smile. "I know, of course, now that I've been a mother myself four times over, that she probably stopped holding me that way when Jimmy was born. He was a colicky baby, and she didn't have the energy for it all. She said, 'Jean, if you do this to Jimmy again, your own brains are going to scramble, just like this morning's eggs.'

"I pictured the parsley and onions in with the eggs and imagined them in my brain. Then Mom said, 'What goes around comes around. Don't you forget that. You'll get what's coming to you, good or bad. It's karma.'

"I asked her, 'What's karma, Mom?'

"She answered impatiently, 'Just what I said, honey. Now be nice to Jimmy.'"

Jean leaned forward, touched her hand to Jim's, and then took it back again, signaling a big moment coming up.

"So then I was sitting on the back stoop and Mom started screaming, 'Call 9-1-1! Call 9-1-1! Jimmy's stopped breathing!' I ran to the phone, dialed, and yelled for Mom to come talk, but she had her mouth on Jimmy's in a big kiss—that's what it looked like. I told the police operator what I was watching, and she told me to tell my mother to turn Jimmy over and hit him on the back.

"I told Mom and she did it, and then I saw a wheel come out of Jimmy's mouth. I knew it had come from the toy car I gave him. I remember wondering if this was karma. I wondered but didn't dare ask."

Jean noticed the intensity with which Jim watched her. She gave him an I'm-finished-now smile. He said, "So that was the start of your thinking about karma."

"Funny, I haven't thought about that for a long, long time."

"I know you said your mom said karma could be good or bad. But when you think about karma, do you ever think of it as good, or is it always bad somehow?"

"Good question. I guess usually when I talk about it, it's something bad that's coming around."

"What good karma has happened to you lately?"

She grinned. "You know it's you."

Jim loved how Jean's eyes sparkled in the candle-light. "I wasn't fishing for that exactly, but I'll accept it. Tell me some other good karma recently."

"Oh, seeing my kids at Christmas and knowing they're all doing so well. Richie and I are getting along really well as roommates. Work's been good, and my A-to-Z friends are very dear to me."

"Any bad karma these days?"

"No, not these days."

"My own thinking about karma," Jim offered, "is that it's just life. I think of life as pretty random, with the good balancing the bad. Sometimes one or the other gets clumped, like right now you're clumping with good things happening."

"And you, Jim? Any bad karma going on?"

"You're a good thing happening, and you outweigh everything tonight."

"But yesterday, last week, last month …?"

"Let's save that conversation for next time. Nothing terrible is happening; it's just not all good—that's all."

"Okay … for now." But Jean felt herself closing down. She put her hands on both of Jim's and said, "It's getting really late, and I'll admit when I was driving over I thought just maybe I'd be spending the night. Would you mind if we save that?"

"I'm sorry if I took the conversation to a bad place for you."

"It's not that. I guess I'm just not quite ready yet." Jean knew what it really was, though. She didn't want to be the only one in the relationship baring her soul. Until Jim told her the bad things going on for him, she wouldn't feel they were on equal footing. But she did understand that Jim might need more time. She had needed five years.

22

JANUARY

In which Madame Selene agrees to a business proposition; Richie keeps his ma in the dark; and Angie starts hiring.

SELENE DIPIETRO AGREED to see Angie for free Tuesday night when Angie asked for a special session that could benefit them both. Selene tried predicting what might be on Angie's mind, but her powers failed her. She knew Angie had been flattened by flu the first week in January. So she'd either had too much time to think, or finally time to think. Either way, Selene predicted this would be an interesting evening.

Angie arrived five minutes early, but Selene didn't quibble. She let her in quickly and they both shivered at the cutting wind that came in with her.

"Want some hot tea? I just poured one for myself." Selene had never offered a beverage to Angie before, but tonight was already different.

"That sounds good, yes." Angie hung her coat and scarf on the coat tree, removed her high-fashion stiletto boots, and followed Selene to the kitchen. She stood in the doorway while Selene poured water over the tea bag. Selene made a show of sniffing the comforting aroma that billowed up with the steam. Then she noticed Angie rubbing her arms to warm herself.

"I think this will warm you up, but tell me if you want me to boost the heat a little."

"Would you mind? I'm frozen from the walk over."

Selene turned the thermostat up two degrees and then led Angie into the home parlor, across the hall from the working parlor. Normally she kept the door closed.

Angie said, "Ooh, I'm being granted access to the inner sanctum. It's beautiful, Selene. Colorful and warm like you. I'm going to grab this velvet chair and make use of this throw while I'm at it." Angie put her cup down on the antique side table and settled in under Selene's great-grandmother's crocheted afghan.

Selene felt a twinge of regret at letting Angie into her personal space. She knew Angie better than Angie knew herself, and she didn't trust her. As a natural intuitive, Selene was capable of friendship and love; she didn't think Angie was. She only trusted that Angie would always do what Angie thought best for Angie. Others didn't enter the equation. Still, just knowing that much gave Selene an advantage.

She remembered that she was the first psychic to caution Angie about a potentially dangerous mix inside her. In that first session, she told Angie to watch out for her Aries propensity to be quick-tempered and impatient, which Angie said was no surprise. But then Madame Selene focused on a part of Angie's palm that Angie hadn't known about. In an area called Lower Mars, well below the index finger, Angie showed a capacity for evil. Madame Selene had the same shape on her own palm. She cautioned Angie to watch out for evil thoughts, especially if she was feeling impatient about something. Angie commented that that would only be a problem if she cared about being a good girl, and both women chuckled at this answer.

Ever since that first meeting, Angie had consulted Selene before making any important decisions, whether in her business life or personal life. Now, taking the love seat opposite Angie, Selene lifted her cooling teacup and sipped before speaking.

"So, now that we're settled in, what's this mutual benefit you see for us?"

Angie put her hand up while she finished her own sip. Then she cleared her throat and started in. "You know I was walloped by the flu last week. The timing worked, actually, since this is the worst month for business. But I had reserved ad space with the *Southern Maine Herald* announcing a January postholiday sale, so a few people might have come by to redeem gift certificates. I put an apologetic note on the door that we were closed due to illness and would reopen January 10." Angie tilted her head, looked away a moment, and then added, "Do you know, not a single person called to see if I was okay?"

"What did that tell you?" Selene couldn't help asking.

"Either not a soul came by the shop last week, or anyone who did was soulless."

"A lot of customers might have come by who don't know you personally."

"Well, it wouldn't have been 'a lot' of customers in any case, not this time of year."

Selene nodded, wondering when Angie would get to her point.

"My favorite bachelor, Jim Beall, never did call me after our date I told you about." Angie squinted and made a slight headshake. "The holidays would have been busy times for both of us, of course, enough to delay picking up on a new relationship. But I keep remembering a comment that woman Mallory Cooper made at the cocktail party. She implied that Jim and the hostess, Jean Trent, might be dating. Whether that's true or not, I aim to find out." Angie shook her head more strongly, as though to dislodge that thought and make room for the next.

"Anyway, once I was on the mend after the delirium stage, I had a lot of time to think and I took advantage of it. As I said, I have a business proposition for you." She took another sip of tea, put the cup back down, and scooted forward under the afghan. "You've never been happy with the location of your 'storefront,' and I need a better draw than I've had lately. So what would you think of setting yourself up in the Byways display window for crystal ball, palm, and tarot card readings on Saturday afternoons? You can give people your business card afterward and get more people coming to your regular place too."

Selene took a quick breath, excited by Angie's idea, but didn't say anything. She wondered what ulterior motive Angie might have besides the obvious one—namely, that displaying Madame Selene in action would be a draw indeed. But would it benefit Selene enough? Was there a downside?

Angie's hands were sweeping back and forth over the nubbly crochet stitches as though they were letters on a Ouija board. "And there's more. You know I've been working with some people who agree that a cinder path will help Great Wharf attract visitors. The deadline for getting a written plan to Town Council is the end of February. They want time to read and think about it before the March meeting. The path won't even need to grab anyone's personal property, just a sliver of some town-owned land between Wyeth and Newman. The rest of it can be constructed along the eastern edge of Burnham Bog. It can fall under the aegis of that trust's mission statement, the part about having a 'public benefit' to the conservation land.

"How this applies to you, Selene," Angie said as her fingers stopped moving over the nubbles and grasped hold of them instead, "is that the cinder path will probably stop at Newman Lane. It won't continue the couple blocks more to your street. Being a Saturday fixture at Byways will allow you to benefit from the extra visitors the path will bring."

Selene didn't need to think further. "Oh, I love this idea. Yes! Even though Saturday is my best day, I can leave a sign in the window for people to come two streets over to your shop. I do think this could up my clientele over time. What would I have to pay you for the use of your location?"

Angie leaned in with a wide grin. "That's part of the mutual benefit! You'd pay nothing to be there, and I'd pay nothing to put you there. If it works, we'd both benefit from increased business down the road." Then her grin wavered and she looked down briefly. "Well, there is one added cost. Could you put in, say, 20 percent for an electrician to set up special lighting and whatever? I'll pay for 80 percent of it."

Selene didn't know if Angie was telling her the whole story, but she couldn't find any fault from her own point of view. "It's a deal. How soon can we get moving on it?"

"As soon as you can come by the store to show me what you'll need."

* * *

Two days later Richie Trent went to Byways for a sixth bottle of Spirits-Up. His mother had been in a great mood lately. The holidays had been good for everyone in the family. Ma didn't share anything more with the other kids than she had told Richie about her first two dates with Jim. "It went well!" was basically all she said after each date. But she wore a Cheshire cat grin, so everyone knew something was afoot. She had a third date in January that the other kids hadn't even heard about yet, but Richie could tell by her mood that it was another success.

He considered not buying any more Spirits-Up, but the second he thought about it, he knew he'd have to keep buying it and slipping it into Ma's tea and his beer. He didn't want to jinx anything.

Fear of jinxing applied equally to his own mood, which was soaring after two secret dates with the beautiful Amanda. They had agreed not to tell his mother anything at all yet. Neither wanted to worry about what Jean might make of them pairing up until they knew what they made of it themselves. Toward this end, they had scheduled each date so far for lunchtime on a Saturday. This way, Jean wouldn't miss either of them from their usual places in her life. Richie was often doing volunteer or freelance work on a Saturday, and Amanda generally only saw Jean during the workweek.

Now, while trudging along the snow-packed Newman Lane sidewalk toward Byways, Richie revisited the second date with awe and warmth. They had met for lunch in Old Orchard Beach at the same restaurant as on the first date, at the O.O.B. House of Pizza. And as before, Amanda paid for her salad and Richie paid for his pizza. But this time, at Amanda's suggestion, they shared their orders.

"That pizza smells amazing, Richie." Amanda held her blond hair back as she made a show of breathing in the aroma over the pizza.

Richie agreed 100 percent. "I know, doesn't it? But you're eating what I should be eating—more fiber, less white flour."

"Let's share."

"Wha-?"

Amanda shifted her gaze from the pizza to Richie. She moved closer to him, kissed him, and said, "This can be our first sacrifice for each other. I mean, our first gift to each other. Well, I guess it depends on your point of view."

Richie's heart raced with the kiss and then skipped a beat in a good way when Amanda used the pronoun *our*. They shared their orders. Lunch went from there, with Amanda telling funny tales about work and Richie telling how much he missed working full-time and being able to afford a place of his own. Whether she was talking or listening, Richie sank into Amanda's beauty. He hoped she didn't have plans for after lunch. He purposefully hadn't made any.

Near the end of the lunch, he asked, "What're you doing this afternoon?"

"Nothing in particular. I was kind of hoping to show you my room at Zoey's."

Richie jumped up from his chair, tugged at the back of hers, and said, "I hope I don't seem too eager."

They made love all afternoon. Zoey was out visiting a friend and never knew—not that she would have been surprised. She was thrilled they were seeing each other and had agreed not to say anything to Jean. "You two and Jean," she had said, "have to play out your own stories. I'm not getting in the middle."

"So," Amanda said to Richie with a giggle as they lay in each other's arms, "which one of us will tell Jean we've done the deed?"

"Ha-ha." He squeezed Amanda to acknowledge her humor. "But yeah, I will. I mean tell her we're seeing each other—I'll omit the part about 'the deed.' But do you mind if I wait a little longer? I'd really like to know where Ma and Jim are headed before I tell her about us. If their next date goes badly for some reason, I don't want to hit her with the glory of our own. I think she's been scared of dating again."

"Okay, and of course it's better if you tell her, not me. But let's make a pact that you really will tell her, say, by Valentine's Day? It's wicked weird at work with Zoey and me knowing but Jean not having a clue."

"Deal."

＊ ＊ ＊

Richie's reverie had to end when he opened the door to Byways. He spotted Angie at the cash register and waved to her. She was ringing up another customer, so he went directly to the shelf where the Spirits-Up bottles were displayed. There was only one left. This was often the case, and he always alerted Angie when he took the last bottle. He grabbed it and went to the register to wait in line.

When he had bought the fourth bottle, a couple of weeks after the party, Angie opened the conversation with a comment on his cat. "That was quite a scene with your cat, Richie. How long have you had that pretty calico?"

"Not long. She's a stray I found right after she delivered a litter. The animal shelter found homes for the kittens, and I took the mama home. We named her Celestine."

"Like that book we sell here about a prophecy. Have you read it?"

"No, but Ma has. By the way, I just took the last bottle of Spirits-Up off the shelf, so you'll want to restock."

"That stuff flies out of here. I think it's the lavender essence that people respond to, even though the ingredients list it last."

When Richie bought his fifth bottle, between Thanksgiving and Christmas, Angie asked him what he knew about Jim Beall. Was he dating anyone? By then, Richie knew that Jim and his ma had been on one date and were planning another. He just said, "Nothing serious I've heard about. So you're interested, huh?"

Angie smiled, handed him his change, and said, "I only know him from your party, but he seemed very nice. I can't believe he's not married, a handsome doctor like that. There must be something wrong with him, but no one's talking."

"He's a great guy. The only thing wrong with him is he works too hard."

Today, buying his sixth Spirits-Up, Richie was in a happy and outgoing mood. He placed the bright orange bottle on the counter and, knowing there was no one behind him, asked, "How're things, Angie? Dating anyone yet?"

She jerked her head back, and her hand went to the angel necklace. She glanced beyond Richie to confirm no one waited in line and said, "I guess you're remembering I asked you about a certain someone last time, but no, you convinced me he's too busy. How's your mother doing? Is she seeing anyone herself?"

Richie knew better than to talk about his mother's thoughts, especially when she wasn't even sharing them with him. So he fudged. "Not that she's talking about."

Angie tilted her head to the side. "I think you're being coy, Richie. Tell me the truth."

"No, seriously, she's not telling me anything."

"Humph. Okay, then." Angie scanned the bar code. "I was hoping you'd be coming by soon. I've just had the worst case of the flu. Oh, don't worry—I'm okay now. But it made me realize I should have a helper around here for times when I can't do all the work myself. Do you know anyone who might want to work here part-time?"

"How about me?" Richie felt a surge of hope.

"Have you done retail before?"

"Not really. But I do work with the public when I volunteer at the trolley museum. Sometimes I help out as a guide there."

"Well, that's nothing to sneeze at, is it? But what would happen to me if you get an electrician's job and then I've put all this time into training you for nothing? No, I need someone who will stay with it awhile."

Angie took his ten-dollar bill and gave him his pennies of change and receipt.

Richie said, "There's a high-school girl, Cassidy. You might remember her from our cocktail party."

"Was she the fat one?"

"Yeah. I wouldn't really call her fat, though. Anyway, she's looking for a way to earn money part-time."

Angie's hand rested on the bag containing his Spirits-Up purchase.

"You know, Richie, even though I said no to you for the floor-helper job, I may have a need for some electrical and handyman work. Can you freelance, or do I need to go to a service company?"

"I can freelance, no problem!"

"I've recently come to an agreement with a psychic named Madame Selene. Do you know her?"

"No, but Ma might. Every now and then she'll—"

"Anyway, Selene does palm readings, tarot card readings, that sort of thing. I want to put some special lighting in. And I want to set something up outside to lure people in."

"Awesome! I can use the work. I'm really good at all kinds of things too, not just the electrical part. I'm an all-purpose handyman now, thanks to my work at the trolley museum. So if you need roof repair, painting, soldering, whatever, I'm your man. I can probably borrow any special equipment too. If you need—"

"Yes, yes, that's great. Listen—will you have Cassidy call me? Or tell her just to come by the store sometime so we can talk about a part-time job for her?"

Richie's skin tingled at the curt dismissal. He said, "Sure, okay," and turned away. In polite hopefulness, he added, "See you later then."

On his way out Richie wondered how he'd ever found Angie Weller attractive. I've got the real deal now, he thought. At the same time, he realized that

Angie's behavior had changed too. Her body language was no longer seductive, at least not toward him. Their interaction just now had been totally job-focused, which suited him fine. He texted Cassidy on his way back to the car.

EPISTOLARY EXCERPT FROM UNPUBLISHED MANUSCRIPT:
Runaway Legacy

September 30, 2010

Dear Caitlin,

That is so cool, your history teacher assigning grandparent interviews for homework. Thank you for sending the draft copy of your work with the questions you still need answered. You did an excellent job remembering things about us that we've talked about over the years.

> When did our daughter leave home? In 1986 (Twelve years before you were born—and here you are asking that question twelve years <u>after</u> you were born—maybe 12 is your lucky number.)
>
> Was she a good student? Average (Sorry—no geniuses on our side!)
>
> What were her likes/dislikes as a child? She seemed to like helping her mother (me, Vera) harvest and

dry lavender and make things from it like potpourri and lavender brownies. She seemed to like sitting on her father's (Sergeo's) lap while he read to her. But, to be brutally honest, she especially liked horrible headlines. She was utterly fascinated, for instance, by the recall process on Tylenol products that occurred in 1982, when she was fourteen. Seven people died in Chicago after taking Tylenol that turned out to have been laced with cyanide. This was the first known, or at least publicized, case of product tampering. Mary kept a whole scrapbook on that story. (Maybe she became a journalist or a writer or ...?)

What did she want to do when she grew up? She never talked about the future except to say she wanted to make money. Journalism or writing don't usually translate into much money, but one can make a living that way. (Maybe she's using a pseudonym?)

Honey, if you ever want to ask any questions of your own—not just your teacher's—you know you can ask us. A lot of times, someone else's questions lead to more in our heads.

We're sad our own move to Florida never worked out, but we do love being pen pals with you.

Hugs and kisses,
Nonny and Nonno

23

JANUARY

*In which the Coopers get a surprise visit; and
Dwight asks Mallory on a date.*

IT WAS 18 degrees below zero and 5:14 in the morning
on the second Saturday in January when Mallory's
uncle Bill Owen and his wife, Cynthia, found the
Coopers' house. A parking spot sat open just across the
street. The black Chevy Tahoe's tires crunched on the
icy, snow-packed surface as the SUV backed into position. The sound was audible only to the raccoons still
trying to sleep through the coldest month.

Bill stopped the car and cut the engine. The car
cooled. Their bodies cooled. They shivered with nervousness. They waited until two lights went on in the

house. The first, they assumed, was a bedroom or bathroom upstairs. In this typical colonial, the second would be the downstairs hallway to the kitchen. It was 6:30.

They waited fifteen minutes after the downstairs light went on. Then they got out of the car, crossed the street, and started up the walk. The ice made getting to the front door a treacherous journey, but neither of them had predicted that it would be otherwise. Bill rang the bell and also worked the knocker. Then he and Cynthia stood back. They would not hide themselves.

* * *

When the bell and knocker simultaneously announced a visitor, Mallory and Dwight jumped and looked at each other like a bomb had just gone off in the neighborhood. They had been sitting in their bathrobes, enjoying coffee and microwave-heated banana nut muffins.

"What the hell?" Dwight said.

"Will you check?" asked Mallory. Then, "No, we'll go together." They went to the living room and peeked through the window.

"It's Bill and Cynthia!" Dwight recognized them mostly from their holiday card photographs.

Mallory's legs barely held her up. She whispered, "Don't open it, Dwight. Please don't open it."

"I have to, Mal. They know we're here. Go sit over there, in the wingback."

Mallory felt like her life force had been drained, like she'd never be able to move again. Somehow she turned away from the window and did as Dwight directed.

The wingback was the chair farthest back in the room—the deepest recess in the cave. Dark mahogany pieces, lovingly refinished after their discovery at estate and garage sales, filled the room. Oriental throw rugs scattered over the dark brown floor vied for attention with brocade upholstery in crimson reds and forest greens. High ceilings and cream-colored walls counteracted the heaviness of the colors and materials.

Last summer Mallory felt the dark was winning out. Lately she thought of the whole as scrumptious again. Now she just wished she had an outfit exactly the same and would be strong and camouflaged. Anything but vulnerable in her bright yellow fleece bathrobe and dirty white scuff slippers.

She heard Dwight open the door and greet the Owens as though the only abnormal thing about them being there was the early hour. She watched Dwight take their coats and lay them on the hall settle. She had always loved that settle, and now she thought she'd have to get rid of it on Monday.

When they invaded the living room, Dwight turned on the floor lamp and indicated that they should sit on the sofa. As they sat down, Cynthia spotted Mallory on the far side of the light. "Oh!"

Dwight blurted, "Coffee anyone?"

"No!" Mallory shouted and leaped to her feet. "Why are you here, Uncle?" She spat the word *Uncle*.

"You never answer my emails, Mallory." Bill looked at Mallory and then at Dwight.

"What emails is he talking about, Mal?" Dwight asked.

Mallory stared at Bill. Her ghost from the past was a real presence, right here in front of her. She could hardly breathe. It had never occurred to her that he might simply show up in her house.

"Mal?" Dwight asked again.

She sagged and sat back down.

"He wants me to forgive him."

"I understand you may not ever forgive me," Bill said. "But I want to make sure you have heard me apologize to you. I am so, so sorry for what I did. To say I was drunk is to offer a reason but not an excuse. There can be no excuse."

"That's for damn sure." Mallory felt so confused. She had hated this man and the memory for over forty years. For many of those years, the whole time she was raising her family, the hatred had simmered invisibly on some back burner. Then when his retirement hit the news, and her family and work couldn't keep her busy anymore, the hatred boiled over. The power of it scared her more than any news of a break-in ever did.

Bill took a couple of steps toward her but stopped halfway. "I wish there was something I could do to earn your trust again. Cynthia and I live so near and yet we can never get together as family because of what I did, and I have to accept that. But I want to do what I can to help you accept what happened as something I alone was to blame for. You did nothing to make it happen—nothing. Did you ever tell your mother about it?"

"Aha!" Mallory grabbed onto the arms of her chair. "So that's why you're here. You want to know if your big sister knows what a shit you are. Well, no, I never told her. So there, you can leave now. She still thinks you're A-OK as a baby brother."

"No, that's not what I'm here for. It's really not. I need you to hear me tell you I'm sorry."

"Fine. I've heard it. You can leave now."

Bill looked at Dwight. "I apologize to you too, Dwight, for whatever pain I caused Mallory that may have harmed you after the fact."

"Just get out of here, Bill!" Mallory screamed. She didn't want this bad memory to witness her break apart.

Dwight dashed into the hall and handed the Owens their coats. He watched as Bill helped Cynthia on with hers, and then said to them as they left, "Watch your footing on the ice."

"Let them fall and break their necks," Mallory shouted from the wingback.

* * *

When Dwight returned to the living room, Mallory was sobbing.

"Oh, Dwight, I can't believe I wished a broken neck on Bill's wife. All Cynthia did was stand by her husband. How can you stand me?"

"I love you, that's how. I wish I could do more to help." Dwight walked behind the wingback and started giving her a neck and shoulder rub. "Maybe you should see someone again after all."

"I thought I was doing better, but this was such a shock. You may be right. Let me think about it."

Dwight couldn't bear watching Mallory's despair. He decided to tell her the surprise he'd held from her so long now.

"Maybe this will help. Last July I made a reservation for a special Valentine's Day dinner. How about we move it up and go out this week instead, if I can change the date?"

"Where?"

"I'll hold onto that part of the secret for now. Let me give them a call later, after they've opened, and see what can be arranged."

Mallory sniffled and blew her nose. "Is it in a safe neighborhood?"

"Oh for Chrissakes." Dwight patted her shoulder and kissed the top of her head. "Give it a break, Mal."

That afternoon he made the call and then found Mallory in the laundry room. She seemed to be doing okay now, humming some light tune as she folded sheets. She greeted him by shifting from a hum to a full-out chorus of "Take Me Out to the Ballgame."

He grinned and said, "I'm thinking of a girl on a swing I'd love to go to dinner with Tuesday night. How about it?"

"Put a baseball bat in the car and I'll follow you anywhere."

"I'm going to pretend you're just making a play on the song you're singing and not really saying I might have to practice my swing on an attacker."

"If you like."

* * *

While driving home from Portland Tuesday at five o'clock, a half hour after sunset, Dwight experienced two strong emotions. The first was extreme aggravation with the traffic during this particular rush hour. It wasn't usually this bad, and he usually missed it anyway by leaving a couple of hours before or after. Still, he was more irritated than he should be. That's when he recognized the other emotion, a thrilling excitement. For months and now days, he had kept the Spears dinner plan in a mental compartment of things not to be thought about until the time came. Now he itched to have the evening unfold. He planned to tell Mallory a secret of his own and hoped it would encourage her to do the same.

The tollbooths weren't as backed up as he feared, and he was soon cruising south along Route 95. The last snowstorm was a week ago. Both the roads and the night sky were clear. He punched the speed dial for home.

"Hello?" Mallory sounded hesitant.

"Hi, Mal. I'm on my way. All dressed and ready?"

"Almost. Where are we going? I need to wear the right outfit."

"Wear something you'd feel comfortable in at a four-dollar-sign restaurant."

"Out of how many dollar signs?"

"Four."

"Wow. Okay, Mr. Mysterious, I'll do as directed."

"See you in twenty minutes. Be there or be square." Dwight hated it when he said stuff like that, but he couldn't help it. Sometimes dated lingo just rolled off his tongue like he was in a Flintstones rerun.

Twenty minutes later he steered his truck into the drive and parked beside Mallory's red Subaru, which they'd be taking to the restaurant. The sedan was a lot cleaner than the truck. Dwight had told Mallory to dress up. She probably wouldn't appreciate truck dust clinging to her outfit.

He ran upstairs for a quick shower and change of clothes, calling to Mallory on the way. "I'm home! I'll be ready in ten minutes!"

"I'm at the computer when you're ready."

Almost exactly ten minutes later, Dwight poked his head into the kitchen.

"Ready if you are."

Mallory was putting a glass in the dishwasher rack. She stepped back with a sweep of an arm and asked, "Do I look okay?" She had selected a full-length maroon dress and a white cotton shawl, neither of which she'd had occasion to wear for too long.

"You look great, as usual."

"So do you, but I'm not kidding."

"Neither was I."

Dwight walked over to give her a kiss, but Mallory put her hand to her mouth and said, "I need to brush my teeth. Give me just a sec." She scurried off to the bathroom, but not fast enough for Dwight to miss the note of wine in the air. Did she really feel the need for a sip before going to dinner with her husband?

24

JANUARY

*In which Mallory and Dwight splurge; and a truth
from Dwight spurs two truths from Mallory.*

DWIGHT HAD CHOSEN a restaurant in Ogunquit.
According to *Bon Appétit*, Spears was one of
the ten most romantic restaurants in the whole coun-
try. For years the Coopers had said they'd have to go
sometime. When Dwight steered the car southward,
Mallory got extra curious.

"Just where are you taking me, Dwight? Boston?"

"Much closer than that. Wait and see. Did you
hear anything from our babies today?"

With that, Dwight successfully changed the subject, and they talked about the kids until he entered Ogunquit center and then hung a right out of town.

"Oh, Dwight, really? Are we really going to Spears?"

"Yup. Thank you for waiting so long for your dense husband to finally come around and get us there."

"What a treat! I wish I'd known. I would have posted it on Facebook so everyone could think of us in this great setting tonight."

"Well, I'm glad I didn't let you know, then. That's creepy—everyone thinking of us here, when I'm looking forward to just us."

"It would still be just us, silly."

"No, it wouldn't, Mal. Not really. What's happened to true privacy? There's no such thing anymore. Everything's right out there for everyone to comment on and throw their thumbs up or down about. It's crazy. That comedian we both like so much, what's her name? Wanda Sykes. You know what she said about social networking? She said, 'When did we all start liking each other so much?'"

Mallory started laughing, and that was just the right response to get Dwight off the topic that was aggravating him to the point of pouring vinegar over the whole dining experience. He couldn't believe how great her laughter sounded.

They arrived at 6:20 for a 6:30 reservation and used the extra time to look around the grounds. They started by breathing deeply in the attached greenhouse herb garden. Mallory plucked a sprig of lavender for her purse and a mint leaf for her mouth. Then they re-entered the main building, a rustic farmhouse that had been renovated to include a commercial kitchen. The rest of the first floor was sparsely decorated and maintained the original feel with wide pine floorboards, chair rails in the dining area, and oil-lamp sconces on the walls. Antique botanical prints added more beauty and detail. Mallory took a brochure for her memorabilia box—which she hadn't culled through for years, saving that activity for old age. If she lived that long.

After being seated, Dwight and Mallory spent extra time looking at the wine selection and the menu. Then Dwight said, "We're going for broke tonight, Mal. I want the eleven-course Indulgence tasting menu 'at the whim of the chef.' Hey, it's only $135 per person." Dwight chuckled but meant it.

"Dwight, are you sure? What if the roof starts leaking this winter, or one of the kids needs to borrow money, or—"

"We could count on one hand the number of times we've just plain splurged." Dwight held up one hand to emphasize his point. "We've earned it." Then he caressed the fresh white tablecloth with all ten fingers.

"Call it a celebration and enjoy the fact that we can do this, period." He brought his hands over to cover Mallory's hands, resting nervously on the table edge. "Besides, we haven't taken a vacation in years. Think of all that money we've saved."

"Give me a minute to adjust." Mal closed her eyes. A moment later, she opened her eyes, grinned broadly, and nodded. "I'm ready."

"Hooray. Waiter?"

Each of the first two items was an amuse-bouche to whet the appetite and demonstrate the chef's range. With the first, a bite-sized ball of goat cheese rolled in freshly chopped chives, Dwight raised his tasting glass of pinot grigio to toast Mallory. "To the love of my life. Thank you for keeping our kids alive."

Over the second, a surprisingly yummy union of passion fruit essence with warm cabbage shavings and sushi-grade tuna, Mallory toasted Dwight. "To the love of my life. Thank you for getting me out more."

Over the third item, Maine shrimp cocktail, they kissed three times. Each kiss carried more emotion. Conversation during courses four and five (a cold cucumber dill soup and a lemon sorbet) centered at first on the food and wine but veered to whispering about the other diners. What were they ordering? What might they do for a living? Are they with spouses or lovers, or on first dates? The mood was extraordinary. Light and carefree.

By the sixth item (corkscrew pasta with pesto) and attendant Muscadet wine, Dwight figured the time was right. "I met a woman last summer who reminded me of you when I first spotted you on that swing."

Mallory squinted. "Why did she remind you of me?"

"She was young and beautiful, and she had a very kind way about her."

Mallory put her fork down and sat back a little, watching his face. "Should I be worried about this, Dwight?"

"Well, let me put it this way. I was worried about it."

He told her, without mentioning the name, how Elizabeth Easley had bumped into him, and how he had invited her for lattes and she had accepted. He told her as much of the conversation or gist of it as he could remember. He could tell from Mallory's posture that the news hit her at a gut level, but he had to get it all out.

He finished up while the waiter brought the seventh course, pork with a raisin sauce, served with a small glass of pinot noir. Some pasta went to waste.

Mallory said, "I don't understand why you're telling me this. What's your point in telling me?"

"I'm telling you because I've never lied to you, even by omission. Not about anything important anyway." Dwight tasted the pork. "This is delicious. Please eat."

She took a tentative bite, wondering what more he was going to tell her. "Ooh, it's terrific!"

"Here's what I need you to know. The experience made me realize how much I miss you. We raised the kids and helped them each get started in life. We kept improving the house and yard. We had common goals for so many years, and then—poof! We reached them and didn't have anything to replace them with. Because of that flirtation last summer, I started trying to talk with you about missing you. And thanks to your own feelings for me, we've been making love more often, which has been great, of course."

He paused a minute, seeing Mallory's brow furrow as the concept sank in. He finished eating quickly.

"Are you telling me you want a divorce, Dwight?"

"I'm telling you the opposite, Mal." He took another bite and sip of wine. "I want our marriage. But I want it in a new and improved form."

"You mean kinky?"

"Jeez, no. Come on—that's not what I'm saying at all." Dwight took a deep breath. "You know, nothing you tell me, nothing, can possibly make me love you less than I do. Do you think, in return for my opening up about being attracted to someone else, that maybe you can see your way to tell me about what happened between you and your uncle Bill?"

Mallory's eyes widened. She sat back slowly as though he had put his hands on her shoulders and pressed. Her gaze shifted from Dwight to her new wine glass, being set in front of her with course eight (a salad of brussels sprouts and currants). When the waiter left, Mallory began, "I was twelve years old."

Dwight hid his surprise. A powerful mix of relief and love welled inside. Mallory's voice had dropped down to such a soft level Dwight had to lean in.

Mallory didn't look at him but fondled the wine glass. "I had started developing, and Uncle Bill had been teasing me about it for a while.

"I was embarrassed by his teasing, but at the same time I liked the special attention. He was in his twenties and very good looking. I knew I shouldn't be attracted to him, because we were related, but I was attracted to him. What I didn't like was that he was usually drunk by the end of an evening. He never came over to the house except for family gatherings, and everyone just figured his drinking was part of the partying, something he'd outgrow. You know, like a juvenile sense of humor or something."

Mallory's mouth twisted and she shot a quick look at Dwight, and then turned her eyes back to her glass.

"The party was a backyard barbecue to celebrate my parents' twentieth anniversary. We had an aboveground pool, and this was the first summer I could wear a two-piece suit and not look like a little kid in it. I was excited to show myself off, to prove I was grown up.

"The party was in full swing when I saw Uncle Bill watching me take off my terry-cloth robe. My parents were oblivious, so I took my time and gave Bill a small performance. I didn't look at him while I folded the robe slowly and then bent in his direction to place it on the ground. Still not looking at him, I climbed up the ladder very slowly. I had an image of myself as Elizabeth Taylor in one of her sexy scenes. When I got to the top I looked straight at Bill, then held my nose and made a backward arc into the pool."

Dwight started to put his hand on her arm, but she said, "Just let me get through this. If you touch me, I'll chicken out." He withdrew his hand.

"When I swam over to the side to catch Bill's eye again, he wasn't where he had been. Then I heard him clear his throat right below, next to the pool, holding my folded robe. He said, 'That was quite a show, Mallory. Do you mind if I keep your robe as a souvenir?'

"The cold water had already sent one shock through me, but now I knew I had started something I didn't know how to finish. I started shivering and I asked Bill to hand the robe up to me. He said he'd meet me in the kitchen, where he was headed to get another beer.

"So I did. I raced out of the pool, down the ladder, across the lawn, and in the back door to the kitchen. Bill was alone in there. He put his arms around me and said, 'I'll warm you up, gorgeous.' He started rubbing against me and cooing; then he said, 'C'mon, Mal, let your uncle show you what you have to look forward to, now that you're becoming such a beautiful woman.' Then, while he gave me my first French kiss, he took my hand and brought it down between us and placed it on his goddamned, out-there-for-all-it's-worth penis.

"I yelled 'No!' at the top of my lungs." Mallory stage-whispered the "No!" to avoid making heads turn in the dining room. Then she returned to the low voice she'd been telling the rest of the story in.

"Bill lurched back and zipped up. He threw the robe at me and said he was just kidding around. He lurched out the back door. As I was putting the robe on, shaking, I heard him tell whoever was right there by the pool that I had no sense of humor, that everything was fine."

Mallory stopped looking at her wine glass and looked directly into Dwight's eyes. "You know, I yelled so loud, and my parents never did ask me about it. I've always wondered what they thought happened.

Every time Uncle Bill was around after that, and he was around way too often, I found excuses to leave the house or at least banish myself to my room."

Mallory picked up her salad fork and attacked the course in front of her. "I better eat this quickly. It's been here a while!"

Dwight said, "You do know, don't you, that none of that was your fault? You were doing nothing but being a normal kid just starting to test her wings. Your uncle Bill was way behind you on the maturity scale."

She finished a few more bites before responding. "Yes, I know, at one level. But at another level I still believe it was my fault."

"You set up a situation that your alcoholic uncle was unable to handle. He was the one at fault. You were a kid."

Mallory finished her salad. "There's a postscript to this story." She gave Dwight a quick glance and then sat forward in her chair. Her shoulders hunched, and she stared down toward the empty plate just as it was removed and replaced with the next course. Dwight could tell she wasn't seeing the roasted quail, which made him sad. He waited.

"You never knew this, but my family had another parcel of land besides the one the house sat on. My parents never did anything with it, just held onto it as an investment. They had a right-of-way across someone else's unused parcel, a wild section of land that was more elongated than square. When I was ten, they and the other owner pooled funds and built a cinder path to mark the right-of-way. Both thought it would add value."

Dwight automatically asked, "And did it?" Then he noticed Mallory's mouth set in a Mona Lisa smile. He made the connection, slumped, and said, "Oh jeez, Mal. What happened on that cinder path?"

"I loved that path. It was a highlight of summer and winter both. I had a lot of time to myself. My siblings had their own friends and activities that didn't involve me. My parents believed none of their kids needed supervision beyond the basic care. I had friends, of course, but that cinder path was where I went to draw and think. It was a quiet, safe space. And every now and then, Uncle Bill showed up on the path and walked it with me."

Mallory paused. She stopped looking at her plate but took a long sip of the red Bordeaux blend. She put the glass back down, sat back, and hunched over even more as she stared down at her dress. Dwight watched her hands twist the white cloth napkin protecting her lap.

He asked, "How old were you, again?"

"Starting when I was ten, and still undeveloped. I felt safe with my uncle, and I think he really thought of me as a fun kid. We tossed a Hacky Sack footbag to each other as we walked along the path and just talked about life and family and whatever. Looking back on this—which obviously I've been doing a lot of lately—" Mallory glanced at Dwight before looking down again, "I think Uncle Bill was struggling to find his own place in the world and honestly didn't have designs on me except as someone to chat with during that time.

"But then, a couple years in, the pool incident happened. And the next time he showed up on the cinder path, he was drunk again." Mallory rubbed her arms. Then she dropped her hands back down and began twisting the napkin again.

"He apologized for being drunk, but he was grabbing at me. I fell, and he landed on top of me. There was a moment when we looked surprised at each other, and I thought he'd roll off and laugh. But no. He started feeling my breasts and shoving his tongue into my mouth. I kicked and bucked and bit his tongue. He rolled over with a groan—his hands on his mouth now instead of on me."

Mallory's voice had dropped so low that Dwight was now leaning in three inches from her face. "Oh, Mal."

She stopped molesting her napkin and straightened her shoulders. She placed both hands on the tablecloth, one hand on each side of the plate. She looked straight at Dwight and raised her voice to a normal level. In comparison, she seemed to be shouting.

"I got up, kicked him in the shins, and yelled at him to stay away from me, and then I ran home. I never walked the path again. I hated him for taking my path away from me. I hated him for the betrayal of our friendship. And as an adult I have hated him for doing what a trusted adult must never do to a child."

Mallory took her wine glass in both hands and swallowed the little bit of (now) Shiraz that was left.

"When I first read Angie Weller's letter to the *Gazette*, I hadn't thought about the cinder path since I was twelve. My enjoyment of it was long gone, and all that took its place was submerged fear and anger. And eventually, I understand now, a hovering over our own kids."

The waiter appeared and asked if the *langue de boeuf* was not to their liking. They apologized, said they hadn't even been aware that it had been served, and asked what it was exactly. When the waiter said "beef tongue," they cringed in a shared grimace and then laughed in a much-needed release.

Dwight told the waiter, "You can have that one back. No offense."

"None taken. Would you like coffee or tea with your dessert?"

When dessert came, the heart-shaped pecan tarts brought tears to their eyes. They shared one of the tarts and asked the waiter to wrap up the other. They would eat it for breakfast in the morning. On the way to the parking lot, they agreed that they would need to come again, order a less expensive option, and talk about something completely shallow.

25

February

*In which Jean gets a strange call; Richie admits
to hiding a truth; and Portland is for lovers.*

J EAN ANSWERED THE phone. It was Angie Weller.

"I thought I should tell you, Jean. There's a rumor floating around Great Wharf here about Jim Beall
having a secret past. He was at your party, and I didn't
know if you two were seeing each other. But I thought
you should know, just in case."

"Gee, Angie, that's awfully nice of you. What's the
rumor?"

"Are you and Jim seeing each other?"

"We're friends, but he hasn't mentioned a secret
past."

"Yes, but are you beyond just friends, like dating?"

Jean's jaw dropped. She said, "I don't see what difference it makes. Are you going to tell me what you know, Angie? Otherwise, why this call?"

"I certainly don't want to plant any seeds of discontent. Maybe I've made a mistake calling."

"Maybe you have."

Jean let the silence grow.

"Okay, then. I'm sorry I bothered you. Just forget I called." After another moment of silence Angie disconnected.

Jean put the phone down. She hadn't talked with Angie since the party. Angie hadn't sent a thank-you note or made any effort to communicate, until now with this strange news flash. What could she possibly have meant about Jim having a secret past?

Jean already had high hopes for her Valentine's date with Jim. Maybe she'd add this question to the conversation.

* * *

The night before Valentine's Day, while cleaning up after a spaghetti and salad dinner, Richie told his mother about Amanda and him. Jean was still sitting at the table, waiting for her tea water to boil.

Jean said, "I'm not surprised by this news. I mean, I figured you two would get together, but I kept thinking it hadn't happened yet. I couldn't imagine what was holding you back. How did you manage to keep me so in the dark?"

"We only saw each other Saturdays or Sundays, when I could pretend that I was working. It felt weird cheating on my mother."

Jean made a face. "And that's a creepy way of putting it."

"You know what I mean."

"Yes, but why didn't you tell me?"

"Why haven't you told me how your dates are going with Jim?"

"Touché. Sort of. At least you knew I was seeing him."

"Yeah, but I thought if you guys were cooling instead of heating, I didn't want to be all euphoric in front of you."

"Great word. And I think maybe we can use that word for me too, about Jim. We're going out tomorrow night, like you, but all I know is I'm supposed to dress for a nice dinner."

The teakettle screeched. Jean got up, poured the water over her tea bag, and carried the cup back to the table. Sitting back down, she said, "And I may as well tell you—Jim said I should pack an overnight bag."

Richie asked immediately, "So can Amanda stay the night here?"

"Wait—what about getting excited for me?"

"I'm psyched, Ma. That's really great. Can she?"

"Of course."

Richie beamed. He had put off telling his mother until the very last minute and now saw how silly that had been. Ma had never been anything but supportive of him, including encouraging him to ask Amanda out in the first place. Now he had made Amanda wait until the last minute to know where they'd be spending Valentine's Day night. He vowed to make Amanda's feelings at least as high a priority as his own from now on.

* * *

Jim and Jean had seen each other twice since their dinner at his place in early January. But after that dinner, Jim knew he had to quit hiding from emotional intimacy if he and Jean were going to have the physical intimacy they both wanted. Jean wasn't being coy; he understood that. She just knew what she wanted and how to ask for it. He promised they'd both get what they wanted on Valentine's Day.

He started making arrangements a month ahead of time. He lined up a limousine and booked a room at the historic Portland Regency. He wanted to take Jean to vegan-friendly Green Elephant Vegetarian Bistro, but they didn't take reservations. So he figured they could arrive at the five-o'clock opening time. Then he and Jean could go to the hotel lounge for a nightcap and more talk before going up to the room.

He called Jean three days ahead of Valentine's Thursday with three instruction-requests. She should get off early from work, wear something dressy-casual for dinner, and pack an overnight bag. "You can decide later if I'm allowed in the room when you open it."

Jim had put the past October's dinner with Angie into a secure compartment in a deep mental recess. After a week or two had gone by without Angie trying to call or see him, he hoped she was going to let it drop. He had been shaken by the memory of his younger self so easily lured into the broom closet by a minor, albeit nearly eighteen.

Angie had dropped a time bomb on him. Even though it was so long ago, it would be horrible if his patients learned he had ever behaved that way. And in reliving the experience last October, he realized he might have misled the young Angie. Had she fantasized that Dr. Beall valued her? Had she dreamed and then been cut down when he completely ignored her after that one time? These thoughts made the older Jim Beall shake his head in commiseration. But that was so long ago and surely not hurting the Angie Weller he'd come to know. He strongly suspected he wasn't the only doctor she'd lured into a broom closet.

Then when Jean started occupying his thoughts in November, Jim fought with other feelings rising up inside him. He was attracted to Jean physically, but she wasn't looking for that. At least, not just that. She wanted a partner in all aspects of life. What shook Jim at first was the realization that he did too. Why did that terrify him so?

The driver idled the limo in front of the building while Jim went in to escort Jean to their ride. A warm flush of pleasure ran through him when she saw the limo and said, "Oh, Jim, this is too much. A limo? Really?"

"I almost rented a stretch limo. Then I thought I'd better save that for if I ever need to up my game."

"If you ever need to up your game, ask me for ideas. I'm pretty sure I won't suggest a stretch limo."

They kissed before getting in. The driver kept his eyes on some distant point. Inside, chilled champagne waited. Jim was pleased and would recommend this professional driver to others. He poured one glass and offered a sip to Jean.

* * *

The dinner at the Green Elephant, both agreed, was excellent. Their conversation over the food started with the mundane—how their work was going, recent events in Great Wharf and Biddeford—and then Jean shifted in her seat and said, "I think it's time I finally told you the rest of the truth about me."

Jim had just put a big bite of curry noodles into his mouth, so all he could do was nod in encouragement. Curious, he hadn't thought Jean was keeping anything at all from him. She was always so open. He was the one holding back, the one they were waiting on for revelations and deeper digging.

"I have a history, ever since Edward died, of mood swings. I've been seeing a psychiatrist, starting in Massachusetts and a different one here in Maine. Dr. Sterns thinks I'm going to get beyond this, but I have to tell you it has been nearly disabling at times." Jean stopped talking and waited for Jim to respond in some way.

Jim had put his fork down while Jean talked. Mixed feelings churned. He never wanted to get involved with someone who had a bipolar disorder. But she said the psychiatrist thought she'd get beyond it, and you don't do that if you're truly bipolar. So maybe she wasn't. But if she was, he thought he might already be too far in love to extricate himself now. And if she was, he would want to help her because he loved her. Why had he let himself get involved to begin with?

What he said was, "What does 'nearly disabling' look like?"

"It looks like me heading to bed the minute I get home from work. It looks like Richie hearing 'no, thanks' when he offers to make dinner for me. It looks like my friends wondering if I'm avoiding them."

"That's it? No manic buying sprees, no thoughts of suicide or running away?"

"I guess that's why Dr. Sterns hasn't put a bipolar label on me. I'm in a clinical trial with my meds, and he says I might already be clean, just on a placebo or something."

Jim clung to that idea. "I've seen no evidence since we've been going out that you have anything like a serious mood disorder. You're always beautiful and sparkling and ..." Jim stopped talking and put his hand over hers. "There's nothing wrong with you."

Jean's eyes watered. "Thank you. I've been afraid to tell you, and I'm so relieved at your reaction. The swimming and yoga, not to mention getting to know you, may have brought me to a new reality. But I've been afraid to trust it, you know?"

"I do know."

"Your turn."

Jim had just picked up his fork and now put it down again. He knew this was the night he'd have to tell Jean about Sheila. He wasn't going to mention Angie, ancient history of a different sort. But he did want to tell her about Sheila. And about the police.

"Tell you what. Let's finish dinner first. I promise to open up over a nightcap in the hotel lounge."

* * *

The wood-paneled lounge at the Portland Regency hummed with muted conversations. Jim led Jean to one of the cozy alcove tables. He needed to shake the memory of having just seen Angie's pixie red hair in a car passing their limo just after it pulled curbside at the hotel. He decided it was someone else with the same hairstyle—or it was Angie and a coincidence. After all, Angie had as much reason to be in Portland on Valentine's Day as he did.

This is what he told himself as he brought his chair closer to Jean's and ordered a scotch on the rocks. Jean made a rare concession to try a banana daiquiri. By the time the drinks came, their chairs were next to each other and Jim placed his arm gently across her shoulders.

"Look at the people in this room," he said. "What do you see?"

"A lot of well-dressed people happy to be here. Just like me."

Jim caressed her hair and let his fingers play around her ear. He couldn't remember ever feeling simultaneously so comfortable and so unnerved before a "first time" with any woman. He leaned in and whispered, "No one's happier than me right now. But I need to take my chair back to the other side of the table and look at you with some distance between us. Otherwise I'll never get said what I need to get said."

"I'll miss you."

Jim had started moving away, but stopped and grinned at Jean. "Maybe we should just head upstairs."

"Ha!" Jean laughed. "You have something to reveal before you get to reveal upstairs. A secret past perhaps? Start sharing, mister."

"Okay, okay." Jim moved his chair to the other side and started talking before he could chicken out. He had never told a soul about Sheila's and his relationship, short of admitting to his lawyer and the police that there had been one at all. Now he told Jean all about it. He started with, "I'm going to tell you about an important woman in my life who died this past September." Then he told her about Sheila, about their friends-with-benefits arrangement, about the precautions they took to keep their friendship a secret, and about his own surprise at the depth of his sorrow when she died.

Jean stayed silent during the entire telling, but her eyes—the way they opened wider or closed a little, the way her eyebrows furrowed or raised—told him she was listening, sympathizing. When he talked about his surprise at the depth of his feelings, she spoke for the first time. She said, "Our inner selves go on without us sometimes, trusting we'll catch on eventually. Sometimes it's too late when we do—too late to let the other person know what we've learned. I'm so sorry that happened to you."

Then she cocked her head and asked, "But why couldn't you tell me this before, Jim? In January, at your place? Was it still too soon after her death?"

Jim sighed. "There's a complication. It seems the police think she may have been murdered, and it's possible they have me on their list of suspects, though they haven't said so."

Jean's hands leaped to her gaping mouth. "Oh my God, no. Oh, Jim."

Jim sat back in his chair. "A real mood killer, isn't it?"

"Well, of course you didn't kill Sheila. That's ridiculous. Who are the other suspects or possible suspects? Have the police told you anything at all?"

"They've actually left me alone, since that one time they questioned me. And I got myself a lawyer, even though they didn't arrest me or charge me with anything. All they'll tell my lawyer is that no evidence has shown up implicating me. The main reason I'm on the list at all is because I was a colleague who referred quite a few patients to her. And I'm sure they got further suspicious when I clammed up during questioning. My amateur theater background should have given me better acting skills than that."

"I'm sure you were too upset and shocked to be thinking about acting. Why do they suspect murder? Anyone could have fallen down those steps in the winds of a nor'easter. And you said there was a bad step too."

"Yes, and her home had been broken into just the night before."

"In 'crime-free' Great Wharf? That's interesting. And scary. I see why you didn't want to talk about all this before, Jim. Please keep me informed going forward. Let me be your friend as well as your lover. Speaking of which, can we go to our room now? I'm lightheaded from this daiquiri and need to be taken advantage of."

26

FEBRUARY

In which Richie and Amanda make plans; and
Richie stays after five to help Angie.

F OUR DAYS BEFORE Valentine's Day, Richie sold his
car to Angie. But not knowing yet about his mother's plans, he asked Angie if he could still use the car
one more time, on Valentine's Day, to take his girlfriend to dinner. Angie said okay but he mustn't ask
for it again. She planned to use it as an interim car between selling her own and getting one she ordered that
wouldn't be delivered for two more months. She hadn't
sold her car yet but thought it would happen soon.

Richie and Amanda enjoyed a candlelit dinner in
a small restaurant that only the locals knew about.

When they returned to his apartment, the first time they'd been there as lovers, they talked about how strange it felt being in the place partly rented by his mother. They didn't want to do that very often.

They had one other very important conversation that night. They discussed what would be the most difficult thing for Jean when the time came for Richie to move out.

"I know," said Richie. "She's grown accustomed to me being here."

"That's not it," said Amanda. "She's going to miss Celestine."

Richie laughed. "More than she'll miss me?"

"Sorry, Richie, but your lovely calico is my true goal. If your mother won't part with her, we're through."

Richie knew she was joking, but he felt an anxious pang anyway. Then he felt anxious because he didn't actually know whether his mother thought of Celestine as more hers or more his. They had never talked about the cat that way. This had to be worked out over the next few months. He and Amanda had agreed that they'd like to be in a place of their own by July.

Richie drove Amanda home the next morning before Jean came home, and then returned the car to

Angie by the time he was due there for some freelance work.

* * *

Three days after Valentine's Day, Angie kept Richie busy on some backyard shoveling and other odd jobs most of the day but asked him to stay a little later than usual. He said he'd be happy to. She asked him to get the tall ladder from behind the store and bring it to the front.

"I need you to make sure the gutter is clear and then string these flashing lights across the roofline. Also hang this banner in front of the eaves." It was five fifteen. The store had closed, and the sun had just set. But Angie said she didn't want this work going on when customers might be there.

There were a gazillion icicles hanging from the eaves. Richie positioned the ladder with an eye to keeping its feet off ice patches. He had been sanding twice a day since an ice storm two days earlier. Careless placement could make for a hard landing.

Up on the ladder, Richie confirmed that the gutter was clear. He enjoyed swiping all the icicles off the eaves as far as he could reach. Then he had an unsettling déjà vu moment, one of those where you can't exactly predict what's going to happen but you know something's going to happen and so you turn your mind to it and try to squeeze the knowledge out. Nothing came. He shrugged and turned his attention to fastening the banner on the left edge. Then he strung the first section of lights, starting at the left and going right as far as he could from his current position.

He climbed down the ladder and moved it over, again being careful about where the feet were. He took hold of the loose end of the banner and climbed back up to hook the right end of the banner and finish stringing the lights. Damn but it was cold out. He started daydreaming about Amanda and a warm fire.

* * *

Inside the shop, Madame Selene talked to the carpenter behind the display window. An adjustment was needed to the platform being constructed for Selene's performance. Out of the corner of her eye, Selene noticed Angie outside in her red winter coat kneeling by the ladder. Selene had a fleeting thought that the posture was odd, but then she didn't give it another thought as she continued directing the carpenter.

A moment later, Selene saw Angie walk toward the driveway at the side of the building. Not two minutes after that, she heard Angie screech, "Richie! Selene, call 9-1-1. Richie's fallen. He's unconscious!"

* * *

Richie woke up slowly, rising through a thick fog. He felt a huge weight on his chest and another on his right leg. "Move, you beasts," he mumbled. "Off me."

He heard his mother's voice from across an ocean. "Richie, wake up. Can you hear me? Wake up, honey. Wake up."

He managed to raise his eyelids halfway.

"You were electrocuted, and you fell off a ladder! Do you remember anything?"

"No. Yeah. Sort of." He was still working through the fog, but at least the elephant on his chest had turned into a baby elephant. The one on his leg was still an adult.

Beyond his mother Richie saw Angie walk through the door.

"Richie, sweetie, you're lucky to be alive. I told you not to touch that wire." Angie stopped by his bed, holding a fake flower bouquet he recognized as having been on the Byways discount shelf for months.

Angie had said something about a wire. "What are you talking about?"

"You know, that winter-lights wire you were tugging on after cleaning out the gutter. I guess after the shock and fall you had, it's no wonder your memory isn't so great."

"I wouldn't—" Richie was interrupted by the arrival of his friend Jim.

"How's my less-than-coordinated patient doing?" Jim's baritone bellow matched his beaming smile.

Richie took a moment to realize that his friend Jim was now his doctor too. While he processed that thought, Angie turned her back to Richie and Jean. Even half-lidded, Richie could see Angie straighten up, raising her boobs in Jim's direction. She held the bouquet behind her back.

"Oh, Jim, I was hoping to run into you!"

"Uh, hi, Angie. Excuse me." Jim sidled by her to get to Richie's bed. "So, Richie, how are you feeling?"

"Not much of anything really. Just foggy. Hard to move."

With practiced hands Jim prodded Richie's arms and legs, felt around his neck, and then declared he was going to be fine. That was the last Richie heard before falling back asleep.

* * *

Jean waited anxiously for Jim to finish his examination. The two of them hadn't talked since the morning after their perfect night, when he'd walked her from the limo to her door with his arm wrapped tightly around her waist. His parting words were, "Let's be sure to do this again next year."

She had asked, "On what planet is a year the same as a day on Earth?"

The tenderness with which Jim kissed her felt like he was saying good-bye forever, heading off to war.

Jean had hoped all day at work that Jim would call, but she knew he'd be busy. Maybe he'd call that night. Instead, she got the call from the hospital that Richie was in the emergency room. And now, seeing Jim here, she understood firsthand the time and energy his job demanded of him.

Over his sleeping patient, Jim told Jean that Richie's broken leg would be in a cast for at least six weeks, although he could start walking with crutches in a week. He didn't think the electrical shock would have any lasting effects. It looked like the shock had entered through Richie's fingers when he grasped the wire. But the contact wasn't long enough or the voltage strong enough to harm his system. Jim put a hand on Jean's before heading out of the room. Except for the lingering touch, he was all doctor.

When Jim had put his hand on hers, Jean noticed Angie pivot and leave the room.

27

FEBRUARY

*In which Jim puts Angie's name on a list; and
Richie makes confessions to two women.*

JIM STARTED UP the corridor toward the elevators.
He hadn't gotten much sleep last night. His mind
swirled with images of Jean, and his body ached for
her. At the same time, an old fear crept up his bones.
The last time he'd had this combination of feelings,
only one time since Beverly, he had stopped seeing
the woman after only two dates. Now he and Jean had
been on six dates, with the supreme connection three
nights ago. He knew he was in love, and he needed
time to think.

Just steps away from the elevators, he stopped short when Angie appeared in front of him, seemingly out of nowhere. With a demure look she said, "So, Doctor B, aren't you happy to see me?"

Jim's jaw clenched. "Not really, Angie. What are you doing here?"

"Richie's terrible accident happened at my place. He's going to be okay, isn't he?"

"Yes." Jim looked toward the elevators. "I need to see another patient."

"Listen—I know you needed time after we went out that night. But it's been months. I thought I'd hear from you after you had time to think about it. I'm not going to make trouble for you. I just want to get to know you better. You're not seeing anyone, are you?"

Jim had a fleeting thought that Angie might be exactly what he needed, instead of getting more deeply involved with Jean. But the thought nauseated him.

Angie lifted herself slightly toward him. "It's been a cold winter." She giggled and added, "Won't you come see me sometime?"

"Listen—I'm sorry about not calling, but things have changed for me. I'm seeing someone, in fact. So we'll just have to leave it there."

"I see. Who?"

"I'd rather not say anything more."

"But do I know this lucky lady? At the party, Mallory Cooper mentioned you and Jean Trent. She also mentioned you and Hank Sanborn. Either of them?"

"I'm not going to talk about it, Angie."

Jim saw her eyes turn flinty just before she swiveled and walked away with a booty swing that would get anyone's attention, and he did watch. When he turned around he saw Jean's winsome figure walking in the other direction. He turned to the nurses' station and put Angie's name on the private "I'm not in for her/him" list that he had set up twenty years before and now used for the first time. On his way to the elevator he wondered what had possessed Mallory to have such a conversation with Angie.

After Jim left the room, Jean had checked to make sure Richie was really asleep and not about to wake and look for her. Just in case, she said out loud, "Richie, you're going to be fine. Now I'm leaving for a minute, but I'll be right back. I just have to check on something."

Jean wanted to take the initiative and catch Jim before he disappeared into some other patient's room. Leaving Richie's room, she saw Jim three doors down, his back to her. He was talking with Angie, who was looking up at him and giggling. This was no professional interaction. Jean turned and walked in the other direction down the hall. She would get some tea in the cafeteria and then come back to Richie's room. Maybe she'd wait for Jim to call her after all.

Jean had kept the true seriousness of her dates with Jim a secret from everyone, except for letting Richie know about the plan for an overnight. It was one thing for Richie to know they were dating, but she withheld the part about being in love. She didn't want Richie to worry about his own future. How silly. Richie was almost twenty-two years old, after all. But he had been such a help to her during her low time. He kept applying for jobs and not getting hired. He needed help with rent, just like she did. She hadn't wanted to scare him. Still, what would she say to Richie if Jim never called again?

And was Jim's relationship with Sheila the "secret past" Angie had mentioned in that awful phone call? Jean hadn't wanted to dig deeper to find out. It was enough that night to learn about Sheila and the police.

* * *

Amanda learned about Richie's accident indirectly. Jean wasn't at work. When Amanda asked after her, their supervisor said Jean's son had fallen from a ladder and was in the hospital. Amanda had to hide her love-sized fear for Richie. Zoey knew they were seriously involved, and by Valentine's Day Jean knew, but no one else did. Amanda wouldn't feel right announcing the relationship without Jean present.

She waited about a half hour and then told her supervisor she wasn't feeling well and better go home. She didn't want to risk infecting others if she was coming down with the flu. "Absolutely," said her super, leaning away from her. "Get out of here, and good luck."

Amanda drove to the hospital in record time. Bypassing any gatekeepers at the front desk, she found the elevator and took it to the third floor. She started asking where someone with a broken body might be found. Within a minute, she walked into Richie's room.

Jean, reading aloud from a magazine, looked up when she heard the footsteps. "Amanda! Is Zoey here too?" But then she saw the look on Amanda's face as Amanda looked at the living, breathing Richie, and she realized she should just disappear. "I'll just leave you two alone a minute." Jean smiled at Richie on her way out, but Richie wasn't looking at her.

"It looks like your face is safe to kiss." Amanda leaned over the bar and planted a soft kiss on his warm lips. "What happened, baby?"

"I can't really remember much. I climbed up the ladder at Byways to clean out the gutters and hang a banner. Angie said I was tugging at the winter lights up there, but all I was doing was positioning them. Even if they did carry a charge, they wouldn't have packed that much of a wallop."

"You were electrocuted?"

"It seems so, plus I fell off the ladder and broke my leg."

"Oh my God, Richie, you're lucky to be alive! How much pain are you in?"

"Not much. I guess the pain will increase as the drugs wear off. Something to look forward to." Richie laughed but had to stop. His ribs reminded him they had been bruised in the fall.

"Can't laugh, huh?"

"No."

"I guess we won't be making love for a while."

Richie gave Amanda a sad smile that turned into a quiver, and then he started crying.

"Oh, sweetie, I shouldn't have tried making a joke. I'm sorry."

"That's not it. I'm remembering my dad."

"That's right—you told me he'd been electrocuted. I'm not surprised your accident brought that memory back."

"What I didn't tell you was that it was my fault."

"What do you mean?"

Richie sighed. Amanda walked around his bed to sit on the chair in his field of vision. "Tell me."

Richie grimaced as he shifted his body. "I was a sophomore in high school. There was a wicked thunderstorm, and I was riding my bike home in it. Branches were flying around and I was scared to death. Lightning crashed twice within a few blocks of me, and just before the second strike, the hair on my arms rose up."

Amanda murmured, "That's so scary." She rubbed her own arms as she imagined the feeling.

"When I finally swung into the driveway, I saw a crumpled old trash bag lying in the gutter. Normally I'd have stopped and picked it up, but I wasn't about to give the lightning more time to find me," Richie said in a self-accusing tone.

"I hoisted my bike onto the back porch, went inside, and dried off. Ma had a stew of something amazing on the stove. I remember the warmth in the kitchen and the smell of oregano and onions. I grabbed a soda out of the fridge and went into the living room to watch the storm from there."

Richie closed his eyes a moment. Then he opened them again and gave Amanda a searching look. Her patient listening told him he could trust her love.

"A minute later Dad's car turned into the driveway, but I saw him stop midway, and I knew he was going after that stupid trash bag. He didn't see, just like I hadn't seen, the end of the live wire hidden by the bag. I'll never get rid of the image of him going rigid before he fell."

Amanda got up from the chair and leaned over to hold Richie's hand.

"If only I had grabbed that bag instead of leaving it for Dad to take care of. Maybe I would have grabbed it differently and lived. I don't know. But I tried to get rid of the guilt by training to be an electrician like he was. When I graduated, Ma told me I had honored Dad's memory, that I'd brought everything full circle and it was time to forgive myself. But you know, I still felt like I could never do enough. And now I'm lying here electrocuted but alive. What am I supposed to make of this?"

Amanda said, "Mainly to be glad as hell you're here—and I'm here. I know that's what I'm making of it. Also I guess this ties in with that wonderful part of you that wants to help others and to fix things, like you're trying to put things right. If your dad's watching, he's awfully proud."

Richie's new tears were powered by a joy he hadn't felt since sometime before his father's death. Amanda watched his mouth change shape as blame gave way to forgiveness. They both said "I love you" at the same moment.

* * *

Richie stayed in the hospital three days. The next time Angie came to see him, she brought a bottle of Spirits-Up for his mother.

"Now, Richie," Angie said with a conspiratorial wink, "I don't want you to feel neglected, but this is a gift just for women. Your mother's been through a lot of stress. Not that you haven't, of course, but a mother's pain runs deeper than her children's pain."

Jean accepted the bottle. Neither woman mentioned Angie's strange call the week before about Jim having some sort of secret past. "How thoughtful of you, Angie. Thank you! I'll have some with my tea tonight."

Richie cleared his throat and admitted, "I confess, Ma, I've been slipping Spirits-Up into your tea for a while now."

Jean stared at him, her mouth slightly open. "What are you talking about?"

"The first time I ever went into Angie's shop, it was because of her Spirits-Up display. I was feeling kind of down, and you'd been in a big down for weeks. This was last July. So I bought some and started giving it to both of us. I really think it's helped too."

Angie said, "The best way to use it—when you've been under extra stress like you have—is morning, noon, and night for at least three weeks. You'll find it works wonders."

Jean ran her finger over the bright orange label. "So much has happened since last summer, most of it really good. Sounds like this little bottle will help me relax for whatever's coming up. And it obviously won't hurt me. But Richie, please promise you'll never fool me like that again. It's not honest and could have been dangerous alongside what Dr. Sterns has been giving me."

"I promise, Ma. Sorry."

Jean noticed that Angie gave Richie another wink, and she wanted to slug her. Instead, she said, "Thank you again, Angie, for being so thoughtful. I'll have it morning, noon, and night as you suggest." To herself, Jean thought it was ironic that someone Jim might be interested in would be trying to make her feel better.

28

FEBRUARY

In which Jean and Mallory hit Byways on different quests; and Doris relays a sighting.

THE NEXT SATURDAY Jean decided to go see the scene of Richie's accident. She hadn't been to Byways since her visit in September, when she had bought the invitations. When Angie gave her the bottle of Spirits-Up at the hospital, Jean remembered the nature of the store. She remembered, too, the bouncy angel Angie had worn at the party, and that her store offered a great variety of such angels. Jean thought they'd make perfect birthday gifts. She thought it might be healthy to see Angie in her workplace, to carry a different memory than the one of her flirting with Jim.

The more she thought about it, the more predestined another visit seemed. Until last fall, in three years of living in Biddeford, Jean hadn't met a soul who lived in Great Wharf. Now within the past six months she had acquired a beau there (Jim, at least she hoped he was still a beau), a doctor (her new one, a colleague of Jim's), and a potential friend (Mallory), plus swimming and yoga at the YMCA. Richie had three friends in Great Wharf (Cassidy, Jim, and Dwight) as well as freelance work, the Community Players, and weightlifting at the Y. Yes, Great Wharf was turning into great karma. If you didn't count Richie's accident, of course.

It didn't take Jean long to find a parking space on Newman Lane. She only had to walk a quarter block to the store. The going was tough over the uneven packed snow. Jean had been feeling peaked and thought it might be due to worrying over Richie. She'd been making good use of the elixir Angie had given her. It helped her sleep through the night better than she would be doing with just the chamomile tea. But now as she felt herself tiring so quickly on this walk, she wondered if something else might be going on with her.

She hadn't gotten the results back yet on all the tests her new doctor had ordered. He wanted her to get them done so he would have a baseline on things like her fasting blood panel and a mammogram. She decided to call him this week and see whether anything had shown up that might be causing her to be feeling extra tired. Or was it just worry? Maybe she should give Dr. Sterns a call. Maybe she needed to go back on her earlier stress meds.

Gypsy music interrupted her thoughts. She looked up from the snow and saw that she had reached Byways. The energetic music came from a speaker above the door. Jean was impressed by whatever technology kept the noise confined to the area in front of the shop. Looking farther up, Jean saw a bright red banner strung from the roof over part of the upper level. It hung between two windows in what she understood to be Angie's apartment over the store. The banner would have been hung by Richie the day of his fall.

Jean shuddered at how high off the ground he had been. He could have died. She felt herself start to sway and brought her eyes back down to the display window. There, a fortune-teller caressed a huge glass ball. The woman wore a bright yellow gypsy-looking outfit with billowing sleeves, a necklace of colored glass beads, and a red scarf weaving in and out of long tresses of black hair. She must be making a prediction.

Feeling weak and vulnerable, and having just had thoughts about karmic predestination, Jean decided it was time to have her future told. She hadn't done this for years, not wanting to spend the money. But with Richie's accident and the appearance of a true love in her life (and why hadn't Jim called her?), she concluded this wouldn't be a bad way to spend a little money today.

She opened the heavy door to the shop. The citrus-lavender mist smelled like a welcome back. A display easel announced that the fortune-teller was called Madame Selene. Jean spotted Cassidy at the cash register in the middle of the store.

"Cassidy, hello!"

"Hey, Mrs. Trent. How ya doin'? How's Celestine? How's Richie?"

"Everyone's doing okay, all things considered. I thought I would buy a couple of angel necklaces for gifts. Is there still a good selection?"

"Sure is! Here, on the other side of the counter? They're under the glass."

Making her way around the counter, Jean said, "I thought I'd give Madame Selene a try today too. Will she be done with her current customer soon?"

"Yes, that customer will be done in about five more minutes? There's no one after her for another hour."

"Good. I only want the fifteen-minute version the sign mentions. Oh, these angels are precious."

As Jean was deciding which angels to buy, the door opened and the gypsy music came in again, along with Mallory Cooper.

"Hey, Mrs. Cooper. Look who else is here—Mrs. Trent!" Cassidy's amazement matched that of an infant when a parent plays peekaboo.

Jean caught Mallory's eye, and they shared a smile over Cassidy's ebullience. Mallory said, "Jean, Dwight told me about Richie. The trolley museum just posted the notice about him yesterday. In fact, I came in here to buy a get-well card for him. The cards on Wyeth Street are insipid. How's he doing?"

"Much better, thanks. It was so frightening at first—such a terrible fall. The electrical shock turned out to be nothing to worry about, but the fall really could have killed him. Did you know a lot of electricians die falling from ladders? I'd forgotten that, but my dear husband, Edward, used to comment on it. So now I have a new worry to add to my arsenal."

"I know what you mean. I can't count how many times each day I worry about Jess in the military."

Jean nodded in commiseration and then decided to tell Mallory another of her thoughts. "I've always believed that, over the course of time, events in life describe a full circle. What goes around comes around. Since Richie's accident I haven't been able to stop thinking about how his father died—accidentally touching a live wire during a terrible storm. So when Richie got electrocuted, I figured that's what would be the death of him. I never thought to worry about a stupid ladder."

"That reminds me of the old death-and-taxes adage. One way or another, it's going to get you."

"I don't know," said a new voice. "I think there's a way to avoid both death and taxes." Angie had entered the shop from the back stairway out of her apartment.

Jean and Mallory turned to look at her. "Really?" Mallory said. "I guess if you believe in reincarnation or something, you can cheat death in that sense. But how to avoid taxes, well, I need to learn that one!"

"I'm so pleased to see you both in the shop. Jean, I was glad to hear Richie went home on schedule. What brings you here today?"

"I want to buy a couple of your angel necklaces." Jean wondered why she had decided to support this woman, her competitor, in her enterprise. She realized she still couldn't believe Angie might have a stronger hold on Jim's emotions than she did.

"Aren't they adorable? Tell me—has the elixir been helping you get a good night's sleep?"

"Excuse me, Mrs. Trent," Cassidy interrupted. "Did you want to see Madame Selene? She's free now."

Jean gave Mallory an embarrassed look. "What the heck. I figured I'd give her a try. Have you ever had your fortune told?"

"No, I haven't. I'm tempted, but not enough to hear anything I don't want to hear. Well, go ahead—and good luck. Sometime let's meet for coffee. Hey, how about when you're done with Madame Selene? My house is only a ten-minute walk from here—we can have a cup there, and the noise level will be much better than in the coffeehouse."

"Yes, let's do that. I'll still have another hour or so before I need to get back home and start dinner."

"Cassidy can give you the directions for how to walk there from here. She lives right next door to us."

"Great. And Cassidy, please hold these two angels for me." Jean pointed through the glass countertop. "This one with the heart next to her halo, and this one with the halo tilted over the hat."

Angie inserted herself to say, "Well, ladies, nice to see you. Let me know when you expand the coffee klatch to a larger circle, will you?"

Jean and Mallory exchanged another quick glance and told Angie they certainly would.

* * *

Mallory squeezed her car into the garage and squeezed herself out the car door's narrow opening. She and Dwight had agreed that they would transform the structure back to a two-car garage someday this spring or summer. In the meantime, space was held captive by the kids' old outdoor toys mixed in with Dwight and Mallory's objects "to be fixed."

Usually Mallory would have just left the car in the garage and walked downtown. Today, however, she combined her need to go out with her need for another practice session behind the wheel, this time without Dwight. She had freed him to spend the day however he wished, and he'd decided on the trolley museum. No surprise there!

As soon as she had extricated herself from the garage, Mallory, excited to prepare for a guest, raced to the back door. Not fast enough, though.

"Mallory, I've got news!" Doris waved her arms from an upstairs window.

"What is it, Doris? I'm in a hurry."

"I'll be right over. I'm not going to yell it for the whole neighborhood to hear." With that, Doris disappeared from view and slammed the window shut.

Mallory swore under her breath as she unlocked the back door into the kitchen. Now she'd have no time to prepare for Jean's arrival. She wanted to set a nice table and get the coffee percolating. Maybe she could still … but no, the doorbell went off like a call to battle.

Mallory raced to the front door and kept her body in the doorframe as she greeted Doris.

"At least let me stand in the vestibule, Mallory—it's freezing out here."

Mallory stepped back to let her in. "I'm sorry to be so rude, Doris, but I have someone coming over any minute now and things aren't ready yet."

"Oh? Who?"

"Never mind who. What's your news?"

"I just thought you'd like to know what my physical therapist told me during my follow-up with her yesterday. It'd been months since we'd seen each other, since my insurance wouldn't pay beyond a certain number of sessions. But as part of my wellness program, I'm allowed a six-month follow-up, so I made an appointment. Heather and I have become nice and friendly, and she's got her finger on the pulse of what's happening in the medical community. I like to keep up with things, you know."

"Yes, I know. Time's a-wasting, Doris. What's your news?"

"For Heather's thirtieth birthday, her parents took her to a very fancy restaurant in Kennebunkport, and guess who she saw having dinner there?"

"Please do tell me."

"Our very own Doctor Beall with Angie Weller, the Byways owner. Say, did you ever meet her?" Before Mallory could respond, Doris said, "Oh yes, I remember now. Cassidy said she was at that party you all went to but I wasn't invited to. Cassidy said Ms. Weller flirted like Catwoman in a Batman movie. Well, I guess it worked on Dr. B, because there they were at that expensive restaurant, and Heather said they were totally into each other. He never saw Heather, and she didn't try to interrupt either."

Mallory fought her desire for more information. "Well, I'm glad to hear that Jim has a social life. Good for him. Now I really do have to get ready in here. I'm sorry to throw you back out into the cold, but ...," Mallory said as she reopened the door and put her hand gently on Doris's arm to nudge her out. "Thanks for letting me know the good news. Say hi to Cassidy, won't you?"

Doris stepped outside and made a shivering motion. "Let's have a cuppa sometime, okay, Mallory?"

"Sure thing, Doris. Bye now."

Mallory shut the door as gently as she could. She knew she had already offended.

29

FEBRUARY

*In which Madame Selene has told Jean a lot
more than her fortune; and Angie discovers a lie.*

JEAN ARRIVED AT the Coopers' house thirty minutes
after she and Mallory parted at Byways. She arrived
breathless. "Mallory, you won't believe what Madame
Selene told me."

"Come in, Jean. You look a little crazed, if I may
say so."

Mallory wanted to get Jean inside as quickly as
possible. She knew Doris would have her eyes peeled.
It's possible she might not recognize Jean in her winter
coverings, but why give her more time to look?

"I am crazed, yes. I'm also exhausted. Can I sit, please?"

Mallory led Jean to the kitchen, where the table was now set with two coffee cups, sugar and cream, and a little bud vase. In the vase were the remaining two blooms from the rose bouquet Dwight had bought her for Valentine's Day.

"How sweet!" Jean exclaimed. "And I think a cup of highly caffeinated black coffee may be just what I need right now. I love your house, Mallory. We had a colonial style in Massachusetts, but it was really a knockoff of the classic you have here. It's so nice to walk into a house that has its original wood trim and wide-planked floors."

"Yes, it's part of what we loved about the place when we bought it as a fixer-upper early in our marriage. This kitchen is the only room we modernized."

"The yellow feels like an early spring." Jean released the shiver she'd brought inside with her. She sat with a thump, clearly relieved to be sitting down at last.

"Mallory, let me tell you about my fortune. You really do need to get yours done sometime. I know it's probably silly, but if nothing else, it's fun. You know, these fortune-tellers hardly ever tell you anything really bad. And Madame Selene is no exception, but she hinted at some dark stuff."

"Do tell me. I'm fascinated." Mallory poured the coffee while Jean talked.

"Well, first she said she could see that my son and I were struggling to make ends meet. I didn't think that counted as a major insight, since it would be a good guess for a lot of people lately. And I'm sure she'd know that Richie had just sold his car to Angie. It's hard to miss that paint job. He sold it to her two weeks ago, before the accident on the ladder. Besides, Angie whispered something in Selene's ear as I was getting settled in the chair in the display window. That's another weird thing, being so on display during the process."

"I would think so," Mallory said while Jean paused to sip at the coffee. Jean seemed to be in a slow-motion movie, the way she lifted the cup like it might fall out of her hands.

"Anyway, then Madame Selene commented on how I'd been feeling poorly lately and needed to get more rest. And again, I figured that was probably pretty obvious, given how pale I am."

"You really are, so yes, that would be an easy one."

"But then she said that my worries about Richie may not all be in my mind, that maybe I had good reason to worry about him."

"What?" Mallory sat upright from the relaxed position she'd been in.

"When Selene said that, her voice dropped really low. I had to lean in to hear her. It felt conniving, like she didn't want Angie or Cassidy to hear. And yet, before this part, she had been using a loud voice and I wished she'd stifle herself a little. With the other comments she made, she probably wanted her colleagues to notice what a good job she was doing as a fortune-teller. But now, telling me I might have reason to worry, she was almost whispering."

Jean took another sip of the coffee. Mallory could see that her hands were still jittery.

"Well, as you can imagine," Jean continued, "I was stunned. I asked Madame Selene what she was talking about, and she said something like, 'The ball is a little foggy here, but there may have been some foul play going on. Or maybe just a rickety ladder that should have been recalled by the manufacturer. Yes, that's probably it,' she said. 'You should find out what ladder was used and see if there have been complaints about it.'

"That's what she said, Mallory, and now I'm not sure whether I should say something directly to Angie, or wait and ask Richie, or what."

"Oh my!" Mallory's danger-alert alarm was going off. "No, I don't think you should ask Angie. There's no way she'd admit to having given Richie a bad ladder to use, even if she didn't know it was a recall or something. But what about the first part of Madame

Selene's statement—possible foul play? What's up with that? From the other things you said, I'll bet Selene and Angie talk about a lot of things when their customers aren't listening. What if they had some kind of falling out? Maybe Selene is trying to make trouble for Angie."

Jean thought about this, and then she said, "You know, maybe she was just making up something so I would think I had spent my money on her wisely."

"I suppose that's possible, but how sick would that be? I don't know, Jean … I think she knows something. But I don't think you should talk with her or Angie again—about this, I mean. Also, I just learned something about Angie that could be why Selene might be trying to make trouble for her. It turns out that Angie is dating my doctor, Jim Beall. Maybe Selene is jealous of that?" Jean's coffee cup clattered down on the saucer. Mallory continued, "There's no way we can figure out what's going on, though. I think you should go see the police. It can't hurt to tell them what you just told me."

"No? They'll just think I'm crazy—that's all." Jean's voice had dropped practically to a whisper.

"No they won't. All you're doing is providing information. You're not saying you believe it or have anything to go on. You're just passing along information. The fact that a spiritualist gave you the information doesn't have to make it suspicious. In fact, you should say that to them. Tell them you're not really a believer—even if you are, sort of—and that's why you think something's fishy." Mallory realized she was talking quite fast. She worried that Jean might think she was overreacting. "No normal psychic would have told you what she told you. It just doesn't make any sense."

"You're right," Jean said with a sigh. "I'm kind of scared, in fact. Where's the police station in Great Wharf? I guess I'd better stop there before heading home."

Mallory stood up, went to her computer station, and got a pencil and some scratch paper. She brought them back and started drawing a map, assuming Jean's car was back at Byways.

"I have to come clean," Jean said while Mallory drew. "I know you said it was just a ten-minute walk from Byways. But I drove here and parked on your street. The snow-packed walks would have felt like shifting ice floes under my unsteady legs. I feel like such a wuss admitting this, but I knew I couldn't manage a trek like that."

"Of course, Jean, you've gone absolutely white. Are you going to be okay?"

"I'm sure I am. Maybe I'm coming down with something. If so, I apologize in advance for infecting you today."

"Don't worry about that. I've had my flu shot, and I'm healthy as a horse in general. I weigh like one too, but I'm working on it."

Mallory walked Jean out to her car and then, without letting Jean know, raced back through the house to lock up and follow Jean to the police station. She didn't want her new friend to decide she had a problem with being overprotective. But she was worried. She waited outside the station until Jean reappeared and drove off. She decided that was as far as she should take the hovering over her new friend. Later, she'd brag to Dwight about her self-restraint.

Back at Byways, Selene listened to Angie berate Cassidy for not relocking the cabinet as soon as she'd removed the necklaces for Mrs. Trent. Angie was having a bad day.

It had started earlier that morning, when Angie told Selene she'd been up until three in the morning rewriting what her cinder-path group had drafted. They called it ready to submit, and she called it disjointed and rambling. "For heaven's sake, can't people write anymore?"

Selene wondered if that was the problem, or if Angie wouldn't like anything she herself hadn't written. In any case, the late night had meant a rough start to Angie's day. And then over breakfast, Angie had skimmed through the *Southern Maine Herald*.

"There was the article by that reporter Elizabeth Easley," Angie fumed. "You know, the one I told you about from last summer? I didn't think it would run this far ahead of tourist season."

Selene tried to mollify her. "Maybe February's a slow news month. The reporter can't control when an editor decides to run an article. In any event, just think—you and the store are getting free advertising."

"The article does say I'm a knowledgeable businessperson. At least the other retailers will be forced to sit up and take notice. But the article doesn't make a single reference to my spearheading the cinder-path project. And worse than that, even though she promised not to, she wrote all about the Spirits-Up display. She lied to me. She outsmarted me!" Angie's face burned an angry red.

Last August it had perplexed Selene that Angie didn't want the reporter writing about the Spirits-Up display. Since then, however, Selene had figured it out. One day when Cassidy called Angie to the cash register to calm a belligerent customer, Selene snuck behind the curtain. She discovered that the Spirits-Up bottles were being tampered with. Used latex gloves lay next to a bottle of lavender essence. Half a case of untouched Spirits-Up containers waited under the workbench. The bottle on the workbench hadn't been resealed yet.

Selene knew immediately what was going on. In Angie's certainty that lavender had soothing, healing powers, she had been adding even more of it to each Spirits-Up bottle. The manufacturer wouldn't be pleased to learn someone was reselling its elixir with a different ratio of ingredients than listed.

Selene decided to wait for the right time to tell someone. No way she'd let Angie implicate her in the ruse. Selene also knew she might never tell. Instead, she might end up owning Byways herself, in which case she was perfectly comfortable with the idea of doing her own Spirits-Up tampering. Who knows— maybe Angie was onto something.

Just the other day Selene had suggested to Angie that they should put both their names on both the leases they currently held separately. "It just makes good business sense, Angie. If anything were to happen to either one of us, a livelihood would be ripped away and affect both of us. We women without husbands need to look out for each other. If both our names are on both leases, we'll have two of us watching our backs."

"Good thinking, Selene. I'll have my lawyer handle it. Even though I plan to get married again, to you-know-who, I've never been completely dependent on anyone. I'll keep our arrangement a secret from him."

Relieved at Angie's willingness to cosign both leases, Selene hoped all this could happen before Angie's grand retirement plan disintegrated. Selene knew it was going to, and she didn't need her tarot cards to tell her so. If Jim Beall were that interested in Angie, he'd have made a few appearances in the store by now.

EPISTOLARY EXCERPT FROM
UNPUBLISHED MANUSCRIPT:
RUNAWAY LEGACY

December 31, 2014

Dear Caitlin,

Have you ever been subjected to bullying
or gossip? We have been subjected to gossip.
Sometimes gossip is lies, and sometimes it's
the truth. Rarely is it in anyone's best interest.
When your mother left us, when she was eighteen, we had no idea about the sort of life she'd
been living behind our backs. Our neighbors
did, and they were gossiping about it, but they
never told us at the time. So when your mother
left town, we were caught completely unawares,
even though our neighbors had been talking
about Mary's problems for years.

Young people these days have a lot to deal
with. The recent news about bullying and
about kids' peers gossiping about them has us
worried for you. Sweet sixteen can be a beautiful age. Please, please, please tell us if anyone ever makes you feel bad about yourself, or

makes you think you are any less than the perfect human being you are.

Bullies and gossips are people with their own problems. But they are people who tend to hurt others because of these problems. We all just need to be a bit kinder—to ourselves and to others.

Call if you need us.

Love,
Nonny and Nonno

30

FEBRUARY

*In which Dwight and Mallory benefit from a
change in scenery; and Mallory makes two phone
calls.*

THE LAST SUNDAY in February—the day after
Mallory followed Jean to the police station—the
forecast was for an unusually balmy day in the fifties.
Dwight suggested they treat themselves to a day trip
and walk around the botanical gardens in Boothbay.
Mallory drove the two hours northward, and Dwight
would drive coming back. They walked for over an
hour, enjoying the unusual warmth and commenting
on the variety of plants hunkered down for the winter.
Dwight waited until he saw the right setting with the

right amount of privacy before making the comment he had planned the outing for.

He steered Mallory to one of the granite benches positioned a few steps off the path for people who wanted to rest or meditate during the walk. This one had a beautiful view of the Sheepscot River. The gray-blue water gave the intervening stand of fir trees a softly undulating background. Dwight turned to face Mallory.

"What is it, Dwight?"

Instead of talking right away, Dwight put his hands on the sides of her face and caressed her cheeks. He drew her toward him. Trusting, she relaxed into his pull. He gently placed her head on his shoulder and put his lips near her ear.

"I need to tell you something, and I need you just to listen." He could feel her tense up. He quickly held her even closer and continued, "Remember I love you, and we are in a safe and private space. No one can hear what I'm saying. Just you. I hurt so much that time I found you crying over the computer, and then that terrible scene with your uncle. Whether or not you can forgive him, you have to let go of the anger, Mallory. It's hurting you. It's hurting both of us. I thought after you told me everything at Spears you'd be better. But I can tell you still hurt. I know you're still drinking more than you should."

Mallory started shaking. At first she thought she was shaking with anger, but then she realized it was fear. She tried drawing back from Dwight's firm hold. "Dwight, let me go now. I'll stay and talk, I promise. I won't avoid it this time."

Dwight let go, and Mallory stayed seated. She put her hands on his hands.

"Ever since the girls opened my eyes to how over-protective I was with them, I've been thinking about why that might have been so. I've realized it had to be directly related to my experience with Uncle Bill. By never dealing with it, I acted out in a protective, I'm-there-for-you way, the way I always wished my mother had acted. Once I saw how I'd actually driven my own children away—the girls anyway—I kept rereading Dr. Nies's case file from her sessions with me. And I'm figuring it out.

"The open question before Dr. Nies died was, what was I afraid of? And just now, listening to you talk in my ear, close and loving like that, I realized how secure it made me feel and what I've been afraid of. I've been this twelve-year-old girl afraid that her mother doesn't care what happens to her. I've been afraid that if I tell her what her beloved baby brother did, she wouldn't get mad at him but at me."

Dwight knew enough to be quiet.

"She would think I was the bad person for letting it happen, and she'd never talk to me again from a place of love. She'd talk from a place of suspicion. And the amazing thing is, as I think about it now, I never did have the mother I hoped I had. She never did feel close to her children—any of us. All Mother wanted was to move forward in her career with the least interference from her brood as possible. She had the brood because that's what her husband wanted. It was expected. But really, neither one of them knew how to be loving the way kids need."

Mallory stood up and walked a few steps toward the fir trees, then stopped at the ground cover. She leaned over and picked off a leaf. She caressed it as she continued talking, but now she faced away from Dwight, toward the river. Dwight was worried he wouldn't be able to hear her, but he didn't want to interrupt. He could hear well enough.

"So, what I figured out is that forgiving my uncle means I have to forgive my parents—my mother, really. And you know what?" Mallory turned and met Dwight's gaze. "I think I'm ready to do that. The scene with Bill helped me come to grips with this. Cynthia wasn't an abused or terrorized wife. She was a partner to him, just like you are to me. I realized he must not be a bad person. His devil is alcohol, and he's been in AA forever now. My anger at Uncle Bill has really been tied in with anger at my mother.

"Dr. Nies kept asking what I was afraid of. I was afraid of disappearing in my mother's eyes. I was afraid I had already died, and Mother didn't even know. Worse, she couldn't come stand over my grave because she didn't know where to look. I was buried deep inside myself is where I was buried."

Mallory threw aside the leaf she had been rubbing. "I'll call Mother the minute we get home. I won't put this off."

Dwight made no effort to stop the tears that were streaming down his cheeks, and now Mallory's began. "Thank you for giving me the time to get to this point." They hugged and brought their faces together again. They went from tears to smiles before heading down the path toward the parking lot.

"Hi, Mother. It's Mallory." She was making the call from the kitchen alcove but didn't turn the computer on.

"Hello, dear. How are things?"

"Fine. Well, in fact, better than fine. Do you have a minute to talk?"

"I can talk for a half hour if you want. Then I've got to start dinner or we'll be eating too late for your father. He can't eat after seven o'clock anymore. Doctor's orders. Your dad's been diagnosed with acid reflux disease. Can you believe that? What's he got to be nervous about?"

Mallory took a deep breath and wished she had turned on her slide show after all. But she'd been using it as a crutch to get through these calls. This call would test her will, and she had to get an A on it.

"I'm sorry to hear that. I'll send Dad a note and see if I can find out, if he's not telling you himself. But Mother, I want to talk with you about something important, okay?"

"Of course, Mallory. What is it?"

"I'm sorry this has to be done over the phone, but I can't afford the plane fare down to Georgia, and I can't put off talking about this any longer. I've waited too long as it is."

"Please get to the point, Mallory. You don't need to worry about giving me bad news over the phone. I'm a big girl now, you know."

Mallory felt herself tense up, but she made herself relax and then started talking. "Mother, do you remember how Uncle Bill was when he had been drinking?"

* * *

Dwight listened from the hallway settle. He wanted to make sure Mallory got a chance to say everything she wanted to say. If he heard her hang up without getting it all out, he'd help her make the call again. He and Mallory had agreed this had to happen if she were going to put the past to rest.

As Dwight listened, he felt himself growing lighter and lighter. By the time Mallory hung up, he practically had to reach up and push himself away from the ceiling and back into the living room, so she'd find him on the couch where she'd last seen him. He waited for her to come into the living room. And when she did, he waited for her to say the first words.

"Did you hear everything I said?" she asked.

"Yes. It sounded like you said everything you wanted."

"I think I did, Dwight. I really think I did. And you know what Mother's final pronouncement was, when she had heard it all?"

Dwight shook his head, afraid to speak.

"She said, 'I hope you know your uncle wasn't in control of himself in those days. I hope you don't blame him, or me, for this. These things just happen, and you have to move on in life.'"

Dwight shook his head again, and again kept silent.

"Dwight, I almost screamed bloody murder, but I knew it would make no difference and kept myself under control. I realized what I wanted was a mommy who would kiss my pain and make me feel better. And that sure wasn't the mother I was dealt. So I just said, 'Yes, Mother, I know. I just wanted to tell you about this so that I could walk away free.' I know you heard me say that. And then—oh, Dwight, get this!—Mother said, 'What do you mean, walk away free? You've always been free.'

"She never got it, that I've never been free of this memory and the pain of it. Well, I'm getting free now. I'll never hold an expectation about Mother again that she can't live up to. I finally see that."

Dwight judged this to be the time to speak. "I love you, Mal. I'm so happy that you got through that phone call the way you wanted to."

"And now I'll go call Uncle Bill." Mallory started to walk back into the hallway but stopped halfway there and turned around. "Honey, it's still a mild evening out. Would you mind taking a ten-minute walk while I make this call? I need to know I'm alone for this one."

"Happy to." Dwight jumped off the couch, took his jacket off the hook in the vestibule, and shut the door quietly behind him.

31

FEBRUARY

*In which a disappearance is solved but throws the
Coopers into a tailspin.*

THE NEXT MORNING Mallory woke up and got out
of bed without thinking. Usually she spent a few
minutes with her eyes open, struggling to bring some
order to her thoughts before committing to the day.
Now she had gone to the bathroom and started brushing her teeth before she realized, facing herself in the
mirror, how well she felt. The conversation with Uncle
Bill had been brief but long enough to communicate
forgiveness. Had the past lost its terrible hold on her?
Was it really done and over?

In the afternoon she got a call from Dwight's office manager, Lindsey, asking if she could babysit Friday night. Lindsey and her husband had reserved tickets for a dinner cruise in Portland to celebrate their second wedding anniversary. Friday would be the first time they would leave their baby, now five months old, with a sitter. Not only would they be unable to come home quickly, but the mealtime also would not be cell-phone friendly. They wanted to make sure the sitter had lots of experience. Dwight had told Lindsey that his wife was trying to earn money for tennis, and Lindsey jumped at the chance to hire Mallory.

Mallory knew how nervous new parents were, and she could put them at ease. She reminded Lindsey that she and Dwight had raised three children of their own. They had all grown up healthy and happy—and that was before cell phones were in everyone's hands.

What Mallory didn't say during the telephone call was anything about her own fears. What if something goes wrong? And am I really ready to drive myself home so long after dark? She talked herself out of the worries by focusing, instead, on the fact that she'd be doing something nice for Dwight. He relied on Lindsey to handle all sorts of emergencies at the office, and Lindsey had never let him down. He let her bring the baby to the office every day. When her baby was sick with some baby thing, she enlisted help from a friend or relative and never missed more than a couple hours of work. Even then, she called in to the work voicemail system every half hour to return urgent calls or alert Dwight to problems.

Dwight was thrilled when Mallory told him she had agreed to babysit for Lindsey and her husband on this special occasion. At four thirty that Friday afternoon, two hours before Dwight was due home, Mallory backed the car out of the drive. Doris waved from her upstairs window, and Mallory pretended not to see her. What?—she thought—I'm supposed to look over at her place every time I go somewhere?

Defensive fuming got her down Temperance Way, through a couple of turns, and onto Log Cabin Road. Sometime before she turned onto Route 1, however, the fuming gave way to nervousness. Mallory reassured herself that Lindsey's place was only two blocks from the Trents'. So snap out of it! Then she wondered whether Lindsey's place was in a better or worse block.

Her hands were shaking a little bit. She started humming, not a tune but a random set of notes. She looked at her speedometer and saw she was going too fast. She lifted her foot off the accelerator to let the car slow on its own. In that same moment, a small animal ran in front of her car. With trepidation,. Mallory raised her gaze to the rearview mirror. Oh, dear God. Too big for a squirrel. Too small for a raccoon.

Mallory pulled over onto a side road and walked back. Someone's pet cat. She watched as the gray tabby's heaving side went still. Blood oozed and pooled dark red around the flea collar. Mallory felt herself going faint. She backed away and made it to her car, where she lay down on the backseat, her mind a blank.

* * *

At five thirty Dwight got a call from Lindsey.

"Dwight, do you know if Mallory's on her way here? She was supposed to be here a half hour ago. We need to leave for the dinner cruise in fifteen minutes. Her phone just keeps putting me in voicemail." Lindsey, his normally self-possessed office manager, sounded near hysterics.

"I don't know, Lindsey. Let me call her and then call you back."

Dwight felt the cold hand of dread on the back of his neck. Mallory seemed to have been doing so much better, but he knew something had to be very wrong for her to be so late for a business commitment. Her cell phone put him, too, into voicemail. He knew that Mallory's latest habit, now that she was starting to drive again, was to put the phone into quiet mode so she wouldn't be startled by a call. Then before getting out of the car she would put it back in regular mode and check for messages.

Dwight left a message for her to call him right away, that Lindsey was worried. He left the same message on their home landline. Then he called Lindsey back.

"She's in the car, I'm pretty sure of that," he said. "But she keeps her phone off until she gets where she's going. I'm sorry, Lindsey. I'd run over there myself, but I've got to wait here for that new tenant. Is there anyone else you can ask at the last minute?"

"No. Otherwise, I would have had my sister or Jack's brother race over to cover until Mallory got here. But that's why I asked Mallory to begin with. I'm sorry, Dwight, and I do hope Mallory's okay, but damn it, if she's not here in the next fifteen minutes we'll miss the boarding for the cruise. The money's nonrefundable and we're just screwed."

"I understand, Lindsey. And if that's what happens, I'll repay you for the expense, but I know that doesn't get you the anniversary you were looking forward to."

"No, it doesn't. Well, we should both hang up in case she's trying to reach one of us. Let me know if you hear anything."

Dwight's tenant walked in a few minutes later, and their business was handled quickly. When the tenant left, Dwight tried Mallory's cell again, but it was still inactive. The home phone too. He locked up the office and drove home. Seeing that her car wasn't there, he drove the route she probably would have taken. It was now six thirty, over an hour after sunset.

He drove slowly down the streets leading to Route 1. He didn't spot Mallory or her car before turning onto Route 1, and he didn't spot anything between there and Lindsey's place either. He didn't let Lindsey know he was in the area; it would do no good. He turned around and looked hard again on the return drive. Nothing.

At eight o'clock Dwight called the Great Wharf Police Department and the Great Wharf Hospital, and was about to call the Kennebunkport police when the phone rang.

* * *

When Mallory woke up, having fallen asleep in the backseat, it took her a minute to get oriented. Then she remembered the cat. And the blood. She knew she couldn't just leave the cat there. She'd have to get a look at the tag on its collar and make sure the owner was told about the accident.

Then she remembered where she'd been going in the first place, and she groaned out loud. She turned on her cell and called Lindsey, who was understandably icy. Then she called Dwight, who said, "Thank God you're okay. Now just come home, Mallory. We'll talk about whatever happened after you get here." Mallory despaired of his love, hearing the controlled anger in his voice.

She got out of the car, removed an old blanket from the trunk, and walked back from the side road to the cat's body on Log Cabin Road. It was near enough to the shoulder that other cars had avoided running over it again. Mallory turned her face away and took sideways glances at the carcass while she gathered it up in the blanket. Back in the car she forced herself to look at the tag, a rabies tag with a number on it. She called the police to report the incident, and they said they would let the owner know. She left the remains with the police on her way home. She used their restroom to wash her hands.

All this she did in a desolate haze. When she got home and saw the front porch light on, she felt a glimmer of hope that Dwight wasn't too angry with her. She locked the car and walked up the steps and into the vestibule. There was no light on in the hallway, but the kitchen was lit. She found Dwight at the table, finishing a beer. His features were set hard.

"What the hell happened, Mallory?"

Any hope she had that he might be sweet disappeared. She started, "I'm so sorry—"

"You know what? I don't really want to hear what happened. Poor Lindsey! I can't believe you let her down like that. I can't imagine anything that can make this okay. You're obviously fine. I've been so damn worried, and so damn embarrassed at the same time. They missed their dinner cruise thanks to you, and whatever agonizing mental throes you may have been experiencing can't compare to ruining their first evening out in five months. Five months of worrying over a new baby and worrying over PCJ Company almost as much. She's the best employee I've ever had. How could you? No, don't answer that."

Dwight downed the rest of his beer, got up from the table, put the bottle in the bin, got a new one from the fridge, opened it, and carried it upstairs. On the way up, he said, "I'm just getting what I need to sleep on the couch tonight."

Mallory squelched a sob but couldn't stop the tears. She had made huge strides in overcoming her anxieties. Dwight had been so encouraging, and she had come so far. But for some reason the sight of blood had still made her dizzy. She needed to do something more. Had she missed something in Dr. Nies's notes on her? And she needed to find a psychiatrist who would give her something for her nerves. She needed, she needed.

* * *

Dwight couldn't get comfortable on the couch, either physically or mentally. He threw the blanket back and swung his legs out to get up, but they caught the edge of the coffee table and something crashed. He turned on the lamp. When he saw the broken neck of the clay giraffe Carol had made in second grade, he wept. "How broken are we?" he whispered into the shadows. He lay back down, suddenly bone tired, and fell into a deep sleep.

The sunlight streaming into the living room around seven o'clock woke him up. His eyes went directly to the giraffe. It was gone. He knew he hadn't dreamed what happened. Mallory must have looked in on him and removed the pieces. He heard her now in the kitchen.

After shaving, showering, and dressing, Dwight still didn't want to talk to his wife. He wanted to love her; he did love her. But today, he had decided, he was going to call Elizabeth Easley. Everything had been focused on Mallory's problems for so long. What about him? Even as he had these thoughts, he suspected they weren't truthful. But he felt driven to do something, somehow, to stand up for himself.

Dwight backed his truck out of the driveway and drove off without a word to Mallory. He went to a fast-food drive-through near the highway for breakfast. While he drank coffee and ate an egg sandwich in the parking lot, he imagined a good phone conversation with Elizabeth. He'd ask how her article went. She'd say she had been thinking about him. They would slide into a deepening flirtation. He'd see her that night.

Dwight said out loud, "Oh criminy, what a fool." His father had had more than one affair. Exactly how many was anyone's guess. But Dwight remembered his mother's despair, and the pall that fell over their home for months afterward, every time. She kept taking him back, believing his promises. Dwight knew he'd never be able to forgive himself if he was unfaithful to Mallory. His guilt would ruin their marriage.

He crumpled the food wrapper into a small ball, threw it into the paper bag, crumpled the bag, and threw it into the waste bin by the car. He drove to Portland to face Lindsey, who always worked with him on Saturday mornings. At least he hoped she still did.

32

MARCH

In which Dr. Sterns takes on another patient;
and new friends compare notes.

MALLORY LOOKED DOWN the list of psychologists and psychiatrists that Dr. Nies's estate lawyer gave to clients who asked. Every time she thought about the horrible night, not quite a week ago, when she had ruined Lindsey's plans and let Dwight down, she cried. She felt like a walking rain cloud.

The day after the fiasco, Dwight had come home from work in the evening and hugged her briefly but tightly. That released her tears immediately. But then he had stepped back, and instead of providing a soothing response, he just said, "We need to put this behind us and get back to some kind of normal." She felt the chill in the air and knew it meant a slow thaw. At least he was talking to her.

Conversations—even now, days later—were still strained, if only because she had to control her tears when he was around. This remained difficult for her, and when alone she was as nervous as ever. She still kept a knife inside her purse when she ventured out.

Mallory placed a call to the first psychiatrist on the list, a Dr. Eli Sterns. Dr. Nies had been a nonprescribing psychologist, but now Mallory wanted someone who could prescribe some sort of tranquilizer. A psychiatrist would be her best bet.

When Dr. Sterns's office learned she had been a client of Dr. Nies, they made an appointment for the next day. The time slot was available thanks to a last-minute cancellation. Mallory brought her file with her, and Dr. Sterns reviewed it while she sat there. They had a ten-minute conversation that convinced him she was a candidate for a mild tranquilizer, and he wanted to see her again in April.

"Please understand, Mrs. Cooper, that you are not to drink alcohol while you're taking this medication. Dr. Nies's notes mention that wine is your drink of choice and that you needed to cut down on your intake. How have you been doing with that?"

"I have cut down, generally to three glasses a day now. Will the tranquilizer remove my desire for it?"

"Let me know if it doesn't, but it should. The main thing is, do not do both. Can I trust you on this?"

"Yes, Doctor. I'm done hiding from myself."

* * *

By the end of the round-robin semifinals in early March, Mallory and Elizabeth learned they would be going up against each other in the finals a week later. They never had gone out for coffee after their original meeting. They decided they definitely should get together before the final battle. Besides wanting to befriend each other, they agreed it was wise to know one's opponent in more ways than just on the court.

Mallory asked Elizabeth if she would like to come to the local Great Wharf Coffeehouse or meet somewhere in between. Mallory admitted that she wasn't quite ready to drive into downtown Portland traffic. Her goal was to feel fine with that by summertime.

Elizabeth smiled to herself. She had enjoyed playing tennis with Mallory during their first match, and she did want to get to know her better. At the same time, the competitor in her kicked in—she liked knowing that this particular tennis opponent had a fear of driving in traffic. It was a weakness Elizabeth thought might play out for her in the final tennis rounds, although she didn't know how she'd relocate the courts to downtown in order to freak out Mallory trying to get there. Still, the thought amused her.

A less amusing thought was that this could be the meeting during which Elizabeth enlightened Mallory about her husband. Once the women had exchanged last names in January, Elizabeth had checked her notes from the meeting with Dwight Cooper and confirmed that Mallory was his wife's name. Last summer she had wanted to interview them as a couple, but she had decided to leave well enough alone, not wanting to hurt anyone. Calling Dwight at the time would have run the risk of setting something regrettable in motion.

Elizabeth's decision had not been easy for her. It meant finishing the article without knowing what every loose thread in front of her might lead to. For once, she let consideration for others win over her ambition. She liked how this compassionate decision made her feel. Now, if she and Mallory were going to be friends, it would be smart to put everything on the table to start. If being the bearer of bad tidings ruined the budding friendship, then better to ruin it before it took root.

She told Mallory that the Great Wharf Coffeehouse would be fine. She suggested ten o'clock Saturday—three days away. Elizabeth decided she could combine that trip with a visit afterward to Byways. She wanted to apologize in person for revealing Angie's display "secret" after promising she wouldn't. Elizabeth turned her attention to how she would start the first of two difficult conversations now planned for Saturday. While the apology to Angie could be handled straight on, telling a wife about a near-errant husband needed finesse.

That Saturday started out dreadfully. First, Elizabeth's alarm clock failed her, so she woke up an hour late. This meant she wouldn't get in her usual hour of exercise before heading into the day. Second, her front left tire needed air, so she knew she'd have to fill it up in the rain. Rain was the third reason the day sucked. Elizabeth hated driving in rain. She laughed at herself. Here she had been smirking about Mallory's reticence to drive in Portland traffic, and she was nervous about driving in rain.

By the time she arrived in Great Wharf, Elizabeth felt as discombobulated as a Dalí painting. The wind had blown the hood back on her raincoat as she filled the tire. She had fixed the runny mascara before getting out of the car again, but she knew she'd have to fix it all over again when she got inside the coffeehouse. She couldn't wait for the day she made a good salary and graduated from cheap makeup.

She grabbed a parking spot on Newman Lane, unsure how far that was from the address of the coffeehouse Mallory had given her. But there had been no spaces open on Wyeth and she was running late now. She just had to trust this was close enough. Elizabeth didn't realize, until she got there, that this was the same coffeehouse she and Dwight had been in last summer. She quickly decided to make this her lead-in when the time came to tell Mallory about her unexpected interview with Dwight.

Entering the coffeehouse, she spotted Mallory waving her over to a table.

"Over here!"

Elizabeth made her way to the table, took her coat off, and let the water slide off before draping it over the back of the chair.

"Are you laughing at how wet I am?" she asked Mallory.

"Well, yes, that, and also all that black stuff running down your cheeks."

"Damn, I was afraid of that."

"I hope you don't mind that I told you."

"Are you kidding? I'd be angry if you didn't! Why don't you stay where you are and I'll make a quick dash into the restroom to clean up and then get lattes for us. Don't want to lose this great seat."

"Fine," said Mallory, "but Dutch treat. Get me a pound cake too, okay?"

Elizabeth stood in line and got them each a latte and a piece of pound cake. When she came back to the table and put everything down, Mallory handed her the exact amount and said, "I'm sort of a regular here; that's why I know how much to fork over. When I was working on getting out of the house more—long story—I often made this place a destination and a reward."

"I do a similar thing," said Elizabeth, "when I finish exercising each morning. There's a coffee shop on the ground level of my apartment building. I head there directly from the treadmill, hoping the aroma of my workout won't offend the others standing in line. I feel guilty that I don't just make my own coffee, three flights up in my galley kitchen. But it doesn't taste nearly as good."

Elizabeth thought Mallory would laugh or nod agreeably. Instead, Mallory sat motionless, her eyes fixated on the fork Elizabeth held aimed at the pound cake.

"Mallory? What is it?"

Mallory seemed to be waking from a nightmare. She slowly brought her gaze back up to Elizabeth's face, her eyes gradually focusing again. She blinked a few times and then said, "Elizabeth, oh my God. I just remembered something from a long time ago. That huge blood blister on your finger made me think of it."

"I hope this didn't creep you out too much," Elizabeth said, putting the fork down and wrapping her other hand around the offending finger. "I got it the way a lot of people do, by stupidly catching my finger in the car door. Guess it's pretty gross looking. They say it's best to let the blister fall off on its own, so I've just left it for all to see. I probably should wear a bandage over it."

"No, no, don't worry about that. It's just that it has triggered a childhood memory I'd totally forgotten about. And it may explain why I've been squeamish about blood the last few years. Funny it wasn't a problem earlier, but I guess I was just too busy raising the kids to let a little blood stop me. And now that I have this memory back, I know what to work on next. I'm so glad you brought that blister with you, Elizabeth!" Mallory did laugh now.

"Glad to be of service! Speaking of memories," Elizabeth figured it was now-or-never time to tell about Dwight, "I sat in this same Great Wharf Coffeehouse last summer, having a latte with a lovely man. He was maybe fifty or sixty. Oh, I guess we should get that question out of the way. How old are you? I just turned thirty-two."

"I, gasp, turned fifty-five last birthday."

"You don't look fifty-five—honest you don't! Well, anyway, I'd say this guy was about fifty-five. I had quite literally bumped into him on the street, bowled him over as he was retrieving some kid's Frisbee. Knocked him flat. He was very forgiving. When he saw who had bumped into him—this is when I didn't have mascara streaming down my cheeks—he asked me to have a coffee with him. This is the place we came to. I think this was even the table we sat at!"

Elizabeth watched the information sink in and realized Mallory might already have heard this story from Dwight. She could recognize the look on a person's face when unwelcome news had just been delivered. Mallory's chin lowered, she broke off eye contact, and she had gone especially quiet.

"What is it, Mallory? What'd I say?"

"Well, let me put it this way. My husband has excellent taste in women."

"Your husband? Are you kidding? Is his name Dwight?" Elizabeth played her planned act of ignorance well.

"Yes, it is."

"Oh! But nothing happened, Mallory, I swear. Nothing happened. It was just a sweet blip, and I could tell he loved his wife. And I think he realized that too—the minute I reminded him he had a daughter who was about my age. Be honest, now. Hasn't he been a good husband to you?"

Mallory nodded. "Dwight and I do have a strong marriage. He told me about meeting you and being attracted to you, and how it made him realize he still wanted us to be together. Last summer feels like a lifetime ago—so much has happened since then. I'm not worried about my husband, Elizabeth. It's just very disconcerting to hear this story from you, because Dwight never used your name. I had no idea."

Suddenly Mallory gasped and a tentative smile started. She said, "He doesn't know we know each other. I can't wait to spring it on him, who my newest friend really is."

"I'm so glad you can take this attitude about it." Elizabeth nodded in appreciation. "You really do have a good husband, and it sounds like a great marriage. Still, I guess you're going to come to our finals match ready to wipe the court with me."

"You've got that right. Get ready for a real showdown on Monday."

Elizabeth grinned in agreement and then changed the subject. "Did you happen to read my article in the *Southern Maine Herald*, about tourism and Great Wharf?"

"Sorry, no. I don't usually read newspapers except the *Great Wharf Gazette*."

"That's okay. It's just that that was the article I was gathering information for when I knocked Dwight over. Anyway, that article ended up in two parts. The second part will be published in April or May. It's about the proposed cinder path. Dwight was the person who first told me about it, just before I met with Angie Weller, the Byways owner. And now I'm going to see her again, after this coffee with you. What's your take on the path?"

Mallory's eyes darted down to her right and then immediately up to her right. Elizabeth knew from her neurolinguistics training that meant Mallory's reaction included both a visceral memory and a consideration of her answer.

Mallory adjusted her glasses and brushed her hair back. "At first I hated the idea. All I could see were problems with it. I'm actually shocked to hear myself say this, but I've done a one-eighty! Now that I'm walking regularly, I like the idea of experiencing the sights and smells of a bog environment on one side with the reassurance of civilization on the other side."

Elizabeth sighed in relief. "Then you're of the same mind, I'd say, as most of the people in Great Wharf. I'll be refining my article on the plan after Town Council meets later this month. And then you can skip reading me in print again."

"It's possible you can shame me into buying that edition, or at least reading the article online. Pay me enough and I'll write a glowing letter to the editor."

"How about you just let me treat the next time we get together?"

"We have a deal."

Having finished their lattes and cakes, the two women bundled up, agreed to compete ferociously on Monday, and headed in opposite directions down the rain-swept street.

33

MARCH

In which Elizabeth makes an apology; and Richie
makes his first call to 9-1-1.

E LIZABETH STOOD OUTSIDE Byways and gaped at the
display window with the fortune-teller in it. That
Angie Weller was too, too much! The fortune-teller
wore a flowing, deep red peasant-style outfit. A tiara
twinkled in her hair, and a sparkly shawl covered her
shoulders. She was making exaggerated hand motions
over the tarot cards laid out between her and an enrap-
tured customer. The violins and dulcimer typical of
gypsy music blared from over the shop door.

When Elizabeth entered the shop, she recognized
the fragrance and was glad the music muted when the

door shut behind her. She quickly wiped her cheeks with one of the tissues she carried in each pocket. A sign at the front of the shop announced that Madame Selene would be there between 11:00 and 4:00 today.

Elizabeth went over to the pudgy girl standing behind the counter.

"Hi," said Elizabeth. "Is Ms. Weller here today?"

"Yes," said Cassidy, "I'll go get her."

Cassidy went over to the curtain at the back of the shop and called softly to Angie that a customer was asking for her.

Elizabeth heard Angie ask, "Man or woman?"

"A woman."

"Oh, well, okay. I'll be out in a minute."

Cassidy went back to where Elizabeth waited by the counter. "She'll be right out."

"Thank you." Elizabeth kept her eye on the curtain of dream catchers. She'd seen a flap in the curtain open just a little as Angie took a peek before committing to entering the shop. Now she swayed toward Elizabeth like a model walking down a runway.

"Well, hello, Ms. Easley! How nice to see you again. I read your article with great interest some weeks ago now."

Her voice dripped sarcasm. Elizabeth thought back to the moment, months ago, when she'd decided—with a mix of ambition, stubborn naïveté, and wishful thinking—that Angie wouldn't really mind if she described the Spirits-Up display in detail. Elizabeth wanted the newspaper's managing editor to give her more bylines. She needed this article to demonstrate investigative reasoning so she could climb to the next rung on the reporting ladder.

Still, Angie's Dorothy ploy was, in fact, fairly ordinary as window displays go—no better or worse than any experienced marketer would be expected to come up with to promote a feel-better product. It's not like every storefront isn't throwing subliminal messages in front of customers all the time. And so, Elizabeth had begun her article with reference to a thriving New Age shop and its Spirits-Up display. She had wondered at the time if she should tell Angie about her change of mind but had ignored the niggle.

"Oh dear, I was afraid of that. And please, call me Elizabeth. Listen—I came over here to apologize to you for going back on my word about—"

Angie interrupted. "Not to worry. Come over here where we won't be in the way of the customers." She led Elizabeth to an unoccupied end of the shop.

"You were saying?" Angie's foot started tapping.

"I wanted to apologize, Angie, for not sticking to my word. When it came to writing the article, I realized that you needed to be the star of it. You showed such brilliance in the way you handled your store display, and I hoped in the end you wouldn't mind if I shared that with the whole of York County." Elizabeth knew she was handing Angie a line of bullshit, and she could tell she wasn't fooling Angie in the least.

"You're too kind, E-liz-a-beth. Don't you worry. I hope the article has been well received. I hope it helps you make a name for yourself. You are obviously an up-and-comer. I wish you well—nothing but the best."

Elizabeth noticed Angie's hands clenching and unclenching. Her words were carefully measured and her voice was low enough not to raise curiosity in her customers.

"I must say, I was quite surprised to read nothing about my cinder-path idea, which can only be good for the town. You never even checked in with me to see how it was progressing. In fact, our committee submitted its plan to Town Council just over a week ago, to be discussed at the March meeting. Work might begin as early as April. Now that, E-liz-a-beth, would have been news worth spreading."

Before Elizabeth had a chance to respond, Angie continued, "And now I must get back to what I was working on. Don't be shy about picking up a gift for someone while you're here. Drive carefully in this storm."

She swiveled and marched back to her curtained hideaway. Whew, Elizabeth thought. Those black eyes were gun barrels aimed right at me. It's not my fault my editor decided to save my cinder path write-up until April or May. Well, I'd better buy something before I leave.

Elizabeth looked around, hoping Angie would notice, and bought a bottle of Spirits-Up. It would make a great gift for Mallory when she beat her in the finals. She really liked Mallory and anticipated a strong friendship. At the same time, she hoped the over-twenty-year difference in their ages would give her the final edge on the court.

Elizabeth alternately smiled and fumed as she drove. This had been a roller-coaster day, starting with getting up late and moving down through rain, up-down-up with Mallory, and down again with Angie. She looked forward to luxuriating in steaming hot bath-water enhanced with her favorite lemon-scented oil. Then, snuggling in a heavy afghan, she would make notes about today in her journal.

First, though, she had to keep her car on the road while this high wind whipped at it and her eyes were stinging from the mascara. The tires weren't gripping as well as they should. Was the bad tire low again, or even flat? Just as Elizabeth thought about slowing down and getting off the road, a car sped up beside her. She had no time to react, but she did see that the driver was a furious-faced Angie Weller. Her moment of recognition coincided with Angie's car slamming into her car, sending it off the road and into a massive tree ten feet away.

* * *

"Oh my God, did you see that?" Richie asked Dwight as they were about to exit the trolley museum onto Log Cabin Road. Richie had just finished maneuvering his crutches to the backseat and getting his cast leg settled in the passenger well.

"Yeah, that could have been on purpose—damn straight I saw it. I saw who did it too."

"So did I—it's not like I don't know my own car. Holy shit!"

Dwight pulled his car over to the side of the entranceway.

"Richie, call 9-1-1. I'll go see how the driver is."

When Dwight got to the crumpled car, he saw that the driver was slumped over the wheel, her face turned away and down. He didn't think he should touch her, but he opened the door and yelled over the rain and the already rubbernecking traffic, "Miss, are you okay? Can you hear me?"

He decided to reach in and feel her neck for the left carotid artery. He found it. The heart was still pumping blood, so he just kept talking and waited for the ambulance to arrive. He couldn't be sure, but he'd only seen that lovely skin and curly auburn hair once before. "Don't worry, miss; you'll be okay. Help is on the way. I'll stay right here and watch over you. If you can hear me, just relax. You're going to be okay."

Elizabeth, who had been thinking for years now that she should get a car with air bags, didn't hear a thing.

As the EMTs got the unconscious driver out of the car and onto a stretcher, the police interviewed Dwight and Richie separately. When the friends compared notes later, they confirmed reporting similar takes on the "accident."

Dwight watched as the stretcher went by. Though he recognized Elizabeth's face, he didn't say anything. He knew the police had her purse, and he'd call the hospital later to check on how she was. He felt guilty, even though he was as innocent as could be. He wondered if he'd tell Mallory and thought he probably wouldn't. Why remind her of that bad stretch in their marriage, especially on top of their recent crisis?

The Kennebunkport police brought Angie into the station that night about eight o'clock, after getting a warrant for her arrest for driving to endanger. Even so, she was free on bail the next morning. Her lawyer, the same one who had helped her and Madame Selene draw up their property and business agreements, reassured her that she would not be convicted. Angie swore she had no idea that her new used car had driven another car off the road. She explained that she had successfully passed the car but then, she thought, hit a pothole, and that's why she kept driving. The lawyer believed her story when it was given further weight by a wet street and bald tires.

This particular lawyer, normally of average intelligence, had never been able to take his eyes off his client's two best assets, either now or in earlier interactions. After gaining her freedom, Angie fired him, saying, "If there's going to be a court case against me, I can't have a lawyer who keeps looking at my bosoms."

34

MARCH

In which Mallory and Dwight fess up; and Richie makes his second call to 9-1-1.

MALLORY WAITED AT the tennis center for a half hour after the scheduled start of her finals round with Elizabeth. Five other players had shown up to yell encouragements. No one knew why Elizabeth was late. Calls to her apartment and her cell phone went unanswered. What started as a lively time of practice serves and loud voices gave way to a somber knowledge that something was wrong.

Finally, Mallory asked the tennis organizer to call the *Southern Maine Herald* editor Elizabeth had been freelancing for. The editor reported that a traffic accident in Kennebunkport two days before had landed Elizabeth in the Southern Maine Medical Center's emergency room. By now she had been transferred to the rehab department at the Maine Medical Center in Portland. The editor would be visiting her over the weekend but hadn't talked with her yet.

Mallory won the round-robin finals by default. It was a terrible way to win, but it was still a win and would always show as a win in the record. But when Mallory thought about her new friend in pain, she felt awful. Also, she had avoided telling Dwight the name of her new friend and finals tennis opponent because she wanted to stay focused on winning the match first. But now she knew it was time to fess up.

Over dinner that night, after toasting each other's happiness with their dinner glasses—wine for Dwight, cider for Mallory—Mallory opened the topic.

"Did you remember that my tennis finals match was today?"

"I forgot to ask! Did you win, my athletic goddess?"

His compliment was not lost on Mallory. It warmed her, as an indication that they were back on a good marital path.

"Well, not directly."

"Meaning?"

"I won by default because the other player never showed up."

"You're kidding. Do you know why?"

"We did finally track down what happened. Long story short, she was in a car accident and is now in re-hab at the Maine Medical Center. I'm going to drive in to see her tomorrow. This will be the impetus I needed to brave the city traffic. It'll be good for me."

"It'll be great! But I'm sorry about your friend. Do you know anything about the accident itself?"

"No, that's all the information I have for now. Well, that's not quite right. There's something I've never told you about my tennis friend, Dwight. Her name is Elizabeth Easley."

Dwight had just taken a sip of wine and now choked. He recovered in time to avoid spraying it all over their dinner table.

"Mallory, I saw the accident happen! Richie and I were just leaving the trolley museum. I had offered to drive him home. You know he's sharing a car with his mother these days. To help pay the rent, he sold his souped-up car to Angie Weller."

"Yes, Jean told me about that."

"So now and then I help out by giving him a lift. We were about to enter Log Cabin Road when we saw Richie's old car start to pass what turned out to be Elizabeth's car. And instead of passing, Richie's car slammed into Elizabeth's and forced her off the road—right into a tree!—and then just kept going.

Richie called 9-1-1, and I ran to see if the driver was okay. I could tell she was breathing so I didn't move her. I didn't know for sure it was Elizabeth until the stretcher went by. Unbelievable."

Mallory gave Dwight a minute to think, and he didn't fail her. Suddenly, his eyes opened extra wide. "Hey, I never told you her name. How did you know?"

Feeling victorious, Mallory grinned. "I didn't know until Saturday." She told him the whole story about the aha moment.

Dwight said, "I should have told you about her accident the very night it happened. I was just waiting for the perfect time. I guess this is it."

"Uh-huh. It's okay, honey. I mean, I'm assuming there hasn't been a true infidelity." Now Mallory's chin quivered. She hid behind the glass of cider, not sure what Dwight might say. "Would you tell me, Dwight?"

"I can't really answer that, Mal, because I've never been unfaithful to you. When it comes down to it, depending on one's point of view, I'm either a wimp or a hopeless romantic."

"I've always suspected the latter, and counted on it." Mallory rested a hand on Dwight's cheek and caressed his wrinkles with her thumb. "I was afraid to ask."

"I've counted on you too; that's why nothing did happen."

Mallory's tensed muscles relaxed. "Anyway, like I said, I'm going to drive in to see Elizabeth. Normally I'd ask you to come with me. But I need to do this alone, and not because I don't want you two to see each other again. I need to drive in Portland traffic and succeed on my own. I also need to see my friend without the added complication of your own history, for lack of a better word. Later, sometime, the three of us can get together. She'll be fascinated that you were the one who made sure she was alive, and I'll tell her that when I see her. But for this trip, I'll go alone."

"I understand, Mal. I especially love knowing you're going to drive yourself in and out of downtown Portland. You're clearing a major hurdle."

"I may even get to see some blood and find out if I can handle it now."

Dwight grimaced. "That's a bit gruesome, even for you."

"I can explain." Mallory leaned forward in her excitement to share what had been on her mind since Saturday. "When Elizabeth and I had our tête-à-tête at the coffeehouse, she had a blood blister on her finger that triggered a memory. Only you will fully appreciate this. The memory goes back to Uncle Bill, after he had thrown the robe at me and left the kitchen. As I put the robe on, I noticed a smear of blood on the front panel and then another on the belt as I tied it. I looked at my hands, and there was a fresh cut on my finger. A big red bubble grew as I watched."

Mallory sat back.

Dwight said, "I give up. Where'd it come from?"

"In my haste to get out of the pool—I've remembered it now—I cut myself on a rough spot on the ladder. I was so focused on getting into the kitchen that I ignored it."

Mallory sat forward again and took hold of Dwight's wrist.

"Now here's the cool thing. Remember you commented that I didn't used to get queasy at the sight of blood, like when the kids got a cut or whatever?"

"Yes."

"I'm sure I blocked that memory as a way not to deal with the abuse itself. Then when the kids and the job were gone and I had all that time alone, fear of blood became a clue from my unsettled mind. Like when someone sends up a flare to alert searchers to their location. Then, when I got paralyzed by the cat's blood, I still hadn't remembered that crimson connection to the abuse."

Dwight asked, "So what do you think? Are you still afraid of blood?"

"From now on I'm going to remember blood for how it must have smeared Uncle Bill's penis. If I can reinforce that vengeful association enough times in my mind, blood will become a symbol of strength for me instead of weakness."

Mallory raised her near-empty glass of cider and tapped it against Dwight's glass of wine. "Here's to Uncle Bill's bloody penis."

* * *

The next morning, as Mallory drove through Biddeford on her way into Portland, she watched an ambulance headed the other way. She said out loud, "I hope that's not one of the Trents." Jean and Richie were the only people she knew who lived in Biddeford, and they'd both had health problems lately. It occurred to Mallory that she needed to call Jean later on and check in.

* * *

Richie had been home most of the time during his own recuperation. His time at Seashore Trolley Museum on Saturday was his first visit back there since his fall. Other than that, when he wasn't on the phone with Amanda he was worrying about his mother, who seemed to be sinking into a depression. She had returned to spending a lot of time on the couch. As far as Richie could tell, she and Jim hadn't had a date since Valentine's Day, almost a month ago. Ma had been going to work, but she dragged through the day and then fell asleep with Celestine curled up next to her on the couch each evening. Richie had to wake her up to go to bed. Now she hadn't gone to work for two days.

He called Amanda. He explained how dry mouthed Ma had been, and dizzy, and complaining of blurred vision. This morning she had even been delirious and had a hallucination that Celestine was flying near the ceiling, but then she'd snapped out of that.

"Richie," Amanda finally said, "this sounds really serious now. You need to get Jean looked at. And I mean right away. Call 9-1-1 and worry about repercussions later." So he did. He just kept falling deeper in love with Amanda, and now he could add to his list of her best features that she was calm and practical in a crisis.

When the ambulance arrived, the EMTs noticed that Jean's lips were swollen and her heart rate was rapid. They asked her to describe her symptoms. She was almost too weak even to talk, so Richie answered for her. He repeated everything he'd told Amanda earlier.

The recording EMT asked what medications she was on, and what she had been eating and drinking. Richie listed what he knew. He mentioned that the pills prescribed by Dr. Sterns may or may not be placebos and showed them the container. The recording EMT put two of the pills in a plastic bag for samples. Then Richie listed typical foods, mentioning granola, soy milk, chamomile tea, and salads. His mother whispered, "Don't forget the Spirits-Up."

"What's that?" asked the EMT.

Richie said, "It's just a harmless elixir she's been using from one of the gift shops in Great Wharf. It was a gift from the owner of the shop."

"Give me the bottle, please."

The EMT sniffed at it, read the label, and then put it in a plastic bag to take along for analysis.

35

MARCH

*In which Richie has Jim paged; Chief Burnham
gets an earful; and the latest word from Doris
sends Mallory to the hospital.*

"D R. BEALL?" A nurse hurried down the hall toward Jim. He had just finished consulting to
one of the internists about a problematic patient. Even
though he had his own practice as a general practitioner,
Jim had specialized in internal medicine. He enjoyed
the opportunity to work with others when called on.

"Your pager doesn't seem to be working—probably just needs a new battery," the nurse said. "There's
someone asking to see you in ER, a Richie Trent?"

"How bad is he?"

"Oh, he's fine. It's his mother. She was just brought in. They don't know what's wrong with her yet, but her son is asking to talk with you. He made it sound like you're friends."

Jim hurried over to the emergency department and found Richie in the waiting room. Richie told him what his mother's symptoms were. "I just thought I should tell you, Jim. I know you and Ma have gone out a few times, and that's all I know. But just in case, I thought you should know she's here."

"Thanks, pal." Jim was about to leave to go find Jean, but then he turned back, remembering to ask, "How's your leg doing?"

"It's great, thanks. The pain is gone. But go find Ma now. I have a feeling seeing you will help a lot."

Jim wondered if that was a dig because he hadn't seen Jean since Richie's accident. His emotions were in turmoil these days. Still, it had only been a few weeks, and he had called and talked with her a couple of times. Yes, he had rushed the calls. He had pretended to be overworked and tired. But the real reason he kept the calls short was to put off turning his life upside down. He knew one more date with Jean might well mark the end of his bachelor days. He had to decide soon what he really wanted.

When he entered Jean's room, he found an empty bed.

"They're pumping her stomach," said the nurse in attendance. "They'll have her back in her bed in a half hour or so."

Jim decided not to wait but to track down wherever they were doing the stomach pumping. He found her only a few doors down the hall. He couldn't believe the thoughtlessness of that nurse, not telling him she was just a few doors down. He felt anger flaring up inside, but then realized he was overreacting out of concern for Jean. He consciously lowered his blood pressure.

He watched while the attending technician finished the procedure. Then he watched while they wheeled Jean back to her room and got her settled into the bed. When everyone had left, he went over to her. Her eyes were closed, but her color seemed good. He read her chart and saw that there was a suspicion of poisoning.

Poisoning! What the hell?

And then Angie's face (and the rest of her) flashed across his mind. He remembered something Richie had told him before he was released from the hospital. He described the rough year his mother had had, and confided he'd been slipping Spirits-Up into her tea. Then Richie said, "But I don't need to do that for a while now because Angie gave her a bottle during her last visit."

Jim knew he'd have to tell the police his suspicions. He didn't want to. They had left him alone since the interrogations after Sheila's death. He hated to call attention to himself again. The near death of another woman he'd been seeing would look very bad.

At the same time, if someone had tried to kill Jean—well, he needed to help the police get to the bottom of it. The strength of his worry alerted Jim to what he'd been shutting out of his mind for weeks. No amount of denial would change the fact that he had fallen in love with Jean. She touched chords deep inside him. Even Beverly had never reached as deep as Jean. Jim didn't know he was looking for a romantic love relationship until he had found himself in one. The emotional connection during their Valentine's celebration surprised and scared him, and he had shut down.

He had it figured out now, and now that he did, he was damned if he'd lose her. The more he thought about it, the more sure he was that Angie was responsible for what was happening to Jean. He remembered sighting her in that car in Portland but then talking himself out of thinking anything about it. Angie had seen him with Jean on Valentine's Day.

Jim picked up the phone and called his lawyer, who agreed to meet him right away at the police station.

Before they hung up, Jim told his lawyer about his broom-closet history with Angie, just in case that came to light. His lawyer actually laughed and then reassured him that in Ohio the age of consent was sixteen. "Who knows what was true back in the 1980s, but in any event, I don't think you'll have a problem, Jim. Sounds like Ms. Weller's got the problem."

* * *

Police Chief Bren Burnham looked up from the papers on his desk. Dr. Jim Beall stood three feet away, also staring at the papers on the chief's desk. Beall looked like hell. He looked like he had forgotten to comb his hair that morning. Either that or he had been running a nervous hand through it for some time. He had the vacant, stunned look of a man who wasn't sure himself why he was standing there.

"Hey, Doctor, what brings you here?"

"Chief Burnham, I'm glad to see you instead of your deputy. I don't think he likes me very much. Anyway, I'm here because of a bad feeling about someone, other than your deputy. Is having a bad feeling a good enough reason to come see the police?"

"Hell, yes," said the chief. "Sometimes that's the best reason of all. I'm not saying I believe in extrasensory perception, and we don't have our own medium on staff, but I know that when I have a bad feeling of my own, I follow up on it. It works in reverse too. For instance, I had a good feeling about you, Dr. Beall, which is why we've sort of let you alone for a while these last few months."

"What does 'sort of' mean, Chief?"

"We've followed you around a few times. Just sort of kept an eye on you for your own safety and for our own reassurance."

"What have you found in the process?"

"We've learned that you have a new woman in your life, but we're not sure how serious the relationship is."

"Welcome to that club!" Jim grinned. Then he stopped grinning. "I'm worried, Chief. That's why I'm here. And here's my lawyer, just in time for us to get this conversation rolling."

Jim told Chief Burnham about his suspicions. And Chief Burnham, for his part, told Jim nothing. The lawyer took notes.

* * *

Mallory hummed, whistled, and sang as she drove home, turning onto Temperance Way just before three o'clock. She had driven to Portland for the first time in almost three years. By timing the trip between rush hours, she had avoided any major traffic problems. On top of that, Elizabeth had looked much better than Mallory had prepared herself for. The physical therapist was predicting that her patient would be released from rehab in two days. Mallory was glad she'd been able to visit Elizabeth while she was still stuck in the health system, when visitors are most appreciated.

Entering the driveway, Mallory felt as happy to be safely home as she felt energized by her success. She groaned when she spotted Doris standing on the stoop. Doris turned around and waved at her. Mallory waved back. She stopped the car short of the house to have the conversation there in the drive. She knew if she continued driving to the garage, she'd end up having to invite Doris inside, out of the raw March wind. She put the window down, turned off the ignition, and called out from the car.

"Hi, Doris. What's up?"

"Mallory, did you hear about Richie Trent's mother, Jean?"

"No, what's happened?"

"Well, I was looking into auditioning for the next Players' production." Doris spoke as she took the steps down from the stoop and walked toward the car. "You know, I do wish they'd send information out in some kind of regular way so we wouldn't always have to call to find out—"

"Doris, I swear I'm going to strangle you. What's happened to Jean?"

"Oh, well, no one really knows—that's the strange thing about it. She's at the Great Wharf Hospital. It seems she's been brought low by something, but whether it's a virus or food poisoning or something else, no one knows."

Doris put both her hands on the car door below the open window and leaned toward Mallory. "I hoped you could shed some light, seeing as how you and her seem to be good buddies all of a sudden. I saw you let her in a while back. When was that now? Maybe two weeks ago? Was anything wrong with her then?"

"Nope, she was fit as a fiddle." Mallory just couldn't give Doris the satisfaction of being right.

"All Richie told Cassidy was he was at the hospital with his mother, and she should tell Ms. Weller when she went to work this afternoon. I gather Richie was supposed to do some odd job for her today."

"Listen—thanks for letting me know, Doris. I'm afraid I've got to head back out. I just remembered something I forgot to pick up." Doris stepped back, looking resigned, as Mallory started the car again. While closing the window, Mallory kept talking. "You take care now. It's nice to see you walking so well these days."

Backing out of the drive, Mallory felt terrible for two reasons. Her rudeness to Doris seemed to know no bounds. And she realized, too, that her automatic lie about Jean having seemed "fit as a fiddle" came so easily because she was ashamed of herself. She had been meaning to call and see whether Jean felt better, but the tennis competition and her paying work as a babysitter and now Elizabeth's accident—all combined with the internal work she was doing—had kept her from getting outside her own head for a while now. Funny that just this morning she had thought about Jean and Richie when she'd seen that ambulance.

Pulling into the hospital parking area, Mallory aimed for an empty space, only to be beat to it by an aggressive driver. It looked like Richie's car, but the driver was very short. She didn't get a good look. Mallory decided Richie was just on her mind now that she had come to visit his mother.

That's when the idea hit to invite Jean and Richie to dinner with her and Dwight. If Jean looked halfway conscious and chomping at the bit to get out of the hospital, she'd offer the invitation today, during her visit. She'd make it for a month from now, say, when Jean should be fully recovered. That would help keep Jean's mind on something positive in the future.

This plan put Mallory back in a happy mood as she walked by that car with the racing stripe and on into the hospital reception area. Then it hit her. She remembered Jean telling her that Angie Weller had bought Richie's car sometime before the accident on the ladder. Well, okay then, mystery solved. But then she remembered Dwight telling her that that same car seemed to have forced Elizabeth's car into the tree. This made zero sense. All Elizabeth said today was that some maniac had driven her off the road, and the police were looking into it. Still pretty drugged up, Elizabeth had trouble forming sentences.

At the reception desk, Mallory inquired after Jean Trent. She learned Jean was in Room 315 and her condition was listed as stable. This made Mallory wonder what her own condition might be labeled. She came up with words for that on the elevator ride up. Improving? Greatly improved? On the near side of excellent? And then she remembered that she hadn't taken her tranquilizer pill for two days. She was having trouble getting into the new habit of it. That meant she had made the trip to and from Portland all on her own!

When she stepped out of the elevator, it further occurred to her that she hadn't minded the ride up at all. A few months ago she would have been uneasy in the closed space of an elevator. She never actually had claustrophobia, but a small enclosed area wasn't where she'd put herself if she had a choice. Now it didn't matter to her. She decided "beyond excellent" made a good label.

She looked at the signs on the hallway wall in front of her. Room 315 was immediately to the right. She peeked in and saw Angie leaning over Jean's bed. It looked like Jean was sleeping.

"Is she asleep?" Mallory whispered as loud as she dared.

Angie jumped back from the bed and glared. Mallory wondered at the venomous look. Meeting once at a party and twice in the Byways shop kept them from being total strangers, but just barely. Then Mallory realized that Angie might remember her more as an opponent of the cinder path last summer. Or as the one who had been snarky about Angie's treatment of a pregnant cat. Or as the one who didn't invite Angie for coffee when she invited Jean. Come to think of it, Angie might have a number of reasons to foam against Mallory.

Mallory spoke in a regular but soft voice. "It's nice to see you again, Angie." She hoped that might be enough to smooth over past disgruntlements.

Angie was fussing with something in her purse but stopped and looked at her again. "Yes, of course. Hello again."

Jean's eyes opened and she tried to sit up, but she was weak and seemed surprised by the restraints on her wrists. "Angie. Mallory. Are you two having a party without me?"

Mallory wondered about the restraints too. They looked Velcro-fastened, probably used when speed was needed. Did the hospital use them when someone tried to take their own life? A wave of sadness came over her.

Angie said, "I was just leaving." She brushed hurriedly by Mallory, and called over her shoulder, "I'll be back, dear Jean!"

36

MARCH

In which Jean slips in and out; the police discuss a nearly cold case; and Mallory and Jim get an unusual workout.

JEAN AND MALLORY watched Angie leave; they looked at each other and shrugged. Jean relaxed into her pillow. She said, "I knew I liked you. Another mother on the other side of raising great kids. We have the same degraded sense of humor."

"I was thinking the same thing, Jean. You know, when I had you right there in my kitchen a couple weeks ago, I forgot to apologize for never sending you a thank-you note for that wonderful party. I'm so sorry about that. At one point I even wondered if your call last November, asking about Jim Beall, was really an excuse to make me feel bad about my atrocious manners. But now I can ask what you think of him as a doctor."

"Mallory, you won't believe it."

"What?"

"Never mind. Let's talk about something else."

"Okay. So why are you in the hospital?"

"Damned if I know. I'm still waiting for the toxicology report from blood tests and having my stomach pumped. But I can tell you one thing: I didn't try to kill myself."

"Then we need to get the hospital to remove those awful restraints from your wrists."

"Oh yes, can you talk to them about these? I hate for Richie to see me like this. I don't know when they put them on. They weren't here earlier." Jean's voice was getting weaker.

"I'll go talk to the nurse at the station and see what's up. Don't go anywhere."

"Ha-ha."

Jean stayed conscious just long enough to wonder why Jim hadn't come to see her yet. And why he had only called her a couple of times since their big night, and even then it had been to talk more about Richie than about them. She felt lonely and scared, but exhaustion pulled her back down into a foggy sleep.

* * *

Chief Burnham called his deputy right after Jim left with his lawyer. "Get a search warrant fast, Pete, and head over to Byways Gift Shop. It's time to check out this Angie Weller. You know, it's a good thing we have friends on the Kennebunkport police force. We might never have made the connection with her name on their car-accident report. I've been replaying a chance comment by my old friend Frank there, about criminals with attitude. After Weller's car ran that reporter off the road, Frank's own suspicions were raised enough to ask me what I know about the proprietor of Byways. And now Dr. Jim Beall just left my office. He has provided us with the motive we've been looking for. It appears that Ms. Weller might be an insanely jealous woman."

* * *

Feeling that he had done the right thing, and reassured that the police were pursuing the investigation, Jim returned to the hospital. It was time to see Jean and tell her how he felt.

In the meantime, Mallory had talked to the floor nurse, who seemed to know nothing about the restraints. She wouldn't talk to Mallory about that anyway, since Mallory wasn't Mrs. Trent's health proxy. But she did say she'd follow up. It was a short conversation.

Mallory headed back to Jean's room and almost bumped into Jim as he rounded the corner from the elevator.

"Jim! How nice to see you! And how sad, in these circumstances. Is Jean going to be okay? And how's Richie's leg?"

Jim laughed at all the comments and questions. It was clear Mallory was feeling much better these days. "Everything's fine—not that I should be talking to you about my other patients, of course. How are you doing yourself?"

They were heading toward Jean's room when they heard a short raspy scream. They started running.

* * *

Jean had fallen back asleep after Mallory left the room earlier. She was awakened by a slicing pain in her restrained left wrist. When she opened her eyes, she saw Angie standing there with a razor blade, moving toward the right wrist. When she screamed, Angie grabbed the pillow from behind her head and slammed it over her face. Now fighting for her life, Jean thrashed as hard as she could with her legs and upper body. She heard an insane cackle coming from Angie.

Suddenly the pillow flew off and she saw Jim, her beloved Jim, holding Angie in a vice grip with both arms. Her peripheral vision took in the gleam of a razor on the blanket, lifeblood spurting from her left wrist, and Mallory running toward her with a gleaming white towel. As Jim held onto the writhing and screaming Angie, his eyes locked on Jean's. Mallory, now holding the towel tight against the cut, yelled, "Security! Security! Security!"

Jean fainted.

* * *

Mallory stepped back when one of the nurses pried her hands from the bloodied towel. She looked at the crimson on white and then at her hands, also stained. She snorted and then laughed to herself. Well, well, Mallory, looks like you've moved on. Here's to Uncle Bill's penis.

Security handed Angie over to the police. The nurse finished attending to the wound. Jim lifted his stethoscope from Jean's chest and said to Mallory, "You may have saved her life holding that towel to her wrist.

Since I'm going to marry this woman, if she'll have me, I can't thank you enough."

"What? You and Jean?"

Jim smiled and looked back down at Jean's unconsciousness. "I guess your neighbor Doris hasn't caught onto this one yet."

Mallory smirked. "I guess not, and I'm not going to be the one to tell her either. Well, I'll take my leave, Jim, so you and Jean can be alone. I'm so happy for you both."

She gave Jim a hug and left, feeling safer than she had in years.

* * *

When Jean came to, the room was darkened and Jim sat next to her on the bed. The wrist restraints had been removed. Her cut was dressed.

Jim leaned down and kissed her. Then he kissed her again.

"Can you forgive me? I'll have to see a psychologist to figure out what the hell my problem was. Because all I know now is that I love you. I can't believe you almost had to die before I'd figure that out. Please forgive me. I love you."

Jean closed her eyes, and then opened them again.

"I'm kind of woozy, Jim. Did you just tell me you love me?"

"Yes. I love you."

"Did you just save my life?"

"Well, Mallory Cooper and I did."

"Remember I told you what goes around comes around?"

Jim nodded.

"By that logic, I should love you back and give you my life. Would that bring you over to my way of thinking about karma?" Jean's freckles—which had gone pale and still—started bouncing again.

"Ah, you toy with me, vixen." Jim felt himself relax into the pool of loving acceptance that was Jean Trent.

"I love you, Jim. I've missed you so much."

A cascade of tears bathed his cheeks and fell onto hers. The warm salty drops were a proof of passage.

* * *

Seeing his deputy's name on the ID display, Chief Burnham answered the phone on the first ring. "What have you found at Weller's place, Pete?"

"We've located the ladder Mrs. Trent mentioned when she made her statement about that spiritualist's comments a few weeks ago. It's completely sturdy and a reputable brand name—probably a model that's been around forever. I doubt there's any recall on that baby, but we'll check, of course.

"Second, Weller keeps a Taser in a drawer by the register that could explain the hot spots on Richie Trent's fingers. Third, there's a rope in the garage that may have been used to pull the ladder out from under him. Weller's colleague Selene DiPietro—that's "Madame Selene"—turned us on to this. She also suggested we get a chemical analysis on the Spirits-Up bottles in Weller's shop. She said we'll find everything listed on the label plus some additional quantity of the homeopathic essence of lavender. It's supposed to help with stress, she said.

"Every single one of the bottles in the boxes waiting to be sold has been tampered with, Chief. The stupid Weller bitch left all the evidence right there behind a curtain in her shop. Unbelievable.

"Anyway, we can't arrest her for product tampering if it's nonmalicious. We want to get her for adding something harmful to the bottle she gave Jean Trent. That's going to be harder to do. All circumstantial right now.

"But here's possibly a major find, Chief. In Weller's closet upstairs, in her apartment over the store, is a pair of boots with lethal-looking heels. I do mean lethal. I've sent them over to forensics to check for blood and match against that wound in Nies's neck."

37

April-June

*In which Mallory and Dwight go visiting; Richie
tells a fib; and Mallory makes an overture.*

E LIZABETH HATED THE cane but was thankful she
had graduated to it. The exercises she had learned
at the rehab center had helped her dramatically. She'd
be playing tennis again before the summer was out.
When the buzzer to her apartment rang, she grabbed
the cane and made her way, almost painlessly, to the
intercom.

"Hi, Elizabeth. It's Mallory and Dwight."

Elizabeth buzzed them up. She was not at all nervous about seeing Dwight again under these circumstances. She and Mallory had hatched the plan for

them to come see her when she had healed more, and now, in mid-April, the chosen Saturday morning had arrived. She had baked her grandmother's sour cream and cinnamon coffee cake and had brewed a pot of French roast coffee.

"Come on in!"

Mallory swept in with a gentle hug. Dwight hung back in the hall, twirling his woolen cap in his gloved hands and wiping his boots on the doormat. Elizabeth held her arms out. "Welcome, Dwight. This is going to be a wonderful friendship. Give me a hug—but carefully!" Dwight stuffed his cap in his coat pocket and walked over the threshold with his arms spread wide.

At Elizabeth's kitchen table, warm cake and hot coffee melted any embarrassment ice that remained. Mallory talked about getting into the next tennis round-robin, hoping to win "for real" this time—and before Elizabeth was back in the game. "I'm going to need the exercise to keep me strong and energized for my new job."

"What new job?" Elizabeth put down her cake slice before it reached her mouth.

"You're looking at the first-ever office manager for the Burnham Bog Cinder Path Foundation." Mallory leaned in and patted Elizabeth's hand. "Your article about the plan—very well written, by the way—coincided with the town's posting of the job. I couldn't believe their list of requirements. It fit me to a tee!"

"In what way?"

"They wanted a native of Great Wharf, someone seasoned—love that word—as well as organized and computer savvy. Town Council has fast-tracked the construction of the path, so I'm lucky to get today off at all, even if it is a Saturday.

Elizabeth said, "You look made for the role with your new pixie hairstyle and au courant glasses. Very nice, Mallory!"

"Thanks. I do love this new look." Mallory touched her fingers to both sides of the short cut and glasses. "I got the pixie idea from Angie Weller. She may be an insane sociopath, but you have to admit she's a sexy one."

"I feel like I'm cheating on my wife now when I kiss her," Dwight said.

Mallory avoided looking at Elizabeth, lest they snicker. Instead, Mallory let her hand graze Dwight's cheek and said, "I doubt anyone will mistake me for Angie Weller."

"Just don't dye it red," said Elizabeth. "That would be weird."

She nudged more slices of the coffee cake over to her guests. "Here—don't make me fat on leftovers. Dwight, how's my other savior, Richie Trent, doing?"

"I don't see as much of him at the museum anymore, now that he has a full-time job. The hospital's electrician-slash-handyman is retiring and convinced the hospital to take Richie on full-time during his last month to ensure a smooth transition."

"Good for him. Hope it works out. I have job news of my own, in fact. I'm now on staff as an investigative reporter with the *Southern Maine Herald*."

"Fantastic news, Elizabeth! We wondered about that when we saw your byline the other day."

Elizabeth put another slice of coffee cake on each of the three plates as she continued talking. She ignored Mallory's dramatic cringe.

"I'll finally have a steady paycheck. The timing couldn't be better, since one of my first assignments is to cover the Weller trial. I have a personal interest in the outcome, of course, and so the newspaper will make sure someone's reading over my shoulder. But they also think my involvement in the case will provide an added hook to get even more readers."

Mallory said, "Well, we're certainly hooked. We can't get enough of it."

"It's hard to believe," said Dwight, "that that woman who seemed like such a normal person at the Trents' party might be a murderer."

"I wasn't there," Elizabeth reminded them. "Did she really seem normal?"

"Well … Dwight and I probably have a different take on that," said Mallory. "But she was dressed loaded for bear, clearly looking for a man. Any man. What was your take on her, Dwight?"

Dwight made a pushing-away motion with his hands. "Uh-oh. No opinion here. Elizabeth, what have you learned so far?"

"Police forensics did match blood found on Angie's boots to Sheila Nies's blood. But they never found an incriminating bottle of belladonna, so it's going to be hard to pin Jean Trent's poisoning on her. And pulling the ladder out from under Richie— they think she tied a rope to her car and yanked it that way, and then Tasered his fingers after he hit the ground—but who could ever prove that? She also hired herself a pretty decent defense attorney. So, I just don't know. But it's mighty scary to think about Angie Weller walking around free again. At least there's no question she tried to murder Jean in her hospital bed. Right, Mallory?"

"Ha! That's one thing I'm sure about."

Mallory leaned forward. "Please, this isn't for publication—but Dr. Nies was my psychologist. I was pretty deep into therapy when she died."

"No! Wow. How'd you cope with that?"

"It was terrible. Dwight's helped a lot. But I still have moments when I wonder if Dr. Nies would have declared me truly stable yet."

Mallory and Dwight had arranged to have lunch with Jean on their way back from Portland. They'd meet her at a local Biddeford lunch spot on the ocean. They weren't terribly hungry after all the coffee cake, but they planned to take an extra-long walk later. After the cold start, a beautiful, sunny spring day had materialized. The raw wintry air was finally a thing of the past, at least for this year. The gloves and wool cap Dwight wore to Elizabeth's were in the trunk now and would stay there until fall.

"I can't remember the last time I had to follow directions with this many twists and turns in them!" Mallory complained as she drove. "Look at those directions Jean gave us. We could have just taken Route 195 to Main Street, but no-o, Jean's giving us a look at Saco's back roads first. Then after lunch, she wrote on there, we can head over and check out the University of New England's Biddeford campus instead of driving straight home. I think she's missed her calling as a tour guide."

Dwight chuckled at the harangue. He was so glad to have the initial reuniting with Elizabeth behind him that nothing short of a flat tire in an ice storm could have bothered him now.

Jean had staked out a table near the window with the best view. "We're so glad you wanted to meet here," Mallory said. "We've always wanted to try this place. I never knew they offered vegan options too, but I assume they do, else why would you suggest it, right?"

Not a word did she say about the twists and turns, Dwight noted to himself. He thought again how improved his wife's outlook—and drinking—were now that she had a job. And the past with Uncle Bill really seemed to be past. After the phone conversation during which he had taken the walk, Mallory looked peaceful in a new way. The look hadn't left her. All she'd say was that the call went well. Dwight hoped that if they did see the Owens again it would go okay, but he worried. The fallout from an experience like Mallory's never completely vanishes.

As though on cue, Mallory, who must have been playing with the edge of her placemat, said, "Ow!" and held up a bleeding finger cut. Dwight stopped breathing as he watched her put her finger in her mouth and suck on it. Then she winked at him. "Sorry, Jean," she said. "Go on with what you were saying." He smiled back at his wife with cautious hope.

Jean finished chatting about how much she loved the restaurant and had been waiting all winter for it to reopen. During her animated—perhaps manic—small talk, she was moving the condiments and bud vase back and forth on the table. Mallory took hold of her hands to calm her down. That's when both Mallory and Dwight noticed the sparkling diamond ring.

"O-M-G," said Mallory. "You're engaged!"

Jean beamed and nodded yes.

Dwight said, "The last time I saw Richie, he was wondering why Jim hadn't proposed yet. He must be relieved."

"I haven't told Richie yet," Jean admitted.

"Why not?"

"Well, he still hasn't proposed to Amanda, and I've tried not to get on his case about that, even though I know they were made for each other. They're young and don't need to be in a big rush. I'm worried that if I tell him I'm engaged, he may think now he has to propose to Amanda. I don't want that to be the message."

Dwight had no response; he was once again stunned by how women's minds worked.

"Well, just say so," Mallory said. "Just tell him you're not implying anything about his and Amanda's relationship or timing. Say you're just sharing your own good news with him. In fact, offer to tell Amanda yourself at work on Monday. Then he won't have to be the one who tells her."

"That's brilliant," Jean said. "That's what I'll do. Thanks!"

"You're welcome. Is there a date yet?"

"Yes, we've decided on the last Saturday in July. More friends and relatives may be able to make the trip as part of a vacation."

"Let us know if you need a couple rooms for overflow guests. With late July being the height of tourist season, it may be difficult to find enough rooms. We have two empty bedrooms just crying for company. We can even clear out a third if Dwight's willing to burn two tons of archives."

* * *

That afternoon, Mallory and Dwight went to the trolley museum for their walk. As Mallory slowed the car to turn in at the main entrance, Dwight pointed to the tree where Elizabeth's car had crashed. Mallory groaned. She wondered whether Elizabeth had nightmares about this. It wasn't fair that the perpetrator should sleep well at night while a victim might toss and turn for years after. Even though Angie was in jail during the trial, Mallory assumed she was sleeping just fine.

They set out around the grounds at a good clip, knowing they had coffee cake to walk off today. Dwight started talking really fast. He delivered his guide speech at a double-time rate because of the speed with which they were passing the sights. Normally each sight required him to stop and stay a while so people could examine the cars while he talked. His supersonic delivery had Mallory in stitches. She begged him to stop so she could catch her breath before continuing the walk.

They stopped near car number 48. Richie was backing out of the old San Francisco cable car with a screwdriver in his hands.

"Whoa—behind you!" Dwight yelled over.

Richie jumped back toward the cable car before he realized he wasn't really about to ram anyone. The Coopers were at least ten feet away. Too late, his weak leg gave out and he fell against the trolley.

Mallory murmured, "Oh dear."

Dwight said, "Sorry to knock you off balance, Richie. Your leg okay?"

Richie winced as he got himself upright again. "It's holding me up, at least usually. Jim says I might have a slight limp the rest of my life, but I'm planning to prove him wrong."

"That's the spirit. What were you doing in there with the screwdriver?"

"Just checking that the hardware's all secure."

"Well, have a great weekend. We're doing a museum walk today—gotta keep moving. Keep on truckin', right?"

As they walked on, Mallory cherished how the friendship with Richie kept Dwight's spirits up. She laughed to herself when she recognized the term *spirits up* as ringing a bell these days in a new way, thanks to what the trial was disclosing about Angie Weller.

"What just made you smile, Mal?" Dwight asked.

"Life's an odd mix, isn't it? We laugh at Angie's over-the-top seductive antics and harmless sale of Spirits-Up, and yet she's a deadly serious combatant who killed a wonderful person and tried to kill at least one more, maybe three more. My smile was in reaction to the new meaning of the term *spirits up* and because I'm feeling so good these days. But at the same time, the world is as dangerous as ever. You never know where the next shock is coming from."

Dwight quickstepped in front of Mallory and stopped the walking. "True," he said, staring at her. "But it's a choice—to focus more on the good or more on the bad. Right here, right now, so good. Now keep walking."

Mallory started to say something, but he was already five feet ahead of her and walking fast. She shook off the dark and caught up with Dwight and his light.

* * *

The next morning, looking down from the upstairs bathroom window, Mallory watched Doris stretch from weeding in her backyard garden and then walk, cane free, into the house. She thought back over the past year and felt the burning heat of shame rise up her neck. How many times, in her own self-focused agony, had she been rude to Doris? And then last week she read in the *Gazette's* reprinting of the police blotter that Doris Hillobenz, that pinnacle of judgmental gossip and holier-than-thou sniping, had been caught shoplifting. She'd probably be fined a couple hundred dollars and given some weeks of community service.

Doris had been single parenting for ten years. Her husband, Cassidy's grandfather and adoptive father, had deserted their family with a short, meaningless note of apology. Cassidy would be heading off to college in another year or two. Mallory couldn't think of a single true friend Doris had. Most people avoided her, and the few who sought her out did so only to trade gossip.

Mallory remembered how, four months ago, she had blithely passed Doris's gossip along to Jean about Jim and Angie being seen together. What a blow she had delivered! And yet had no idea.

She finished dressing and made up her mind. She walked around the hedges by the driveway to ring Doris's front doorbell. If she hadn't been on the mission she was on, she would have cackled at the incredulous look on Doris's face when she opened the door.

Mallory blurted, "I was wondering, Doris, if you might join me on a walk around the neighborhood, say, two mornings a week, before my work. We could both benefit from the regular exercise and fresh air. My only condition is no gossiping. What do you say?"

Doris stared. Then she blinked, looked down at herself and up again, and said, "I'll be at a loss for words, but let's try it."

Behind Doris, a well-maintained hall area displayed artfully arranged ancestral photographs on the walls and a lovely Oriental rug over a hardwood floor. But a door left ajar to Doris's right revealed the magazine-piled living room of a hoarder. Mallory wondered what she had gotten herself into. But she knew one thing for sure: she wouldn't start any gossip about it.

EPISTOLARY EXCERPT FROM
UNPUBLISHED MANUSCRIPT:
RUNAWAY LEGACY

June 16, 2015

Dear Gallant,

You will not believe this. We had rather a large shock in April but didn't tell you about it for fear of disrupting your happy life with Blair, Caitlin, and her stepsiblings. However, we now have reason to tell you.

Our Mary has resurfaced. We recognized her in a news release after her arrest in a small town in Maine on suspicion of murder and a number of related charges. Whatever plastic surgery she's had done over the years has been truly excellent because—except for her hair, which she has dyed an awful red—she looks almost exactly as she did in high school. Imagine! For weeks we surfed the Net and hung onto all reports we could find about what was happening with the case, which rarely hit national news thanks to even more shocking or at least more recent events or the usual politics gone haywire.

Long story short, we have been in touch with an intellectual property lawyer, who got in touch with an agent, and we have ourselves a book deal. The publisher thinks this is a best seller in the making (do publishers always think that?).

As you know, we've had a bit of a tough time the last few years, between unemployment and living on Social Security plus battling with our various health issues. And your generosity in helping us stay afloat has been such a blessing.

This past weekend, we decided to set up a college fund for Caitlin and her stepsiblings, to be fed two-thirds of any revenue we're fortunate enough to earn from the book.

Well, back to the manuscript! We're still discussing what the ending should be. Any ideas?

Love,
Vera and Sergeo

38

JUNE–JULY

In which Elizabeth stays on topic; Madame Selene does a jig; Celestine is resourceful; and karma abounds.

EXCERPTED FROM A feature article by Elizabeth Easley, appearing in the *Southern Maine Herald.*

BIDDEFORD, Maine, June 30: Great Wharf business owner Angela (Angie) Weller was found guilty at Biddeford Superior Court yesterday of depraved indifference homicide—a form of criminally negligent manslaughter—of Great Wharf psychologist Dr. Sheila Nies and the attempted murder of Biddeford's Jean Trent.

DNA evidence matched Nies's blood with bloodstains on a pair of stiletto-heeled boots owned by Weller. Nies's body was found at the foot of a staircase outside her office-residence after the nor'easter last September. The prosecution claimed that Weller was standing at the top of the staircase when Nies climbed it during the storm, perhaps after retrieving a traffic cone that had been placed there to mark a bad step. Handprints on the landing railings were matched to Weller's hands. The diameter of a hole torn in Nies's neck matched that of a boot heel in Weller's closet. The prosecution described Weller raising herself on the railings and thrusting the stiletto heel of her boot into Nies's neck, hitting a jugular vein and causing Nies to bleed to death even as she fell backward down the stairs.

The police had withheld information about the neck wound during the investigation. The motivation for the murder seems to have been jealousy over a man (name being withheld as he was not a party to the events). Once Weller was in custody, physical examination revealed she wore a tattoo of the human brain that matched one worn by the victim. Weller's tattoo was estimated to be six to nine months old, prob-ably inked after the murder.

Depraved indifference murder carries a sentence of 25 years to life, with life measured as 70 years. Attempted murder could extend the sentence another 15 years. Weller was also found guilty of nonmalicious product tamper-ing, which could result in a sentencing of any-thing from time served plus fines to time in prison of up to five years. Exactly how Judge Keyes will structure the sentencing overall will be known two weeks from now. Weller's attorney indicated an appeal will be filed.

Other charges brought against Weller were the attempted murders of this reporter and Richard Trent (Jean Trent's son) and an earlier murder attempt on Jean Trent. In the latter charge, Weller stood accused of having attempted to murder Jean Trent by poisoning, though the original source of the poison—bel-ladonna—could not be found. The accused at-tempted murder of this reporter allegedly by running her off the road, and of Richard Trent by allegedly causing him to fall off a tall ladder. The jury, preponderantly male, reported to a stunned judge and a stunned courtroom that they could not convict on any of these other charges. The jury believed the circumstantial evidence that had been amassed against Weller in these cases could not be used to convict. They were especially cautious, they noted, because Weller had no prior criminal history.

Weller is being transferred from York County Jail in Alfred to the Maine State Prison in Warren tomorrow morning.

* * *

"Well, Pete," Police Chief Bren Burnham sighed, "you still did a helluva job gathering what evidence you could in this case. It's still hard for people to see a beautiful woman and think of her as capable of the same kind of evil they can see men capable of."

"Yeah, well, at least we got her for Nies's murder, and she'll go to prison for a good long stretch. We'll sure keep an eye on her if she comes back this way."

"You got that right, Deputy."

* * *

Madame Selene did a quiet but energetic jig behind the Byways curtain when the news came out about Angie's convictions. Then she left the hideaway and said to Cassidy, "Don't worry about your job, Cassidy. You still have one here if you want it."

"Oh, thank you, Madame Selene. I was wondering whether I should leave or what. Do you own the store now?"

"Not exactly. My lawyer met with Angie's lawyer, and papers were signed. With Angie's conviction, I can purchase her products at a reduced rate. Now I'll run the business on both our behalves until she's free again. The lawyers also had us sign that if either of us dies—whether in prison or attacked by a moose on the cinder path—the business portion of the estate reverts to the surviving party. So don't worry, Cassidy; your job at Byways is safe."

Cassidy giggled. "You're funny, Madame Selene—about the moose, I mean. It's not funny about one of you dying."

"I knew what you meant." Selene patted her shoulder. "And now, I'm going to talk with the owner of the spa scheduled to open next door two months from now. I'm proposing we add products that will appeal to their customers and have the spa hand out coupons for discounts on purchases at Byways. Angie was certainly right about the cinder path attracting new businesses."

* * *

Celestine was running scared. She couldn't know that there were pictures of her posted in coffee shops, police departments, post offices, the animal shelter, and all the local veterinarians' offices in a ten-mile radius around Great Wharf. She couldn't know that leaping out of Amanda's arms—as she was being carried from the car to be introduced to her new home—was the worst mistake she could have made. But a loud car horn had terrified her. And now she was starting to feel like she had once before, the time her human had lobbed her out of a car into a strange location.

Now she stalked the periphery of Burnham Bog (not that she could name this place) and caught a whiff of something edible that wasn't a mouse. She'd found lots of mice to live on, but this new aroma reminded her of the food delivered on a plate. The smell was just a jump away, coming from the open door of an idling vehicle. In a straight shot Celestine leaped upward into the dark slot behind the driver's seat. She was slinking toward the smell when the driver returned and slammed the door behind him. Celestine dropped and froze as the vehicle accelerated. When the motion became consistent, she picked her way toward the enticement.

* * *

Hank Sanborn still had nightmares about cats, shrimp, and toothpicks, to the point that he kept a nightlight on and serene music going all night long. He hadn't slept well last night, and then he overslept, such that he skipped his usual breakfast of ham and eggs. On his way to work, he stopped at a convenience store. There he bought coffee, a Danish, and, while he was at it, a prewrapped tuna-fish sandwich to eat at lunchtime. When noon approached, he was driving the jail's van. He lifted the bag containing the sandwich off the passenger-side floor, dumped out the contents, and expertly steered with his knees while opening the cellophane wrapping.

With his first bite, Hank realized he needed to take a piss. He hadn't had time to relieve himself for several hours. Luckily he was on the stretch of Wyeth Road by Burnham Bog that was devoid of buildings on the other side. He saw no traffic coming from either direction. He swung the van onto the berm and ran ten feet into the conservation area.

Two minutes later, Hank climbed back into the driver's seat, buckled up, eased back onto Wyeth, and accelerated to the speed limit. He kept his eyes on the road as he reached to the right for his sandwich. Instead of the anticipated pushback of soggy white bread, his fingers sank into … fur? Hank's ailurophobia—the fear of cats that had ruined several of his relationships with women—got the best of him. As he felt all strength dissipate from his body, his head fell back against the seat in a swoon. Later he would wonder if he'd imagined the moose in front of the van that caused him to swerve so violently toward the telephone pole. He certainly wouldn't admit to a cat-induced swoon. As far as anyone else might be concerned, there was simply a moose on the loose.

BIDDEFORD, Maine, July 1: Convicted murderer Angela (Angie) Weller was killed this morning when the van transferring her from York County Jail to Maine State Prison crashed into a telephone pole on the high-speed southern stretch of Wyeth Road. The driver, correctional officer Henry (Hank) Sanborn of Biddeford, protected by a seatbelt and an airbag, sustained a broken arm and two broken ribs.

An investigation is planned into the accident, but Sanborn said he swerved to avoid a moose. Several sightings of a moose in and near Burnham Bog have been reported during the past year. Recent cinder-path construction activity on the town side of the bog might be driving the moose closer to the other side. Neighbors blame, too, the presence of a new broccoli farm west of Wyeth, which might be reason enough for a moose to cross the road.

A calico cat was found at the scene and taken to the Great Wharf Police Department for holding and observation overnight. Its fate has yet to be determined.

The evening news ran a gawker's smartphone video of the scene that showed Hank on a stretcher and a calico cat being put into a small animal carrier. Richie and Amanda started yelling at the same time. "That's Celestine! That's Celestine!" They put on their shoes, grabbed IDs and keys, and raced out of their new rental. Their car's squealing tires as they pulled out of the driveway reminded them to watch the speedometer. They didn't need a speeding ticket in their new hometown of Great Wharf. They drove as fast as the law allowed to the police station.

Richie and Amanda begged the desk officer to release Celestine to them. "She's had all her shots. Please let us take her home. She can't possibly tell you anything about the accident."

The desk officer called over Trudy, Chief Burnham's assistant. Then the two of them conferred with a few others at the station. Finally, Trudy and the desk officer returned to where Richie and Amanda stood waiting with their arms around each other.

"Tell you what," Trudy said. "We'll open the door to the carrier. If she comes to you, she's yours. Just be sure to bring her papers over here tomorrow."

A hush fell over the station as Trudy brought the carrier out from behind her desk and set it on the floor twenty feet away from Richie and Amanda. Amanda whispered to Richie, "You call her. You saved her once before. She won't forget that."

And she didn't.

* * *

Richie knew now that his own life was under way for real, separate from his mother's life, separate from his father's life. If his ma ever went through another bout of depression, she was with Jim, the right person to help see her through it. Besides, her psychiatrist, Dr. Sterns, hadn't hurt the health of his own practice when he testified at the trial. He spoke about the spectrum of bipolar conditions versus other mood disorders, the correct use of medications, and the value of placebos.

Richie threw away the last, long-emptied bottle of added-lavender Spirits-Up. He had held onto it as a keepsake but then decided it might be bad karma.

He was especially happy about the metal plaque now hidden and firmly attached to Seashore's cable car number 48. He did feel guilty about secretly defying museum code, which prohibited permanently affixing anything to an artifact. But his queasiness over breaking the rules was trumped by his need for peace. He had found strength over the years in his mother's philosophy that things come full circle if you just give them enough time. He knew he'd experience an inner calm whenever he thought of that plaque the rest of his life.

> *Dedicated to the memory of Richard C. Laskey, possibly killed by this very cable car in 1910, for which it's very sorry and would take it back if it only could.*

* * *

On their seventeenth walk, and their first on the new cinder path, which was completed in time for the Fourth of July festivities, Mallory showed Doris her new, larger spring-assisted knife. "Dwight gave it to me, instead of putting in an alarm system. He says it's a lot cheaper and I can use it indoors and out."

Doris lifted her blouse enough to reveal a holster. "I bought this Smith & Wesson .38 Special the day after Cassidy's father left us."

"And here we are living in one of the safest towns in Maine."

"We both know safety's an illusion."

"I guess safety and comfort are two different things."

The women's conversations had been slow and cautious over the first several weeks. Children were always a safe topic, as were tales from their own childhoods. Personal concerns were fine if they didn't beg judgmental responses.

Mallory had to hold her tongue a lot at first. And it was many weeks before Doris dared to bring up a topic of her own. But they were beginning to trust each other.

"Did you hear about Angie Weller?"

"Is this gossip?"

"No."

"Because it was in the news?"

"Yes."

"I'm still struggling to understand the rules."

"I know. Me too."

A moose grunted from somewhere in the bog. Doris grabbed Mallory's arm and, in compassion, Mallory quickened her pace.

ABOUT THE AUTHOR

M EREDITH MARPLE IS a former independent publisher and current writer of memoir and fiction. With a B.S. in zoology from Tufts University, she spent many years in educational publishing before switching to trade publishing and then writing. She may have left the "hard science" aspects of her education behind her, but she never lost her love for the life sciences, evidenced by a fascination with human and animal behavior that permeates her writing. With her husband, Marple splits her time between Maine and Florida. Her website is meredithmarple.com. She tweets as @authorMMarple and has a Facebook page at facebook.com/authormeredithmarple.

Reading Group Guide

What good things happened when Mallory Cooper got out more? What bad things happened?

What things did Mallory have control over, and what things would have happened anyway?

What were other characters afraid of? Were the fears real?

How did different characters show courage?

A thematic thread throughout the book is the power of truth and lies in people's lives. Which do you think, truth or lies, won out in this book? Which truths hurt, and which lies helped?

Many of the characters were looking for love. Some, like Jim Beall, didn't know they were and felt off-balance when they found it. Dwight knew he was and had to decide where to find or re-create it. How did different characters look for and react to love?

Another theme could be the strength we gain from friends and loved ones if we let them help us grow. How did Dwight help Mallory and Richie? How did Mallory help Doris? What other relationships helped people to improve themselves?

Mallory hated gossip but sometimes participated in it despite herself. Does that happen to you?

Which character did you like/dislike the most? Why?

Have you ever been to the area of Maine that Great Wharf is set in, and did the author's descriptions feel true to you? How might the story have differed in a different setting?

What scenes in particular have stayed in your mind since you finished reading?

Mallory was able to put her upset with her mother and history with her Uncle Bill on a back burner while raising her children and then holding down a job. When she had time on her hands, however, after the kids had

left home and her job disappeared, she couldn't ignore
the pain inside anymore. Have you had old memories
or experiences surprise you like that?